I0564354

THE IGNITED MOON

ANDREW JOHNSTON

CONTENTS

ALSO BY ANDREW JOHNSTON

The Discarded Knight

Iron Frost Universe

The Ignited Moon

The Ignited Moon is a work of fiction. Names, characters, cultures, and incidents are a product of the author's imagination. Any resemblance to actual persons and cultures is entirely coincidental.
Copyright 2025 Andrew Johnston
All Rights Reserved.
First Edition
Artwork by Catrin Russell
ISBN: 979-8-9909874-2-5 (e-book)
ISBN: 979-8-9909874-9-4 (paperback)

To My Nephew

MUTAFAKARA

NEMA

CRIZALBOLT

HAUSARA

NATLEND

CILLNAR

NIEV

B

THE WORLD OF
IRON FROST

◇ CITY
◉ NOTABLE TOWN
•• COUNTRY BORDER

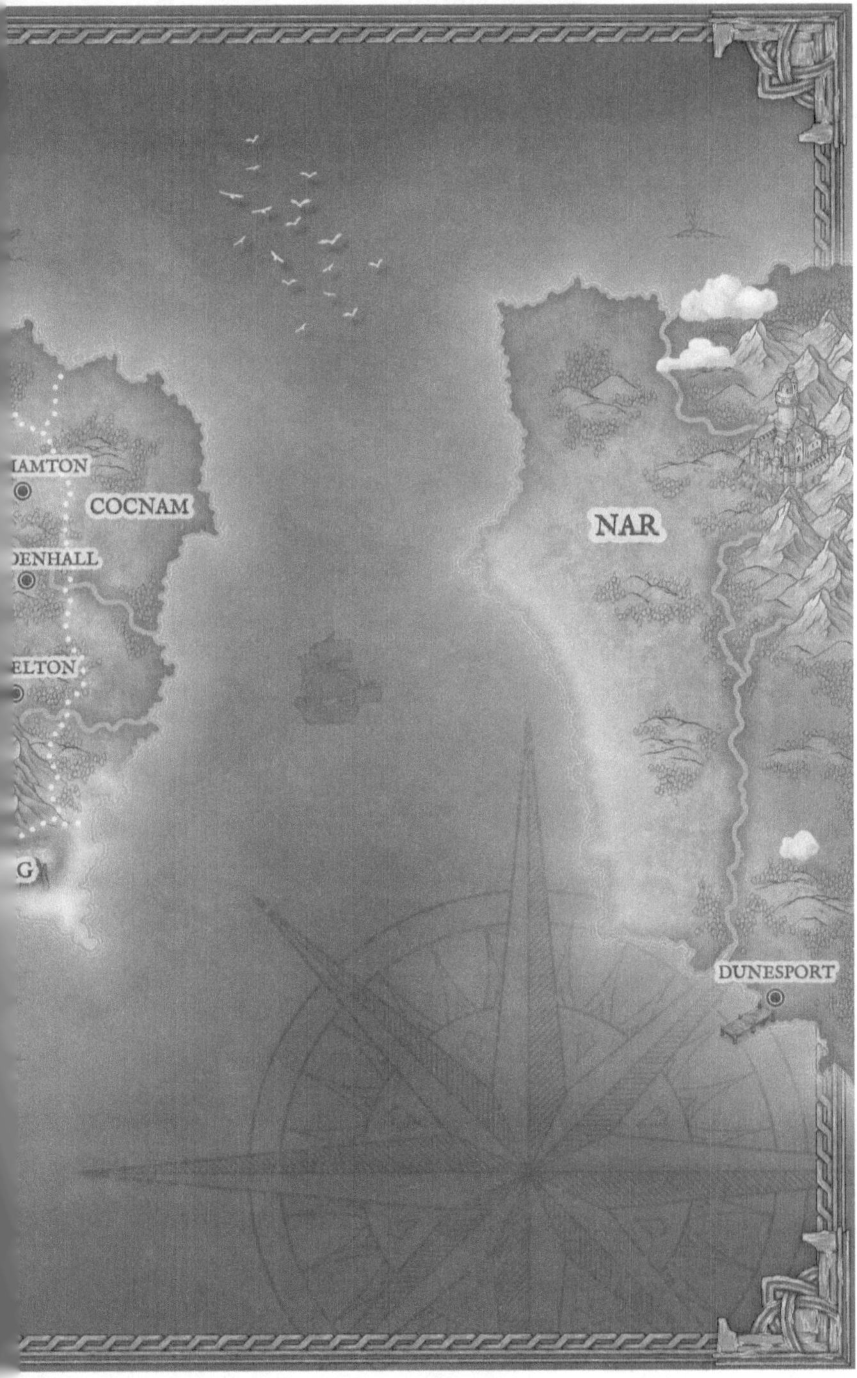

AMTON
COCNAM
DENHALL
ELTON
NAR
DUNESPORT

CHAPTER ONE

"I beg you, Non, goddess of oceans. Grant my one request. Dissolve my marriage to the Storm King."

Yatzil took a deep breath and opened her eyes. The reflective sheen on the polished tile floor muddied the reflection of her slender figure and ice blue skin. She rose to a kneeling position, closing her eyes in a last desperate plea with Non. The goddess remained silent, following the lead of those in her pantheon. Did they believe her marriage would keep the city of Niev and her father's kingdom safe? Yatzil shook her head and opened her eyes to the dozens of columns supporting the pyramid above. Her crown's weight made the praying position she had taken difficult.

She groaned from the soreness in her neck and craned it to look upon Non's likeness. The statue was crafted from onyx and towered at the far end of a grand pool. It was eye level to the dais she had been positioned beside for hours. The pool's salty aroma relaxed her, but to meet the ocean goddess's immense eyes and jade beak boiled her blood. A great hook rested between the goddess's eyes, sharp like the

frequent cramping in her calves. Yatzil focused her frustration upon her hands and ground her teeth.

She flared her nostrils, ice ran over her skin, crackling
over her cheeks. Her eyes ignited yellow, but then she
remembered her brother was present. His calm meditative
state on display brought her patience. Yatzil thawed her
features to flesh and decided perhaps Non required more
time. Her brother opened one eye to the smooth white tile
steps leading out of the multileveled room they were in. A
faint grumbling emanated from his belly. Yatzil drew back
her curiosity at how he was hungry once again, focusing on
her time with him.

It was their final ocean ritual, but she didn't want it to be,
even if it meant just being his older sister. His calm, light
brown eyes rested upon his hands. Her brother's face was
framed by long black hair that shrouded the formation of a
double chin. He wore a snow-white lumao around his waist.
A jade owl clutching his name in its talons over the surface of
a full moon kept the fine silks in place. Yatzil eyed his gut as
it hung over the owl's piercing round eyes. Their mother had
convinced him a hungry prince would make a strong ruler, a
god among their people, and master of the harem. His arms
remained muscular, but his ornate wrist and arm bands
needed to be let out. She worried their mother's lies might
leave him vulnerable someday. It tugged at her heart, and
with it, a wish to speak with their father surged.

Drumbeats removed Yatzil from the storm of worry in
her mind. Without her noticing, priests and priestesses had
entered from the palm-and-oak doors to the left of Non's
likeness. Men in green silk robes stood to either side of the
sacred pool. Her focus raced from the oars in their hands,
through a growing cloud of burning incense to the grand
stairs beyond.

Her parents descended them one step at a time. Their feet

garbed in sandals inlaid with jade and gold squares. She sneered at her mother, slightly relieved for the hollowed-out frigagator skull upon the queen's head. Six eyes lined it, stopping before a long, cavernous skull of faded red bone. Her king father wore a larger one, its eyes lined with gold leaves. He slouched a little, taking away from the tall and muscled king she grew up admiring.

Yatzil believed his decision more than the month's rituals weighed on him. During their last meeting with King Yanter, her father had not wished her to wed the proud nol royal. When night had arrived, he had come to no decision and Plunemar had phased into the west, leaving the south moonless and his second option gone by tradition's demands. She had gone to bed that night and her father had chosen not to make peace through marriage. It meant life would remain the same except when she woke the next morning, the opposite had come true. She refocused upon her father. His posture straightened.

The royal couple's pace was slow and purposeful, stopping to acknowledge her father's lesser wives and potential heirs. Her mother's grip tightened in his. Yatzil wondered if such youthful and noble women gave the queen cause to feel threatened. The royal couple passed through a forest of towering support columns. The columns carved in the image of Non, grasping a fish in her beak. A collective swishing of robes sent Yatzil's eyes to Non's servants bowing to her parents.

She followed their lead once the couple were within reach of the dais. The queen eyed her through the skull's teeth before the king aided her up its steps. A wheezing resonated from her mother's movements. Yatzil still didn't understand why a woman considered a goddess could be so weak. Or that with weakness frowned upon for a royal, how disgusted whispers of it had not reached her ears. Yatzil shrugged off an unsettling feeling and watched two priest-esses approach the dais.

They took one step at a time, chanting as they joined her parent's. Yatzil adjusted her posture, raising her hands to align with her brother's. The priestesses removed the friga-gator skulls as the royal couple knelt upon a long white cush-ion. And then, like always, her father gave Yatzil a wink with his sightless left eye. Yatzil secreted a smile in return, thankful for the incense filling the room like fog in a harbor. Footsteps breached the calm of its sweet smell.

A prince, ten to Sachihiro's sixteen, ascended the steps beside her carrying an ornate chalice upon a tray. Yatzil recognized him from court but did not know his name. The chalice held an elixir to strengthen the king's connection to Non. The prince wore a lumao like Sachihiro's but unlike her brother, a green moon graced his brow. It marked him like many of her father's other children as uncrowned children of the king. He bowed. The chalice rattled freeing droplets upon the queen's dress.

The boy's eyes widened as the queen's jaw formed her lips into a scowl. He raced past her to join the other children and wives. The drumbeats increased, matching the prince's speed. His mother gathered him within her arms and settled him by her side. Yatzil closed her eyes to pray for the prince and asked for her marriage to be dissolved. She scrunched her nose and scoffed. Silence.

Plop. She opened her eyes at the faint sound then eyed her father. He hoisted the chalice to his lips and drained it. He stood with his hands raised, every finger bent like talons. Her mother removed his lumao, folding it upon her lap. After a moment of chanting, tremors ran down his scarred back and shaven legs. The king who Sachihiro may resemble someday gasped, but he made a fist and remained upon his feet. Sweat ran down his back like sea spray against a rock, sending

Yatzil's mind into a frenzy. *No nescaran perspires.* Yatzil moved to one knee as her father descended the steps to Non's sacred pool. The cushion under her hissed against the tile. Sachihiro waved for her to remain still, confusion escaping his thinly painted eyes. But soon, the gold Friga-gator claws pinning their father's long hair were out of sight. Yatzil rose with her brother and climbed atop the dais. An unsteadiness ran through Yatzil's legs as she watched her father stride with uneasy steps. She knelt beside her mother and fought to convince herself what troubled the king would pass.

An odor pried at her nostrils from the chalice perched before her mother. It was familiar to previous ceremonies but there was a hint of difference. She reached for it. *Slap.*

"Your attention must be," her mother wheezed, raising her hand to eye height. "On your king."

Yatzil seethed for a second, rubbing the pain from her hand. Ahead, the oarsmen churned their oars faster, and priests pounded their drums harder to resemble a thunderstorm on the sea. Her new life required the welcoming of harsh weather as a Storm Queen. But worry flooded her veins, drowning any thoughts of future duties. Her father aimed his fingertips skyward, dived, and swam for the pool's center.

A minute passed, and then another, and then a flock of priestesses lined the path her father had taken to the pool. The priestesses swayed like waves until a third minute passed. Bubbles surfaced at the pool's center, scattering as her father shot up. His lips begged for air and hands clawed for aid.

"Father!" Yatzil cried, hearing her brothers and sisters panic before their mothers hushed them.

"What troubles my father?" Sachihiro said, a slight crack in his voice. "I command the ceremony to cease."

"You both will remain silent and … still," the queen sneered.

Sachihiro leapt to his feet, kicking over the chalice and sprinting down the steps. The chalice rolled slowly past Yatzil, nearing the dais's edge. A wave of priestesses crashed upon Sachihiro, holding him back like a current high enough to pull him under. The priestesses spoke of a disagreement with Non, that this was punishment, but Yatzil had never witnessed the ocean goddess in conflict with her father. Yatzil seized the chalice and sniffed it. She froze, afraid to breathe, the blade pressed close to her ribs.

She glanced at Sachihiro. Ice formed over his flesh as he pushed to be free. Non's servants dropped to bended knee as he increased his strength. But still, there were too many of Non's priestesses and they were too eager. It doubled her suspicion, adding to why no one, not even her younger siblings, called for guards to seize the one holding her hostage. She winced. Her mother's thin fingers dug into her neck.

"Keep silent!" The queen's labored breaths chilled her ear. "Your father's death shall protect all nescarans."

"Why—?"

Slender fingers clamped down at the arm she used to keep steady. They were too warm to be her mother's. Warm like the heat from a meal-maker's oven. To frost may cost her life and possibly Sachihiro's. Her mother thrusted her face toward her father and pointed a bony finger.

"He is already dead."

Sachihiro barreled through the priestesses and halted short of the pool's edge. The pool's waters calmed to a standstill. And from what she could see, her father's body had morphed to a mass of black ice.

"You dare leave my father to drown," Sachihiro said. His eyes burned bright with rage. "I'll execute you both myself."

The oarsmen collapsed to their knees and trembled. Sachihiro dove into the pool. Seconds passed. He burst from the water, holding their father close. Yatzil watched the priests rush to aid him.

Tears blurred Yatzil's vision, every breath grew labored, as if she had climbed a great height. Her brother climbed free of the water, thawing, his hair clung to his face. A rush of footsteps revealed her siblings and their mothers coming to see if the king lived.

"I will allow three days for mourning," her mother whispered. "But … utter a word to your brother, and you will be warming your husband's bed before you have time to curse my name."

The queen's grip yielded, and the stranger's fingers retracted with the blade. Stumbling to her feet, Yatzil found only distant faces of priests along the temple walls. She raced to Sachihiro's side.

"Leave us!" Her brother's voice was weak at first, but he deepened it, "Go! Or I shall have you all stripped of your duties and banished."

Shuffling filled the air until only faint sobs from their father's youngest was all that could be heard.

"How can Father's control over the oceans fail, Yatzil?" Sachihiro took her in his arms. "Neither he nor Non have disagreed before."

"I do not know," she said. His chilling breath raced then retreated across her bare shoulder. "He was devoted to Non and us."

Yaztil buried her face in his chest, dizziness taking over at the great length and depth of the pool before them. Their father never looked so vulnerable. His legs were pressed together and pulled to his chest. His hands gripped at his stomach as if in great pain. Yatzil kissed Sachihiro's cheek, not caring that affections were publicly frowned upon. Her lips trembled once she lowered her gaze upon her father.

Every measure of strength fled. Sachihiro held her close, guiding Yatzil to the floor. His strength brought her comfort, but questions ran to her tongue. What reason did their mother have for poisoning her king and husband? Who had kept her from aiding Sachihiro? Yatzil peered up at her mother to find disgust on the queen's aged face. There was comfort in knowing her mother would no longer rule. But becoming Mother of the King meant influence and control, and not just over Sachihiro.

CHAPTER TWO

T he journey north in two days drew closer. Yatzil withdrew the cloth from her painted eyes, its silks stained black. Sleep had deserted her, leaving the sweet bate-nich to be relied on for energy. Its juices and ripeness left Yatzil pining for more. Several of the fruit's purple cores lay on a plate at the end of her bed. She had abandoned her bed's raised mattress above its white granite steps, their cushions scattered. Her desire for solitude outweighed any need for comfort. Her toes brushed the large pillow resting against the balcony's balustrade. Yatzil rested the cloth atop the balustrade's wide rail. The wind snatched it away like her mother had with her hopes.

Tears ran then froze upon her cheeks, on full display, but since isolating herself, the worry of judgment for weeping remained absent. She rested her gaze on the finely chiseled homes stretching out beyond the palace. High thick walls halted their columned halls and rich silk overhangs from reaching the sea. A mile-wide moat bound the city like a serpent's coils below its walls.

Her stomach lurched at the thought of having a diamond-fang smuggled into her bedchamber to end her marriage before it began. To have the serpent wrap itself about her body and poison her meant freedom from her unwanted future. *She shook her head. I would be abandoning Sachihiro. He barely held his own at father's burial.*

All within a day, chosen priests and priestesses had prepared her father. And, before the sun vanished upon the horizon, a pounding at her bedchamber door had come. Yatzil rolled her shoulders, finding they ached from the task demanded of her. The great key to seal her dynasty's tomb had been hard to turn even in frost form. But Sachihiro was there to share in the task that both hoped they would never have to perform. Rituals followed, robbing him of wanting to mourn, forcing him to hide the tremors she noticed. Once all had come to an end, she knew his rein would be met with struggle. After the tomb had been sealed, when all royals had gone but her, the elite priest guard halted her grieving. The guards were duty bound to the king and queen, but it appeared her mother had already allied them to her schemes.

Yatzil shuddered, remembering how their eyes flared red in place of yellow from within their intricate owl skull helmets. She ignored the creaking of her bedchamber doors. It was most likely a handmaiden asking if she required more bate-niches. A breeze sent her hair back, freeing the frozen tears from her cheeks. Yatzil returned to yesterday's rituals, to Sachihiro placing a jade mask upon their father's face. It was crafted to their father's likeness and preserved his features. This act made Sachihiro king, and even with so much power at his disposal, his present duty held his emotions at bay. She drew in a breath, recalling the priests raising her father upon their shoulders before carrying him into her dynasty's tomb.

Yatzil rested her hands upon the balustrade. Though it was her desire to dissolve her marriage, it risked war. And after yesterday's proceedings, she possessed no desire to thrust her wishes upon her brother.

"I have troubling news."

Yatzil gasped. She spun to find Flor.

"I was sent to tell you something." She bowed before Yatzil could collect herself. "Your husband has been killed."

The stale gloom of the morning felt brighter. Every bit of strength absent from her muscles returned as she spun to face the city and sea. Yatzil flashed the owl eyes tattooed upon the dorsal side of her hands and called out like a battle had been won. But when she faced Flor again, tears filled the handmaiden's eyes.

"This is cause for tribute to the Four, Flor. A thousand temple mice or five hundred …" Yatzil tilted her head, noticing a scroll clutched in Flor's fist. "What is that? Has Mother married me off to…?"

Flor's hand shook. Yatzil ran her fingers over it and removed the scroll, slipping free its tiny eagle pin.

It is with great sadness that King Yanter has fallen to a bear's rage at the Lid's foundations. Succession of all lands earned by the first to hold his name and wear his crown will pass to the last of his dynasty, Prince Amteer. As viziers to our Storm King we must keep the peace made. The marriage to Princess Yatzil will…

Pain squeezed her throat to continue reading. Any hope of remaining home was lost, and there was little to be done but wait. Yatzil checked to see if the doors were shut to her bedchamber, dropped the scroll, and embraced Flor. She sobbed into the handmaiden's chest, every breath heavy, splashing upon her cheeks. Flor caressed her long black hair, smoothing its tangles.

"I have never seen his son," said Yatzil. "What if he is arrogant like his father? Or takes me to bed without sacred dance like some fish thief?"

Flor pressed a cheek to Yatzil's brow.

"You can defend yourself," Flor said, parting from Yatzil. "You have power over cold like all nescarans." Flor folded her arms. "How else have women of your blood and beyond stood proud for so long?" she sighed. "I can see you doubting yourself."

Yatzil faced the city and dammed up her anger, discarding tears with a bawled fist.

"I doubt nothing."

"May I be bold in your presence?"

"When have you ever not been?" Yatzil said.

Flor grabbed and spun Yatzil, pulling her close. The bareness of Yatzil's feet squeaked against the polished tile as she shook free. She backed away, drawing herself up to full height as ice replaced her flesh.

"Have you lost all sense?"

"How dare you, my only friend, doubt yourself?" Flor snapped, jabbing a finger at Yatzil's chest. "How dare you refuse to take responsibility? Why do you hide away instead of seeking what poisoned your father?"

The soft silks engulfing Yatzil's chest like crossed wings loosened from ice made flesh again. Her rage faded with the glow of her eyes. She stumbled onto the pillow against the balustrade. Her long gray dress hid her feet as she pulled herself into a ball.

"You are right," said Yatzil. "And you must think me a delicate royal unlike the queens who once froze thousands to the core."

"I will," Flor offered her hand. "Only if you allow your

mother to win."

The *plop* remained clear in her mind as if she still kneeled within Non's temple. Yatzil took in where her misery had brought her. And then as clear as it had been in the final moments of her father's struggle, her mother's words surfaced. *He is already dead.* Yatzil grabbed Flor's hand, standing nearly eye to eye with her friend.

"Let's prove Mother a traitor."

———

DEEPER INTO THE PALACE, every hall possessed panther statues layered in dust and frost. The Four once possessed the form of such predators for many a millennium until the new age of nescaran royals seized power.

"We are close to the Wisdom Room, my princess." Flor whispered. She increased her pace and pointed. "It's only a little further in this direction."

They turned left down a narrow hall. Faint footsteps caught Yatzil's attention, but Flor kept her stride, the caution existing since they first met was absent. Yatzil pulled her friend behind a statue of Urrra, brushing against a ring of armored white granite avalanche warriors surrounding the goddess. The goddess's paws were plated in bronze, and her helmet contoured to her fierce muzzle.

Two guards rounded the corner, passing them at a brisk pace. Flor patted to her shoulder and waited until both guards were gone. Yatzil rolled her ankles and flexed her toes to relieve their ache, taking comfort in her friend's eagerness. Their journey felt as though it was the longest ever made. It was certainly the longest Yatzil had gone without being carried upon a palanquin.

As they passed through the Wisdom Room's triangular entrance, a darkness beyond what Yatzil had ever witnessed loomed over them. Shelves filled the room's length and breadth with an oldness to their dark wood. Everyone she passed was stuffed with scrolls foxed and browning. Their faint moldiness scraped the inner shafts of her nostrils. A faint trickling caught Yatzil's attention, growing louder the closer they came to the Wisdom Room's center. Eight oval pools aligned in pairs below statues of the Four. They hoisted by their wing tips in unison an orb of pure silver.

"I have never entered this part of the palace, Flor," said Yatzil. "What purpose do those pools serve?"

"If we find what we seek," Flor said, peering over her shoulder to the entrance, "and your brother believes us, I will show you how those pondering pools work."

A thin film of broken ice covered each pool, accompanied by small tables, sporting chalices and decanters at steps leading out of them. They stopped at a ring of tables encircling the pools and statues. Yatzil's eyes widened, running her fingers over etched maps of the Wisdom Room upon the table's surface. Flor nudged her, pointing to a shelf marked, *Dangers of Toxins.*

"Come, Yatzil." Flor took off at a run. "It is beyond Limpe's likeness."

Yatzil raced to catch her friend, their footsteps echoing in the cavernous room, overpowering the light trickle of water. The water running below the Four's talons made them appear as if balancing atop a waterfall. Yatzil caught up to Flor and stared, curious as to what she meant earlier. She could see that the pools were deep from the many layers of rock that were visible; they were clearly carved from stone. None of them matched the depth her father had drowned within. And though her bedchamber bath did not come close, it frightened her to be immersed in water she could not step free from. Yatzil quivered at a rush of heat up her spine and turned from the pools.

"What do you mean by how they work?" Yatzil held onto her wrist firmly, ignoring what was absent from it. "Is there some magic to them?"

They scanned each crowded shelf until Flor pointed to a bronze plate of gray whale bone marked, *Dangers of Toxins.*

"There is no magic in those waters. I wish to remove your fear of drowning," Flor ran her eyes from the bareness of Yatzil's shoulders to her sandals. "And see you wear what bracelets and shoulder necklaces brought you such joy."

"I do not miss them."

Yatzil released her wrist, remembering how the gold of such items almost cost her life. Flor removed several scrolls from their crammed cousins, straining. Yatzil reached out to help, but her friend pulled away.

"I am fine," Flor said. "You need not help me, but if we can sever our new king's loyalty to your mother, will you learn to swim again?"

Yatzil turned from Flor, resting sight on Limpe's likeness. Her wings raised and her body was wrapped in fresh boar fur of green, red, white and ocean blue. Yatzil faced her friend again, noticing a scroll under her arm marked, *Bites by Flight.* To be less plain was something she did miss, from earrings extending to her shoulders, and coin bracelets about her ankles. But no amount of riches measured up to the wealth of her father's kindness. A secret he shared with her most among all his children. His stories of voyages to save ships from fish thieves were a thrill she missed.

"Yes." Yatzil grinned, grabbing a handful of scrolls. "And may Sachihiro join us in such lessons?"

"You are my princess." Flor laughed. "I don't see why not."

Moving to one of the closest tables, they rolled out scroll after scroll. Most of what Flor gathered spoke of fruit you could eat but the seeds were poisonous if not planted immediately. Several went into grand detail about diamond-fangs.

Yatzil swallowed, pushing aside the scroll after learning what one prince and princess had done with the serpent's poison. They had poured the creature's stone melting poison down their father's throat. The couple married soon after, entombing their father within his own border wall to christen their reign.

Yatzil unfurled another scroll, its writings spoke of poisons specific to royals that were found weak by nescaran definition. She turned her nose up at the text of the king's brothers, believing him to be weak. King Planudurn had pardoned an old man for mispronouncing his name. His brothers had started a riot and threatened to poison him, should he not punish the old man. Yatzil gulped. The thirteen-year-old king refused his brother's demands.

Yatzil's eyes grew heavy with the passing of time. She smirked at a scroll written of sickle wings, great swooping silent creatures. Yatzil showed Flor an image of a sickle wing releasing its sought-after droppings on the shoulder of who penned the scroll. Yatzil rested her head on Flor's shoulder as they laughed, losing focus from their unstoppable joy.

"How dare you touch my daughter that way?"

They pressed themselves to the table.

"Mother?" Yatzil gasped.

"Separate them," said the mother of the king from her high palanquin. "Bring no blemish to my daughter's ... flesh. It is still sacred no matter her foul actions against ... me."

Guards separated them in seconds, scrolls toppled like a collapsing wall of loose bricks. Just one may have formed the foundations to bring her mother down from so divine and prominent a position. Her mother snarled, revealing darkened jade squares emblazoned upon her teeth. Yatzil frosted but thawed with the prick of ice spears to her skin.

"Release her!" Yatzil screamed. "I command it as Storm Queen of the nol and Princess of Niev."

"Take my daughter's … friend to my bedchamber. I will …
silence her myself lat—"

"No. You shall not take my friend like you did my…"

The spears lengthened as she snatched words back, every
point pressed deep into her flesh. Yatzil sniffed back pain,
contemplating freezing the guards from within to bring
them to their knees. Flor kicked and pulled, every tear falling
and freezing before hitting the ground. She planted her feet,
but they were yanked into the air, and soon the girl whose
bravery was beyond an avalanche warrior was far away.
Yatzil turned back to her mother.

"You dare … make friends with a highborn committed to
servitude, to holding piss jars? And now… Now you wish to
take away what is … mine. My divine right!"

Yatzil whipped her hair back.

"She has been my friend longer than you know. Now,
why kill my father?"

The former queen straightened upon her ornate palanquin, forcing its bearers to compensate and hide their clear
sorrow for Yatzil. She focused on the faint wrinkles waving
from her mother's unrelenting eyes.

"As I have said, it was … meant for all nescarans," said her
mother. "And though your father bent to my will thanks to
acts beneath my … divine position, he would no longer do so
if he learned of what I helped put in motion."

Yatzil craned her neck to find her friend still resisting,
and then she was gone. "YATZILLLL!"

"I shall return!" she screamed. "And with an army at my
back, have you executed for taking my friend and my father."

Her mother cackled. Her aged lips peeled back,
narrowing her gaze. "Come here my, foolish daughter."

The guards squeezed her limbs tighter, swiftly raising
her. Yatzil gasped, clamping down on her lower lip. The
guards aligned her with her mother like a drifting log against

an anchored ship. She dared not struggle, fearing the pain following a fall. What good would she be to Sachihiro if injury came from her efforts? Her mother dug her fingers into Yatzil's cheeks, exposing the jade squares upon her teeth.

"Try if you must, my … daughter. And if you … make it to your brother's city, have those unwashed nol bathed before the Four's guardians eat them."

YATZIL RUBBED HER EYES, shading her face against morning's light. The west's frequent storms would keep such annoyance at bay at least. Yatzil leered at the baskets stuffed with cod and ice chips being tied to three immense eagles. The birds nipped at their feathers near the grand steps leading down from the palace. Sachihiro emerged from the silhouettes of the birds. He embraced her to bid farewell. She brought him close, struggling to stay awake, wishing not to leave him behind. She knew he had duties to witness being done, rituals to perform, but for once, her brother ignored them. She had no plan on how she would deliver on her words, and if it came to seducing her husband. She shuddered.

A rumble broke off their goodbye from the palace's thick palm-and-oak doors. Their mother emerged, crowned over the brow by golden owl eyes before a dome helmet ringed by talons. Between the owl eyes, a jade queen held a crowned child. Yatzil hid her emotions from the guards and elderly priestess following close behind. The Mother of the King bowed to Sachihiro, spreading her hands to greet the waiting nol vizier. The wind tousled the vizier's white feathered head, his garb was made up of an arrangement of fur Yatzil had never seen before. Her mother granted the old man a thousand blessings and a safe journey for his guards. Yatzil bit her lip to contain herself.

"I must go, sister," said Sachihiro, peering over to the palace entrance. His crown was snug, crafted to match their mother's but with a moon between the owls' eyes. "I'll ... miss you."

His queen waited for him at a distance inside, wrapped in heavy black robes. Thin streaks of lightning danced down her smooth pearl white cheeks. Yatzil smiled at Queen Sute, surprised to receive one in return but there was pity in it. Whether from Sachihiro's sorrow or sympathy for Yatzil, there was no way to be certain.

"And I you." She released him and bowed before backing away. She crossed her hands and flashed their owl eyes. "I shall return. Be safe."

He rubbed at his eyes, but once he withdrew his hand they widened. "Mother comes," he whispered. "Call upon me if the Storm King brings you harm. Goodbye, Yatzil."

Yatzil messed up her face as he left, trailed by his royal guards. Labored breaths battled the constant wind as her mother drew closer. Her mother's crown partially hid one of the three immense eagles. It made certain the baskets were secure about its ankles. Beside it stood a handmaiden noticeably young in features. Yatzil had only seen her once at court. Her mother stood before her casting out a hand.

The old priestess knelt before it, hoisting a bowl with her bony arms. Slowly, as the wind gathered strength, she found a distraction from her mother's presence. Yatzil eyed the golden statues of the Four. They stood as watchers of the sky, seeking out disruptions to royal arrivals and departures. Her mother dipped a thumb in the bowl and gently painted glyphs on Yatzil's cheeks.

"I saw you noticed my replacement for the *other one*."

"Have you at least the benevolence to give Flor's body to her family?"

Yatzil winced. Her mother drew her thumb away then finished one set of glyphs. No blood came yet her cheek stung. Her mother pursed her lips.

"Do not speak, daughter. I wish not ... to leave a blemish. Believe it or not, I am proud of your beauty."

Rougher strokes ran over her left cheek until gold coated her mother's thumb.

"She escaped." the Mother of the King called up the priestess and made for the doors, peering over her shoulder, "but did not get far. You may say she fell of her own ... choice."

The doors rumbled shut, leaving her with three nol and a handmaiden she wished was Flor. Weakness ran over her knees; her breaths grew labored like a stonemason hoisting a great block. To escape the avalanche warriors sent, Flor had taken her own life. The nol vizier hobbled over to her side. His wrinkles drew taut, asking if illness was upon her. Yatzil reassured him and returned to proper posture.

"Go ready the eagles." she said, waving him away.

The handmaiden went to one knee, bowing at her approach. She appeared fresh from her womanhood cere-mony, no more than twelve. Tremors unsettled the bow she gave, and a gold moon remained solid and clear. Yatzil recalled her own ceremony, although a noble girl had the option of a boar over the obligation of a criminal to freeze from within. The vizier helped Yatzil upon the center eagle. A faint gasp made her turn before she settled herself. A collective flap signaled the takeoff of her guards' eagles. A shudder ran down her spine as her eagle cocked its head and strutted to the crest of the stairs. Yatzil shut her eyes, unsure of where the handmaiden went. Deep down, doubt battled within her gut for the change to come, but now it appeared her mother had new plans.

"Do not move," said a voice.

The scent of frost lily oil made her wish not to obey. Flor held her close as a great jerk and flap pressed them close together with the eagle taking flight. Yatzil kept her eyes shut, unnerved by what breathed between her legs. The eagle let out a long lingering screech. Flor relaxed her arms against Yatzil's clenched stomach.

"I fooled them," said Flor. "I took the hidden passage within your mother's bedchamber. I made them think I leapt from her balcony."

"I am glad it wasn't so." Yatzil opened her eyes to wipe away tears. "I was afraid to do this alone."

The eagle climbed higher, making a final pass around Niev city. Its high, thick white granite walls stood behind the still waters of its moat. Yatzil thought she saw an armored scale, that one of the Four's guardians pierced the water, but it was only a stretch of ice. The homes and high farms numbered in the thousands. A divided immense mansions from the rest of Niev, joined at its center by a gate. At the city center, four step pyramids aligned in a square, connected by a hollow jade moon. Beyond the city lay the Trunk, stretching to Nema's mainland, its two distant coasts dotted by fishing villages.

"You need not worry," Flor said over the wind. "And even if all was upon you, my princess, you are your father's daughter."

Her heart felt lighter, but doubt remained.

"Yes." Yatzil peered over her shoulder. "I … believe so. But I still have no plan or know how the nol shall survive Niev's guardians."

"Then. We must form a plan together."

CHAPTER THREE

Pain emanated from her palm as she eyed the sewn cut made by the priest. Drinking at the feast left her a little dizzy, but her senses remained like the pain of her blood trade. There was a faint pounding above, growing louder the more steps she climbed. Its pace fell behind the racing of her heart. The pop of braziers kept her nerves in check. Yatzil had witnessed the act of intertwinement done by her father in tribute to Fertilida. Every move he made brought the priestess closer, and to think of doing it made her stomach churn.

The pounding grew in speed, tempting Yatzil to ask her husband what the noise may be, but her wish to flee was stronger than her curiosity. The handmaiden kept a slower pace, molding her face without emotion and, like Yatzil, didn't know how to fly an eagle if escape was their original intent. Flor wore a white boar fur shawl over a close-fit dress and followed with less apprehension in her steps.

Yatzil shut her eyes to fend off unnerving thoughts, hearing whispers from her husband and Flor. Her mind spun and suddenly felt a presence. Frost lily oil filled her nostrils once she opened her eyes. Flor held her close. Yatzil gaped over her shoulder at King Amteer. He nodded and turned away, leaving her to wonder how long he would wait.

She slowly accepted her friend's embrace, wishing to wear the same scent on her skin. The Nol to her misfortune found such fragrance unnatural, and thus, didn't permit it. Yatzil swallowed and forced her to focus on her wants, on her husband and how their union would aid in ending her mother's corruption of Sachihiro.

"It must be done, Yatzil," Flor whispered.

There was a hint of nervousness in Flor's words which brought Yatzil's courage to its knees. Neither favored the plan they had in place, but it was no use wishing for a scroll they had never found.

"Above all," said Flor. "You must bend him to your needs or there will be no—"

"But I am not ready." Yatzil interrupted in a hushed tone. "There must be—"

Flor rested a finger to Yatzil's lips, focus narrowed her friend's unpainted eyes. Yatzil peered over her shoulder again. Amteer folded his arms and met her gaze with a soft curiosity.

"If you do not commit to this," Flor said. "Who will?"

Yatzil carefully rubbed the tension from her emotions, feeling the paint of the glyphs upon her cheeks. They were meant to protect her if the storm king took leave of his senses. Flor possessed the skill to protect her, and Yatzil knew she too possessed strength to do the same.

"I shall keep to our plan," said Yazil.

The handmaiden bowed, and they continued with only ten braziers before a pair of immense doors. Yatzil sifted through her mind to piece each nol dance move together. They mixed with ones meant to grant her hopeful future army passage into Niev. The passage dance partnered with glyphs of the Four around her navel. They chased one another in an oval with nescaran glyphs of war, fertility, cleanliness, and sea. Nema was said to have been danced into existence, and those who wished for children were to emulate the dance from which kingdom they resided. She prodded at the mint leaves wedged between her teeth. Their abrupt freshness bothered her but pleased King Amteer enough to have them leave the feast early.

Dust glazed the wolf head nobs to King Amteer's bedchamber. Flor took hold of the rings within their snarling jaws. The passage dance remained more prominent than the nol dance, no matter how hard she focused. Time was close and, even if a move was forgotten, the Storm King had an air of forgiveness. Yatzil readied to remove her pale green top, its dangling frigagator teeth around its trim tapped against her flesh. Her husband fumbled the knot to his half kilt. It left bare one leg and blanketed the other in feathers embroidered with a golden eagle. Her fingers were slick with sweat, something she'd seen plague her father after poisoned. She shot a gaze upon Flor and found droplets on her brow.

"You may open the doors, handmaiden," said Amteer. "And close them once our dance is done."

Flor pushed open the doors and gasped.

Yatzil's eyes widened, struck by a wave of heat. A flash blinded her for seconds, stinging and jabbing her eyes. She rubbed them before a dark shape collided with her. The crown tumbled off her head, yanking at her long black hair in the process.

"What has happened?" Yatzil said, recognizing the shape. Amteer was upon her, eyes clamped shut. "What was that light?"

She peered over his shoulder and saw through the door and beyond a balcony fire rained. The flames bombarded one of the toothed cities surrounding Wolfstrong. A great flash of light forced her eyes shut. Echoes of panic reached her ears from down the hall.

"Who attacks, Storm King?" said Flor.

"Someone," said Amteer, peering back to see, like her, the city engulfed in flame. "Someone..., I thought it was only a story."

Yatzil rose with his help. His hand shook over her own, but despite his fear the young king led them down the hall.

They found a bedchamber a few paces away. Dust fell from the beams protecting the room like ribs over organs. Flor slammed the doors shut and pressed her back against it. Yatzil guided King Amteer to a bed. His stomach rose and fell in quick successions. She averted her eyes to his long dark feathers held aloft in his crown and made a face. *His garb is torn, and I can see...* She commanded Flor to find something to cover him, but there was nothing. Flor offered her shawl and bowed, tension ran through her fingers. She rested the shawl in the nol king's hands. *It was her favorite.* Yatzil grimaced.

"Please, Amteer, who invades us?" said Yatzil.

King Amteer tossed aside his torn garb and wrapped the shawl about his waist. Yatzil hesitated, then caressed his cheek. She hoped it would calm him and retrieve his fleeing courage, but his lips trembled. It made her question if he had seen battle, or if whoever laid siege to Wolfstrong was something worse than war. She kept her frustrations at bay until finally Amteer spoke.

"They're the Palenore," said Amteer. "Long ago, the kingdoms united to defend Nema from a great burning star."

He eased her hand away, plodded to the doors and pressed his ear to one.

"I know we won and imprisoned the palenore behind Plunemar," He sighed and faced her. "Their Queen Aagono murdered all but the Fifth Nemamoon. I'm sorry our wedding night was ruined."

Yatzil moved toward him, unsure, raising her hands slightly. His fists were bawled, and tears lingered at the corners of his eyes.

"I have failed you and my people before I—"

"Shhh." She hugged him. His back tensed at her touch. "There shall be time for such things."

She gulped, hesitated, and then kissed his cheek. To act sure of herself was foolish, but she needed him on her side. If they lived, his forces would aid in overthrowing her mother's influence on Sachihiro's subjects. And yet, as the dust fell and the palace quivered, how could any of that be possible?

"You have not failed yet," she said, ignoring the damp smell all rutoe of the west possessed. "Come! Let's help everyone we can."

———

THEY CREPT DOWN several sets of cascading stairs. The skulls of wolves lined every wall, everyone a reminder of the first dynasty to rule the west. The ribs of the largest wolves supported the palace itself. No bones of dead eagles graced their way, but statues of previous storm kings and queens, cloaked as the large birds, guarded every room.

A finely detailed tapestry caught her eye, telling of four armies fighting the palenore on separate lands. The first army were immense yellow-fanged and gray-furred wolves. The second a legion of fearsome ice blue panthers. A third creature spewed yellow lightning from its immense red jaws. Yatzil thought Sachihiro's raton queen strong, but not fearsome like the dragon emerging from a mass of black clouds.

A faint glow peeked from down the hall. It highlighted a being of shadow and vines farthest from the other armies.

Shouts came when they were short of the corner. Above the towering set of doors, a tapestry showed five rutoe women, whom she believed were the nemamoons Amteer spoke of. They stood tall wrapped in flowing robes, reaching out to the five armies. Each were identical in face but possessed the skin tone and hair of the rutoe alive today.

Amteer peered around the corner, urging her and Flor to stay back. Yatzil rubbed her eyes, the brazier light convincing her the fifth woman above the others had winked. She squinted, peering over Amteer's shoulder to find the light's. She gasped.

Black arrows protruded from two guards sprawled on the floor, a third crawled toward them. An arrow pierced through his knee scraped at the stonework. Further down the hall, two pale men emerged, laughing, and shouldering their bows. A third ran up and severed the crawling guard's head, brandishing a sword forged from a diamond. Blood dripped in a pattern as he danced. He chose a brazier and dropped the head, sending up flames and stirring smoke. Yatzil squinted to make out the others. Their skin made them invisible in the light except for their black leggings and arrow stocked quivers.

"They were no use." said one.

"The First Son and Daughter will be displeased," said another. His voice sounded like he had swallowed fire. "If we return without those brats, it'll cost us our heads."

One stepped from the light, resembling the thickly muscled palenore streaming from their burning star upon the largest tapestry. Yatzil searched for a way to get past them, rubbing her eyes again. Amteer jabbed his thumb at the rookery. The doors were marked by perched red stone eagles on either side. Fingertips hissed across her shoulder. Flor ran down the hall and fell to her knees, short of the light.

"No." Yatzil screamed. She clamored around Amteer to find her friend begging, but every plea met only laughter.

"Run." Flor shouted; ice raced over her formed fists. She swung, but a palenore caught her wrist. Flor swung the other and cleaved skin from the man's jaw. "Run now."

Amteer grabbed Yatzil's hand. Her other hand reached before the three palenore called for them to halt, flinging the rookery doors open they stopped cold. Eagles lay bloodied and spread across the floor, chained to a metal rail above. Some eagles lay headless, littered with arrows. The coppery scent filling her nostrils was something she was used to, but such carnage churned bile in her belly.

"There you two are. No death by beheading for us."

A yank at her shoulders forced Yaztil back. The palenore's arms wrapped around her as another pressed a short sword to the small of Amteer's back. Trickles of blood ran down it, and straw crunched the more Yatzil struggled for freedom.

"Let us go." said Yatzil.

Her captor's thick fingers sank into her arms like a hungry diamond-fang. There was a familiar warmth to them the deeper they dug.

"Take me," said Amteer.

The tallest palenore ran his fingers through his scarlet quills, their black rings clicked against one another. His breath muddied Amteer's eyes. A yellowish glow flared through the tall warrior's teeth.

"The First Son and Daughter want you both," he said. "I wouldn't be a good captain if I brought just one of you."

Amteer's face turned black the more the captain's breath cooked his face. Yatzil bawled her fists and struggled faster. She might not have wanted this marriage but 'aiding one who offers aid to you' was her father's way. She cried out for the captain's mercy. The captain chuckled. Her skin faded and hardened to solid ice. Yatzil narrowed her eyes as they ignited yellow. The breath of the palenore holding her misted against her neck. His teeth chattered like her sacrifice had when she proved her womanhood. Yatzil twisted free, but he grabbed her wrist.

The yellow highlighting his muscles faded with his strength. She smiled when the cold forced him into a coughing fit. Her iced knuckles could shatter his jaw, but she needed to remain a delicate frost lily. The palenore warrior dropped to his knees, spitting ice crystals at her feet. Amteer's tormentor focused his sword at her, pushing Amteer to the ground. She hadn't even moved and already he shook. He lunged, gagging, collapsing to the ground with a thud. The Storm King yanked free the dagger she hadn't noticed under the captain's belt.

One palenore remained as blood dripped from the dagger. Yatzil edged a toe forward, sending him cowering off. Her husband grinned. *He believes his use of the dagger is why.* Yatzil thought, containing her disappointment.

"What was that?" Amteer shook his head. "I thought a nescaran's power over cold was just a rumor."

As her fingers thawed, she bit her tongue at his assumption and felt the cut on his back. It was a nick, yet pretending it was worse might further earn his trust.

"This must be bandaged," she said, withdrawing her hand swiftly. "Our wish to help others has cut you deep. I can numb the pain."

"I'm fine." he said. As he removed the captain's belt, his tone was more confident than earlier. "It will fast."

Screech. She jumped, kicking up straw, ready to frost again. *Clank* went a chain on the rail above. It spun and went taut, colliding with the limp chains beside it. Yatzil remained fused to the spot, eyeing the chain. Amteer applied the belt and approached the struggling chain. It grinded at a stone pillar, tormenting her ears.

"A nescaran's power the over the cold is very much real."

"I'm glad," Amteer said. "Or else I would never see you again."

She folded hand over hand and smiled. *I need not hold back.* The eagle was smaller than its dead brethren. The way eagles cocked their heads gave her nightmares. She covered her stomach, picturing its beak tearing away ribs and gobbling her heart. This one was young, possessing dark brown feathers. It wore a thick iron collar around its neck, rust chips fell from it as the eagle clicked its beak.

"Come, Ringna." Amteer slid a thick pin from the collar, then removed it. "She is my wife and won't hurt you." He caressed the matted feathers around the bird's neck. "Come, Yatzil. It's all right. She won't harm you."

Ringna dipped her neck before Yatzil had a chance to stroke it. Amteer rubbed the eagles back, coaxing her to lower herself. He offered a hand. Yatzil hiked up her dress and took it. The fabrics and boars' teeth from her dress dug deep into her legs. Footsteps sent her focus to the hall entrance. She made a fist, but the bird bucked, and she grabbed hold of the ring of feathers at its neck. Amteer edged toward the entrance. Yatzil gasped.

"My Queen."

CHAPTER FOUR

A need to weep ran through Yatzil's very being at Flor leaning on a broken spear shaft. The handmaiden hobbled towards her, breathless, pressing her frosted fingers to a slowly expanding stain of red at her stomach.

"Thank the Four," said Yatzil. "Come with us."

"Ringna can carry only two," said Amteer.

The bird's tail feathers were close to where Yatzil's bottom slid to remain mounted. She found herself without words to say. Her friend's courage was equal to the nescaran queens of old. The handmaiden moved toward the rookery doors, panting, blood seeping between her fingers and shattering in frozen droplets.

"It will be well, my queen," she grunted, and with a whisper, snatched Yatzil's breath away, *"I will miss you."*

Flor pushed with all her might, sliding an old iron studded board from across the doors. Yatzil flinched at the press of Amteer's lips to her forehead before he mounted Ringna. The board slammed into the floor kicking up dust. Black ice expanded between Flor's fingers. And with another heave Flor swung open the doors. Light blinded them for seconds. Footsteps echoed from the entrance to the hall.

"Take her someplace safe, Storm King," said Flor.

Yatzil's vision blurred with light and tears, wrapping her arms around Amteer. Shouts came with the palenore growing closer. Flor steadied herself against a worn wooden support beam. And with a leap Ringna took off.

Wind tangled with the light above and the black of Yatzil's hair. Beyond the relentless winds, Flor raised a hand to wave but instead, she shrieked and dropped to her knees. Black ice raced from her wound consuming the agony in her face. Shadows crept swiftly upon the handmaiden's blackened, frozen pose. *Smash.* A short sword burst through Flor's chest and shattered her to pieces, shredding her dress. Yatzil screamed, readying to leap from the eagle and freeze a path. The wind whipped against her fingers, but she could not grasp at any moisture in the air. Palenore filled the archway, slipping on and kicking her friend's remains, scattering them. Their disregard unleashed the rage Flor had taught her to tame. She withdrew her hand, feeling her eyes burned with fury.

Heat rose from the churning river encircling Wolfstrong. The palace's arched tongued peak was peppered by fading black pillars of smoke. The white fang-shaped cities surrounding it were blackened. Fireballs barreled through apple orchards circling the face of each city upon wide cliff farms. The fireball smoldered until a palonore emerged with a main of red quills. The ash slid down his shoulders forming a bow, sword, arrows, and leggings down to his ankles.

Screech!

Three large eagles flew toward them. Amteer jabbed his foot into Ringna's side, sending the bird bolting over a stretch of maples. Further and further until the palace and cities sank out of view. The trees formed lips over the cities like a wolf's mouth. Amteer said the First Son controlled the Highnonstar above for it was his namesake. *His fear was justified.* She thought, witnessing Plunemar red, covered in cracks of black, flashing and then releasing more fireballs upon the west. *The moon is gone.* she thought. *What will become of Nema?*

They headed north over a churning river. Yatzil licked her lips, craving the cool droplets of the west's storms. The sky was empty of clouds and only the salt of her sweat reached her tongue. A wish to tell her husband to turn around came but the risk was too great. It would not help Flor to get a proper burial and her remains may already be lost.

Screech.

Yatzil's eyes darted to an arrow jutting from Ringna's left wing. One palenore made it within reach, but Amteer urged Ringna to spin right. It freed the arrow, thrusting Yatzil's stomach into her throat. She regained her breath, witnessing the red quilled warrior barrel roll into a stretch of trees.

Two remained, gaining once Amteer coaxed Ringna further north, shrinking Wolfstrong, blinking it out of sight. She gasped. An arrow wisped and dropped past them. It was not the arrow that had come so close but the faded glyphs on her husband's back. *May these entrance glyphs remain like their dance within my mind.* She edged toward Ringna's tail.

"Stay close," said Amteer. "You'll slow Ringna."

"My apologies." Yatzil edged within inches of his back. "I wished for a better look at our pursuers."

"They'll be gone before you know it. They don't know the west like I do."

A lake appeared before a vast domed mountain. They dipped towards it, gliding a few feet above the lake's surface. Their pursuers were distant, but Yatzil feared the smaller bird may tire soon.

"We'll head for the Lid." Amteer pointed to the mountain. "Their eagles can't manage its maze of trees."

"How can you be certain?" said Yatzil. "They seem swift and powerful to me."

"A smaller bird like Ringna has the advantage."

Twisting and turning through every stretch of trees, they came within a scented range of pine and maple. With the shade growing denser, the strain in her eyes eased. Amteer gave Ringna another nudge at her side just as an arrow whizzed past Yatzil's head. She peered back to find they had lost their advantage.

"Go back up, Amteer." She squeezed his shoulder. "He will hit us—"

"No, just one more turn."

He pouted. Yatzil bit her lip, cursing behind her teeth, and found her lack of faith had returned his hopelessness. His back tensed when she apologized. He kicked Ringna so hard that the bird veered before striking a long stretch of jagged boulders. The force of it threw off his crown and freed his feathers. Yatzil ducked as they reached outward. A crack and screech summoned a scream sending the remaining palenore into the ground. Her mouth gaped as Amteer laughed. He brought Ringna up high again. The glyphs upon her stomach remained intact, but with Amteer's risky behavior she doubted his ability to command.

They landed in a narrow clearing above a village. Smoke sifted through the trees, yet it was not of homes burning but the scent of meat. Meat she had only tasted at her wedding feast, making her mouth water. Her husband helped her off the eagle's back, a scowl contorting his face. She took a step back and pressed down the wrinkles of her dress.

"I am sorry for my misjudgment."

"You should be," said Amteer, stepping back, the dagger

tucked in the captain's belt. "I know what I'm doing. You said I have not failed yet, and now you doubt me like—"

"Who doubts you? I was afraid."

She stiffened her lips only to have them quiver. None, not even Flor had ever shown such childish nature to her. Yatzil was thankful to be permitted more emotion in the west, but to experience this was strange. Amteer clamped down his teeth like she had taken his crown. She hoped the anger she saw could be forgotten and made well.

"My father tested me frequently and called me useless when I would fail. He tested me, because among my brothers and mother, I had survived the raton's *giftnos*. But he's the one dead."

Amteer slammed his hand against a pine tree, loosing dozens of nuts. One tapped Yatzil's shoulder as her husband rubbed his palm.

"I think only of myself, don't I?" He snatched up a branch shaken loose by his anger. "I'll return with food and firewood."

His footsteps kicked up pine needles, leaving an easy trail to follow but she didn't. She rubbed her cheeks, smearing the glyphs into her skin. It was better to be careful with what she said. *His father lied about him, and they both are prideful.*

Her worry of glyphs relied more on the ones upon her stomach. Every glyph and owl goddess were smudged, but the ones upon her thighs remained untouched. She swallowed and gathered words to convince the Storm King of Sachihiro's troubles. Her troubles. Yatzil let her dress drop, swinging with an iced fist against a tree. *Crack!* She yanked her fist free, losing dozens of splinters.

"Why have the palenore decided to return now?"

Yatzil dropped to her knees, crushing many nuts. Her fist thawed with each deep breath to ease her frustrations. A crack ran up and down the tree from her strike. Ringna cocked her head toward her. Yatzil covered her stomach, heavy breaths keeping her fingers from further blurring the entrance glyphs. Ringna turned away as if in disgust.

She rested her hands in the grass and let her mind drift to the forest Flor had shown her around Niev. Those forests of the Trunk were safe with Plunemar in its western phase, but with the moon gone, and the Highnonstar in its place had those phases stopped. Yatzil contemplated prayer for the Plunemar's return, but neither Urra, Non, Fertilida nor Limpe had bothered to answer her of late.

Snap. Yatzil spun, pushing against the ground until the teeth of her top clicked against the tree left in ruin by her rage.

"What happened?" asked Amteer.

Yatzil eyed the eagle nipping at her feathers.

"Your bird attacked me." She held up her hand to Amteer. "My bracelet was missing, and I thought…"

"Ringna." Amteer dropped an armful of broken branches on the ground. "You give her what she wants." He squeezed the back of the eagle's thick neck. "I'm sorry, I'll find it."

"It is likely gone with our pursuers." She focused on the leaf-like pouch stuffed into his belt. "Is there food in that pouch?"

Amteer slipped it from his belt, unfolding its leaves. Berries with purple and white streaks piled in his palm.

"They are called *tootens*," he said. "If you eat three you will not be hungry for a day."

She plucked three from the pile, plopping one in her mouth. The juices were sweet. Her stomach was as full as if she ate two plates of roasted boar.

"What gives it such a name?" she asked.

Yatzil ate the other two once Amteer swallowed his.

"I'm not sure. Food earns a name for how it makes you feel later."

The Storm King gathered up the branches and stacked them. Yatzil licked her lips, savoring the berries' juices. Her husband struck tiny stones plucked from behind his ears. She hadn't noticed them amongst his long dark feathers. The nol appeared to be always well equipped. Feathers grew from their heads, but in the south a feather acted as a tool to record events. He stuffed grass into the wood and coaxed a tiny flame with slow breaths until smoke rose. Up through the trees, the Highnonstar pierced some of the branches forcing her eyes to her toes. What leaves remained drooped, as if missing the rain. Bushes around her clutched at their green like a wife to her warrior husband.

"I am troubled by my rush to judgment," said Yatzil. "Can you forgive me?"

Amteer sat silent for a moment, poking at the fire with his dagger.

"I'm more worried about the Palenore."

Now she had the need to tell him what she was worried about most. He rubbed his eyes, resting his chin against his chest. If she were to give him another worry, then why not hold his eyes open to the Highnonstar's brightness. Yatzil pursed her lips and felt the same wish to save Nema, but the drive to help Sachihiro was stronger.

"My mother murdered my father and holds the loyalty of my brother's subjects."

"What?" Amteer sat up straight, jamming the dagger into the dirt. "But he's king. Without him, we can't unite the kingdoms like before."

"We must gather your people to save him then." She breathed deep through her nose to channel the anger building. Her mother's face flashed across her mind. "He knows not of her treason."

"We must do as you have said then. I hope the east and north are still free." he sighed, pressing thumb and forefinger to his brow. "If we can save him, it may cost more of our people."

His worry was justified, and if she kept the glyphs upon her stomach intact and remembered the dance, then the Nol had a chance. The wind gathered speed, swaying trees, teasing their fire, and hadn't come yet for some reason. She dismissed her final thought, overwhelmed by the thought that what she wanted felt so huge only a Nemamoon could accomplish it.

CHAPTER FIVE

T he night never arrived. Yatzil eased her eyes open to a brightness she had never experienced with the sun. She frowned and groaned at the ache in her back, rising from behind a bush. The *tooten's* were perfectly named, leaving her flatulent for many hours. It wasn't only the berries forcing her to sleep alone, but the fire worsening the rising heat. Her people required no heat for warmth. She eyed her husband wondering what possessed him to build a fire when there was no need.

The treetops were browner than earlier, and Yatzil saw no way of knowing how long she had slept, or if morning had arrived. Yatzil frosted her hands to be certain her power over cold had not been stolen by Highnonstar. They dripped, so she frosted her entire self, and smiled from the chill consuming her. Amteer stirred, and as he did, she held back a deep sorrow for him. King Yanter had boasted of Amteer's skill as a warrior while doubting him. Yatzil wondered if Amteer's wavering mood made him fit to lead his people to save her brother or battle the Highnonstar. For now, she focused on keeping him on her side.

"The mud is drying. I miss the storms of my lands." Amteer said. He sniffed the air. "Do you smell something?"

She closed her eyes for a moment and sniffed. Her mouth watered at the seasoned scent blended with something unfamiliar.

"It is stronger in this direction." she said, taking in the aroma once more. "It must be from the village I saw. Let's head that way so the villagers will surely aid us."

Branches snapped as Ringna followed with her tail feathers brushing tree trunks.

"Stay here." Amteer brushed a hand over Ringna's beak. "We'll return."

"Will we need a coin?" said Yatzil, ignoring the flustered eagle. "I carry none on me."

The forest floor slowly sloped with each step they took. Whatever kind of meat was cooking, it was seasoned for certain. Yatzil had spent much time in the palace kitchens as a child. Her *lamodun* warned against it, but the meal makers honored her presence, teaching of spices, glazes, and when meat was ready for eating. Her *lamodun* also gave her lessons and kept her safe, for which she was grateful.

"We use trade. Our people … know about my father but not us. I'll need warmer clothes to head south." He looked her up and down. "You'll need something to blend in with our people, if the palenore come for us again."

She gazed at the muddy and wrinkled mess of her wedding garb.

"I understand."

The journey north came with one stop, a grand villa built in nescaran style. A small step pyramid of white granite with rooms within and a high thick wall surrounding it. She forced it to memory and hoped if Amteer sent his people south that the villa's noble would keep his promise. *He understood and swore upon his sons' lives.* Yatzil focused on every move Flor taught her to appease the Four's guardians as the village drew near.

Amteer spun the palenore dagger in his fingers like a performer baton. He stuffed it beside the captain's sword. Its pommel was round and had a red gem like a burning comet she had once seen.

The huts appeared from between the trees like mud covered domes, ribbed by bent trees stripped of bark. Yatzil snatched Amteer's hand when men rose from turning a rump on a spit. Grease dripped from it and hissed into the fire. Eyes laced with suspicion peered from strips of hide bound nol heads. Yatzil drained her face of emotion, wishing for something to protect her own eyes from the brightness. A young man smiled, noticing her straining eyes, offering his own strip of hide, but was elbowed in the gut by an older man with long gray feathers.

With each step the huts grew more clustered, some in fine shape or in need of mending as they stretched down the Lid. Children ran past her and through a bustling market of wagons and baskets arranged on blankets. Yatzil picked up a handful of apples, gazing at them, not familiar with their taste, but recalled them from the wedding feast.

"How do you like this?"

She rested the apples atop a full basket and bit her lip. Amteer's choice was plain unlike her own grab. Small stone coins with etched images of storms lined the dress's V-shape collar, polished, outlined in amber. A beige made up its color, and the material was from an animal. Its smoothness was more suitable for a cushion. There was a sash to accompany it possessing long strips of fabric trimmed like eagle wings. Yatzil smiled to appease the old woman sitting behind a canopied wagon bearing a mound of clothes. Amteer picked a pair of dark leggings, a wide stringed loincloth, and a fur lined coat. He offered the old woman the palenore dagger. Its pommel glistened in the light.

"Will you take this dagger for all of it?"

The old nol peered over her mound of clothes. Her gray feathered head was shaded by her wagon's red fabric canopy. She stroked her chin, admiring how the light glistened off the dagger's diamond blade.

"You can keep it and what you have chosen, Storm King."

The two youths gaped at her, wide eyed. Yatzil saw the old woman staring blankly at the symbol of Amteer's dynasty on his chest. A proud golden eagle with wings long and wide, its talons balled like fists.

"But she must offer something of hers," she hissed through white gums at Yatzil. "That nescaran will bring you trouble."

Yatzil's stomach churned, laying the dress down.

"She is my wife and your storm queen," said Amteer. "Our kingdoms are at peace."

Amteer scowled. The old nol leaned back as the Storm King strangled the rail of her wagon. He climbed atop a nearby barrel as the crowd gathered from his commotion. It was like the panicked boy of before had disappeared again.

"All of you would be wise to see our real enemy is who torments our eyes. It's Highnonstar that robbed us of our sacred storms."

The men turned to their wives and children and after a moment bowed to her and Amteer. By the look on the aged silver faces, and the youth in others, his words had removed some suspicion. A few nol men furthest away shook their heads and stormed off.

"I'm sorry for my anger," said the old nol woman. "You may have the dress. I need to find my grandchild. She's likely hiding in my daughter's hut."

She hopped off her stool, wincing with each step over tiny stones littering the ground.

"Wait," Yatzil said. "I may have something for you."

Yatzil slipped off her jade encrusted sandals.

"These were my grandmother's."

She held them tight for a moment, exhaled, and handed them to the Nol woman. Stones pricked at her well-groomed feet, but the pain went away after receiving a thankful smile.

"You are most kind. I'm Haseya."

Haseya slipped on the sandals.

"May your journey be as smooth as this boar leather feels. You are young but must have an idea as to what we all must do."

"Go south," said Amteer. "My queen's brother needs our help."

"Does he, my queen?" Haseya had a glint of worry in her eyes. "Why should we help him if he raids our border villages?"

"Raids?" said Amteer.

Panic slithered through Yatzil's body at this news. Had Sachihiro missed her enough to risk war? Yatzil gave Haseya a queer look. Amteer stepped between them. His face gripped by disappointment.

"Head for the Gaping Mouth," he said, peering down at Haseya. "Its tunnels are vast with places to hide." He glared at Yatzil. "If this is true, we have two enemies to deal with, and you lied to me, Yatzil."

"My brother is no fool." said Yatzil, pleading, her eyes strained by light and panic. "What peace my father made with yours is binding, and my mother did as I have said."

Every villager shouted for her to leave, making harsh remarks about the wrinkled mess of her garb and how Nescarans were traitorous. She raised her hands, quieting the rising din.

"My brother keeps to tradition, and by it will not dare make war without the moon in the south."

Amteer relaxed a little and raised his hand to further calm everyone.

"We will head south first and send winded word if it's safe. Everyone, head for the Gaping Mouth mine." he said, lowering his hand as he did.

The old nol woman bowed and the rest of the village followed her lead. Yatzil and Amteer gathered what was given to them as all began to clear the market. His decision sank her hopes to the bottom of her belly.

As they headed back to Ring the whiff of cooking meat calmed her nerves. A few slightly charred slithers were carved off by the older Nol from earlier. His smile calmed her nerves further, handing her the meat wrapped in a leaf untouched by Highnonstar's rath. Yatzil tore off small pieces like her *lamodun* taught her. But when the herbs and juices met her tongue, all lessons disappeared.

She savored it, a plan formed on how to send the villagers south. Yatzil grimaced at the thought of seduction, but it meant a guide. She peered up at the nol going about their business. The villagers emptied their huts of fur and garb, struggling to manage with the hide over their eyes. She sighed, hoping the task before her will encourage Amteer to unite his people and grant her the army she needed.

Amteer was given them a handful of pouches stuffed with dried meat and grasses to fuel fires. Yatzil was given a knife which by the heft of its blade surpassed the palenore dagger. Unlike a nescaran dagger the hilt was without decoration and the blade possessed only one edge.

As her and Amteer went up the Lid, a faint trickling came from her right. She scratched at mud, smeared up her arm, missing her three daily cleansings and begged that they go wash. The young king frowned at first but then followed her.

It was clear he missed his old life and was troubled by Haseya's words. Yatzil frowned, missing the chill of the south, but most of all Flor. To not have Flor at her side was like losing a limb. She yanked her mind to the present and realized Amteer had stood up for her. If only he had not dashed such a surprise by disarming her intended plan. The nol priest during their wedding ceremony told them, loyalty bonded them in more ways than their vows. Amteer's choice had weakened her loyalty to him, but this was more important.

Yatzil dipped a finger in the mildly cold stream. Her eyes stung more than earlier from the Highnonstars rays. She parted from him to wash alone.

"Stay with me, Yatzil."

"I shall be fine," she said, wanting time to think. "Can you fill those ... water skins they gave us?"

The villagers had given them what looked like dried out lungs. Bile ran over her tongue at their odd shape, their shriveled look. Amteer sighed, then nodded. She left him, avoiding large stones, pleased giving up her grandmother's sandals brought trust, but winced at a sharp misstep. Yatzil let out a breath at a bush tall enough to give privacy.

She dropped her new clothes on a boulder. The glyphs upon her thighs bent and merged with her movements as she removed her dress to make water. Leaning against a tree made it easier since no chamber pot held by handmaidens was possible. Yatzil regretted having them do this, but it was another minor tradition her mother insisted on.

She removed her top then shuddered. It had to be done. Flor had reminded her throughout their journey that seduction was their strongest option, but to take it was to emulate her mother. Every breath caught in her throat; her mind fell like Flor's remains to Wolfstong's encircling river. She sighed and wet the end of her dress to rub away mud. There was no way to honor her friend with a burial necklace. Flor deserved one of jade, and *not* bronze whale bone. *Snap.* Yatzil cocked her head upstream, finding Amteer struggling with the leggings.

Yatzil shook his awkward movements from her mind, wishing only to focus on loss. The light hid the stream bed, and the owl eyes upon her hands glared at her.

"I must for Sachihiro. I … cannot afford to fail."

She made a face before snatching up the sash. Her body swam within how large it was, so she wrapped it around her waist. Its fabrics were smooth like the throne cushion from her wedding feast, but it made her feel bone thin. Abandoning her dress, Yatzil drew in a breath and wrapped her top about her chest, not wishing to discard what Flor had chosen. She grabbed the Nol dress and knife. Every move the nol childbearing dance required crawled back into her memory.

"I wanted to ask at the feast." Amteer said with a light tone, admiring the palenore sword. "How do you speak my language so well? It must have been hard."

Yatzil let the slight against her go, dropping the knife and dress on the ground. Language was what she excelled at most in her lessons.

"It was far less complicated than you may imagine."

"I don't know," said Amteer. "I'm still…"

An unsureness crept over his face as she rested a hand to his chest. But as if remembering her words, at Wolfstong he cast aside the palenore sword. He raised his arms and then cocked them to begin the dance. Yatzil cursed under her breath and raised hers in the same fashion, brushing a foot against his shin. He did so in the same fashion. They circled like a pair of eagles as a chill ran over the cut on her palm. The nol priest had placed her hand in Amteer's after giving it to her. Time slowed dramatically making her wonder if this was from the merging of their blood.

"We must come together, you and I." She puffed up chest, arching her back to make her breasts more prominent. Her eyes fixed on his own as she untied and removed her top. "And then we shall make everything right."

Yatzil undid the sash, letting it puddle at her feet. And in seconds, Amteer slipped off his clothes, tossing them to the side beside her own. She slowly rested her hands at her hips. They brushed cheek to cheek like birds their beaks, laying down where they had danced.

"I'll keep you safe."

She rested her lips to his and gasped. Yatzil braced at the sudden, heavy thrust as he began. She shrugged off the press of his lip to her neck.

"And I you." she whispered, pressing her back to the ground to grant him a view of her breasts.

She pressed her legs about his waist to entice him. And as his thrusts grew deeper and more frequent, it felt as if there had been meaning in her words. His lips pressed roughly against her own, burrowing his tongue, touching her own. Yatzil pulled his face to her chest and swallowed the compulsion to vomit.

CHAPTER SIX

Intertwinement wasn't what she imagined it would be. She was sore from his rough, hammering efforts. Yatzil ground her teeth when he had raked his fingers through her hair. And when they changed positions, Yatzil had to pretend that doing all the work as ladies of her father's court called it pleased her.

"We'll keep going south together," Amteer said, breathless unlike herself. "The Gaping Mouth is safest for our people, Yatzil."

Amteer turned over, shrugging away Yatzil's touch before falling asleep. Despite her gentle words once they had finished, Yatzil found she possessed none of what her mother did in getting what she wanted. Yatzil snatched a leaf and crushed it. *Does he not understand?* Snoring rumbled out and drew in from him, and the longer she dwelled, the clearer it was Amteer would be no help.

She shut her eyes and slammed her fist into the dirt with a soft thud. She wasn't certain if Ringna remained where they had left it, but she half hoped it was gone. Yatzil curled into a ball and then felt her heart stop. Her eyes shot open, gold was smeared over her legs and up her stomach. Yatzil focused on what the glyphs looked like and every move their dance required. She exhaled, repeating what each glyph was, how each dance movement went until sleep consumed her.

Wind held back her hair with its fierce strength, neither warm nor cold. Her eyes rested on what she believed no longer existed. Long black spikes ran down the dragon's back, with red scales over its body, as it flew amongst clouds. Yatzil braced herself to one of its spikes, but somehow, she remained steady as if standing on solid ground. Below, an ocean swelled, and above dark thunder clouds filled the sky with lightning bolts going off at the storm's edge. An island lay ahead with wide leaf trees.

Yatzil saw a woman strolling along the shore; a yellow shawl wrapped loosely around her chest and shoulders. A long flowing black dress held tight to her hips, splaying like flower petals about her ankles. Her arms gestured in graceful patterns of spirals and thrusts. The woman was like the figure upon the walls of Wolfstrong, silencing any doubt of her not being a Nemamoon. Yatzil admired her grace as the dragon circled the island. The Nemamoon was untouched by age, yet Yatzil found no rutoe kingdom in Nema to place her. The others, whose garb was familiar to her, represented Nescarans, Raton, nol and Lijani.

No words formed from the goddess's lush lips, but a voice surfaced in Yatzil's mind, saying she must come to this very island. Yatzil swallowed, sniffed, then shook her head. The deep longing to remove her mother was stronger than answering a stranger's invitation. And by what words flowed into her mind, the Nemamoon sounded desperate.

"I must help my brother."

The Nemamoon nodded and continued to dance.

Yatzil woke to a figure lying on the ground beside her. She leaned over and found it wasn't who she wanted. Amteer's dark feathers were long like Flor's hair. His feathers remained stiff as if caught in a heavy breeze. Yatzil snatched up her top, held it close, and then rose from the ground.

It was time. The dream had been strange, yet she was compelled to make up for her refusal someday. She dressed, grabbing the knife, a water skin and two pouches of dried meat. Every step was slow at first until only the tips of Amteer's feathers were visible through the overgrowth. The storm king had defended her from the villagers. She found trust existed with him, yet the risk of having him act as he did when they were chased was too great. She left him dried meat and a waterskin to show gratitude.

A low hum met her ears before she found the eagle asleep. *She snores?* Yatzil ignored the scattered bones and blood streaks erasing Amteer's fire. She frosted a fist but realized an eagle was not a tree and frosted entirely. To be frosted brought great strength, and she dared to believe, with so much at stake, the near invincibility Sachihiro spoke of.

Blood coated the eagle's beak. She reached to stroke Ringna's neck with every finger trembling and her stomach in knots. Yatzil yanked her hand back, cradling it like the sleeping bird had snapped. Every thought went to her stomach being ripped apart. Amteer used foot thrusts to Ringna's sides and light tugs at her neck feathers to fly her. Stretching out her hand once more the eagle stirred. The bird's eyelids twitched open then shut. Yatzil wrinkled her nose, spun, and then took off at a run.

Low branches whipped against her face, their very tips tugging briefly at her hair. She stretched out her fingers to freeze a path, but there was again no moisture in the air. Stones jabbed at her feet, reminding her of her cowardice, but there was relief in knowing no nescarans were around to mock her for it.

Halfway to the village no scent of cooking meat met her nose, and no voices carried to her ears. She stopped short of the first domed hut and leaned against a tree to catch her breath. Beyond its wide bending trunk, the market was gone. Its wagons had been overflowing with goods, but there were no beasts of burden to remove them. Yatzil crept through the bushes.

"Hello" she shouted. She gasped, immediately covering her lips at the echo. "You fool. Amteer may have heard that."

She cursed and ran, finding the nearest hut. She peered inside and yanked back its dry, dusty flap and slipped inside. Darkness enveloped her once the flap swayed shut. Her eyes relaxed, finding it was easier to see. There was no place to sit but upon the dirt. It felt wise to stay here, away from the Highnonstar and out of sight of her husband. To be alone though was discouraging in a time like this one.

Her thoughts filled with the falling pieces of Flor. Their mission had failed, and a time may come when a sign of her recent failure would press upon her shoulders. Both made saving her brother more and more difficult to imagine.

A decoration hung from the hut's center, crafted feathers of different lengths and colors. Some were black and others gray like the ones of the eagles. Yatzil reached to stroke the longest and grayest, but a slight breeze did first.

"Where is your husband?"

Yatzil swallowed, turning slowly, searching for an answer for the old woman.

"He is back at our camp asleep."

"Why come back to us alone then?" said Haseya. "And why choose my daughter's hut, with no offering in your hands?"

Haseya stood taller wearing Yatzil's grandmother's

sandals, yet age kept her from doing so fully. There was no reason to even be in the hut except to hide, and only what she had fled with held value. Yatzil firmed her grip on the knife and patted the pouches she had slipped into the shawl under her dress. The water skin dangled by a cord around her wrist.

"I had no way of knowing this was her home," she said. "As to my husband, I have—"

"You can tell the truth, my queen," said Haseya with a slight grin that wrinkled her face more. "I saw how uneasy you were the moment you stepped up to my wagon."

"Fine." Yatzil huffed. "My plans have changed some with the Highnonstar taking control of Plunemar... I witnessed something I never expected, only to be sent—"

"And that is why you married the boy in a king's body?"

Her jaw dropped. If her father were spoken to like this, a scar on the cheek would have been expected. The old Nol woman was bold, too bold, but she had to agree, despite the loyalty Amteer had displayed.

"I was given no choice but to leave him. What I witnessed breaks a law all kingdoms share. My heart even more so." She squeezed the wooden hilt of her knife. "There was someone I was able to trust most to help me but..."

Haseya smiled again. This time showing more of her toothless mouth.

"You are safe with me," she said, softly. "Was the one helping you a better man in temper? I am eighty and have always found the golden eagle dynasty cocky unlike the silver wolf."

"Yes."

It was true, Amteer's father always held his chin with pride and spoke as if he were better than anyone else. She grinded her teeth for the assumption that Flor was a man.

How could a woman even short and fragile, but fierce in her own right make such a guess?

"Don't worry how you feel for him," she said, breaking the trance Yatzil was in. "I did not like my husband, but he helped me have the daughter I wanted."

"Is this not a blessing?" Yatzil asked. "Why dislike a man able to do such a task?"

"He farted too much and couldn't hunt to save a village."

Yatzil stared at her for a moment. The light from the hut flap crept to Haseya's feet. Her grandmother's sandals were speckled with mud. She refused to cringe, reminding herself how the Nol didn't cling to purity of appearance like a Nescaran.

"I must apologize for my ignorance. That is a choice of words not taught by my *lamodun*."

"Do Nescarans not break wind, my queen?"

"Oh."

She giggled. Haseya placed a hand to her faded silver of her cheek and laughed too. A bad provider wasn't so humorous yet none of this explained the magics of the cut on Yatzil's palm. Nor did the guilt she wished didn't exist for leaving Amteer. The old nol woman's face grew serious, halting their moment of joy.

"I'm sorry to say this, but he will find you. You have bigger problems. All of us do if the Highnonstar dries everything up."

"I do not know how to defeat it except to save my brother." *I still do not know how I shall do that.* "And ask him to offer up sacrifice to summon all Nescarans to fight. And his queen might be able to summon raton support."

"You'll need the Lijani too. Though I know," Haseya sighed. "... they won't help. They shy from courage, and all the nemamoons are gone."

Yatzil explained the dream she had about the massive

waves and the red-scaled dragon. The Nemamoon called for her, wanting her to come to an island. And, by the expression on the goddess's face, there was an understanding.

"Until you can prove your dream is true," said Haseya. "I'd try and save your brother. I have my family to look after. I returned for our hang-in-down-dingle-dangle."

Turning to the ornament, it was too high for the aged Rutoe to reach. Yatzil stood on the balls of her toes, the dirt filling between them. She untied it and ran their softness over her hand before handing the ornament to Haseya.

"It is beautiful. You must have collected it from many birds."

Haseya chuckled before wrapping the ornament in a piece of fabric.

"Thank you. My family always keeps their feathers free of bugs and mud."

"Oh… That is … interesting."

There was a long pause as the air was growing thicker with heat, sending sweat down her forehead. Yatzil brushed a strand of hair behind her ear. *They really use everything in many ways.*

"I ask you to take them to Niev instead. With my brother's help, your people shall be safe."

Haseya squinted before lifting the huts flap and then gave Yatzil a queer look.

"Don't you mean our people?"

Yatzil bit her lip at such misuse of words, wanting to frost to hide her shame. Light pierced through the treetops. They were green in places and less so in others unlike earlier. It was like Nema was fighting against the way the Highnonstar aged its forests.

"I am sorry. You are all my people."

Haseya didn't meet her eye, gently placing her family's feathered ornament in a sack at her side. There was a knife stuffed beside it as well. Yatzil hesitated, ready to tell the old nol woman everything. Load distant screeches rang out. A small eagle bolted overhead as three larger ones swooped in behind, blanketing them both in brief darkness.

"Amteer?"

"Your husband's in trouble," said Haseya. "You can tell me later what you're really up to."

They ran down the Lid leaving the village behind. Yatzil's face tensed, and her breath quickened, finding she had made a terrible mistake. *I have put him in harm's way.* Yatzil slowed her pace to allow Haseya to catch up, but she was soon outpaced. Amteer called out, dodging black shafted arrows. The neck feathers of each scarlet quilled warrior's eagle had been burned away. It was hard to tell, but their talons glistened like they had been tipped with metal.

"Follow me, Princess. They are heading for Lake Wet Iron."

The Lid grew steeper with dried mud and fallen leaves. It sent unease crawling up her chest, so she slowed, but the boulders and fallen trees didn't bother Haseya. Haseya maneuvered around a patch of jagged rocks. How someone so aged was so swift was a mystery for another time.

"Yatzil!"

Amteer's voice was faint, desperate, almost sad. She strained to hear him and lost sight of where Haseya had gone. She ducked under a branch then slowed to find Haseya had stopped. She slumped onto a stump and tried to regain her spent breaths.

"We must continue." Yatzil said once by her side. "They did something to their eagles that will tear him to pieces."

"I must catch my breath, and I have ruined your..."

Haseya slipped off the sandals. Their jade squares chipped or missing, and their straps were snapped. Yatzil took them and held them close to her chest. A screech frightened her out of tunneling grief as tears welled up in her eyes. Her grandmother had been kinder than her mother dared speak the truth of. Flashes of Ringna's winged shadow raced across her face, though, by its reactions, time was short.

"Go help your husband," said Haseya. "I may despise his family, but he is still my Storm King."

Yatzil rubbed her eyes, holding tight her grandmother's sandals, the scar upon her palm tingling with Amteer in a danger she didn't intend. This must have been what the priest meant by no great distance can the clouds of a storm marriage be separated. Yatzil laid the sandals down, flashed the owl eyes upon her hands and rose. The lake lay near the base of the Lid. It was the same as before, but lower and faint steam rose from it like the river around Wolfstrong.

Amteer flew below a palenore while another chased him. He thrust his sword into the eagle's belly. The eagle cried out and snatched the sword from his hand. The palenore and his eagle dropped suddenly, splashing in the lake. Two more remained, and Yatzil focused on forming an ice spear but had never done so before. She huffed, concentrated, and rehearsed in her mind how her father had shown to throw one. Pressing her fist together she squeezed them tight. *Screech.* Her fists lost their tensity, unnerving her focus.

"Ringna." Amteer cried and fell.

One palenore urged his eagle to grab Ringna, placing her in a vice of immense talons. A whoosh scattered dried leaves into Yatzil's face. Ringna struggled to be free, squawking and reaching with its beak for its king. Yatzil felt helpless, allowing herself to thaw. The second Palenore caught Amteer on the back of his eagle. Her husband crawled to the eagle's neck, seized it by the feathers and...

"Amteer, watch out!" she cried.

The palenore swung his dagger, and, in a second, Amteer collapsed. Yatzil fell to her knees, craving to follow, cursing her nerves, and feeling ashamed for not being stronger. Her brother had been allowed to spar and join their father on voyages around the Trunk to fight fish thieves and... No, it was her fault for keeping to a selfish plan. The palenore flew south until Amteer and Ringna were gone from sight. A shuffling sent her spinning to find Haseya.

"Why have you stopped? My king heads south. Is that not where you want to go?"

"I wish to help him in place of it."

Haseya eased down next to her; all her youthful speed spent like a coin. She clutched Yatzil's grandmothers' sandals in one hand and wiped her forehead. The sandals had lasted four generations, and now they were torn, chipped and without their purpose. The faint tingling in her palm tightened as if Amteer's hand pulled hers in the direction the eagles had flown. She rubbed it, searching for a reason the Storm King had to forgive her.

"Come with me," she said. "I must save him."

Yatzil stood and offered a hand to Haseya.

"It's strange how the young change so fast, Princess." She offered her hand but yanked it away like it had been stung. "Are you sure saving him is what you want?"

Yatzil scowled at Haseya's stubbornness. It was no longer revenge that drove her, but the need for forgiveness, and possibly if she found the Nemamoon, defeat the palenore. She kept Sachihiro in her thoughts and promised, when Amteer was rescued, that he would be next. But first trust needed restoring with Haseya, who, by her furrowed brow, saw her no longer as a queen.

"It is. And if you wish not to come with me... I shall go myself."

The lake's eye shape added distance to her journey. Its shores sloped at a steep angle; dry mud and dying fish laid at the water's edge. Faint steam rose from the water sending sweat down her brow. She frosted to fend off the heat but found her energy fleeing faster than the wind was blowing. There was little of the dried meat to restore her energy, so she untied the water skin from her wrist. From a distance, her growing loneliness vanished to see Haseya had changed her mind. There was still reason to learn, as she finished drinking, how someone old had outpaced her.

A slight breeze toyed with her hair, doing the same to Haseya's feathers. The old nol stopped dead and dropped the sandals. Yatzil dropped the skin and kept still.

"Don't struggle." Haseya whispered. "They don't know why you're here."

Twigs snapped, yells came, and Haseya quickly crossed her arms and knelt. Yatzil frosted, each finger almost ice, until her eyes ignited yellow then faded and ice returned to flesh. The largest man she had ever seen made bushes bend to the vastness of his height. His head was a mass of sharp quills and arms were the width of tree trunks. Yatzil kept still and embraced for once the nescaran tradition of lack of emotion. A sharp quick pain forced her head forward, releasing spit from her tongue. Yatzil's eyes rolled shut as her lips found dirt.

Every tree blurred when she woke, and the ground was murky like dirty water. Pain zipped down her back as she turned to make sense of where she was being taken. A tall figure loomed over her, his face shielded by reaching branches. Her head doubled in pain the more her captor refused to watch his step. The smell of blood caught her attention, but none trickled down her skin. Ahead, a long-necked creature was tied to a smooth shaft. Its head hung in a noose close to its hooves as two men shared its load. Words came to her, wanting to be put down and released until more throbbing pressed her eyes shut.

CHAPTER SEVEN

A single shaft of light highlighted the blue of her toes. There was darkness like the hut, but once she stretched, her fingers found smooth fabric. Fur brushed her face as her eyes adjusted. They rested where the light fell from, its shape like a cinched knot. She licked her lips, and they tasted of bile. Yatzil wiped her mouth then rose to a position beaten into her from birth. An arm to prop oneself up, legs pressed and bent off to the side. The calming chill of home and multiple cushions would have been better than the furs or heat.

Voices sent her scrambling to stand but her arms lacked strength. Yatzil shielded her eyes as a figure passed through a flap across from her.

"You …" Yatzil frosted, the chill of her eyes following suit. "Are you with them? Those …"

She readied to rise, but Haseya raised a hand from the basket in her arms.

"Calm down, Princess. I brought food. I explained to them that you married our storm king and that he was captured."

Yatzil slowly thawed but frustration bunched up her nose. She plopped down to rub her head. Frosting seemed to dull the pain, and if she were released, she'd frost longer and then... She gasped. She patted her sides. The pouches of dried meat were gone and so was the knife. Yatzil scowled at Haseya's confused gaze.

"You should have explained before I was struck. You still must explain how someone of your age and in need of sandals to manage stones can be so swift ..."

The old nol perched in front of the flap and opened the basket. A sweet burnt aroma wafted from it. Haseya rested three small apples atop its lid and slid it forward. Yatzil moved back, bumping her head against the surrounding fabrics. Hunger licked at her insides.

"Well, my grandmother told me, age truly means nothing to a nol. I'm sorry. I moved slow, Princess, because I didn't trust you at ..."

Yatzil silenced her with a raised hand. Haseya sighed and sat up straight, outstretching her arms in a welcoming manner.

"And do you trust me now," she said, not trusting in Haseya's familiar pose. "I feel guilty. I found him arrogant too before he protected me."

"But, your highness," Haseya looked down for a moment as if finally considering her words. "Why did you abandon our king? Many depend on you both, and my village heads for the Gaping Mouth."

Yatzil swallowed and tried to call back the courage leaving her. She rubbed her nose, blaming her lack of courage for the loss of her friend. But even deep within her home's wisdom room, she was certain avenging her father alone was impossible. Their search was a rush of encouragement for what needed done. Flor's friendship at that moment was a break from the sadness plaguing her.

"Who aided me was no avalanche commander, nor a noble with a fleet of fishing ships," she said. "She was a servant meant to bathe and hold my chamber pot when I ... A companionship was forbidden, and when I witnessed my mother's act of treason I... The task of proving my mother's guilt should have been on my shoulders alone. My father had already arranged my marriage to King Yanter. He was against it, except my Father gave into Mother's demands like always and this time she rewarded him with death."

Tears collected in her eyes as faint chirping came from outside. There was something soothing about it, but Haseya's eyes kept her from its bliss. There was neither amazement, nor anger, but curiosity once Haseya's mouth shut from dropping open. She moved to Yatzil's side with the basket lid weighted with apples and plopped down beside her. Yatzil watched Haseya take the largest apple, nibbling at it like a babe sampling its first morsel of solid food.

"My question is answered then," said Yatzil, allowing herself to breathe. "You trust me enough to share a meal. I can only guess you find no fault in why I'm so far north."

Juices clung to the old Nol's lips after another bite. Yatzil took an apple, eager for confirmation of her words. She bit into a tiny, slightly burnt part and found it pleasant. If sliced it would go well beside the meat from the village. Haseya wiped her mouth, setting down what remained of her apple.

"If we survive the trial ahead, my queen. I'll help you kill her."

BEFORE HER WAS A MAN, older than any Yatzil had ever met. They introduced themselves in the same way she had with Amteer upon Wolfstrong's tongued tip. A bow with hands raised high enough to align with her chest to symbolize the giving of an offering. It was less ceremonial without actual offerings, but she kept to nol ways. He kept his balance upon an uneven boulder. Yatzil stood upon layers of fur provided for her.

"I'm Ahigan, leader of those among you."

She nodded and held her nervousness at bay. Haseya rubbed her palms, standing not far amongst the other nol.

"I am Yatzil, Storm Queen of the nol and Princess of Niev."

Ahigan returned her nod ruffling his white feathers. They were so long that, in her mind, if he dove from a cliff the feathers could act as wings. Yatzil caught sight of the long knives around his finely stitched lumao of deer hide. The knives' hilts were crafted from animal bone and their blades were the length of her hand. She rested gently on her weathered furs, matching his tested gaze.

"So," he said in a deep voice. "Our new Storm King is in the hands of the First Son and Daughter. And from what Haseya tells me, you are a nescaran of royal blood sent to marry him?"

"Yes."

To not be on a higher perch than him jabbed at her like the uncomfortable ache in her back. She had to restore such a position of honor, and most importantly earn Ahigan's respect. His son Clod emerged from one of what she learned were smiftas and stood beside him. His father's face remained stern and drawn in by disappointment.

"I have been selfish," she rasped, throat dry. "I admit to it and ask I be released to save King Amteer and his eagle."

She swallowed to relieve her throat, but it was no use. The trees clung to less of their green once her judgement began. Haseya's village had joined them earlier. They glowered from beside her, whispering, setting her nerves on edge. Haseya had called them to her location with winded words, using a form of nol Yatzil didn't know. It was used in a whisper to the strongest breeze, but without the storms of the west, her words met frequent silence. Some villagers ate the apples offered to them, and a few tossed thin cores at her feet. She felt so much of their respect was gone, that they saw her now as but a servant. Yatzil forced herself to ignore them and folded her hands to restrain anger.

"If you'll pardon me for rudeness," said Ahigan, "even though you are meant to be worshiped as a goddess, there is no royal guard to help you leave. We have reason to save King Amteer ourselves and tie you up for him to decide your fate. It will be a fine gift for our new king."

Around her many chuckled, their whispers were of the tradition inlaid upon her teeth. She clenched them to resist lashing out at their assumption of greed. None of them understood what an honor it was to wear jade this way, to be royal and possess teeth like the beaks of goddesses. A chill ran through her with the assumption of being vain. Ice replaced flesh, understanding all were against her but Haseya. To freeze them from within may bring them under heel like nescaran queens of the past. But unlike a single palenore, a hundred, if not more was too much. Her glowing yellow eyes faded when she saw the children and mothers.

"Father," said Clod, in a rumbling voice. "We should kill her after what her father did to my…"

"Hush boy," said Ahigan. "I have told you the crimes of her father are his alone. I do not and will not follow the *guilt is blood* tradition. The nescaran is responsible for…"

"Speak of what my father has done."

Yatzil stood, her eyes flashed bright, narrowing upon the father and son. Her father had been unique, kind unlike most of her dynasty, and desired no conquest beyond the Trunk's border wall.

The very tips of the fur beneath her feet had frozen over.

All who mocked Yatzil fled to the very border formed by the towering smiftas. Haseya was left out in the open, shying from the chill ebbing from Yatzil's anger. Clod stood like a monolith, braced against the chill, wielding his axe. His thick fingers strangled the axe's rough wooden shaft toward the nob that was capped by a skull.

"You need to calm yourselves." Haseya said, raising her shaking hands, edging between them. "You're both needed to save our Storm King. My Queen, your brother will never be saved this way."

Ahigan cleared his throat and joined them, placing a firm hand on his son's thick wrist, and within seconds his son calmed.

"I still wish to know what you say my father has done."

Ahigan sighed then rubbed his short nose. "My wife was killed by a nescaran raiding party months ago."

Yatzil wanted in her heart to believe him, but her father had never lied. It was the one thing her mother made sure of above bending him to her will... *It was her.* Her anger drained from her as ice returned to flesh. Her eyes faded from a yellow, bright like distant stars, to the light brown many women of her father's court envied. She let out her breath and relaxed once her delicate lashes returned.

"You are right, Haseya." she said. "I have acted rashly. What your son says is untrue of my father, Ahigan. My mother must have used his name to cause *our* people pain."

"A king letting his queen do that?" Clod growled, stomping forward. "Was he a coward behind those high walls of his?"

Yatzil braced herself before Clod's father grabbed his arm. Haseya moved beside her, hissing her through quivering lips at Clod. She reassured Yatzil with words possessing a softness to them, a caring her mother never bothered with even behind closed doors away from the judging eyes of tradition. She nodded to Haseya and then glared at Clod.

"He was no coward, and my brother King Sachihiro is proof. He made certain those who brought me north were unharmed. There have been other raids, and my brother would never order them."

Clod was about to speak, but his father did first.

"We can guess your mother is responsible. We still have family south who send winded word of more raids after Plunemar disappeared."

Voices filled the air as people returned from hiding. She tempered her rage from their earlier assumptions. Clod glared at her as if none of what was said mattered. Yatzil bit her lip and cursed her mother, watching the giant of a man remain respectful to his father, but he clenched his fists and furrowed his brow.

"I thank you, Ahigan," she said. "My mother is swift in her plans, and many are loyal to her but shall bend to their king's will if she wishes."

Haseya smiled at her but then mushed her lips together. "Then we have two enemies and a captured king to deal with."

Whispers filled the air, with those closest to Yatzil asking if they should join her and fight. There were less certain ones from women desiring to listen to Amteer's recent command. She dared not guess, as some spoke, of how many nol had been killed. Clod's brow relaxed a little but there was distrust in his eyes. *I hope his contempt for me will fade with time.* She weaved her fingers and searched for words to further convince him of her regret. She paled at the thought, but not enough time had passed to worry about it.

"Let's save my husband and his mount swiftly before doing the same ... for my brother." To place Sachihiro second pinched at her heart, yet their help was needed. "I give my word as your Storm Queen; no harm shall come once at Niev's gates."

"I'll make sure you keep it," said Clod, readying his axe like she was a tree to be cut down. "If those metal serpents eat my people … I'll add your skull to the others."

Clod tapped his hip with two oar sized fingers to his belt. Unlike his well-armed father, Clod's barreled waist displayed a row of skulls from rutoe and beast. The one mounted over his groin was like the creature she saw when captured. She ceased the faint quivering of her lips. His size frightened her more than his trophies. They paled to the salvaged skin taken by an avalanche warrior. He stomped off, followed by the others, leaving a silence in his wake.

They agreed to return to the smifta Yatzil had been held prisoner in. It was north, amongst trees wider than ten rutoe. She had not noticed how far it was before. Every tree, bush, and mossy log clung to new life. Nema acted like a cut healing and being reopened. Yatzil smiled, finding hope in it, but what needed to be done to save Amteer still eluded her. If her words proved foolish, the nol might follow Ahigan in place of herself. Her throat remained dry but worry over-powered it, so she took shorter steps to bide for time.

She drank in the darkness of the smifta and rested at its rear to face its flap. Ahigan untied from his hip what looked like a small tortoise shell stuffed with a thick fabric. Yatzil uncorked it, sniffed, and then drank, relieved it wasn't the bland wine served at her wedding. She offered it to Haseya. The old Nol took it after raking her boney fingers through her feathers.

"I still don't think searching for an island is wise," Haseya said. "After saving two kings."

"If we can save them," said Ahigan, his frustration of earlier gone. "My son will listen to me if I come. What island, Haseya?"

"Only our Queen can tell you. She dreamed of a nemamoon. I heard all of them disappeared long ago."

Haseya had placed her on a dais, a high place of honor she always feared. Her father held open his palace's courtyard to public complaints upon one. The demands were always deafening. It was just Haseya and Ahigan, unlike the crowds blocking escape to the palace. She held her chin to proper height, replacing nervousness with courage.

"I dreamed of a woman upon an island thick with trees. She danced below me for I was upon a dragon. It matched the one I saw upon the walls of Wolfstrong."

Ahigan scratched his chin then ran his fingers through his feathers.

"Before the *giftnos*, it was rumored no dragons were left in the east. And if there were, only a raton could speak to one. Your island will lie in that direction."

"Do you believe my dream is enough to search for someone who may no longer exist?"

Ahigan sat beside her, his shoulders sunk, and his back hunched. There was when the Nemamoon winked at her, but she wasn't certain he would believe it. Yatzil kept her focus on how he ran his fingers through his long-feathered mane, contemplating her words. In the dream, the Nemamoon held a beauty she wished she... Ahigan rose, breaking her stream of thought.

"No matter what the Highnonstar has done, there is green in the trees and ... only a nemamoon can make that so."

Yatzil released breath through her nose, releasing her inner lip from her teeth. A stiff breeze whistled through the hole above them.

"I suggest we head for the Gaping Mouth if the east brings danger," said Ahigan. "Legend says Wolfstrong spawned from it, and its tunnels are fortified. Its craftsmen to this day forge the iron weapons of the west."

Yatzil finally understood her husband's earlier decision. If not for the palenore, so much suffering would not be hers to remedy. There was no need to leave the smifta to witness what the Highnonstar had done. Redness replaced the white around Haseya and Ahigan's eyes. Her own widened, understanding when she had been defending her father, why the women whispered to their children. None of the children possessed aim to their sight, and if not for their mothers being older, she guessed, they too would have suffered blindness from the Highnonstar.

"We must plan immediately. I can feel where my husband has gone." She displayed the scar upon her palm. "If I am right, he is at the villa I once visited."

Panic slithered through her at the thought of what might have happened to the noble and his sons. Ahigan scratched his chin and raised an eyebrow. Yatzil searched his eyes for trust and told him of the villa's thick walls and minor pyramid.

"The enemy having eagles gives them an advantage," he sighed. "I know the west well, but there is a great risk with large numbers."

"I ask only a few men to save our king." Yatzil stood to meet Ahigan's eyes, matching his height. Haseya and Ahigan stared at her with intense focus, but all recent judgement had hardened her nerves at this point.

"Let's gather the best of our people," said Yatzil. "What weapons do we possess that can bring down an eagle?"

"Do you have a plan?" Haseya said with pride in her voice. "I have to stay with my family."

"I wish it no other way. Protect them." Yatzil smiled at Haseya and then turned to Ahigan. Her heart skipped in its pace. He crossed his arms, likely expecting strategy, but her mother never permitted the learning of battle tactics, preferring language and history lessons. *History possessed princesses knowing strategy,* Yatzil thought, *and tradition demands I do.*

"We have arrows tipped with the same iron on my waist," said Ahigan. "I suggest we head south after some …"

"Rest." Yatzil took a step back, regretting finishing for him. Ahigan drew himself up to full height, exhaled.

"Yes, rest," he said. "I am trying to trust you as a Nol must his Storm Queen, but I cannot remove what you did from my mind. You are right to where he is because you both are connected, yet I have never seen such selfishness."

The room blurred for a moment to find her efforts trampled. Yatzil hardened her face, forming it into a blank slate. She found herself alone. Haseya touched her shoulder, but Yatzil brushed her hand away and stumbled toward the smifta's flap. She ducked out into the world, feeling everyone's lives compounded upon her shoulders.

"I shall do all of it alone," said Yatzil.

Without care for provisions, or a weapon, she pushed through the brush. Haseya called after her in a shrill cry like she had given birth to Yatzil herself. It pinched at her heart to leave Haseya, the one person who supported her. Haseya had a family in greater need though, and Yatzil dared not rob them of an elder.

She entered the encampment. Clod emerged from a smifta like an owl, a hollowed-out tree nest. His brow crinkled, leading out by a hand a woman her mother's age.

Yatzil ignored the growl in her stomach, the dried grass clinging to her feet. Rabbits skinned and pierced head to rump caught her eye as she drew closer to the woods. Yatzil stopped and watched as a Nol girl no older than nine by her size turned each rabbit. The girl must have been lucky, unlike others her age. There was only redness around her eyes in place of blindness.

The nol girl noticed her, but Yatzil remained at a distance.

Yatzil peered over her shoulder to the grove of trees. No one pursued her.

"Where are you going?" said the nol girl. "Mother said, since Clod didn't kill you, that I can trust you."

Yatzil held back a snort, still in disbelief. The silver skin girl tilted her head before adding wood to the fire. Yatzil edged forward half tempted to ask for a rabbit. Relief spilled over her heart to have trust in this girl.

"I am glad," she sighed, deciding to tell the truth. "But there is no trust between his father and me. I'm leaving to save our storm king and Nema alone."

A pop and shifting of crumbled wood kicked embers into the air. The child before Yatzil was unmoved, her brow unfolded, absent of judgement.

"I'm Sparron. If you'll allow me, Storm Queen, I'd go with you."

"Oh, young one," said Yatzil, a lump formed in her throat. "You are kind. And by your skill as a meal maker, our hunger shall be nonexistent, but I would rather you remain safe with your mother."

"I've got a knife." Sparron rubbed her nose, then drew it from a scabbard on her hip. The scabbard had the worn silver face of a Nol woman. Great black feathers streamed from the Nol's ahead over dark brown hide. "I can help. I can earn my grown name with my knife when we win."

The girl held it by the point with similar balance to Ahigan's on his boulder, tossing it in the air and catching it by the hilt. It was near the length of her forearm. Yatzil leaned forward and smiled.

"I must still have you stay behind," she whispered. "There shall be other times to earn your grown name."

Sparron returned her eyes to the rabbits for a moment.

"Ok," said Sparron. "Take my knife at least."

Yatzil stopped Sparron's little hands before they reached to hand over the scabbard.

"Keep it. It shall remind me to return your knife."

Yatzil patted Sparron on the shoulder and ran her fingers through the girl's feathers. They smiled at one another, parting.

She felt lighter. Her confidence was stronger after meeting someone so young and brave. Yatzil flashed Sparron the owl eyes upon her hands in a gesture of parting. An honor nescarans didn't share to outsiders, but the child had earned it.

CHAPTER EIGHT

The heat had ceased its hasty rise after the third day; dry leaves clung to the ice of her frost form. Yatzil grasped Sparron's knife in one hand, reaffirming the promise made, and in the other her fifth attempt at an ice-spear. The knife's hilt was smooth and pale with a pommel made from a blunt brow tie, but her ice-spear had only reached the length of her fingers. A stabbing pain resonated with her every step, and her head still hurt. She found the coolness of frosting no longer dulled the pain, and the memory of Clod's words worsened her struggle.

Her thoughts fell to his harsh pale brown eyes, the scowl on his face when she had passed him. Clod had been more than willing to add her head to his collection. To have one's head severed sent a rush of heat down her spine. She sighed, thankful to escape such a death, but out alone in a land not her own invited another kind of demise, and one with no guarantee of a proper burial.

Stronger was the feeling of Amteer from the scar on her palm as she plucked tootens from a bush growing under the shade. Yatzil savored them in defiance of her decision to leave unprepared. The tootens amongst the light were shriveled, and she worried with time there would be no shade to protect the others.

She leaned against a tree and slid down to its finger like roots. Yatzil set aside the knife and rubbed her feet as they went from ice to flesh. She raised her finger sized spear to her lips and sucked the water dripping from it. A rabbit hopped passed, sniffed, and then bolted into a bush. Yatzil raised her arm, sniffed, and blamed herself for the creature's troubles.

Yatzil licked her teeth of lingering tooten juices, reminded from their jade squares of home. Wiping her brow, nearly all her spit was gone and there was a longing to hear the faint trickle of a stream. There had been none since before Lake Wet Iron, making the rivers south a distant hope.

"If I had calmed myself, I may have raised Ahigan from his distrust and I'd not be alone."

Yatzil slumped where she sat, both eyes heavy with sleep. To keep alert of the days passing she walked until too tired to go on.

Snap. Yatzil bolted up and readied her knife, its blade glistened in the light. She moved a few paces, then darted her head left at a flash of movement. A growl sent her into frost form, her heart skipped in rhythm. A wolf crept through a thicket. Its fur was gray with black streaks, one of its ears stood erect. The other was chewed to a nub. Yatzil stepped back, wishing it were a palenore. Its tongue dangled the closer it came, and its muzzle aligned above her brow. It stopped and sniffed, eyeing her softly for some reason, pawing at the ground as if welcoming her. And then it shook its head, moving toward her. She reaffirmed her grip on the knife, picked up a stone, and threw it. The stone struck the wolf's cheek. It snarled as she realized she had no clue how to wield her knife.

Neither she nor the wolf moved, its yellow eyes focused. She flinched, cursed, and the wolf charged her and leapt. Yatzil swung the knife, severing its curled chin whiskers and landed hard on her back. She winced, its rear paw kicked, scaping her across the face.

Yatzil rolled over and touched where it hurt. There was no blood, but flecks of ice laid in the dirt like stars in the night sky. Fur clung to the knife. She readied it again, the wolf bounding toward her with its tongue whipping drool. A long-jagged ice crystal laid at her feet. She eyed the wolf nervously, dropped to her knees, doubled her grip on the knife. The wolf was a mere foot away as she snatched the ice crystal, shut her eyes, and thrusted.

The wolf collapsed upon her, blood sprayed and turned her dress a dark shade of brown. It had her pinned with her knees and legs pressed against the ground. The blood was warm and sticky. Such immersion of blood surfaced a memory of what a nescaran princess felt when becoming queen. She knew no cleansing followed, or a long night with a king. Her mother bragged of her own blood baptism frequently to noble women of the court.

Yatzil pushed the groaning beast. It growled then whimpered like it had made a mistake. She clenched her teeth, every breath heavy, begging her to accept a slow death under the wolf for her selfishness.

"Sachihiro," she said. "I cannot give in."

Harnessing what strength frosting gifted her, she dug her toes into the dirt. The creature's jaws shifted atop her shoulder, and it fought to rise as she pushed but the ice crystal and knife dug into its throat summoning a final gasp. Yatzil heaved and threw the wolf off, thawing, every breath hurt, and blood painted her skin. She ran her fingers through her hair, finding, as it softened, that the ice crystal had been a clump of her hair. It streamed from her attacker's throat like a trampled black serpent. She rested a hand to her face and found a thin cavern of missing flesh.

Yatzil licked her lips, drained of strength. Her dress weighed on her shoulders from the wolf's blood. She slipped it off and retrieved Sparron's knife. Without the dress to protect herself from thorny bushes all that remained was her top and the shawl about her waist. The blood coated Yatzil's hands in thick streaks. She decided to use it as a tool to intimidate, but with the nol it was different, none of them shied from blood, yet no statue of a storm queen held a weapon. They may have possessed a magic rendering a spear and dagger of no use.

There were no lessons of past storm queens she recalled from her *lamodun's* teachings, only how to address the Nol and speak their language. Yatzil swallowed, finding he was another whose company she missed, a second father. She sniffed, curling her lips inward until they disappeared. He died in her fifteenth year and without, by rule, allowed to tell her his true name.

Pressing on further, a tree with tiny faded green leaves and low branches looked like a place for rest. She crawled under its lowest branches, finding some relief from the light. Yatzil shut her eyes then turned over to the tree trunk. Yatzil ran her fingers through her hair, tiny dead leaves littered it and clung to her skin. A foul taste resonated on her tongue at how unclean she was, knowing it defied what she was accustomed to. She raked her fingers through her hair to return it to its smooth, tamed appearance, but a bone comb was needed.

She freed her fingers from her hair, pressing them to her chest. Her thoughts drifted to Amteer, of what his words may have been finding her gone.

"Did he throw himself into a rage? I made him believe a trust existed and sealed it with his people's child forming dance. I ... have brought shame to my father."

She shuddered at the thought of her father closing his eyes and turning from her, diving into Non's pool, never to emerge again.

Sweat muddied the blood on her cheeks. She prayed Haseya still cared for her. But with them far apart, and her rash actions to blame, Yatzil doubted that care still existed. Sleep crept through her body with heat draining every muscle of the strength that kept her awake.

Again, upon the same dragon, the clouds were as black as the soles of her feet. She focused ahead and found the island, but its trees were broken and burnt as if the dragon had released an onslaught of lightning. Upon the sands sat the Nemamoon as her red scaled escort descended. She gazed up at Yatzil with a yellow glow fading from her eyes. The dragon landed before Yatzil could brace herself, forming a wall of scales and jagged spikes upon the sands.

"Come down from Crimson Spike, Yatzil." she called, ushering Yatzil with a long slender hand. "We must speak, for you killed the poor creature meant to bring you to the villa."

Yatzil scrambled to her feet.

"It attempted to end my life," said Yatzil, crinkling her nose. "If you wished to aid me, why not say so before? How can I trust you if I do not know your name?"

The Nemamoon sighed. "My name is Sath. Will that aid in you trusting me?"

"Yes. But I believe I shall remain where I am."

Yatzil planted her feet, holding her focus on the nemamoon's eyes that flickered from yellow to a deep brown. She crossed her arms, but her stomach churned, and nerves tensed. The dragon's steady breaths increased, and it moved. Yatzil grabbed for one of its long thin spikes, enveloped by a wave of heat from its immense jaws. No strain tightened her arm muscles, and her skin remained its normal ice blue.

Sand dirtied her toes, and the sea washed them. She let go and spun to scold the nemamoon, but no one was there.

"My apologies, Storm Queen."

Yatzil gasped and fell, but a strong grip seized her wrists. Sath pulled her up right, flashing a small smile.

"I must not rush your trust, but without it a new moon cannot be danced into existence."

"Will it heal my people's children of their blindness?"

"Their time in the Gaping Mouth will do that," said Sath. "To form another moon, a woman of each kingdom, who has mastered their child forming dance is needed."

Frustration rushed to her fingers, curling them into fists. She wondered if this goddess, this Sath, who she had never heard mention of in the Four's temples knew of her greed. She shook her head to be free of worry.

"I shall represent the Nol to make such a task possible."

"That is impossible, for you are not one."

"Why? I am their storm queen and know their dance." said Yatzil. "It is upon my shoulders to perform ..."

Sath raised a hand sending wind through Yatzil's hair, smothering her words. Yatzil shielded herself as ice formed across her skin.

"Settle yourself to flesh form, Yatzil." Sath waved the wind away. "Like Nescara, herself, you are swift to claim responsibility only after committing a wrong."

"You know of?" Yatzil gasped. "I ... have been traveling for days to make up for it. I can feel his hand in my own." She stared at the thinly healed scar in her palm.

"And yet, until seeing him in danger, you had not cared for him."

"So, I must find another nol woman of royal blood?"

"That is not a journey you must make." Sath smiled. "Nol was

not royal when she gave the first moon permission to guide sky
rocks to her mine for her descendants to prosper. Royal is a word
for those strong in magic and leadership like your father. Now, go.
Save Sachihiro and who you wronged."

Everything grew blurry with her lips opening to ask what
was obvious. Her eyes shut and then opened to dead
branches outlined by brightness. She made her way from
under the strange tree, much of what was green no longer
was. She groaned as a rush of weight struck her in the side.
Haseya grinned up at her and released her from her crushing
grip. Branches snapped and fell from muscled arms as Clod
pushed aside thick overgrowth behind them. Ahigan
followed behind his son, eyeing the barren bushes and brittle
bark upon the trees. Yatzil bit her tongue to find he remained
disappointed. There was a bruise across his cheek, swelling
part of his left eye closed.

"Helping this traitor better be worth it, old woman," said
Clod.

"You could have stayed behind," said Haseya. "And
followed the others to the mine."

"Our Storm Queen needs us, my son," said Ahigan.

"You're only saying that because you had a crazy dream
and fell out of your sleeping pouch."

Ahigan rubbed his bruise again. Haseya whispered into
Yatzil's ear.

"I did that when he wanted to ignore his dream." she
chuckled. "It was about that nemamoon you saw in yours."

A smile stretched across Yatzil's face at the nemamoon
aiding in Ahigan's trust, but it faded at the deep sadness on
his face. He carried a heavy sack over one shoulder and
several water skins on the other. She met his eyes, and when
he returned her gaze, he sighed and bowed low.

"I see disappointment remains on your face." She dug
her toes into the dirt and folded her arms. "Why come

then? Has my wish to mend my mistakes altered your thoughts?"

There was a long pause and then like a commander succumbing to surrender he nodded.

"A dream and encouragement," He rubbed his cheek. "Is enough to send a man on his way. I thought on it when you realized your mother was responsible for my wife's death."

"And?" Haseya hissed.

"That you truly want to save our Storm King."

She held up her hands and parted her lips, releasing her breath like she had been holding it for an eternity. Yatzil flashed the eyes upon her hands as she had done for Sparron. It was a gesture of respect she found he deserved more than anyone she had wronged. She had earned what she believed was too far gone and hoped someday to reward it.

THEY WENT FURTHER south for several miles. Yatzil explained the dried blood and Haseya rested a hand to her cheek. Haseya laughed when Yatzil spoke of the wolf's purpose being a swifter way to the villa.

"My guess is you're glad we came."

She wrapped her arm around Yatzil, holding her close as they walked. Yatzil hesitated at first, but when Ahigan reached to remove the old woman, her mind changed.

"Haseya has permission to touch me." Yatzil smiled a warm smile. "She has been kind to me."

"If those metal serpents don't let us in," Clod grumbled, clearing their way with his axe. "Then I won't be asking your—"

"Stop your threatening, my son." Ahigan stomped. "You have been a pain in our backside, so be quiet."

"Yes, Father."

Yatzil gulped and remembered Flor saying the guardians sensed when someone was false. The guardian's rumored size was said to be enough to crush Niev's wall like two fingers a lone grape. She believed she once saw a guardian before flying north but it had been a sheet of ice coasting across the moat. The entrance glyphs needed painted on her stomach were still fresh in her mind but the dance to join them was a blur. Ahigan's control over his son gave some relief, but how long would Clod listen if her dance failed to please Niev's guardians. Yatzil stayed close to Haseya with Sparron's knife clutched tight.

There was still a need for a nol woman to be found beyond just raton and lijani. She peered down at Haseya, curious if Sath meant the old woman. But above all that twisted her stomach in knots as was if they succeeded in Amteer's rescue. Would he be forgiving? The palenore captain had said before Flor's great sacrifice. *"If we return without them, those brats could cost us our heads"* She removed herself from Haseya and kept going before pausing at a clearing ahead. The heat reached toes, teasing her skin.

"What's the matter, my queen?" said Haseya, resting a hand on Yatzil's shoulder. "We are heading south, and Ahigan and Clod are—"

"You should never have come."

"Why?"

She walked a few paces and turned.

"Amteer and I were meant to be captured. For what purpose, … I cannot begin to say."

"My guess is to hold you both as hostages," said Ahigan. He removed his tortoise shell and raised it to her. "Here. I should have offered you water sooner."

Yatzil received it, unplugged the stopper, and took a few sips. Ahigan pulled from the sack on his shoulder a small piece of parchment wrapped around short metal needles.

"I thank you," Yatzil said. "But I must ask all of you to travel west to your families."

"I'm with the nescaran princess," said Clod, removing a twig from a chink in his axe. "Put our smifta away and lets—"

"For the last time, we aren't leaving her, my son. Now be quiet."

Clod wrinkled his brow and reaffirmed his grip against the thick shaft of his axe. His father gave him a sharp look. The giant grumbled allowing his weapon to hang limp at his side. And before Yatzil could raise a hand to stop him, the white feather nol planted the bound needles within the clearing. He dropped to his hands and knees and blew on it. Every breath darkened his face until what was small grew like her frustrations. Ahigan moved to her side as dirt kicked up, each needle thickened and lengthened, expanding what was animal hide and not parchment. A gust of wind encouraged the smifta until it looked able to house them all. Yatzil backed away from them. Haseya gave Ahigan a nod.

"You must do as I command." She huffed, raising herself to full height with her chin in the proper position. To do this felt ridiculous but, to save them, she had to attempt something. "I shall continue to try and master forming an ice-spear. Your families require your shelter, not I."

"They're farther from us than when you left three days ago." said Ahigan. His eyes were soft with concern, and his breathing returned to normal.

"And we can't allow you to rescue our Storm King alone." said Haseya, sadness creeping from her quivering lips. "How will you return my granddaughter's knife, if you die?"

Yatzil raised it, turning it in her hand, its brow tine visible beyond the border of her hand. A lump formed in her throat, the knife feeling as though it had tripled in weight. *She is right. And I do not think I shall be ready for a fight in time.* To only be tested once was another problem she had to consider. Freezing someone from within and in considerable numbers was beyond her. Her dream revealed the Nemamoon needing rest and with that tootens may grow scarce. She eyed them all with nervousness. Even with her connection to Amteer guiding her way, it didn't prepare her for unfamiliar land. Yatzil took Haseya's hand in her own and nodded, wanting to keep her promise to Sparron and the man she had wronged.

CHAPTER NINE

Yatzil bent to leave the smifta with an ache in her back. She tore off one of the tassels from her dirtied shawl. Doubt swam in her belly. Could they save Amteer and Ringna? She hoped so, but she wouldn't allow herself to believe they couldn't. She bit into a piece of dried meat, then swallowed.

She gathered it up and bound back with the tassel. Two weeks they had traveled with dried meats and water to sustain them. Ahigan had gone with Clod to scout the villa after she sensed they were close. Green had returned to the branches, bushes, and grasses in the past few days. She rubbed the scar on her palm, its tingling had risen to a burn.

Chill ran through her throat, rushing over her lips and turning the meat between her fingers into a blackened sliver of ice. Yatzil cursed then tossed it into the overgrowth. The seasoned meat was better than any placed before her at a feast. Her stomach growled and she pretended the great hunger her lamodun spoke of meant something other than a child.

She ran her fingers over her stomach, searching for how

best to tell the others. Another life was at risk by her actions to avenge, who, deep in his tomb under Niev, was disappointed. *Now more than before,* she thought, leaning against a tree, and rubbing her eyes, unease in her fingers. Yatzil wanted to fall to her knees and beg Fertilida for guidance, but if the goddess had stayed silent for her marriage, then asking for aid was pointless.

Branches snapped and fell. Clod charged up to their smifta like an immense beast. His father was close behind, panic creasing his wrinkled face, his feathers bounced on his shoulders. Even with his hulking son under his control, Clod searched still for reason not to trust her. He stopped and leaned his axe against a tree, running his fingers through the sprouting feathers he had allowed to grow out. The skulls about his waist were flecked with dust. Ahigan bowed to her before finding his breath.

"There is ... no cover to overcome the guards, my queen," said Ahigan. "I'm sorry. Age doesn't limit a nol but—"

"It's impossible," said Clod. "Eagles circle its walls. You nescarans have big heads about yourselves with that pyramid. It's on—"

"Fire." Ahigan turned to the forest ahead and then to Yatzil.

She gulped, pressing her lips together and narrowing her eyes to mask her worry. The First Son and Daughter couldn't have burned Amteer alive in the bedchamber in which she had stayed. The noble had offered it to her, willing to believe what she witnessed in Non's temple. She sensed her husband more now, the scar upon her palm remained at a constant tingle. Yatzil took a step back, not daring to believe the noble was dead. Haseya came out to join them. Yatzil frosted to hide her worry further but thawed as all eyes rested upon her.

"I wish not to forsake him or his ... eagle, but I am no warrior."

A hand rested on her shoulder. She flinched then found worry in Haseya's reddened eyes. The old nol was less of a warrior than she was, but it had not stopped her from coming this far. They had learned more about each other, and her granddaughter's knife had been a gift presented by King Yanter's storm queen. The dried meat they enjoyed from days previous was given flavor by spices stored in the sack hanging from Haseya's shoulder. And by a blessing the Highnonstar likely didn't intend, every sliver of meat dried faster.

"We need to try." Haseya leaned in close. "I know you are worried about not being ready." she whispered. "But you must tell not just us but him."

A creeping clawed itself over Yatzil's skin. Was it the hoarseness in her voice, the faint mist of her breath? She had refused water of late, fearing a need to make water. And if she did the ground would freeze from it. The nol dance and glyphs the Fertilida priestesses crafted had worked. Yatzil turned from Haseya to Clod, his arms folded. Ahigan stood eager for her next words.

"You are right, Haseya." she said. "I am... I am with child."

Ahigan stared, expressionless, and turned to the woods dividing them from the villa. She moved closer to him. His silence pained her. Clod applied his axe to the leather holster on his back. The skull on its nob like a man resting his chin on the giant's shoulder. He spat before giving her a look.

"I have revealed much to you in spite of my poor choices." she sighed. "I was afraid to create more worry."

Clod let go of his axe once it was secured but Ahigan spoke first.

"I believe in your wish to make up for your selfishness."

Ahigan let out a tensed breath, but it didn't lessen the worry in his eyes. "You carry the last Golden Eagle should we fail."

"I'll stay," said Clod. "But I'm heading to be with my wife after we save our king." He moved to within inches of her face. "I don't want to be away from her anymore."

"Done." Yatzil gulped.

He passed her, taking hold of a thin string at the smifta's entrance. Ahigan had already moved their supplies outside. Yatzil went to retrieve Sparron's knife, having forgotten it, but Haseya had it in her tensed fist.

"Come, Haseya." said Yatzil. She bit her lip, gesturing forward with uncertainty. "We shall go on ahead while the smifta is drawn up."

Haseya wrapped her arm behind Yatzil and shakingly handed her the knife.

"I'm happy you told them, my queen." She whispered, leaning in close. "Make certain you keep that with you around Clod."

"I shall."

"Promise me."

"I ... promise."

A whine, slip and plop followed a rustling of dirt as the smifta shrunk back to its length of hide and iron needles. Even with two weeks passing, how just blowing on something small grew into a place of sleep amazed her. She wrapped her arm around Haseya's shoulders. The old nol picked up her pace. Yatzil gave her a tight squeeze of reassurance. It slowed the pounding of Yatzil's own heart but with the footsteps of both men drawing close, it picked up speed again.

BEFORE THEY WERE within full sight of the villa and the lands surrounding it, their plan had been brought to a halt. Thick cress crossing of bramble gave her, Haseya and Ahigan cover. Clod peered around the thickest tree he could find, cursing their luck and gripping a bow tall enough to meet his shoulder. He had it stored within their smifta with arrows long like spears. Yatzil peaked above the brambles to find three palenore dressed in red plated armor, accompanied by large, sharp beaked eagles. The plates were diamond shaped, pounded to fit their muscled bodies. Their scarlet quills held no dust or tangles unlike her own hair. She turned up her nose and tied it back to avoid distraction.

Her heart sank, time passed, and none of the palenore moved on. One eagle cocked its head, turned it one way and then the other, then nipped at its feathers. A slicing feeling slipped across her stomach. She cringed and second guessed the need to rescue Ringna but groaned and decided it needed to be done. The bird and Amteer were friends in a way she didn't understand. Haseya tugged on her arm. Yatzil shook free her churning thoughts, the imagined pain of her stomach being ripped to shreds.

"Is there no way around them?"

"No." Ahigan said. "We could travel for a distance under cover and be spotted by palenore on eagle back and there are other patrols."

They were just visible through the twisted branches and withered leaves. The eagles over the villa were like a dark, hovering mass. Their sharpened beaks and metal tipped talons glinted in the distance. She cursed under her breath.

"We must attack them," said Yatzil, with a heavy heart. "I have to mend what I have done."

Haseya backed away, stumbling to her knees. Yatzil had found her to be strong and worried when needed but now the old nol was quivering fiercely.

"We will be killed for sure," said Haseya. "I don't want to abandon our Storm King, but I care too much for you to see you die."

"There is no other way to—"

"Oi. You there."

The palenore rushed through the undergrowth, thorn scraping and snapping against their armor. They unsheathed short swords crafted from diamond and sliced their way at great speed. Yatzil motioned Haseya to hide, ice crackling and forming over her skin. Haseya hesitated. The sun joined Highnonstar beating against her silver brow. Ahigan threw one of his knives, striking a palenore. The light made the expression upon his face untraceable.

"Go," Yatzil said. "And take this."

She tossed Sparron's knife to Haseya. Haseya caught it then raised an eyebrow.

"It is my promise to return alive."

Haseya stumbled to her feet and fled into the woods. Yatzil spun as her eyes ignited yellow, striking her fists together. She grinded her iced fists, hoping her quick and confident promise could be kept. The sensation was instant as she lightened her grip and parted her fists. A palenore swung his sword down, his blade screeching and clicking against her spear. She raised it higher, strain thundered through her arm muscles. Points grew at tremendous speeds until her spear was taller than herself.

Clod tackled the palenore bleeding from the blade of Ahigan's knife. Yatzil pushed off her attacker, found a narrow gap in his armor, and then thrusted her spear into it. Blood flung from the palenore's mouth, a glow brightened and faded from its depths like a dying star.

"Get this prick out of me you southern wh—"

Ahigan thrusted a knife through the palenore's neck. *Boom.* A tower of flame burst from the mouth of the third palenore. His mouth snapped shut, smoke sifted through his teeth. She gasped and tried to focus, remembering the captain's teeth at Wolfstrong. The palenore opened his mouth again, but Clod punched him in the jaw. She yanked free her spear, panicking at distant screeches that sent her skin crawling. All three ownerless eagles took flight and crossed paths with those braking from the formation over the villa. She found herself alone for a moment but then Clod and Ahigan aligned beside her.

"The blast must have been a call for help," Ahigan said. "I fear my son and I won't be enough."

The Highnonstar's heat grew worse, weighing on her focus. What was five eagles through the brightness doubled to ten. They flew at great speed, stolen from the tips of the toothed cities surrounding Wolfstrong, splitting into two groups. The second swiftly cut off their chance of escape into the woods. Around her upturned dirt, frail fallen trees and the half-buried remains of dead animals. They looked to be fleeing from the villa, around it was the same as where she stood. Dead and blanketed in dust. The Highnonstar was positioned directly over the villa and closer than the moon had ever been.

"Then we must stand and fight. If they wish to capture me, it shall be with struggle."

"Good." said Clod, readying his bow, a hint of pleasure mixed with trust in his voice. "I won't go down easy either."

He knocked an arrow and released it at the palenore cutting off their escape. The giant of a nol loosed three more in quick succession, then peered over his shoulder, sneered.

"You can throw that thing, can't you? Get to it. And make another, I've only have ten more arrows and these palenore are fast."

Yatzil swallowed her nerves, planted her feet side face, and threw. The spear climbed but fell short of an eagle's talons. Footsteps filled her ears from the palenore who had landed first. One knocked an arrow and aimed for Clod. She slammed her fists together, spreading them, but panicked, dropping a finger length ice crystal, and ran for him trailed by Ahigan, The palenore loosed his arrow. Another whipped his quills like a frigagator's tail and grabbed hold of Ahigan by his white feathered main.

Ahigan yelped as Yatzil stepped off a large rock and leapt. The arrow struck her iced chest and glanced off into the rough. She landed on her side, clutching her chest, and drawing in a short, pained breath. Dust rose like a brown mist sending her into a coughing fit. Yatzil made it to her knees, panting, unable to believe she had survived the strike.

As she stood, Yatzil smeared dust from her face and pressed her fists together. Clod glanced at her in shock, swinging himself to the fight. He plowed through upturned roots, dropping his bow, and unstrapping his axe. She spat and choked on the dust trailing from his footsteps. Yatzil parted her fists as the spear lengthened. She pressed a hand to the mark the wolf had left. It was packed with dirt. More palenore came as Ahigan freed himself and wrestled his tormentor to the ground. This one was taller than the rest, like the captain she had met, except unlike him, thicker rings emblazoned with miniature highnonstars were looped through his quills. A blood churning scream rose from Ahigan's cracked lips. Yatzil ran to aid him, but her arms were yanked behind her back.

"Leave them." Another captain yelled. His quills were longer than the others with spikes on his rings. "We got her, and that's all that matters."

Every yank and twist were no use, but she concentrated until all palenore shook and mist escaped their lips. Those holding her hostage tensed their grip, fingers slipping down her iced arms. Coughing fits bombarded her senses, soon she was let go, her captors dropped to their knees. Yatzil reached for her spear but suddenly paused. A sharp point pressed to her throat. She raised her chin, meeting struggling black eyes before her.

"You fi … fi … finished," said the captain. "Our First Son and Daughter knew you were coming 'ere. I'll 'ave the giant and old man k … illed if y…"

Yatzil scowled, finding Ahigan pinned down while Clod had raised his axe in time to suck in his muscled gut. Palenore had him surrounded by sword points. She frowned and doubted that the captain would keep his word. Slowly, she thawed until hoisted upon an eagle's back. And then two palenore forced her against the eagle's itchy, dust feathers. She felt flesh against her back, and in those seconds, she saw the fear in Ahigan's eyes, the frustration in his son's. The eagle took flight as she listened for more movement, but the wind made such effort worthless.

CHAPTER TEN

Her guards had doubled once within the villa's outer wall. Its step pyramid was crowned in a raging flame. They ushered her toward immense palm-and-oak doors below it. Statues of the noble's ancestors standing tall along the walls were cracked and melted to their sandaled feet. They once possessed stone orbs engraved with depictions of the Four with their hands opened and raised to the sky. The doors thundered shut behind them.

She winced as a guard yanked at her hair and severed the tassel holding it back. The others joked and sniggered at the tangles and highlighted dust made of her hair from her travels. Being inside offered some relief to her eyes, only flickering braziers lining the hall at intervals troubled them. Yatzil restrained a gasp. Blood lashed out in thick streaks from doorways muddying the dusty white tile. She grinded her teeth and refused to let her captors see her pain or guess her thoughts about the fate of the noble's sons.

She wished to pray for the boys, recalling their generosity before her flight further north. If the Four failed to answer, then they were truly of no use to her. It required her hands upon her chest and kneeling with only the eyes upon her hands open. It opened her body to guidance. Yatzil kept her feet moving, storing away such tradition for if she survived what was to come. *I will not be mocked again by these monsters.*

They pushed her into a columned room. She stumbled then dropped to her knees short of a raised dais tiled with jade. *Slam.* Yatzil flinched, resting her eyes on four ash covered owl statues. Symbols of the Four were just visible upon their foreheads. A hook for Non, a spear piercing a moon for Fertilida, a leaf dripping water upon a bathing woman for Limpe and for Urra, an ornate dagger piercing a small warrior.

Yatzil pushed herself up, approaching the dais with unease, allowing herself a smile. Amongst surroundings so much like home her heart grew heavy with emotion. She kneeled upon the center of the dais and stared at the hall ahead. The jade was warm against her legs as a cloak of colored furs hung on the hall's left harassed and burnt. A light dusting of snow would make the illusion of home complete. Yatzil checked if she was alone, finding no voices from the hall and no one peered from behind the columns. They contained the noble's ancestors posed as she readied to be.

She untied her top and found a small hole where the arrow had struck before folding it under her knees. *I must use this time alone wisely.* She exhaled, finding there was still silence, still time to honor the noble and his children. Yatzil cupped her breasts and leaned back to close her eyes. The Four swooped in with silent wings through the darkness. They landed close to her, with Limpe clothed in a cloak of colored furs. Flor had spoken of offering them a gift once they returned to Niev. It was only right for neither knew the

West then. Yatzil firmed up her posture, taken aback that now, after all this time, the Four had come to listen.

"Great goddesses. I miss the cold I shared with you. Guide Flor..."

Her friend's name caught in her throat, though her prayers were meant for others. She had known her since she had become a woman in nescaran eyes. Flor had shown her Niev's harbor, its snow laden forests around the city's walls and moat. Yatzil focused on the passage they took to see these places but its only semblance to her memory was a damp cave. A quaking not experienced in sometime had caved it in.

"Guide Flor to your halls by my request."

The four ice blue owls narrowed their gaze then screeched.

"It will be done but speak of who you came to us for first."

Yatzil clenched her teeth, tears collecting in her eyes.

"Grant your loyal servant of this house and his sons guidance to your halls."

The Four aligned with their statues around the dais and remained silent, assessing her until her patience was gone.

"Allow me to mourn my friend!" she snapped. "Oh. I ... have forgotten."

Tremors ran down her back finding everything, all her efforts had kept her from keeping her father's memory. The Four hooted and snapped, flying up then snatching her wrists, ripping her hands from her chest.

"Show rage to yourself." They dug their talons into the eyes upon her hands. *"We mourn for him but know not what caused his fate."*

"How can you not?" she screamed. They released her, and she covered herself. "Do you not see all as I have been taught?"

"We know only what we are told and make decisions then."

"I shall tell you then how my father was—"

Non silenced her with a raised wing.

"Allow yourself to mourn your friend first. You have made little time for it."

Her lips edged out of place, ready to demand they hear of her father's killer, but Non's words held her tongue at a point. Yatzil nodded and the Four flew off into the darkness. Her heart pounded against her chest to think of Flor. The last time they had been alone was in the bedchamber burning high above her. She had laid upon the bed's softness, lying still as she had ever been. Its frame carved and inlaid with gold woman and man intertwined, exchanging pleasures. Flor had finished the last of the glyphs for Niev's guardians, leaving the bed, demonstrating the dance to accompany them. They had been fortunate the noble possessed a wisdom room. A scroll at the foot of the bed held faded images of an avalanche warrior performing every move as a king sat upon a palanquin.

They had reminisced about sneaking onto Yatzil's father ship. Neither had ever set foot on a ship before or since. Yatzil swallowed, remembering the kiss of Non's sea breeze that day. How it tossed her father's long dark hair when he reluctantly tried to discipline them. Her lips trembled and her back ached. The rage on his face was for the guards, she knew, before sending Flor and her to the palace.

Yatzil breathed deeply and thanked Non for her earlier words. She squeezed her chest and blamed lack of faith, no, ignorance for not coming to the Four sooner. Their explanation put to rest why they had not dissolved her marriage. They had been told to remain silent, thus allowing events to unfold, and by who at the time possessed more power than Yatzil had with a crown and the west awaiting her rule.

She collapsed against the tile and curled into a ball, ignoring the pain in her shoulder, and the tile's heat. Too long it seemed she needed to be on her guard and with all she had learned there was no care that she was a prisoner. The heat through the sky light pressed at her skin like a dozen blades to a traitor's neck. Yatzil sobbed and pressed her face to her knees, dismissing a faint scuffling for the cloak. There was something upon her shoulder. It was long and slender, gentle like Flor's touch, even cool. Yatzil opened her eyes like water had been splashed against them. The present struck her as she rolled away and crawled back.

A woman stood before her with long evergreen dreadlocks streaming to her shoulders. The woman's ember eyes flashed, brightened as they met Yatzil's. Yatzil covered herself, stumbled to her feet, searching for her top. It was out of reach in a wrinkled heap beside the woman. She kneeled before Yatzil and bowed with shyness, the opposite of how intimate she dared be earlier.

"Away." she screamed, yet the girl with a narrow brim nose and dark bark-like skin remained still. "I did not grant you permission to touch me."

She clasped her mouth, both anger and sorrow had bested her again. Yatzil crossed her arms to feel safe, feeling the edge of the dais bite at her feet.

"Hand me my top," she demanded, but the woman only crawled backwards, flashing her eyes, shielding her face with her hands. "I said hand it to me…"

It was no use. Yatzil wanted to thump herself on the head at such a dull mistake. The woman was neither nescaran or nol, and she possessed none of the calm of a Raton. The scuffling she dismissed wasn't the cloak, hanging still and torn. It was this woman's feet. Lijani were not known to travel south, and they dressed, unlike this one, by growing clothes from their bodies. They shied from the rest of Nema which didn't explain this lijani, nor her temperament.

"I know little of your language," said Yatzil. "It was difficult to learn."

She took one step forward, pressing an arm to her chest. The lijani kept her eyes focused, every inch of her neck turned scraped and hissed. Her skin was flecked in places, seeping black swirling mist. The dress she wore was that of a nescaran handmaiden. It kept the legs close, tiny beads formed its straps, holding firm the breasts. The left arm was covered by a short sleeve of pounded bronze. Yatzil stopped short of an arm's reach. Her eyes went to her trapped top beneath the lijani's knees.

Yatzil let out a hissing wet sound, followed by a conflicted whistling and croaking. She hoped her use of lijani to ask her for top back didn't result in a bit tongue. Even her lamodun knew just greetings, and struggled with them too, deterring her from learning more. Every word she spoke sounded harsh to her own ears. She huffed then contemplated shoving the woman. The frigagator teeth around the top fringe were scuffed. The lijani woman giggled, leaned, and presented its light green fabrics like a gift.

Yatzil grabbed it, keeping herself protected, wrapping and tugging, finishing with a knot. The lijani's lush lips opened.

"We can try a nescaran's swift rolling language," she said, "if you like."

Yatzil's eyes widened at how her home tongue flowed so gracefully. It was like this northern woman was a nescaran guised as a tree.

"I appreciate such change." she said. "I am Yatzil, Storm Queen of the nol and Princess of Niev."

"I am Maua." Maua bowed with a nervous smile. "We have only one royal in Mutafakara. It is a pleasure to meet you, Storm Queen."

Yatzil tucked the knot under her top's silks. The hall behind and the doors ahead were their only choices from the temple. A dampness remained on Yatzil's cheeks. The lijani held her focus with her burning, orange eyes. Maua closed her eyes for a second, before meeting Yatzil's again. Yatzil pursed her lips and refocused.

"You appear to be searching for someone."

"How do you know?" Yatzil asked.

"You were deep in thought, Storm Queen. We lijani spend all our time in it." Maua pointed to the doors behind her. "This way is guarded but down the hall is where you must go next."

Yatzil crossed her arms and eyed Maua a little longer. One thing needed answered before trusting this woman.

"Before I go, I wish to know why you intruded on my mourning?"

Maua folded her hands. Her eyes fell to the jade tile as the evergreen faded from her dreadlocks. And then they darkened, sprouting tiny leaves, her embers eyes bright red as she drew in a long breath.

"I was offered as tribute to the First Couple so the lijani could be left alone. We are born and left to grow alone, coming together only when more must exist. That happens seldom and leaves me to be lonely. I did not wish you to be alone as I have been."

Maua returned to staring at the tile and examined her hands. They had three fingers each and twisted like tree roots. To be alone was familiar. There was a deep void in Yatzil's heart in need of filling now. She raised Maua's chin with a curled finger like her father had when she was sad.

"As to beyond my personal reason for being here." Maua sniffed. "Queen Aagono made it my duty to pleasure her guests if they wish it."

Maua's words struck like a second arrow to the chest. It was an echo of what her mother expected from Flor and every handmaiden if her father received guests. Yatzil let her hand drop. But instead of layering the lijani woman with pity, she stretched out her hand.

"There will be no need to serve anymore," Yatzil said. "I shall find a way to free you and who I seek."

A single swirling misty ball ran down to a spot absent of bark on Maua's cheek. Bark formed removing the blemish on her face. She took Yatzil's hand.

CHAPTER ELEVEN

Yatzil left the dais with Maua at a brisk pace down a hall lined with torches that left scorch marks. The marks stretched across the ceiling like fingers. She chewed her lip at the possibility of being locked away soon but what troubled her more was not receiving Amteer's forgiveness, or if his life had been ended. Their footsteps echoed. She decided instead to believe both him and Ringna still lived. She swallowed and held firm Maua's hand.

She remained thawed and kept her thoughts going, piecing together how best to say. *I laid with you to raise an army.* She released a stored away breath then sealed her lips with a smile for Maua. *Amteer, I left because my brother needed me.* All were true yet she feared he may grow angry regardless... *Screech.* It was faint but when she listened again there were only the whispers of lit torches. There was no mistaking the light youthfulness to it that was Ringna's, but the eagle's master needed her first.

Maua motioned with her chin to aged tapestries on the walls. Their intricacy and depictions sent Yatzil's falling spirits skyward. She was uncertain if the royals blessed with jade inlaid teeth and wearing owl eye and talon crowns were of her blood. But they performed the same rituals of hunting, submersion, intertwinement, and cleanliness atop step pyramids. Below their sandaled feet were the skulls of those who defied tradition. A king held a dagger and piled claimed riches on a decorated plinth.

Three kings placed their tattooed hands above their eyes, and in some images, queens too, offered what the Four demanded. But in truth now such goddesses were like pets to a royal, and whether temple mice or fish of the sea, to her, it was encouragement for doing what they were told. There was a light ahead that disturbed her vision for a second. Yatzil rubbed her eyes to be certain of one queen who appeared sixteen to her eighteen years of age. Faint voices drifted from the light ahead.

"They await you, scheeche nik." Maua said with her words nervously going from nescaran to lijani. "I was meant to present you when ready."

Maua yanked her hand away. The voices were growing louder. Some were impatient as Maua pressed herself against the wall and tiny leaves fell and browned from her braids. Yatzil searched for words to calm her and quickly. Her own emotions pounded at her chest like a distressed prisoner claiming innocence.

"The First Son and Daughter do not scare me," she said, lying to herself more than Maua. "You must be calm."

"No disrespect intended, Storm Queen, but to not fear the Highnonstar is foolish. How will you find who you seek, and free us, when he with a blackened eagle on his chest is so powerful?"

"Eagle?"

Yatzil squinted through the light filled archway. The Four

chased one another as if at play over it. It was difficult at first with light and darkness blending, but two pairs of feet appeared beyond a tall pillar. Yatzil took Maua by the hand and pulled her forward. The lijani wept then tugged back, rubbing her fingers like they had been pinched.

"Please, leave me behind!" Maua cried. "Find who you seek."

"I cannot leave you. And besides, I believe I have found him."

Her heart thundered against her chest the more Maua refused to budge. It clawed at her to know what this First Daughter had done to Amteer. Was he beyond capability to listen to her wish for forgiveness? If he had changed so much, then why not send warriors to fetch her instead of a frightened woman sent to pleasure her before some gruesome end?

"I promise," she whispered. "I shall find a way for us to escape no matter what."

Maua let go of her hand again. She stood up straight and took deep breaths, new leaves and a darker green returned to her dreadlocks. Misty tears fell to the ground and seeped between smooth parted tile, sprouting tiny, pointed leaves.

"I will present you."

Both went forward with a slight speed in their steps, but Yatzil lagged as Maua folded her hands, letting them rest against her dress. Yatzil stopped cold below the arch and shut her eyes like dirt had been flung into them. It wasn't the light but who beyond an open grassy courtyard sat on high, joined by a woman, familiar in face, yet beautiful in a way that excited Yatzil somehow.

"Amteer." She whispered before stepping forth from the hall. "It must not be too late."

The dried grass hissed against her feet. She had been within this courtyard before, but it's pillar was missing a vital piece. The pillar meant for a game which strengthened one for battle or childbirth with hip and chest thrusts. Her eyes adjusted to the light as Queen Aagono stood and placed a hand of ringed fingers on Amteer's shoulder. Her red quills were woven through a golden star crown. It formed a point on her forehead while her quills hung over her shoulders and down her back. This First Daughter, this Queen Aagono as she was to Yatzil wore a near transparent top. It enhanced her round breasts and wrapped behind her, exposing her smooth pale belly, joining with a short skirt that clung to her narrow hips, swallowing her knees.

"You have saved my warriors a search," said Aagono. "Do you wish for my husband to release his host?"

Queen Aagono's words were light, with song to them, yet they made Maua shrink back to where they had come. The way *host* was used sounded strange, and no other man of great prestige was present.

"Yes… I wish for his release."

"But you abandoned him with little nourishment." The queen grimaced and then smirked, flaring her nostrils. "Why wish such a thing if leaving him was your intention?"

Yatzil sealed her emotions away and focused on Amteer's own blank expression and more chiseled features. His eyes were black like the first daughter's and his face was paler than a snowstorm upon Niev's harvest month. His posture was straighter, prouder, like his father's. His lumao possessed thin waves of gold, wrapped tight about his waist. His crown presented a long enough point to skewer a wild boar.

"I did wish to leave…"

It had to be said no matter how helpless it left her feeling. She narrowed her eyes then felt herself falter.

"But our dance has formed a child within my womb and given me cause to find you. I…"

Amteer rose. His quills clicked their thick gold ringlets.

Queen Aagono urged him to remain seated, but his curiosity was too great. His seat was formed of the pillar's missing stone X. His lower lip trembled like it had at Wolfstrong before she restored his hope with affection.

"Why should I believe such a farce after you abandoned him?" he said, in words not of Nol fashion, taking hold of Aagono's hand. The queen smiled as he frowned. "You both were bound by blood trade. Tell me truthfully why you left him, for you led him to believe we... I mean you both were on a noble journey."

She saw in his eyes and heard in his voice the storm king she had married. Amteer craved the truth through this High-nonstar. The black of his eyes melted away but then return to its darkness. It appeared Amteer was fighting for control, for the truth. More palenore flocked in from a hall right of the disheveled thrones. They wore long black robes, viziers it seemed to a grass filled court. To tell him she was with child made her heart lighter yet within the cool chambers of it the complete truth needed released. Yatzil reaffirmed her stance, summoned all courage, and parted her tensed lips.

"I tell you as true as can be husband," A tear raced down her cheek, "a child grows in me like my regret for leaving you. I should have been kinder and understood all you wished was for our people to be safe. I have not eaten in nearly two days because of the child forming from my greed."

"Why starve yourself if you're with child?"

"It is not by my choice."

"She lies, Highnonstar." said Queen Aagono. Her fingers wrapped and tightened over his. "She is untrustworthy and clever like Nescara before I killed her. Make her prove herself."

Highnonstar took a step back with weakness in his eyes.

It gave Yatzil hope. She wished to smile but guards soon joined the viziers. The feeling of chill on her breath was potent, but if it wasn't enough, to make water was no act she dared do to convince them. She turned back to Maua still huddled in fear, the new leaves in her hair were turning a pale green. Yatzil let go a breath, a cool mist rose from it.

"If proof is required," she said. "Then give me fruit."

Queen Aagono ran her hands over and then down Amteer's chest. They halted and caressed ever so below his navel. The queen smiled at the rise of his member. Yatzil made a fist as the First Daughter stood on tiptoe. She whispered something that distanced Amteer further before gave him a soft, assuring kiss. The Highnonstar looked up with a stiff chin and determination back in his eyes. Yatzil strained to remain calm. Amteer had been with the First Daughter too long. Yatzil wondered if her father had been as strong as she believed when her mother could do the same thing with such ease as the first daughter.

"Come forward, lijani servant." Highnonstar called, parting his lips, and drawing in a slow, pleasing breath. "Bear fruit for who left my host to die."

Maua's ember eyes brightened to a beat red. Her leaves had fallen from her dreadlocks to be replaced by thorns. But even with so angered a change, Yatzil found her timid as she stretched out a shaking finger.

"Will you," she whispered. "Abandon me too?"

"No," Yatzil said, lips trembling. "My reason for leaving him was to save my brother, and I regret it."

Maua drew back her finger as it sprouted then withdrew leaves. Yatzil licked her quivering lips, stretching out her hand. Queen Aagono laughed.

"Do as your First Son commands or be burned to roast meat."

"Please," said Yatzil. "I shall never abandon you. If we die, it will be as if I have."

Yatzil glanced back at the First Daughter to find a palenore wearing a thin apron about his waist raising a tray containing gold cups. A film of ice coated them, and by their distant scent the cups held palm wine from noble's private stock. The queen peered over the rim of hers, amusement filled her solid black irises in place of how worried they were earlier.

"Then." Maua stretched out her finger, leaves blooming. "Free us."

A red dot formed between the leaves. It whirled and grew, colored with stripes of red and yellow. A light fuzz sprouted over its skin. Yatzil secreted a smile. It was a bate-nich. They were grown in high farms throughout Niev. Yatzil gave the ripe fruit a tug, expecting Maua to wince but the lijani's eyes flickered with the pop. Yatzil admired it, not having had one in so long.

"She will fail, Highnonstar." The First Daughter wiped droplets from her lips. "And when she does, I will make her a slave as I have the lijani girl."

Furry ran through Yatzil as she gave Maua one last look. The palenore queen wanted her for more than servitude, she knew, and dared not imagine how Maua had suffered. Her eyes grew wide, and breath caught in her throat.

She remembered why Amteer was called Highnonstar. What tormented Nema was the namesake of the god controlling him. Yatzil swallowed then drew in a breath and shut her eyes. A cold mist ran over her lips engulfing the bate-nich. And what was a bright fruit of red and yellow became a black core within a ball of ice.

"No." Aagono screamed, dropping her chalice. "No, no, no. no."

Boom!

Everyone spun and focused on the archway, the First Daughter's guards raced to man it.

Boom!

A tight squeeze nearly toppled Yatzil. Maua knelt before her, arms bound about her legs, her full lips trembling. Amteer descended from the dais, slipping through Aagono's fingers. Amteer took Yatzil's hand as faint shouts reached her ears from down the hall. The palenore guards raced down the hall, their footfalls muted by shouts and then were silenced.

"Do you truly regret leaving me?" he said with both eyes returned to their green. "Am I really a father? Do I have your love?"

If she looked into his eyes the truth would be revealed to his final question that gave no, *yes*. More shouts came and an immense figure filled the hall behind her. She was only able to answer the first two and had done so, but love was never a feeling beyond her brother, father, and Flor. Maua released her legs and hid behind her.

Clod emerged from the hall doused in dust, mixed with splashes of blood, grounding his teeth and wild eyed. Ahigan squeezed past him, brandishing two long knives tipped in blood running down to his fists. The viziers in their long robes swarmed around Queen Aagono like a black curtain as her eyes burned a bright gold.

"I truly," she said, in a familiar hoarseness once the chilling mist left her lips, "hold our child within me. Now let us find Ringna."

"Be silent!" Aagono cried. "He is mine."

Flames formed around the First Daughter, her body its white shifting center. She launched herself from the dais and landed, charring the grass at her feet. Yatzil frosted but such heat sent her ice cowering back into her skin. The flames rose like a wave and swallowed Aagono's viziers. Their screams were brief with their remains vanishing like a field of long grass. A half dozen guards came in from the hall. Clod and Ahigan spun, fighting them off.

"We must go, my queen." Ahigan said, dust swirled each way his feathered main whipped. "Before that goddess burns us too."

"She won't. I will not permit it," said Amteer.

Yatzil reached for Amteer's shoulder as he turned to face the enraged goddess. The First Daughter reached and called his name, her eyes softening their glow. Amteer stared at his hand, turned it left then right and aimed at a wall. He strained and gasped. A ball of flame filled the courtyard with light. Yatzil shielded her face with her arm, frosting, holding Maua close. The brickwork scattered churning dust and crumbling stone.

"How dare you usurp my husband's control of you?" Queen Aagono cried. The First Daughter slapped Amteer so hard he collapsed to his knees. "And for someone who abandoned you?"

Yatzil grabbed Maua's wrist and headed for the singed remains of the wall. Ahigan and Clod followed. Yatzil peered back just short of a second wall blown away by Amteer's efforts. She swallowed then found him drained somehow by the First Daughter's strike. It was a miracle Yatzil never believed possible yet saving him was still obtainable by her words. He had nearly forgiven her because of them. But as for Ringna who she still feared, the eagle remained a prisoner like her master.

"He has rebelled before, Storm Queen," said Maua. "That is the reason for the pyramid being on fire, but she always wins."

They ran for the forest ahead with what palenore flying over the villa diving in to help their queen. Queen Aagono held Amteer's head close and engulfed it in flames. Yatzil stopped as the others continued, Maua's hand in hers. Amteer rose and looked down at the First Daughter, taking her in his arms like he had lost her somehow. Their protectors shielded them behind a wall of feathers and white flesh. Yatzil felt herself raised with Maua shrieking as Clod placed them on his muscled shoulders.

"You will have to reflect on loss later, my queen." said Ahigan, far up ahead. "Our enemy remains distracted for now."

The skull upon the knob of Clod's axe prodded at her back with its chin. His bow strung over his shoulder jabbed at her elbow. Yet through such awkwardness she felt safe, resting a reassuring hand on Maua's shoulder. Maua smiled, but her lips trembled, and her cheeks flaked at Clod's lack of emotion. He gritted his teeth, and every stride increased to catch up to his father.

They ducked at low branches, bushes bearing the brunt of the giant's plowing knees. There was a faint chattering like that of teeth. Yatzil gasped and Clod groaned, finding her frost form had blued his lips. Clod had been shaking without her notice and his fingers were fused to her thigh. She thawed, thumping herself on the head for not doing so earlier. She peered back to the villa, wanting to try again, but it risked those she cared for, and the child residing within her. Yatzil stroked Maua's shoulder. Maua smiled a nervous smile, meeting her eyes.

Clod set them down deep out of sight of the villa. She guided the lijani woman to a fallen tree to rest against. As she turned back to the villa's burning top, visible through what length of trees they had traversed, a rush knocked her off balance.

"See," Haseya said, embracing her. "I told those bolder heads ash and dust from the forest was good for blending. Where? Where is our king?"

"We have to go back," said Yatzil, holding Haseya close. "But another attempt to save him will be a great risk—"

"Not needed," said Maua.

Ahigan offered Maua water from his tortoise shell, its cork still plugged in; Haseya raised an eyebrow, parting from Yatzil.

"What do you mean?" said Clod, rubbing dust from his face. "We failed but our queen is right."

"I... Well, I have been in service to Queen Aagono for a time after Plunemar changed... Oh, it's far too terrible to say."

Yatzil took slow steps, seeking truth in Maua's fading eyes. She ran her fingers over her belly, for some reason imagining it swollen. She shook her head, returning her thoughts to Maua's words. Her eyes grew wide for a moment. She peered over her shoulder to Clod, realizing that for the first time, he had called her his queen.

"Tell us how another attempt to save my husband isn't needed, Maua."

Maua turned away, readjusting her dress, and resting on the fallen tree. Her hands leapt to her lap like something had burned them. Yatzil took a few steps toward her, the others staring intently. She paused when Maua rose and faced them.

"Yes. Well, nol magic is ... I only know what I was told... Oh, I must not tell. We will be pursued soon."

"You better tell us quickly then," Haseya grumbled. "Or..."

"If we are going to trust you." said Ahigan, tying his tortoise shell to his loincloth. "You must tell us what you know." He turned to Yatzil, eyes narrowed, and lips firm. "If you wish her to join us, my queen, force her."

"Or we'll cut her up for..."

"Stop, Clod." Haseya hissed through her gummy mouth. "We aren't going to..."

"Silence." Yatzil said. Her tone was firm enough that it

reminded her of her father. "Look what your anger has done."

Maua had slipped into a ball on the ground. Her dread-locks withered into thin pale green at the roots. The fall had loosened shards of bark from her skin, releasing mist over her limbs. Yatzil fell to her knees and reached to embrace the woman she had freed. Maua flinched at first but quickly gathered herself up in Yatzil's arms.

"Please tell me." she whispered. Faint screeching sent her eyes darting to the treetops. "What do you know?"

"I…"

Maua raised her head, edging her lower lip out of place.

"I sensed when I touched you a connection to the High-nonstar. Queen Aagono knew of it and wanted it severed so his possession could be complete."

"Are you telling me the blood trade of my marriage is what keeps Amteer from being lost to us?"

"Yes," Maua said. "And I was sent to sever that connection, but knew not how, and you were in great pain."

Yatzil threw Maua off her and crawled, finding Haseya. The old nol dropped to her knees and held her close, scowling at Maua.

"I think we better leave you, tree girl," Haseya said. "We know only one way to break a blood trade."

"What breaks a blood trade?" Yatzil said, through trembling lips and eyes blurred by tears as the screeches drew closer.

"It's death," said Haseya. "Blood trades are what keep a nol loyal to who they marry."

"I am sorry," said Maua. "I did not know death—"

"Do not speak of it. I am glad for your pity," said Yatzil. Her mind raced to something she hadn't considered. "If the First Daughter is from long ago, why think I would survive to serve her?"

"I do not know," said Maua. "Am I ... forgiven?"

Yatzil gathered herself up, brushed off the dirt on her fingers. Maua had given Nema a greater chance by not knowing. And as Yatzil focused on the trembling northerner, the chance to dance a new moon into existence had tripled.

"Yes ... I forgive you."

CHAPTER TWELVE

Yatzil brushed the last fleck of ash from her shoulder. Her ears trained for the screech of eagles should they come. At a great distance west of the villa, Clod, Haseya, and Maua remained hidden. Ahigan matched her pace, eyeing both the skies and tree line. His silver skin doused in ash resembled the night sky she hadn't seen in days. She sighed, gratitude abundant in her chest. Haseya's idea of using the burnt remains of the forest to hide from the First Daughter's soldiers had worked.

Despite Maua's words Yatzil took Ahigan to rescue Amteer once again. She chewed her lip, hoping Queen Aagono hadn't abandoned the villa. No eagles circled in the sky and once they reached the courtyard no one could be seen. Yatzil rested a hand to the white granite pillar at its center, sending Ahigan to search. Every blade of grass was scorched, and burns climbed the pillar like the tentacles of a squid.

"The First Daughter could not have fled," she said, withdrawing her hand, the sun pressing upon her brow. "She has no reason to fear a queen with no army."

Pattering met her ears, a figure rushed down the hall from the temple. Ahigan emerged, sheathing one of his long knives. He met her eyes opening his hand. A short, white feather rested upon it.

"I found only this, my queen," he said, keeping his aged eyes peeled. "The First Daughter must have taken our king's eagle before fleeing. I don't see a reason to leave."

"I agree," she said, plucking the feather from his hand. "We shall focus on my brother for now. And if we can free him from my mother's control, perhaps we can free Amteer too."

THEY TRAVELED further south for a week. Yatzil kept constant watch on Maua, remaining with the Lijani woman in Ahigan's smifta. She watched her sleep, much bark that had been lost had grown back. It was less tasking to see today, and she guessed, with all her time spent out of the light, that darkness could aid the children of her kingdom.

She nudged the Lijani after she asked everyone to prepare to leave. A coolness missed glided over her skin from the smifta entrance. They were closing in on the border, and the sun had gone down. She watched Maua roll flat on her back. Light slowly reached her chin as the woman below her opened her eyes.

Maua smiled a tiny smile. Yatzil told her they would be leaving soon to continue the journey the Nemamoon said would resurrect Plunemar. She wrapped an arm under Maua, easing her upright, careful of her lengthy vine-like dreadlocks.

"I have not done the Lijani dance in so long," said Maua. "My people gather to do it and seldom unless a storm claims one of us."

"So then," said Yatzil, a need to practice the nescaran dance dawned on her. "You must practice when within my brother's palace."

"May I do so when we settle for rest again? My strength is nearly returned."

It was true the glow had returned to Maua's eyes. Yatzil stood and helped her up to find a strength in the northerner's stance. The bark of Maua's hands was smoother, lacking the thick knots for knuckles, and replaced by knuckles like her own.

"I have never read of a Lijani dance. I imagine it will be," She sighed, finding a role in her life had reversed. *Flor, I am the strong one now.* She met Maua's eyes. "Most beautiful indeed." Yatzil finished in the scraping and hissing of Lijani.

Maua giggled. "Your lijani has improved. The dance is like a tree in a strong wind. And it is beautiful."

"More beautiful than my use of your language?"

They looked at one another breaking out in laughter. One at a time they went out to join the others. Maua's laughter stalled, breaking into a coughing fit then vanished as if such expression was not frequent. She hoped Maua would grow in spirit and never be withered to near mist and roots again.

She gave a soft pat on Maua's shoulder and said she wished to practice the nescaran dance alone first.

Leaving for the thick overgrowth she thought for a moment and then dropped to a panther-like position. She arched back and splayed her fingers like claws. It was a struggle with the new dress, close fit like the one from wedding, except it possessed beads and not boar teeth. *I must give Haseya thanks for it.* She prowled like the beast, raising her claw-like hands. Strain raced up her back like lightning across the sky. Her mind rested on Flor.

She had come so far and without her best friend. Flor had encouraged her to be fluent in languages. She had been a friend when Yatzil's mother scolded her for wishing to traverse Niev on foot. Yatzil rose, taking in the fact her friend had been gone a month. Unsteadiness ran through her knees, commanding her to collapse and surrender to grief. She planted her hand against a tree and clasped her throat. She discarded encroaching tears and thought of sending everyone away to continue the journey alone. But how could she when they had come so far and given so much?

After a few short steps, the smifta appeared ahead, shrinking as she brushed aside a branch. Clod picked up the smifta, rising and rolling his eyes. Maua arched her arms back, enhancing her slenderness, then bowed forward with every finger splayed. Yatzil felt a deep longing to mimic such moves, but they were only growing friends, and she wasn't a man. And a man was considered by most in Nema to be the only accepted partner for such a dance.

It was a relief without any brightness to tease her eyes like a fly unwilling to leave. No redness surrounded the eyes of those in Yatzil's company, fully settling her doubts for her people traveling to the Gaping Mouth. Yatzil raised her chin and welcomed the chilling breeze against her cheeks. She rested her eyes on Maua, the lijani not bothered by the south's arctic atmosphere.

They sat upon Clod's shoulders, an offer of repayment for Yatzil saving his life. Clod wore a mismatched arrangement of furs from Haseya's wagon. And with the Nol giant being of such immensity the wagon was left barren. His appearance was like a furry beast, but one she no longer feared. His skulls still hung around his waist and as they left where they had camped, Haseya threw her last bit of needle and thread into the bushes, folding her arms, grumbling. Yatzil kept her eyes forward to hide her displeasure. The old Nol's wagon served a new purpose, carrying Clod's bow and arrows. She peered over her shoulder. Haseya stuffed the tiny box with its wheels in the sack at her side.

Yatzil returned her mind to Maua, her nescaran hand-maiden dress discarded. Leaves greener than on the trees slowly covered areas she failed to ignore. It felt as though, with all she had experienced, that her feelings had begun to alter, yet they were familiar somehow. Yatzil closed her eyes, rearranging her thoughts, placing them on the dance steps that granted passage into Niev. Every move had grown easier in weeks passed with spins and turns leaving her neck sore. She rubbed it. Thick vines ran from Maua's chest until dangling unattached and pointed around her ankles.

She felt a slight nudge and was about to ask why Clod had stopped but her breath left her. A great wall loomed ahead. Statues of the Four graced its top, their wings spread and eyes facing north. Their faces were crumbled, and cracked, doused by snow. She flashed the eyes upon her hands at a fallen statue of Limpie, her wings crumbling against the smooth surface of the wall. Clod continued. His long strides brought them between an unfinished section of the wall. Its white granite blocks were large enough to house the nol giant.

Yatzil tapped his shoulder, wanting to let the snow fill between her toes. Snow crunched beneath her feet, its familiar crisp wetness erased memories of dust and dried grass. She frowned before passing through the incomplete section. The glyph of cleanliness upon Limpie's brow were missing their gold.

She had grown distant from Limpie's teachings, and with what she had learned, there was little reason to bother with them. Yatzil rubbed something from her brow, it came away oily, something she never felt before. *I must make time for Limpie's extensive practice of body purity at least,* she thought, snow crackling under her feet. She rested her gaze on the fallen goddess once more and thought of Sachihiro. *He comes first.* She bawled her fist, strolling for the forest ahead, worrying about bringing her mind to the demise of a king from a previous dynasty, and how he had built the wall, and the way his death had come. The king had drained Niev's coffers to build it and had secretly enslaved Nol to move its blocks. His eldest son and daughter overthrew him, and in a way no nescaran royal had ever done.

"You are deep in thought, Storm Queen." Maua said after she thanked Clod. He removed his axe and dashed ahead of the others. Maua's eyes flared a burning orange as Clod raised his axe and sliced, severing low branches. "I wish for him to stop ..." Maua caught herself mid-sentence. "My apologies. I halted my concern for you for that of the forest. Lijani hold all sacred what does so much for so many."

"Hold where you are," Yatzil called to Clod, turning to Maua. "My mind is on my brother and how I shall give him control again."

Haseya cackled as she and Ahigan shared his tortoise shell. Yatzil ran her fingers over her wrinkled dress. Its hide was thicker than Nescaran silks. The old Nol gave Ahigan a hearty smack on his thickly garbed back. *Why was my mother never so bold in kindness?* Yatzil sighed.

"I am grateful for your concern."

She took Maua's hand, tracing a circle over it with her thumb.

"Do you wish your mother were like Haseya? Lijani do not have such women of value but like you I would choose Haseya over your true mother."

"I only hope my brother..."

"Come, my queen," Ahigan said, waving her hand south.

Yatzil shook her head and found they had stopped midway from the wall to the forest. She waved for Ahigan to wait, increasing her pace. The lijani matched it, maneuvering her lips from a hard line to a smile. Clod had ceased his chopping.

"You said he is strong in body and mind," she said. "I do not … think King Sachihiro will allow treason if he suspects it."

Maua's slight hesitation sent Yatzil's nerves into a race. The last she had been in his company they had been saying good-bye. Even then, with the possibility of never seeing one another again, her brother had ceased his sadness once their mother was present.

She released a long breath, drawing in the sweat scent of the palm-n-oaks shading the three nol in her company. Yatzil looked upon them in their furred garb. Ahigan's feathers were slightly less white than snow. And though he had not rolled in it, as she wished to, his feathers were like snow drift on his boney shoulders. Clod rested his axe against his knee then cracked his knuckles.

A lingering worry swelled in the depths of her belly. It told her despite being with child, her appearance like it was before leaving home that not even with the dance would the nol before her be granted entrance. The Nol were spoken of in harmful ways in her father's court before peace was struck. Yatzil withdrew her hand from Maua's, knowing lijani received no favorable words either. She swallowed and let out a breath, steam absent from her lips unlike the others.

"Let us continue." She eyed Clod. He raised his axe to use it again. "No more will you be using your axe, Clod. It unsettles Maua."

"We'll be whipped in the face, my queen," said Clod. "How will we spot danger before we cross the Wrinkled River?"

"You're scary enough and furry enough with my wagon's furs," said Haseya, a hint of bitterness in her voice. "That danger will crawl away."

"Would you rather my son freeze?"

"No more arguments," Yatzil said. "I should have said it weeks ago. I shall have your wagon replenished Haseya, with boar fur if our task succeeds."

Haseya crossed her arms, mushed her lips, and turned her nose up to Clod.

"I did like your dress when I first saw you." she said, meeting Yatzil's eyes, grinning. "Is that top you still wear boar fur too?"

"Silks, but boars are of many colors." said Yatzil, hearing confidence in the old Nol's voice. "The beast's meat makes a feast in the skilled hands of a meal maker."

"Then this argument can be settled." said Ahigan, eyeing Haseya. She raised an eyebrow at him. "I think we need something different to eat and we are low on dried meat."

"What about the forest?" said Clod. "I can crush diamond fangs and cut down frigagators, but I'll need to see them."

Maua stepped forward, spreading her hands, drawing in her surroundings. Bringing comfort to the northerner felt right to Yatzil, but she shared Clod's concern. Their path held much more land to cover with its dangers. A stiff chilling breeze played with her hair, pressing lightly on the furs of her garb. Snowflakes stirred up from a strong eastern gust, reminding her how brave the nol in her company were to face the south's harshness. Maua swiftly made a fist and raised it toward the trees.

"I can clear a little at a time by—"

Launching out of the brush a gray serpent sunk its fangs into Maua's ankle. Yatzil gasped. Maua fell on her side. And before Yatzil had pressed her fists together to form an ice spear, Ahigan severed the head of the diamond fang. It was longer and thicker than both her arms combined. Its fangs released Maua's ankle as she moaned in pain. Yatzil dove without thinking, grabbed the serpent by its gray bloody head and threw it into the brush. She screamed, calling for water as the serpent's blood burned her skin. Ahigan unplugged the stopper to his tortoise shell and poured water over her hand.

The blood washed away but Yatzil seethed, cursing herself for not frosting. Her fingers strained with pain. The skin over fingers swiftly went black, and her palm brightened to a swirl of orange, streaked by gray. The pain came in jolts. The diamond fang's blood reminded her of the king who had built the wall. How his son and daughter had freed the enslaved Nol and sealed their father in it as the serpent's poison boiled him from the inside. That king's death was quick, but Yatzil wasn't certain of how long Maua truly had.

"Maua. Are you?"

"The fangs have sunk deep, my queen," Clod said. He searched the overgrowth for more diamond fangs. "Father, can you help?"

Yatzil fell to her knees, resting Maua's head in her lap, hardening her face to remain strong. Haseya kept watch with Clod. From where Maua had been bitten black mist seeped and swirled then grew thick, dripping like oil from a lamp.

"Can you heal her, Ahigan?" Yatzil cried. "I cannot bear to have her freedom taken so soon."

"I don't know how to draw poison from a lijani," he said, gently examining the bite marks. "I can wrap it and hope she can survive what remains of our journey. There are no snakes like this in the west. I do know a long burning comes from diamond fang poison before death." He looked up at Clod. "My son. Go hunt for more meat. We will need it."

Maua shuttered. Branches cracked and hissed as Clod vanished into the woods.

"I can still help clear our way," Maua croaked.

"No." Yatzil took Maua's hand, find strength in her fingers. "You shall only hasten the poison."

"How long, Ahigan?" Maua groaned. She strained to harness her breath but released it, shaking flakes of bark from her cheeks. "I want to help save Nema. I ... do not want to become mist and return to the ground."

"I'm not certain," said Ahigan.

Yatzil's face darkened. Her tears were enlarged by fresh ones. Her abandoned plan had stepped in the way again. Healing took skill not mastered in a day and Flor held passion in it. Yatzil rubbed her eyes and clenched her teeth. She had focused more on finding what poison that had killed her father. The scroll about diamond fangs had been long but her patience was short.

"I will not allow you to die like this."

She placed her free hand over the one holding Maua's. A few days previous they both had spoken of their homes, though Maua was hesitant, and described how no lijani lived in great complexes of white granite or on high farms. All roamed in thought within a stump far larger than Wolf-strong, rooted at its center in circles of silence. Yatzil compared such solitude to meditation. A week out of every month in the same confined pose with no speech permitted. Her only company was a ring of priestesses who did no more than give nourishment and hold a chamber pot for her to make water.

Ahigan poured water onto Maua's ankle then wrapped it. He asked if Yatzil wished for time alone. Haseya asked the same as Yatzil razed her head from misery.

"Leave us. If you know of a way to bring her to my home without more harm, find it and return soon."

When they were gone for a few moments, Maua forced herself to sit up. Her arms shook, and more so when Yatzil released her hand. Yatzil sat back with her hand over her mouth. The leaves growing at short intervals over Maua's braids slowly wilted. She moved to face Maua and found the glow of her eyes dulling, flickering like a weak star.

"What can I do to slow your pain?" said Yatzil. "I can frost and ease the pain with cold."

"I will not need soothing. What I need is ... trust?"

Yatzil sat puzzled, a light snow crept through the forest canopy. She had trusted Maua, like the others, with every secret.

"What makes you believe I don't trust you?"

Maua raised a hand toward the forest, making a fist. It trembled. A whish and whine shifted the trees, ruffled the undergrowth. A few trees bent and cracked on the verge of snapping in two. Bushes shook, low branches raised and grass poking just above the snow, hissed into its depths. Her hand fell, crunching in the snow. Maua's chest heaved in quick succession. Yatzil watched her teeter, but Maua remained upright, pain laced her face, cracking its bark.

"I ... had much time before trading to dream of someone trusting me." Maua said, pulling her knees to her chest, wincing from her ankles bumping. "I trusted you to free us. I will fight the poison even if it should hasten." she gulped. "By my helping you."

"You have cleared much. I cannot thank you enough for sparing my life and my child's."

Rough lips pressed against her own. Yatzil felt herself drained of fear, all thoughts swirled like great whirlpools. Her father had chased fish thief ships into them to be destroyed. She wished to pull away, but it was strangely soothing. Splendor compounded in her stomach, journeying to her womb, and then, with great speed to her heart, vanquishing doubt. And then the churning joy pressing at her feelings vanished. The moment grew awkward in a flash.

Yatzil pushed Maua away. Snow crunched under Yatzil's weight as she scrambled upon hands and knees, rising.

"Why push me away?" Maua cried." I only wished for further trust, and I find you so…"

"I." She backed off to find her thoughts in a storm. "Why kiss me? I did not invite it."

"I care for you. And what I have done will hasten what lives in you."

They stared at each other with no sign yet of the others returning. Yatzil fought an urge to weep. The kiss was so bold an act that it frightened her. The last time she had tasted another's lips it was not as pleasant as this had been. Yatzil rested her fingers to her lips, and by Maua's affection, she understood why losing Flor had hurt her so much.

"Does this mean my child shall come faster?" said Yatzil. "We have my mother's avalanche warriors to face if we cannot convince my brother of her treason."

"Yes." Maua mumbled. "But not until you feel safest. And I will rest when needed to clear our path to help him."

Yatzil turned away, finding Maua's words confident. Peering over her shoulders the lijani's braids were beginning to thin, theirs clicked and fell, caught by the wind. There was a calming chill in her heart, one she had felt only in Flor's presence. She decided to keep her new feelings in line. In no kingdom had what they done gone beyond the walls of a nobles' home. There was mention of it from noble girls she wanted to consider friends, but they passed on such love as beneath what must be practiced by a nescaran royal. Facing Maua again, what was last said meant hope, but if it was well placed, then Maua would have to possess power greater than could be imagined.

"I hope such safety comes." A faint shudder released from Yatzil's lips as she withdrew her fingers from them. "There are great odds against us. My feelings for you, I know they existed for Flor. But if I am to have them for you, we must save my brother. And after doing so I must get to know you better."

A crunching came from her left as a breeze brought the familiar scent of blood to her nostrils. Clod carried in both arms an immense boar. A gash ran from the beast's throat to where its genitals once hung. Ahigan and Haseya pulled a thick mesh of palm-and-oak leaves. The leaves were sought after, grounded up and aged to be made for palm wine. One leaf was large enough to cradle a small child. To each side of the makeshift liter were tied long wood railings Yatzil was sure belonged to ...

"Don't worry about my wagon, my queen," Haseya said, frustration foaming in her words. "They needed to be replaced anyway."

Yatzil saw relief fill Maua's flaking face, but her eyes didn't brighten at Haseya's kind gesture. There was much confusion in her heart. Haseya took out their smifta and stuck it in the ground and blew. As it grew, Clod dropped the immense boar in his arms. *Thud.* He rose to full height and gaped at the forest cleared by Maua's efforts.

"I did what I could, Clod." said Maua, edging out a small smile.

He stared at her as both Ahigan and Haseya froze in their movement to aid Maua.

"How?" he said, removing a bundle of branches from over his shoulder. "Aren't you dying? I mean not like anyone..."

"...wants you to." Ahigan finished. "It's clear the poison has weakened you."

Haseya's curiosity kept her from helping Yatzil lift Maua onto the litter. Yatzil rubbed her hands together to slow her hurrying nerves. Maua's braids withered, all but barren of leaves.

"I wish to help," she said, looking to Yatzil and then to

Clod's shouldered axe. "Your axe brings suffering of Nema's trees, Clod." Maua shivered until Yatzil met her fading eyes. "Our queen approves."

Yatzil rested a hand on her shoulder, panning her vision, firming her emotions on the three nol. To risk losing Maua's trust sliced at her insides but having the girl before her die was something greater. Yatzil resisted biting her lip, then against her fingers flaking in small pieces.

"I... I must insist you not clear any more of our way."

"What?" Maua shrugged off Yatzil's hand and scowled through flaring ember eyes. "I said I would rest when needed."

"My mere touch removes more of you. It has grown worse than before and Nema needs you more than ... we do for travel."

"There is much ahead, Maua. It may kill you," said Ahigan. "Our queen is wise in her choice and shows care like a Storm Queen is meant to." He rested their supplies beside his readied smifta. Yatzil blushed. "You are needed, and our queen's unborn child must have safer times to grow in."

Maua kept her eyes fixed on Yatzil. There was no way to hide the frustration thickening the bark on Maua's face. She hoped Ahigan's words had worked. Some leaves budded from Maua's hairs as she drew in a breath, releasing it. Haseya threw up her hands and Clod tapped his foot impatiently. *Please choose what shall not end what I am beginning to feel.* Yatzil thought. Her legs shook, growing weak for a moment, begging her to become submissive, to plead for her friend to understand.

"You're right, Storm Queen," Maua sighed, resting her hand in her lap. Dark swirls trailed from missing patches atop it. "Nema is larger than ... any of ... us." She met Haseya's eyes. "May I have aid climbing on the litter?"

Yatzil squatted with Haseya, watching, and looping under

Maua's arms and legs like the old Nol did. Maua buried her chin into her chest. Yatzil strained, grounding her teeth, the task was done, but she had allowed the others to do such tasks throughout the journey. Maua rolled to her side, folding her arms. Yatzil felt alone somehow, even now amongst the rutoe she had grown to trust.

CHAPTER THIRTEEN

White granite pathing stones met Yatzil's feet once within sight of Niev. Its moat and thick, high walls were far more imposing from the ground than upon an eagle. The snow had fallen with greater strength before reaching the capital, burying their ankles. Yatzil stood in awe of the immense likeness of Sachi-hiro towering left of the city's tall palm-n-oak doors. It was made of a dark stone, ice formed over it turning her brother's image black as night. Towering left of the entrance a long robe and intricately chiseled likeness of his raton queen, Sute. Yatzil realized if the royal couple's images remained then her mother had not yet usurped the divine couple's authority. She rested a hand to her brow.

She had no way and no iron to forge a new crown, and though Ahigan appeared well versed in all things Nol, he possessed no skill to craft one. The gold for its eagle was key but there was no way to find it either. Yatzil withdrew her hand, too much time spent on being more convincing to the city guardians would take away from saving her brother anyway. She had, with Haseya's aid, purified herself at the

Wrinkled River. If she had not done so, Yatzil knew, it would lead to consequences that gripped her despite no longer possessing the same respect for the Four. Yatzil drew in a breath and remained captivated by the city.

Her heart steadied at being back, high farms dotted the city's rooftops like scattered embers a dying fire. Far within Niev's center rose in perfect alignment four vast, step pyramids. No matter the thick falling sheets of snow, their craftsmanship still enhanced her confidence, but Maua's silence drew her away from her returning memories.

Maua flaked more with each day. Her braids, as the wind picked up, withered from its harshness, thinning, paling, resembling roots of a pulled weed. The lijani twisted and gasped in pain as Yatzil rested her eyes on her. Every time night fell, and Yatzil had rested within the smifta beside her friend, she wished the serpent had bitten her. Maua's eyes flickered open, their glow a faded yellow in place of the orange Yatzil missed. *Will she never speak to me?* she thought. *She knows I care for her.* Yatzil sighed. She wondered if it was the diamond fangs poison, the weight of saving Nema, or that being of help was too great a risk.

"We have made it, Storm Queen," said Maua. The soft slowness of her voice was a relief from so long a silence. "I hope the armored serpents permit us entry."

"Me too." Clod attached his axe to its leather holster. "I might not want you dead anymore, my queen, but I don't want to end up as serpent shit."

"I have practiced the entrance dance and bear the sacred glyphs." Yatzil rested a hand on his arm, and another to her painted stomach. "If something goes amiss in any way, my hope is the guardians will recognize my position as Storm Queen and Niev Princess."

The paving stones were slick with ice as they continued to the city. Ahigan lost his footing. Yatzil reached, clasping his wrist, her feet found purchase naturally being accustomed to ice. They rose together, nodded, climbing a second of three steep hills. A low rumbling halted them in their tracks. Yatzil sent her focus to Niev's moat, but the water stirred only a little. She took one last look at Maua. She gave Yatzil a small smile. A tremor ran through her, glazing her eyes just before the crested the second hill.

"I'm glad I survived it this far, Yatzil," Maua said. Her breath quickened as she slammed her eyes shut. "I hope the..."

Water rushed up from where the two ends of the moat met like pincers to a bridge. Ornate statues of the Four cast in jade lined either side. Heavy droplets pounded the goddesses by beings Yatzil had only seen in scrolls old and fragile. Both serpents were long enough and vast enough to bind the city as if it were their prey. They loomed over Yatzil, narrowing their diamond shaped eyes. Their eyes burned a solid red and their heads were large enough to swallow everyone in her company in one, swift gulp. Yatzil winced at the loud scraping and slam of their iron scales, and ice fell in sheets from them. The guardians released twin breaths upon her, forcing her hair back, rendering the snow for yards to mud and grass. She remained still, peering over her shoulder, smiling. The others remained firmly behind her. Clod backed away baring his teeth.

"I am Yatzil. Storm Queen of the nol and Princess of—"

"Welcome sister to King Sachihiro," both serpents growled. "By custom demanded of all nescaran, and those not of their kind, perform for us the entrance dance."

Yatzil met the guardians' eyes, clenched her teeth, and then spread her legs before straightening like a pillar. She arched her back until her hair was a foot from the snow. Spinning was hardest as she eyed dead fish trapped between the sharp, many rowed teeth of either guardian. Water seeped from their lips, not in salivation, like some noble lusting, but from the moat's waters. She dropped on all fours like the nescaran child baring dance, but then rested upon her knees, outstretching her arms to their limits.

"I have returned," she said, out of breath. "With child and in as royal garb." She bowed, for even nescarans royals were subject to the Four's guardians. "I ask that my companions be permitted to enter with me."

"Your Nol companions may enter for rutoe of nescaran and nol flesh are at peace," the guardians hissed. They lowered, crossing, their mass hiding the city entrance. "But the Lijani must remain beyond the walls blessed by Nescara whom all nescaran's are descendants of."

Yatzil rested her gaze on Maua, her lips trembled. Maua lay still and weeping, black swirling mist cascaded down her cracked cheeks. The northern squinted with fading, struggling like her eyes had under the Highnonstar's brightness. She paused before returning focus to the serpents. *Why has it not crossed into my brother's lands?* she thought, then faced the guardians. Her nose bunched at their rotted fish breath. All had been prepared for this current interaction, and if only she, Ahigan, Haseya and Clod were permitted through, it meant throwing Maua's freedom.

"With the greatest of respect to Niev's protectors," she said. She stretched out her hand, marked by the diamond fang's blood. It shook and jolted with pain, "my friend needs healing."

Maua rose to one elbow, but it gave, and she reeled in pain, jabbing at Yatzil's heart. Neither guardian made an emotion of caring, their immense lips sealed shut, filling the air with their silence, returning south's icy bitterness.

"From how this Lijani is ailed, a diamond fang is to blame." Both serpents nodded at each other. They whispered to one another for many moments. Yatzil returned her hand to her side, bawled it into a fist and fought the burning in her eyes. "She is close to an end," They said." "You have kept true to your duties, but we must ask you. Where is King Amteer?"

The question hit her like an arrow to the chest and burned like the diamond fangs blood. How was neither guardian aware of what plagued the west? Had her mother's avalanche warriors silenced her brother's? All were sworn to share all their findings to the king and Niev's protectors.

She swallowed her frustration then explained all that had happened. With some anxious satisfaction, and strain in her throat, she told how her father had been murdered. A faint coughing touched her ears with a shuffling of feet. Her lips had closed on the final detail. Haseya appeared at her side. She snatched Yatzil's hand with tears in her eyes.

"I tried to give Maua food, but she can't swallow." said Haseya. Her fingers were clammy, and the cold was forcing them to shake. "We need them to..."

"This sacrilege cannot go unpunished!" both serpents roared. "But we are far too large to enter the city." They rested their eyes on Maua. Yatzil drew her lips inward when every metal plate the guardians possessed flattened then flexed. "You must seek justice for the most admired king in living memory."

"Does this give us permission to," Haseya gulped, "bring our friend into Niev?"

A storm formed in Yatzil's belly of a need to be forceful and demanding as expected, yet both guardians had seen this wasn't her way. They remained still and towering, all the while, despite her fear of what was to come, and great burning ache to save Maua, there was no other way in. Even so close to home the tunnel Flor had used to undermine the guardians evaded her memory. The guardians with their bright red eyes slowly lowered to the bridge's level, churning, and splashing the moat's waters. She dropped to Maua's side and took her hand in hers, but it slipped through her fingers. It had turned entirely into mist. It rested on the boar fur meant to keep her warm.

"I have seen your home at least, Storm... Yatzil," Maua said, every word aching for an end. "I guess being free with you for the time I did is..."

Maua collapsed into a coughing fit, snapping her eyes shut. Cracks ran over her face and down her throat until she was aged like Ahigan and Haseya. Her dreadlocks thinned until they were like the hairs Yatzil's grandmother possessed without a wig to hide them. Yatzil kissed her forehead but even so soft a touch forced Maua to wince.

"In the name of the Four." Yatzil stood. "Open these gates."

There was no movement by either serpent to give their call. A call which shook the ground until Niev's tall thick gates opened. They stared intently, sniffing with their sharp, spiked nostrils to make certain somehow of what she didn't know. Yatzil firmed up her face to match the focus of her brother's statue, a hand to her stomach. Unlike what her lamodun taught of a woman's time with child, it had grown at a greater speed than normal. She guessed, fearful of being correct, that Maua's magic was the cause. Her fingers ran over the glyphs around her navel. She merged her brow and forced anger to fill her youthful face.

"I carry the heir to the west," she shouted. "I shall not leave Maua alone as my fellow Nol and I proceed. Do you wish to leave myself out here to starve and thus kill my child? The lijani is precious to ... me."

It was strange somehow to have said it. Her heart raced faster than her fear of great size and fangs either guardian. They came closer, churning water, leaving spots of caved in snow below them. Yatzil placed herself in front of Maua as did Ahigan, Haseya and Clod. Haseya bunched up her face and placed a foot further forward than the others, holding tight Sparron's knife. Its pommel had begun to jab at Yatzil's swollen stomach during their travels. They kept still through a great burst of cold snow laced wind. The beings before them drew in a sharp deep breath and flared their nostrils. A slow rumbling ran through the ground, rising out of their jaws like laughter.

"Such bravery and love for one whose people braved the world only once is admirable." said both guardians. "Your passage is granted into Niev. We advise you do not idle in removing the mother of the king. Go now Storm Queen and nescaran of royal blood."

They rose above the city's walls, curled back their necks into an "S" shape and then let out a roar. Faint cries came from the city, trees from the forest far behind her rattled. Yatzil had everyone move with caution toward the bridge. Ahigan and Haseya were slowed by their wish not to cause Maua more pain. Maua groaned, turning her head left and right. Yatzil placed an unsteady hand on her shoulder.

"I'm going to save you." said Yatzil, giving it a light squeeze. "I promise."

The liter Maua rested on bowed back and forth, unsettling her thoughts. Clod gave her a crude look sparking doubt in her words. Even he could see, as the ground shook, that little time remained. Her care for Maua was even stronger than her need to save Nema itself. And when both great palm-n-oak doors were opened, her worry turned to fear. Startled faces of bronze inlaid teeth from men and women with long bound back hair or curled locks that streamed down to the shoulders. A woman loomed high on a palanquin, protected by avalanche warriors emerging from the crowd. She shot Yatzil with a stern, unyielding look.

"Mother."

CHAPTER FOURTEEN

The Mother of the King sat upon an ornately decorated palanquin with images of the Four in gold forming two headed armrests. From what Yatzil could see on the back there was an intimate scene of her mother and father giving tribute to Fertilida. The four men that shouldered her on the palanquin turned to face Yatzil. They were the same men from when she had been caught in the wisdom room. In their eyes pity from long ago begged to be released. She bit her inner lip and refused to lash out. She was unsure what may happen to her companions, although she felt tempted to demand justice for the raids upon the Nol living near the border. Clattering of sandal falls reveal many hundred nescarans filling the street. They bowed to both her and her mother, some close enough to her the uncertainty in her breaths. She blew out a slow breath, catching sight of Clod bawling his massive fists. Ahigan prodded the giant's back and then whispered something that lowered the swell of his anger.

Her mother nodded with her usual grace, noting Yatzil's uneven hair and scar on her temple with her painted eyes.

The former queen had gray whale bone shoulder shields joined by a wide ornate shoulder necklace. Upon her mother's head was a crown with large, golden owl eyes and between them sat a woman holding a crowned child of jade on her lap. Hooked talons ringed the crown's dome top. Yatzil noticed similar glyphs graced her mother's cheeks to the ones she had painted on Yatzil's. If Ahigan had not calmed Clod, her mother would most definitely have required their magic.

Yatzil ignored her mother's jeweled bracelets and fang pierced ear lobes. The former queen nodded in return for Yatzil's lack of emotion. Above and to the sides of her mother on iced paths stood royal guards at the ready. They were armored in pounded and shaped bronze, boar tusks pierced their ear lobes, and jewels outlined the shallow collar of their breastplates. They had lowered their hands from icing the paths they stood upon. The paths stretched for miles disappearing through thick, falling snow.

"You have … returned swollen with child. At least you were wise enough to complete the … marriage pact," her mother said, waving a hand for her guards to dissolve their spears. "I see you are not alone, but the handmaiden I gave you was left behind." She smirked. "And where is the one who survived so great a … fall?" Her mother eyed Haseya and Ahigan with contempt and sent a guard to fetch another palanquin. Yatzil clenched her teeth, damming up her mounting frustrations. "And what is this, a lijani in your brother's sacred city?"

Whispers raced through the crowd. Shout of imprisonment for the sister of the king.

Yatzil flared her nostrils as her mother sat up straight and pointed. She took a step-in front of Maua then raised the owl's eyes upon her hands in forgiveness, but it only quelled the stirring crowd some. If they knew what her mother had done such a gesture wouldn't be required for assassination outweighed friending an enemy. *And yet mother does not hold back in her harshness.*

Her mother snatched up the golden handle of white feathered fan from her lap, pressing it to her chest for a more regal appearance. Every feather was familiar. Yatzil gasped. Ahigan took a step forward. *It is from a nols' head.*

"Mother of our Storm Queen. This is Maua of the Lijani." There was resentment in his tone as he stretched out a hand to Maua on her litter. "A diamond fang bit her and we need one your healers to—"

"I did not address you, old man," her mother said. "No dialogue was opened to one in my daughters' service."

Ahigan stepped back and bowed, his finger bent like readied claws. He said no more but Yatzil was certain he had made the same connection. The fan rested again on her mother's lap. Maua groaned. Yatzil knelt beside her when her mother finally noticed Clod. The former queen beckoned to her royal guard to ready their ice spears. Clod stepped in front of them, a hand to his axe.

"I can feel it." Maua whispered. "I will die soon, Yatzil."

She reached to take Maua's good hand in hers, but it was cracked in several places. They had known each other for two months by her sleep count. To tell when days passed, and nights came was easier without the Highnonstar present. And yet why had the Highnonstar or the palenore not invade her brother's kingdom? Maua's breathing was shallow. Haseya gave her the same look from before the guardians opened Niev's gates.

"These nol," said Yatzil, rising to her feet. All looked upon her, but the former queen did so with repulsion, for how Yatzil's words had caught in her throat. She swallowed her nervousness and made her face plain like a stone block. "And Lijani have kept me safe and nourished along my journey.

My husband has been made the new Highnonstar and the Palenore have returned."

Whispers stirred amongst the onlookers, some moving closer to hear better. Her mother plucked up her fan again except this time she raised it and silenced everyone. Yatzil met her gaze and felt her stomach. Even in that moment, with tension high, her mother made her wait until all was quiet.

"A palenore return is impossible," she said, "but I knew your king would not be at your side."

"How so?"

Her mother cocked her head back and laughed. The jade squares long inlaid on her teeth were dark like they had not been cleaned of late. Her mother covered her mouth as her eyes watered from amusement once the second palanquin had arrived.

"Because I have," She pulled a scroll with a gold eagle emblazoned on it. A hole punctured the bird's chest where a smaller iron eagle was missing to seal its contents, "a message from King Amteer telling of how fair the storms have been. Those would not exist with the Highnonstar's return."

The Mother of the King's faintly lined brow creased as she unfurled the scroll.

"He speaks of you being caught trying to leave by eagle." She rolled it up and stuffed it between her hip and armrest. "He speaks of you performing the Nol dance and inter-twining with him. That you order your handmaiden to slaughter Wolfstrong's rookery to aid your escape."

A rush of fury ran from her dirtied feet up into her chest. Yatzil shut her eyes and kept her face to the ground, anger curled her fingers and toes. She imagined her mother as the tree bearing a hole the size of her fist. There was no way that scroll held such information. There was no way anyone had listened to her and Flor's plan.

"Where is my brother? If what you say is true, you knew I was coming. Is this palanquin to carry me to judgement by you or my king brother?"

Maua groaned again, every leaf bordering her neck withered and the bark upon her hand crumbled away. Yatzil and Haseya traded quick worried glances. Ahigan raised his tortoise shell to Maua's lips. She choked and knocked it away, spilling its contents across the clean swept brickwork. Ahigan snatched it up and plugged in its stopper.

"The message arrived on the ... previous day. So, I allowed luck for your return ... home and, oh, ... those serpents are very loud. He orders you to be locked in your bedchamber to ... await judgment."

"I shall have a glace healer come to drum the poison from Maua first."

"What makes you think you ... can make such a demand, daughter?" her mother wheezed. "Only an over fed ... nol protects you."

Narrowing her eyes upon the palanquin, to Maua whose breaths quickened again and then finally to her mother, only one thing remained to say. Sachihiro now believed she had betrayed Amteer in a way less painful than the truth. Regret readied tears in her eyes, but she rubbed them, peering up at the woman above her. *I know what shall turn all of this in my favor.* To use it as a weapon was unthinkable but there was no other way.

"If I must Mother," she said, "I shall tell Niev's people how my father truly died."

GLACE HEALERS WERE SUMMONED IMMEDIATELY after Yatzil's final words. She placed herself upon the soft cushion of her palanquins' chair. It was a nice change to no longer be on her feet as she relaxed and smiled with a hint of satisfaction. Lingering demands of her people reached out in foul tones. They called into question what she meant, but to further torment her mother she kept silent. Her father's statues that once protected the inner part of Niev's entrance had been replaced by her brother's. His statues wielded great stone spears pointed at the doors, and he was lean and muscled unlike her last memory of him.

The former queen had her royal guard disperse the crowd while all four healers drummed a slow beat, sending out great chilling winds. Maua shivered, but as she did her face regained form. The healers wore slow smoking incense lamps tied to their frosted bald heads. Yatzil hoped the time taken to reach Niev had no bearing on the glace healers magics.

As they began the journey to the palace, Clod snarled at the suspicion in every nescaran eye, sending men shuffling back to their day to day. Many stood at wagons filled with fish while others leaned on low walls protecting high farms. Clod followed his father and Haseya as they shivered from drum blasts. Two avalanche warriors had been summoned to transport Maua on her litter. Ten were added to the already disciplined royal guard in their march. Her mother kept her chin up and mouth closed, daring not to look Yatzil in the eye. More vibrations rattled shut doors and shattered pots on high perches. Those frustrated by this remained silent, trying fiercely to salvage their palm wine or spilled boar milk. Every beat jostled her bearers and by their eyes they wished it to stop.

Yatzil reflected on the day her father died, refusing to cry. The salty aroma of Non's pool still lingered in her nostrils. It had been her eighteenth visit, and the month had been in its last day. They passed between Non and Limpie's temple. Yatzil shut her eyes and drew in a breath until it felt like they had passed the temple. Its hook hung between two large onyx pillars over the entrance to Non's temple. Opening them it was out of her vision and Urrra and Fertilida's temples were in full view beyond the hollow jade moon below her.

The splashing and calls for aid her father made attacked her mind. Never had he struggled in a temple or out in ocean depths, but this time, something was different. An elixir in a tall chalice ringed by waves of jade sat in front of the thick cushion he had knelt upon.

Both her mother and father were meant to bless it before he drained it for his submersion. The faint *plop* tempted her to pout, but nesarans filled the city's streets. It echoed in her memory but had been so faint amongst priests drumming and oarsmen churning the pool. There was no question a palenore was whose hand and blade had kept her from aiding Sachihiro.

Homes with high balconies and pale green overhangs filled her line of vision with a great dark image of the palace through the falling sheets of snow. A great arch marked the beginnings of mansion homes to nescaran nobles. Two avalanche warriors thickly armored in pounded gray whale bone and frosted guarded it. They bowed before pushing open doors with crests on the surface of noble families old and in infancy. Many were worn but fierce, possessing images of the panther form the Four once possessed.

She peered over her shoulder. Her heart lit up at the Lijani's brightening ember eyes. She was drowsy but drank Ahigan tortoise shell. Haseya was unable to hide her lingering nervousness but nodded at Yatzil despite it. It reminded her of the unease she failed to hide at her father's burial. Sachihiro's own pain had been sensed by onlookers when his fingers trembled to rest the jade mask likeness on their father's face. She had taken his hand and found it calmed him before they watched their father be carried into their dynasty's tomb.

The glace healers dispersed, lifting their drums, bowing to her and her mother. Slowly Maua's eyes rested shut. Yatzil, finally, in that moment, allowed herself to worry a little less. She sighed and turned to face the tall palm-and-oak doors of the palace. They were thick and had been carved first before the palace itself had been built. And for what seemed a year they slowly opened, revealing a distant young noble. He wore a long red lumao and a golden owl pendant gobbling a ruby bate-nich. He was trailed by servants carrying trays of gold.

As the palanquin bearers passed around an oval dais, she braced herself for the steep steps ahead. Her mother remained poised then scowled.

"How dare you put my life at ... risk?" she hissed.

"You sent me away."

Yatzil released her grief, tears running down her cheeks. She eyed the remaining two hundred steps and saw the top was hidden by walls of falling snow. She wiped her eyes, forgetting she was in the south for a moment. Her mother bunched up her nose, glaring at Yatzil.

"I guess," Yatzil said. "You shall not be imprisoning us then."

"Not by my way of it. You...," her mother wheezed. "Stirred up suspicion. I ... will have to make an excuse for the inquiries to ... challenge my love of your ... father."

The Mother of the King waved at a royal guard. He raced ahead to have the doors opened. Around his neck swung a golden pendant of a sitting mother holding close to a crowned child.

"Why poison him then?" said Yatzil. "Father was good, and you forced me to say nothing with a knife to my back. Sachihiro must be…"

"Your father was ambitionless and easily … manipulated. Had you fallen for a noble, no arrangement of … marriage to an imbecile need be made to make peace. Your … father possessed forces large enough to swallow the … West."

Yatzil squeezed the carved armrests of her chair then turned to Haseya. The old Nol kept her focus on Maua but took each step as if walking on air. Clod and Ahigan did the same but remained wary of the royal guard, who eyed the father and son with suspicion.

"How could you have known what Flor, and I had planned?"

Her mother sat back then hid her lips behind her fan, peaking over it. A group of Sachihiro's personal guards stood upon the plateau that encircled the pyramid's peak. They wore jade pendants of an owl grasping a moon in its talons. The Four's statues were in view ankle deep in snow drifts surrounding their pedestals.

"You have your friends," she wheezed. "And I do mine. If you wish yours … dead, then speak of my husband … again. You will not take away what is … mine."

―――――

WHERE MAUA, Ahigan, Haseya and Clod were sent, Yatzil did not know. Maua had been asleep when they met the choice of left or right beyond the palace doors. Yatzil was about to be carried around the corner when Haseya turned to speak, but she wasn't fast enough before both were separated.

Yatzil folded her arms and remained silent. Statues that were once of her father had now been replaced by statues of her brother. His jaw was stronger than she remembered with

soft painted eyes and youthful features better than his likeness outside the city. The coolness of her home relaxed her a
little despite no longer being with her friends.

A smaller statue of his queen stood between his legs, just
below a long sash, eclipsed by the Raton's tall erect gold talon
crown. The queen, like any princess to marry a nescaran
royal was permitted to wear her home kingdom's garb. She
had stood waiting for him when last Yatzil saw her. Yatzil
frowned, watching her mother's palanquin bearers pick up
speed.

Sachihiro had been who she expected to marry for some
time. She had nearly fallen for him for a time when no
noble's son caught her interest. He had displayed courage on
the oceans, and they bounded well. Yatzil shook her head. It
was during a private game, she remembered, stroking the
faint scar on her elbow, when she had found him desirable.
But with what she knew of herself now, a connection to him
in such a traditional manner was impossible. The way of
keeping her dynasty pure had been abandoned long ago. The
Mother of the King turned back as they were about to be
separated.

"I shall tell your ... brother of your arrival, daughter." She
wheezed, crossing her owl eyed hands. "Give thought to not
being foolish."

Yatzil flashed her owl eyes and then faced front when the
bearers turned up a set of stairs. She returned to reminiscing
again, of the day she had started to desire Sachihiro's affection, to rule at his side and go back to old ways. It was the
first tradition not expected of her and of which she did not
question. Her hand went to the scar again, and as if being
there, at such a young age , having that feeling vanish when
he did not help her from the ground. She shook her head
again once her bearers met the landing to her bedchamber.
Further stairs ahead led to the trimmed grasses and large

stone "X" of the game they had played. *Get up.* He had smiled. *The game is not over yet.*

The doors to her bedchamber opened, letting a breeze in from her balcony between columns crowned by an open beaked owl. Her bed had been made on its high frame, surrounded with cushioned white granite steps. Her bearers lowered her palanquin, and as she stepped over its low floral border a tear surfaced in her eye. The doors closed as one bearer said handmaidens were to tend to her needs. She waved him off. The feeling of truly being home was too much.

CHAPTER FIFTEEN

S he moved to the bed with a grace all but diminished from her memory. Yatzil ran her fingers over its golden footboard, pressing her hand into its mattress. The softness called to her, but there was still the ocean from her balcony to take in. A breeze kissed her cheeks as she savored her bed's silk sheets between her fingers. Yatzil clenched her teeth to suppress emotion, pleading deep down for the handmaidens to be delayed. The wish to reminisce again came but the present and future required her attention. Word would quickly spread of the letter her mother displayed but the same would happen of what she had said. Yet if her mother had such control over Sachihiro's subjects then Niev's people may just as well fall into line. She sighed.

"If I possessed control of the Four," she said. "I would curse Mother to eternal frost form before she had spoken. She is more of a traitor than I am, and deserves being unable to control what happened to…"

Yatzil slammed her palm against her forehead. There was no time for mourning again. Even if she had more control of the Four, they were more loyal to her mother's wishes. She gazed upon her budding stomach.

All thought fell to the child growing within her and what months remained until it was born. There was no kick as to be expected much later, but she ran her fingers over her stomach, finding it more dome shaped, smearing its glyphs that had brought her this far. She sighed, wanting Maua's magic to bring her child faster despite the dangers to come.

She bit her lip, knowing her child was doomed if Sachi-hiro didn't believe her. The walls of her room closed in, making what had to be done harder to imagine. He was loyal to their mother like a guard to his mistress. Again, her thoughts went to her child, a child she hadn't wanted in the beginning. She hadn't expected to find herself to have a change in heart.

A hiss against smooth tile brought her back to where she stood. Light clapping sandal falls introduced ten handmaid-ens, five weighed down by large buckets entirely of ice. They kept their heads down and planted the buckets within her inground bath. It was the width and length of her bed, deep enough to sit within. Every handmaiden lined it with their fingers touching the buckets. The buckets melted, losing their shape, filling the bath with water. A handmaiden moved hesitantly toward her and offered to undress her.

"It is no great task," Yatzil said, untying her dress from her waist. Her face sank at the hair growth over her legs. The handmaiden stepped back, keeping their eye contact broken. "I shall however need aid in shaving."

The handmaiden bowed. "I will fetch cream and a blade to shave one of divine blood, if she wishes."

"I do." She dropped the dress then raised the handmaid-en's chin with a curled finger. "You may all look at me when no one of my blood is present. I shall bend tradition to my will to see beautiful faces."

The handmaidens met her eye as they bowed. A chair next to her bed welcomed her sore limbs. She removed her top, cast it upon the bed and slouched upon within the chair. The handmaiden went to retrieve what was needed. Both the blade and cream were on a tall shelf against the wall. Another breeze tousled her hair over her shoulders.

Though much needed done, to be in safe company felt good. She worried a little for Maua and the others but knew the mysterious death of three nol and a Lijani was not a wise choice to make. She released a slow, easy breath with such assurance in mind.

A LONG SKIRT was applied high enough to cover her stomach. She ignored the tenderness in her breasts that were wrapped in the whitest soft silks. A shoulder necklace with bracelets had been given to her to wear, and though she stared at them with a raised eyebrow, she didn't wish to provoke her mother. It was a desire of Flor's to have her wear such things again, but not even at the Wrinkled River had her fear been faced. *Thank the Four for Clod's kindness.* She had worried for him when he ignored the chill of the river, its current that brushed her toes and soaked his garb.

Yatzil sat upon her palanquin, both hands gripping their rests as if afraid to fall. To be dressed in so delicate a way again bothered her. The bearers raised her after a hand-maiden presented her with a fan. It possessed similar feathers to her mother's, and for that, she pushed it away and gulped back resurfaced bate-nich slices. Though she had been raised with stories of royal and avalanche warrior brutality, killed a criminal in sacrifice on her twelfth year, and brought down a palenore, making such use of a Nol's remains troubled her.

After leaving the last step, taking a right down a long hall, doors met her guarded by statues of Sachihiro. His battles beside their father against fish thieves played out on walls in intricate detail. She yawned and felt a laboring regret for having not slept. Sachihiro had not demanded her arrival after being cleansed. But she needed to speak with him, to know how Maua, Haseya, Clod and Ahigan had been treated after three hours had passed. Once her bearers turned right at the four-way, the throne room doors came into view.

Yatzil's pulse quickened at the mere thought of Clod losing control on a guard. She composed herself and sat up straight to contain her worry. If Clod ever disobeyed his father... No, she refused to imagine the consequences.

She refocused on what required her attention. A need to feel her stomach came again, like it was a way of reassurance, to build courage, to remind her of how she had changed. She covered her lips as they quivered, narrowly avoiding a passing vizier's judging gaze. It made her wish she had accepted the fan. The throne room doors were layered in thick gray whale bone. They opened by the strength of ten servants wearing brown lumaos and in frosted form. They wore the same jade pendants of his brother's royal guard but upon their arms, almost embedded into their skin. They bowed their heads as her bearers brought her through.

A vast legion of panthers in polished onyx supported the room's ceiling upon their heads. Their slender figure unchangeable to the owl form the Four currently possessed. She let out a breath as her bearers rested her palanquin on the floor before a high multiple leveled dais. It sent her heart retreating to her stomach at its immense twin skeletal gray whales. They swam down at her from either side with jaws open to reveal hand chiseled thrones. Polished white tile lined the throne room floor beyond them. She glared at the one with its golden Mother of the King glyphs upon the armrests.

For some reason, her mother was not present upon it. She smiled exposing the jade squares on her teeth, casting her gaze high above. Her heart stopped. Sachihiro had grown in girth. His kilt hefted up to his chest to hide his massive stomach. His queen shared his grand throne of smooth aged palm-and-oak. The young queen's hand rested close to his covered loins. He rested a hand to his queen's cheek but then noticed Yatzil.

"It has been so long, Yatzil." said Sachihiro, through lips pressed by his swollen cheeks. "Leave us door men."

Yatzil moved with desperation in her steps as his lumao's sash hid his queen's efforts. She ignored it, missing him more than being home, or the south's chill. She smiled at the awkwardness in all he wore. His crown imperfectly placed, eye makeup too thickly applied. Even when she had last seen him both sandals had been missing. *He always liked doing things himself.* Laughter replaced worry as they ran to one another. Sachihiro made it to between the whale's heads, his crown snug atop his head. Yatzil shut her eyes for a moment, drew in a breath and opened them within his arms. Frost lily drifted from his neck, from his queen's affections but it boiled her blood less than him believing she was a traitor.

"I did what you have been told." Her insides felt like granite blocks dragging her down. "But not in a brutal way."

She remembered what had perplexed her since passing the great wall marking where his kingdom ended. What did their mother mean by friends? And what other ambition did she have as Sachihiro took her in? *She ... wishes his throne to be hers.*

"I have heard of what you have done," he said, "but do not wish to believe even our own Mother. You must become familiar with my queen. She remains stubborn despite what I tell her of you."

Two months before their father had been murdered, the raton princess had met them for the first time. Yatzil watched her descend the dais's step with her robes dragging like a receding red wave. The clop of her hand carved sandals echoed the room as her thickly lashed eye crackled and lashed out with lightning bolts. She had proven a hunter when killing a boar out beyond Niev's walls. Unlike other ladies of court or harem, Sute cared about Sachihiro's stories.

"I must complement the mark you bear, Storm Queen," said Sute. "But must address your admittance to what we have been told."

Sachihiro rested a hand on her scar. His thumb edged over the surface of it. He drew his hand away with his eyes narrowed upon his hand.

"It is not of importance... A wolf. My intention was to bring the nol south to aid you. Your kingdom is not truly yours."

Both the king and queen stared at her in shock. Sute adjusted her thick black v-collar. It gave a hint to a red scaled breastplate underneath. Yatzil's eyes widened as Sachihiro said.

"Explain, why what is mine by divine right isn't?"

His face twisted with rage when she spoke of her journey, but she was hesitant to tell him of their mother's part in their father's death. It squeezed her throat like an assassin in the night, and to increase the pressure, his queen was another they could not trust.

"I am unaware of raids." Sachihiro seethed. "My avalanche warriors know I abide tradition. Mother would never usurp my throne. She—"

"She speaks lies and so does." Yatzil nudged him out of

her way. "The Palenore wore armor like yours when I was captured."

Sute stepped back and opened her robes. She wore a dark red dragon scale breastplate shaped to her pert breasts and narrow abdomen. The queen's lips trembled, covering herself as Yatzil frosted and scowled. Lightning licked from Sute's fingertips, the finely stitched black cuffs of her robes like storm clouds.

"Make sense of your words, Storm Queen." said her brother's queen. "Do you believe my family and people are in league with the Palenore?"

Yatzil raised an iced fist, her eyes burning, brighter than ever. This princess had done all she had to bind marriage with Sachihiro. She had even been there for him when last, they'd seen one another. Yatzil loosened the frustration in her fist. Sachihiro frosted, moved between them, and stretched out his hands, each finger splayed and thick. He lowered them and eyed his queen and then her. They winced at the loud crack and boom from Sute's hands. And then Yatzil thawed with Queen Sute's lightning vanishing.

"No," said Yatzil. "They are not in league with them. But the Palenore wore armor like that of a raton soldier."

She gave them both a bow, attempting to restore some lost respect. Her brother thawed, moved to his queen's side, and took her hand in his own.

"I can assume something is out of place." Sute's eyes returned to their normal crackle and pop, leaving Yatzil to wonder how the two kissed with the queen's eyes constant brightness. "We swore never to make peace with what killed all but three dragons long ago. My armor and those of my people can only be given willingly by a dragon."

A connection formed in Yatzil's mind of the dragon in her dream, and a need for a woman of every kingdom. She did not know if her brother would permit what might soon be needed of his wife.

"I have something else I must tell you, Sachihiro." She crossed the owl eyes upon her hands and raised them to the royal couple. Suddenly regret struck her heart for forgetting her friends. "It is about Father, but first you must tell me where my friends are."

He acknowledged her gesture and folded his arms.

"They have been placed in the servant's chambers. The large one has frightened those you say may be not loyal to sleep in the hall." He grimaced. "What do you wish to tell me about Father?"

Yatzil let out a low breath, finding relief, but then raised herself to full height.

"Our mother poisoned him."

CHAPTER SIXTEEN

Boom. The sheets tumbled from her shoulders and puddled in her lap. At first, she thought it was an attack like that against Wolfstrong, but this was louder and closer. *Boom.* She wrenched her eyes to the balcony and frosted, snatching up her skirt lying like a waterfall from her bed to the floor. Her mind went to how Sachihiro had dropped to his knees and pounded his fists on the tile in agony. He had thawed slowly, as if he wanted to hide from what she had said. His eye makeup stained her skirt when she had held him close. His queen had knelt to console him as he thanked Yatzil for not allowing him to live further in a lie. "I found that woman vile by every measure." Sute had told Yatzil, guiding Sachihiro to their throne.

Boom. Yatzil cinched the skirt above her belly. Flecks of stone came in clouds over the door as she yanked down the bunched silk top from last night. She slammed her fists together, but her brown leather shoulder padding constricted her arms. Another *boom* flexed open and then shut the doors. Sachihiro must have had her doors frozen over, but where were the guards assigned for double protection? Had their mother finally revealed her intentions, and if so, why not reverse the ice barrier?

The door burst open, splintered, and dented like a ship crashing upon a reef. Clod stepped forward with his chest heaving, and shoulder bruised. Yatzil's eyes dimmed to a faint glow as Maua bounded toward her, trailed by Haseya and Ahigan. A group of men wearing the pendants of Sachi-hiro's personal guard rushed behind them and down the hall.

"What happened?" said Yatzil, overcome by Maua's abrupt embrace. "Have the Palenore come south?"

"No." said Haseya, grinding her gums and wrestling Maua from Yatzil. "Your brother has gone mad. Those nescaran loyal to your mother are fighting your brother's guards." Haseya turned her attention to faint yelling from the hallway as Clod kept watch and Ahigan raced to the balcony. "Did you tell him about your father?"

"He … did not receive it well."

Ahigan left the balcony shaking snowflakes from his head.

"You may have broken your brother's loyalty to *her*." He clenched a long iron knife in one hand and held his other hand to an unsheathed knife. Yatzil tensed, worried about what he'd say next. "But now he may be in true danger."

"We need to hurry and stop hugging her, Maua," said Haseya, holding Maua in the upper of her arms. "You can thank her later."

Yatzil's thoughts blurred with worry as they left her bedchamber. Why had her brother not just summoned their mother and kept his feelings in check like all nescarans? She motioned them right as Clod's long strides placed him at her side. She forced her fists together, every finger uneasy at first. The spear's points breached her fists and grew as she parted them. She eyed Haseya and bit her lip, running a hand over her stomach. *No.* She had to believe her frosted form would shield her child.

"All of you within this room," she said, pointing to her left. "Ahigan. Aid me with this door."

The door's ornate iron owl head knob was heavy. A hint of a smile flashed across Ahigan's face. The palace was older than her dynasty and much more. It was the knob's craftsmanship that did it. They were a glyph of an old alliance from before all she knew existed. Even with her worry for Sachihiro an appreciation for the past came.

Clod slammed the door, freeing tiny icicles from above. Faint shouts breached the doors as they shattered upon the floor. The shouts were light, a handmaiden searching for a place to hide. Ahigan looked to Yatzil for their next move.

"Maua and Haseya must stay within this guest chamber," said Yatzil.

Maua rested a hand on Yatzil's shoulder, her lips quivered. Haseya curled her lips into a frown and plopped on an assortment of cushions at the room's center.

"We have to go with you," said Maua. "I do not wish you to die after saving me."

"She has the *men* to protect her!" Haseya hissed. "I agree with what you will say next, my queen."

"You must understand," Yatzil said, unease clear in her voice. "How important you two are to Nema and … me."

Haseya sighed, crossed her arms, and nodded. Kissing Maua on the forehead Yatzil's worries lessened for a moment. *Thunk.* An ice spear pierced the door. Clod and Ahigan braced against it. Their effort met noise but soon it went away. She ran her fingers through Maua's braids knowing it was time. She nodded to Haseya and made for the door. The old Nol stopped her midway drawing her close.

"Take this."

Haseya placed Sparron's knife in Yatzil's hand. The old Nol folded Yatzil's fingers over its hilt.

"Keep your promise my ... child."

Yatzil nodded as a tear ran down her cheek. Haseya rested a thin fingered hand upon it and whispered. "Good luck."

THEY NEARED THE FOUR-WAY. Statues of Sachihiro were smashed, and a deafening cracking and booming ahead. Men lay dead in black ice form while a handmaiden, caught in the blasts of light, lay melted through her stomach. The hall was bright like the west under Highnonstar's control, yet this light was not ever present.

A red lightning bolt zipped by, and then a distant cry revealed a guard behind them brought down by it. Queen Sute cradled a babe in a sling crib as the lightning faded to her fingertips, revealing five guards kept close by. They removed their hands from their ears. Yatzil's ears rang as she realized the protected babe was her nephew. *He sleeps?* He stirred a little from his mother's kiss upon his thinly haired head.

"How does he sleep through all this, Queen Sute?" said Ahigan.

"More important," said Yatzil. "How have you and my brother a child when your marriage has been only a few months?"

The young queen smiled awkwardly before resting her eyes on the sleeping boy in her arms.

"It took little for my husband to charm me when we first met. Stories of fighting fish thieves are unheard of in Crizal-bolt. And my son sleeps like a boulder as I always have."

Footsteps scraped up the stairs left of Yatzil, leading

down to her mother's bedchamber. An ice spear bolted toward Sute. The queen shielded her son as Yatzil lunged to reach them in time but a rush and groan from a guard at the step's crest led to a loud thud. Ahigan lay before her, the ice spear standing tall from chest. Clod turned to him and then to the noise from the steps. He grimaced and then let out a ground thundering roar.

Clod ran toward the stairs, teeth clenched and ax in motion. Yatzil dove and rolled off an ice chunk. Rubbing her side, Clod smashed nescaran after nescaran ascending the steps. Dropping her spear, her brother's royal guard formed a merged ice wall behind the raging Nol giant. Ahigan called to his son as Clod disappeared slowly behind the ice. He gripped frantically at the spear's long smooth ice shaft. The tips of his fingers were wet with his blood, but he sealed his grip despite the spear's chill. Yatzil crawled over and stuffed her knife in the waist of her skirt and pulled with all her might.

The spear was slick but soon it slowly moved. Ahigan cried out, the wound gushed, running over layers of fur. His eyes bulged with pain as Yatzil yanked free the spear and tossed it away.

"My son." Ahigan reached for Clod. The giant was halfway down the steps and blocked by ice. "Come back and protect your ... Storm Queen."

"We are safe, Ahigan."

He looked up at her. Clod's silhouette sliced a guard in two.

"You need him so your mother will surrender."

Yatzil peered toward Clod. The silhouette of the Nol giant reduced to his head, and soon, it was gone. She held tight to Ahigan's hand, but even as he bled her grip wasn't as strong as his own.

"I am unsure he shall listen to me if we succeed."

"Please tell him this, Storm Queen," Ahigan croaked. "I forgive him for..."

His words died before another flick of his tongue or squeeze of his tested fingers. To her, Ahigan's hands had seen much conflict unlike her own, plagued by pain from the diamond fangs' blood. She slipped her hand free wishing he had strength to finish what death had stopped. A ruffle and faint clop sent her eyes to Queen Sute, whose long black hair covered her son like a blanket as he slept.

"I will do all I can to force her surrender."

Her words refocused Yatzil's mind, but it felt wrong to leave Ahigan's body unprotected. Clod was gone to his rage, but his roars were still as clear as what needed done. She had worried this was inevitable, and now there was no one left to calm him.

"I want your guards to take Ahigan's body to the throne room. Have them freeze the door so my brother's son can be safe too."

"It will be done," said Sute, placing a hand on Yatzil's shoulder. "Let us press on."

A FRIEND WAS GONE, and his son was absent from her sight. Yatzil passed a grand open room alongside the others. Long transparent curtains of a pale green covered its flawlessly carved disk shape. She had been this way three times as a child out of curiosity. Other sons and daughters of her father played beyond the curtain during the day, but by night, by rumor Sachihiro once heard, it entertained their father with women of great beauty from noble houses. Her mother no longer held the queen title, and Yatzil thanked every day for it. This gave her reason to live at the same level and obligation to discipline those meant to please her son. But if Sachihiro was in a rage their mother might play on this and take him captive. *Oh, Four. Forbid such a thing,* she prayed.

Bodies littered their way, but Yatzil was glad Queen Sute was at her side. Sute's rage sent streaks of red lightning from her eyes, across her hair, giving a brief glimpse of an aged queen whose face remained unchanged. Yatzil shook her head to focus on the doors ahead. Unlike some of the halls above, with their long rectangular windows, none were to be found deep in the palace's pyramid section.

Relief washed over her as the royal guard fought at Sachihiro's side against those loyal to their mother in jade encrusted armor. He moved with a grace that overcame the bulk she believed might hinder him. She pressed her fists to form a spear, ready to join the fight. Sachihiro spun and blocked with his spear. He sliced with an ornate dagger of jade and gray whale bone across a man's throat. She gasped.

Clod crumbled to his knees, twisting, and turning, covered in nescarans loyal to two different royals. Lightning bolts shattered those highest on his chest while those about to attack surrendered to cover their ears. Yatzil drew her knife, ignoring the loud booms, as a man circled her with a spear. He lunged but she was too slow as the spear sent up ice flakes from the scar of her marriage. Yatzil screamed and thrusted her knife into the man's neck. Tears blurred her vision as the sensation of Amteer's hand in her own vanished into nothing.

Yatzil held her hand close and called out to Sachihiro, but her voice was shallow. Clod rose to full height, black iced limbs tumbled from his shoulders. He gave Queen Sute a nod then met Yatzil's eye as she frosted more to halt the pain in her hand. Few remained of her mother's royal guard and soon, battered and broken, they surrendered to her brother. They dropped to their knees and pleaded, offering twenty thousand blessings for his forgiveness.

"Brother," Yatzil called again, struggling to remain standing. "We must get within Mother's bedchamber."

She dropped her knife and fell to knees, both arms planted like a pair of orphaned trees in an open field. Sachihiro raced to her side with panic flaring his eyes. She choked and thawed, feeling a hand rest on her back that sent jolts down her spine. Clod snarled below his narrowed eyes at the surrendered nescarans, their mistress's door and then to Sachihiro.

"What ails my sister?"

"I don't know," said Clod. "But one of your mother's puny guards killed my..."

"Please, brother!" Yatzil said, unable to distinguish statue from person, wondering if her pain was part of her severed blood trade. "I wish Mother ... dead as much as you ... but I was given a chance to face trial for my..."

She reached out to him as a soft embrace lifted and laid her against a wall. A face of blurred almost sizzling pearl white spoke in gentle words. What may have been three great booms rang out as Sachihiro readied his spear and his ornate dagger. He ran from her, and she knew by a fourth boom that her mother's bedchamber had been breached. Her eyes fluttered shut. They jarred open at what she was certain was her mother's scream. She winced at a tight tug on her hand. A moaning plea came, and then a harsh command followed that had to be Sachihiro.

Yatzil's head throbbed, and brow grew hot with fever. What last she saw before pain clasped its hand around her eyes was a figure, suspended, twisting, and screaming.

"Unhand my sacred body you..."

It was her mother.

HER HANDS FOUND A POWDERY SUBSTANCE. *Though it was not the snow of Niev, its texture was familiar. Yatzil drew in a breath and opened her eyes to brightness. She rolled over to hide from it as her straining eyes fell upon bare feet. They sifted through what dotted her black hair like stars in the night sky. A hand stretched from the scar on Yatzil's temple until across her forehead. It withdrew and the figure who sat beside her eclipsed the brightness.*

"You will be well, Yatzil. The Four are under King Sachihiro's control now, for he told them of your mother. And they demand a price for your mother's betrayal."

Yatzil struggled to sit up, but it was clear that all this was a dream. And the one who sat beside her with a gentle smile and wind tasseling her hair was the Nemamoon.

"He must have listened then. I remember Mother screaming. She was high above me." she sighed, and yet kind of disappointed in herself. "Before Mother sent me away, if my attempt to prove her guilt had succeeded, I may have told Sachihiro differently."

The Nemamoon brushed her hair behind her ears and quieted the wind with a wave of her hand.

"I wish to ask of you, do you feel after abandoning the Storm King and meeting who you have, and doing what you have done, that your old self was unjust?"

Yatzil suddenly found the need to change the subject. It came to her how much life had returned under the Highnonstar's heat. She tried to bring them both up, but Sath smiled and stroked her cheek when her legs acted like a lazy seal on a shore.

"Your body remains weak unlike your mind and concerns. You shall be awake soon, so I hope you have an answer to my question by then."

Yatzil found her footing but collapsed again, her legs were trapped as if in an invisible net.

"You will only be trapped longer if you don't answer."

It was too much for her to place into words. She had become less ready to seek revenge thanks to Ahigan. He was just in not wanting to have her killed after being told the truth. By Haseya's kind heart, a mother that had been cold and distant was replaced by one who accepted and loved her. Yatzil had redeemed herself entirely with Amteer, but now they were no longer bonded.

"I have learned revenge is not what I want any longer."

A smile crossed Sath's lips as she got to her feet and formed a combative pose. Her hands bent and shifted like grass in the wind, and then her fingertips met at a point like a towering tree.

"Take much rest, Storm Queen. The journey does not grow less difficult from here."

CHAPTER SEVENTEEN

There was a familiar kindness in the strokes against her brow. Yatzil's head swam as the room churned into focus. It was partially hindered by the cool, damp rag over her vision. Yatzil gripped the bed sheets with returning strength and found a bandage shortened her fingers reach. The rag went away like a startled white rabbit. Haseya sat back, dropping the rag in a bowl. Maua sat at the foot of the bed. Her feet poked and tugged at the sheets until swallowing Yatzil in her arms. Frost lilies filled her hair with pale blues that relaxed Yatzil by their sweet scent. A wish to place a kiss on Maua's lips came and went. There was much to learn of Maua still, and larger worries to face beyond her bedchamber. She smiled instead and took in Maua's list of worries.

"When you slept for two days, I—"

Yatzil shot up from her pillows, tossing over the bowl and sending her friends to the very end of her bed.

"Two days?" she gasped. "What has happened since I slept? Has mother been put on trial? Executed at the city center?"

Haseya crawled forward and took hold of her shoulders, rubbing them as the sheets tugged against her chest. Yatzil pressed her hands to her head, gripping great clusters of her hair. Maua offered her water, and Haseya offered a bate-nich slice from the bed's edge. Yatzil waved it away, finding her appetite had gone missing.

"What has happened?" she said. "I demand you both tell me."

They gasped, drawing themselves back, but Haseya was more frightened than Maua. Yatzil's chest heaved, wanting to pronounce sentence instead of Sachihiro. Yatzil felt a need to avenge her father resurface but she slammed her fist on the bed. Haseya contorted her face in disgust. The same disgust from when Yatzil had hidden her intentions up north. Haseya climbed off the bed. Maua sat puzzled, lips quivering, putting aside the water in its gold cup.

"I must resemble my mother," said Yatzil. "She has given me much reason to want revenge, yet I want to be better."

Haseya stopped at the empty bath, her arms folded, and her gray feathered head tucked into her chest like a sleeping bird. Yatzil pushed off the bed sheets and then pressed them to her chest.

"We had to undress you, my queen." Haseya faced her. "Whatever that warrior loyal to that woman you call mother did... It made you burn more than anything I've seen."

"We worried you and your child may die on the first night," said Maua. Her lips went still. She pulled at her long braids until they bounced and formed into spirals at their ends. "Those drums healed me and stopped your fever but for some reason you fell soon after into a deep sleep."

Yatzil looked upon Haseya.

"My mother may have given me life, Haseya."

Yatzil crawled down the bed's steps, pressing the sheets to her chest. She found her footing, but dizziness wrapped itself like a serpent about her ankles. Yatzil stumbled into Haseya's arms, and when their eyes met, her feet found strength.

"But you are my true mother."

"Oh, my queen, my child." Haseya embraced her, pressing her face to the thin sheets hiding Yatzil's nakedness. "This brings joy to my heart. I must tell you something. Your brother has spared her and wants you to decide her fate."

"What?"

"He had her iced up on her throne in that fish's mouth." added Maua.

"Your brother went to those temples and told your owl gods everything. He demanded they be on his side."

A breeze nipped at Yatzil's cheek from the balcony, dancing with her trailing sheets.

"He is a good king," said Haseya. "Although, I think the fight convinced him you were telling the truth."

The nemamoon's words had come true, but it meant the Four wanted revenge like Sachihiro and not of their own will. Yatzil believed her words three days ago had been what forced the fight into motion instead.

"I must dress and leave to make my decision while I retrieve the answers I seek."

Haseya brushed her hair back and rested her hand on Yatzil's cheek.

"If you want to be better by not seeking revenge, why go to her?"

"It is not for revenge." Yatzil sighed. "I believe in my heart that if the truth is heard I shall know why my father was killed. And I must do so, to be certain Flor's sacrifice was worth it."

"I understand," Haseya said. "I know you will choose wisely. But I must know what will happen if you spare her?"

It was a possibility she had not considered before waking

moments ago. To be of royal Nescaran blood and not take a traitor's life meant only one thing.

"Banishment."

Maua and Haseya had left her alone to be dressed. Handmaidens entered with two trays crowned in steam. One had bread and the other boar meat, seasoned, as she found by its aroma, with the finest spices and three more hand-maidens entered, presenting her fresh clothes. A raton eunuch came later with his eyes to the ground and dressed in gold robes possessing black cuffs. He held by the tips of his forefingers a scroll, still not meeting her eyes. She thought it was to shield him from her nakedness, but then he spun on his heels and left without a word. Yatzil unfurled the scroll to find its writing, the eloquent swirl and tug of a raton.

> IT PLEASES ALL NIEV AND ME TO HEAR YOU HAVE RECOVERED FROM THE FEVER WE FEARED MIGHT CLAIM YOU. WORD HAS SPREAD OF YOUR MOTHER'S TREACHERY, AND YOU NEED NOT WORRY OF REVENGE BEING TAKEN.

Yatzil paused to finish her boar on a log. It was her way to blend meat with the soft warm breads of the royal meal maker's ovens. She sloshed her hand in a bowl of bathing salts, had them rinsed and dried. She snagged the letter as handmaidens began to dress her.

THE HANDMAIDEN YOU SAW AT MY FEET WAS A SPY OF
HERS. MY EUNUCH READ HER MIND AS ALL MEN
WITHOUT COINS IN THEIR PURSE CAN DO.
I WISH YOU LUCK IN YOUR JOURNEY. MY ATTEMPTS TO
SWAY MY HUSBAND TO JOIN YOU ARE NOT OVER YET.
QUEEN SUTE
RULER OF THE TRUNK
PRINCESS OF THE RATON

A firm tug finished the knot at her back as she rested the parchment on the bed. A long skirt that trailed like a pale tongue behind her was applied next. Its knot was tied over her stomach and secured with a jade owl pendant clutching her name upon a moon in its beak. She waved off a handmaiden bringing her a shoulder necklace. There was no longer a need to play safe her interests with her mother apprehended. The necklace's inlaid blue gems reminded her of the waters in her dreams. The jade owl was enough, like a soaring protector for her child. She rested a hand to her stomach, finding it had swelled even more after her blood trade had been severed.

Her back ached with each second it took for the doors to open. Four bearers with pinned back black hair, brown lumaos, and pendants of Sachihiro's royal guard presented a palanquin. It had thicker cushions which called to her, offering relief for her pain. She had wished earlier for some reason to walk, to be given time to gather her thoughts. Yatzil strolled toward it but not before placing a crown that took a month to craft upon her head. It was a replica of her own, made of iron gifted by King Yanter to her father. The wait for it had sped her worry for Nema. As she took in its weight, relief washed over her like being blessed by the west's sacred rain.

She sat upon the palanquin and took in the bows of her handmaidens. There was a lingering need to remain with tradition, at least until gone from Niev city. Yatzil gifted them with a plain expression and then squeezed the palanquins armrests, being raised as if it was a signal.

"Proceed to the throne room."

Straining from the weight of her crown there was wonder why Putma, as her mother was named, had not been betrayed by her own bearers. She shuddered and recalled a time when one had tripped. The others stumbled and Putma's crown was knocked off balance. The man was made naked and beaten through the streets with a whale bone club reinforced with ice. The bearers to witness her return to Niev a month ago had contained their resentment like the ones from that day.

Yatzil swallowed remembering what tradition had in store for worse harm to royals.

They descended cascading steps meeting a short hall. As they four-way approached, much of Sachihiro's shattered likenesses had been removed. Fresh white granite blocks manned doorways chipped at by sculptors thickly robed and perfumed more than anyone should be. Every block showed near complete images of Sachihiro and his queen, except Sute stood at equal height with her hand interwoven with Sachihiro's own.

Yatzil sat up straight and held her chin high until her bearers turned down the long hall to the throne room. Resentment made her crush her armrests in a vice to possibly rival Clod's strength. Soon the throne room doors would be opened, and she had not yet found what words to say. Her worry rose more for Clod than what needed to be said to who she, for a moment, did not want to be bothered with.

Neither Haseya nor Maua had mentioned where he had gone. Her focus traveled to Ahigan's last words. There was a sense of sudden frustration for not knowing what Clod had done. *Is it why he has no grown name?* It had taken her willing to be struck dead to earn the giant's trust. When close to the Trunk's ruined wall, he asked to be alone in her presence. There had been tension in his sculpted aged face, a stiffness to the short budding feathers upon his head. Yatzil swallowed but contained her emotion as she recalled him kneeling yet still surpassing her eye level. He had promised not to leave her until Plunemar had been restored to the sky. She pressed her lips into a solid line and hoped for Clod to return in time.

Guards ahead bowed, frosted, and pushed the throne room doors open. Far and to her right two Elite Priest Guard stood wearing long white robes with bronze breastplates laced by finely woven cords. Gray whale bone was hard to penetrate from what Sachihiro once said. But Putma had never shown interest in facing anyone without guards. If there were magics to free oneself, Putma must not have bothered with them and to do so against men more brutal than an avalanche warrior was foolish. Yatzil saw they wore black masks of fabric over their faces under bronze owl skull helmets. They were frosted by the sight of their bare feet and arms.

Her bearers lowered her as fear nicked like a thousand blades over her skin. The priests bowed and raised their owl eyed hands, covering the eye sockets of their helmets. She did the same to her forehead and to stem suspicion allowed her emotions to melt away to a blank expression. They nodded and turned to the gasping, reaching lips of her mother upon her throne within the gray whale. Yatzil gulped and dared not imagine what a month trapped in such agony could do to someone.

Her mother had been held down, placed in posture perfect beyond any Yatzil had ever been forced to perform. Putma's feet were planted, back straightened and her arms were pressed to the throne's onyx armrests with every finger reaching like the claws of a desperate beast. Remnants of her past rage surfaced as she stared at Putma's furrowed brow and exposed teeth, but Yatzil pushed past it. *I must be better.*

"Thaw her until at the shoulders," said Yatzil, forcing her expression to be plain. "I wish for words with her before passing judgement."

They bowed and displayed their owl eyes like before. She swallowed the lingering hitch of worry in her throat. No motion unsettled the priest's eyes, leaving her certain they hadn't noticed. She knew she was softer than her old self in judgement, lacking care of purity of body, but as both men began, old wishes of brutality bubbled. Yatzil shook her head of it. The Elite Priest Guards chanted and made swirling motions with each hand.

Ice became long black hair, strained weathered eyes shut and opened. Putma let out a gasp as if being choked in a snowstorm. She heaved and twisted like she had been forced to bear witness to some horror. Yatzil pursed her lips, gave both priests orders to leave and raised a fist.

"Enough with this," she commanded. "You can breathe imprisoned, and no order was given to seal what permits such noise..."

"You dare ... speak in this way to me?" cried Putma. "I caught your father's ... seed and bore you into this world. You..."

"You murdered him and betrayed our people," Yatzil said. "And then you tried to murder my friend."

Her throat filled with rage as ice raced and coated her skin. Strain slithered through her legs as if the weight gained and strange accelerated growth of her child were zapping her strength. All she wished to do was wrap her fingers around Putma's throat but after what she had gone through her hands remained in check.

"I know you found him unambitious. And Flor meant only to serve."

Putma shook her head and ceased her worthless struggle.

"You were raised knowing strength was … only permitted and those not of great value beneath … you."

"And yet you struggle to breathe," said Yatzil. She struggled to calm herself, to remember the Nol that suffered, swallowing in regret of being so vile. "That was below what I have become. And my father was weak enough to give you what you wanted."

Putma eyed her tall iron feather crowned.

"It is clear you … still believe yourself a queen as I do. Had you not noticed my actions, all may … have gone to plan. But your father was far from weak willed and that is why I used more than my … beauty to sway him."

Yatzil set free her finger, strain wreaked pain through them. but refused to show relief upon her face. Putma must have asked Fertilida for aid to increase her odds. *You are as I have always believed father.* She pursed lips and dove deeper.

"So, he overcame your tricks and was killed for it. Did you know what Queen Aagono intended for me? How did you learn what Flor and I planned?"

"I knew you would be … safe." Putma wheezed. "That noble kept an eye on you for me. I shall tell you more when … released."

She stepped back as Putma craned her head forward and twisted her shoulders. The noble had been generous and provided the gold paint for the entrance dance glyphs. A chill she had never felt emitted from her, making the former queen shiver.

"You face execution by my choice."

Putma ceased her struggle, tremors ran through her cracked lips. To be stretched naked on an altar by Elite Priest Guards made Yatzil almost pity her. Heart and organs would be removed, but first, what made you a man or woman was cut out and offered to appease the Four. Every crime you committed was announced as you were mocked at the city center. *What royal made this a demand of the Four?* She gulped.

"I suppose … you wish for my further embarrassment then?"

"I want answers," said Yatzil. "Death was near my fate, but I was given a chance to repair my selfishness."

Her legs ached like a club had struck them several blows. Her eyes searched for refuge, but the palanquin had been taken when the elite priest guard were dismissed.

"Why betray us all?"

Putma pursed her lips, but they trembled violently like her shoulders.

"I was confronted by a palenore twice before their entrance into the west. Why did this messenger come to me and not your father I … demanded." Putma swallowed and failed to toss her hair out of her face. Yatzil found herself tucking the long dark locks behind Putma's ears. Their lobes were open fleshy rings from removal of frigagator claws. "My thanks … daughter. I know you may no longer think me a … mother, but I am no traitor to our people."

It was too difficult to say allowed. The former queen let her head drop to her iced chest. Yatzil ignored what age had done to Putma's body. Sachihiro had stripped their mother of garb and jewelry as tradition gifted a traitor.

"I do no longer consider you, my mother. You used me like an object to secure an alliance with the First Daughter."

Putma's thin eyebrows linked amongst the long-matted locks of her hair.

"When you returned and almost exposed me," Putma said,

meeting her eye. "I did not believe you would go against my warning."

"I heeded it. I needed time to consider what to do next."

Putma chuckled. Her breath danced with her hair before she raised her head as if she were queen once more.

"For once," she said, "what I have told you found its way through your stubbornness."

Yatzil flexed her toes, tempted to squat, and relieve her aching legs. The skirt had grown tighter as her emotions had surged. The great chill of earlier eased slightly as her rage ebbed away. She didn't know how to loosen the skirt and the wish to sit was unbearable now. Maua's magic had redefined what her lamodun said took months.

She had no reason to forgive Putma, and after what she had just heard Flor's actions were truly not in vain.

"You must answer for Father and the raids upon my kingdom."

"For it all, I ... shall never be ashamed. My son's kingdom is safe and is one of two, and no fool sits high upon..."

Slap. Yatzil drew her hand back as Putma spat blood. Putma cocked her head back revealing contorted lips open enough to draw breath as her cheek swelled. Yatzil pressed her fists together but a faint, yet powerful motion pressed inside her. Her eyes softened as every finger became flesh and spread across her stomach like a net. Refocusing on what angered her, none of her rage seemed to matter.

"My child is close to his emergence," she whispered, looking down upon herself to savor the moment. She rose to full height once the feeling was gone, disappointed, before realizing what she had done. "That was deserved, for Father was kind, even to you."

Putma stared through tear filled eyes. Yatzil closed her own and battled with what to do next. The one she no longer called mother begged and sobbed as if repentant. She traced back her feelings to seconds ago. Hope surfaced in her heart to feel so much life but Putma's groaning, and heaving snapped her back to now. Yatzil opened her eyes, tempted by the angry insistence in Putma's. The former queen had given up on finding Yatzil's mercy. And though it was a betrayal to nescaran royals of the past she was unable to not give it.

"I shall be hated," she sighed, "but imprisonment is forever your fate."

Yatzil went to summon the elite priests and once she returned the former Mother of the King raised her head with softened eyes. They could have spoken volumes, but no more answers could be obtained. The priests presented the owl eyes upon their hands as before. Yatzil returned the gesture of sacred respect. They scowled as if sensing the sadness in her before her lips gave a single command. And even as their eyes narrowed it mattered not. She was to be banished soon, and only those she cared for mattered.

They bowed after commanded once her palanquin arrived. And as she lowered herself into its ornate chair, graced by etched frost lilies over its frame, her mother's pain tormented her heart.

One priest climbed within the gray whale's mouth and seized Putma by the head. Putma groaned and begged, shaking to be free. Her muddied words pleaded for execution. The second elite priest guard waved and pressed his thick fingers over Putma's face to her chest. A scream rang out as the priest's hand sealed over her jaw, tightening until ice had replaced all flesh and there was no sound.

"Take me to my bedchamber." she said, emotion flooding her throat. She firmed up her voice and then gave up knowing it was too late. "I no longer wish to look upon the traitor."

The bearers raised her without a word or sign of discontent at her emotions. She turned back, a tear nearly escaping her eye at the pleading Putma emanated from her eyes. Minutes passed and soon she was too far to see. Yatzil had done the right thing deep down at least. The doors were fully closed and that gave her permission to release a trapped pent-up breath. Her choice had allowed her one great blessing. To move forward with her life.

CHAPTER EIGHTEEN

By a week passing, Yatzil had barely left her bedchamber. The door rumbled shut following the footsteps of three servants, carrying four plates each. She had commanded the royal meal makers to send larger portions of late. Her mood had traveled in more highs and lows than Nema possessed mountains. Four stacks of scrolls sat by her bath, threats on her person from Niev's people. Haseya had begged her in days passed for her to change judgement and execute Putma. She refused to return to her old self. To revenge.

Yatzil sighed and allowed her skirt to drop after splashing water to cleanse herself. The servant at her feet rose with her full chamber pot and gave a hesitant bow before leaving. Yatzil ran a hand through her hair finding it smoother and sleeker than in past months, but it went unnoticed by the ladies of court. They only bowed. They hadn't bothered giving her blessings for her child's safe emergence. She suspected they held a grudge for being merciful but dared not show it with the palace guard around.

Reflecting on a previous hour, Sachihiro had asked her to

court to bear witness to the execution of peasants that had burned likeness of her within the city's center. She had refused but sent word back asking permission for Sute to join in the finding of the Nemamoon. Yatzil eased into a chair beside her bath, grasping a full cup of palm wine. Her brother's silence troubled her more than servants and women of the court. Haseya joined her by the bath.

The old Nol woman crossed her arms with a foul look that worsened her wrinkles.

"I'll kill her. I promised. Remember?"

"No," said Yatzil. "And you spoke of helping, not performing the task yourself."

"It will allow us to come back," Haseya said, insistently. "After we dance a new moon into existence."

"Haseya!" Yatzil snapped. "We may not survive the city with threats so close now."

"I don't believe they will get any closer." Maua said from the foot of Yatzil's bed. Yatzil took a draught of wine as the northerner's sweet words softened her mood. "You have gone through much as we all have. Your child has swollen you to readied size."

"She isn't baking bread, Maua." said Haseya, aiming a queer look at Maua. Maua's braids curled and loosened some of their petals. "Your brother will help us no matter what, my child. And I don't think the nemamoon will allow you to get out of saving us that easy."

It was true beyond reason that Sachihiro would aid her even if it led to every nescaran wishing him dead. She ran her fingers down the soft green silks of her skirt. It was smooth against her skin and not stiff with jade squares and gold coins like most she had recently worn. She rose to think upon the balcony, a cool breeze whispered across her face. She smiled at the bickering between Haseya and Maua on how to cheer her and then...

"Where is Clod?" She sank, unable to understand how a month had passed with him absent from her thoughts. "Why have I not been told of his whereabouts?"

Haseya and Maua traded confused looks as the doors creaked open. Clod stepped through with a better fitting white coat and thick leggings of black boar fur. A jade owl was mounted upon his massive chest, with wings spread to his shoulders. Upon the moon in its beak was her name and titles with his trophies polished around his waist.

"I'm sorry my queen," he said. "I've been gone … but I will keep my promise."

She folded her upper lip over the bottom, pressing them hard against the jade on her teeth. There was no need to question him for not everyone mourns in another's company.

"I appreciate that more than you know." she said, needing to tell him what pined her most yet afraid of his reaction. "Your father said he forgives you."

Clod bawled his thickly gloved fingers. Their layers could pass for the ice boulders said to fly from the immense guard towers upon Niev's walls. Clod buried his face in his coat until calm fell upon him and his lips released a heavy breath.

"I don't deserve it."

"What have you done not to, Clod?"

"I killed someone close… I was practicing with a knife my father gave me and thought it was a wolf … but it was my brother."

Yatzil gasped. Haseya's mouth gaped. Maua clasped her hand to her chest.

"He was smaller and … my twin." Clod's chest gave a great heave, but his eyes stayed dry. "My father was hunting, and my mother saw him before I did. I didn't hear him. Why? Why'd he have to scare … me?"

Clod collapsed to his knees. His tears left unmatchable

patterns over the smooth tile between his fingers. Yatzil moved slowly within reach of him. She hesitated, every thought finding itself on how long Ahigan had held on to such a loss. She raised Clod's head and embraced it, understanding why the giant didn't dare disobey his father. To do so would have made anyone crumble like burning wood. She wept with him as Clod's eyes met her own. She backed off, dropping her cup. It hit the furs about her feet with a soft clang. She felt a slight motion within her as the fur turned a darker shade. Her skirt grew wet and heavy, and joy collapsed upon her heart.

Clod gathered her in his arms and dashed to the bed. Haseya ran to the door as Yatzil took in the bed's softness. Haseya jerked open the thick door with all her strength and called for help. Maua took her hand in hers, its rough bark softening like it were a leaf. Clod backed away to the bath, powerless despite all his strength.

"My queen."

"Yes." Yatzil groaned. Haseya yanked the owl pendant from Yatzil's skirt. She hid Yatzil's legs with a sheet before tossing the wet skirt aside. The pain was like being bathed in a diamond fang's burning blood. "You have been a good friend, Clod. I am sorry for ... mmm ... ahh ... father."

"Thank—"

"You can talk later," Haseya said, cutting Clod off. "Go find those bald big, bellied healers."

Clod ran out the door. He called out yet as Yatzil was propped up by pillows, battling her flooding pain, she worried a healer may flee at the calls and size of a panicked giant.

YATZIL DREW in the familiar damp Nol smell from her daughter's hair. She held her close, breaking another tradition by giving milk of her own breast. It pained her to allow another to nurture her child once her strength had returned. She pulled the furs the babe nestled in tighter to keep her child warm and thought of a name. Her daughter hadn't taken well to the cold unlike most nescarans, and her eyes were a constant yellow glow. It was the nescaran's way to use names of those closest to a babe's mother to create the child's name. But no name came to mind. She swallowed and knew there was so much more left to do, and to not be present for it pierced her heart.

Haseya sat beside her with an admiration that kept Yatzil within the moment. Until after gaining the gray feathered nol's trust and embracing her as a mother, joy was brief. It was just them for now while Maua and Clod gathered supplies for the journey to come. Yatzil sighed as her child fell slowly to sleep before resting her in Haseya's arms. She wasn't certain who was in better spirits because Sachihiro had filled Haseya's wagon with boar fur and new thread. It had come with permission for Sute to join them. But by the tone of his words an hour previous there had never been a greater decision upon his shoulders to make.

He had taken his time, pacing the length of her balcony, every step quaking his belly while his tongue searched for words over his teeth. And when he had rested his eyes upon his niece an answer came.

Haseya gave a light peck on the babe's cheek as Yatzil slipped the soft silks of her top over her breast. Close to the doors an old crib of palm-and-oak stood, carved to the shape of a sail less skiff resting upon the back of an owl in flight. The owl's body rested on a block of ice formed to its belly like an updraft of wind. Yatzil climbed from the bed with more strength within herself. There was a need to tell Haseya something. It battled with her mind at this moment as Haseya rested her child within the crib. But to shatter such peacefulness meant misery for them both. Yatzil rested the hand upon Haseya's shoulder with which he no longer felt what it once did.

"I have kept something of importance from you."

Haseya chuckled. "A mother's child always does, Yatzil."

"It is about Amteer," She tore her eyes from Haseya in search of more peaceful thoughts, thoughts of her child so protected and in her heart. "I can no longer feel his hand in mine."

Yatzil revealed where the scare overlapped the one from her blood trade. She braced for a wave of anger, of unrestrained words but Haseya only crossed her arms.

"I'm glad."

"Why say this?" Yatzil gasped. "We have lost him forever."

Haseya embraced her, drawing in a breath as if not seeing Yatzil for many years.

"Because I didn't have to lose you. I haven't seen my family in so long and to lose you, Yatzil, would be like losing one of them."

Yatzil returned Haseya's embrace, binding her arms tight as if she were saying goodbye to someone doomed to execution. She could think of it in no other way. So much of her life before being sent away possessed more brutal than kind moments. The kind moments with Flor, Sachihiro and her father were all she had then. She looked upon her child, a tiny yawn escaping her silver lips.

"It'll be time for us to leave her soon, my child," said Haseya. "Are you sure east is where to go?"

"No dragons have ever lived in the west and Ahigan confirmed islands exist in that direction."

"And only those serpents guarding our way out exist down here."

"True," said Yatzil, nibbling her lip from Haseya's earlier words. "If only they were able to fly like the one in my dream. Our journey may be shortened that way."

"Ask your brother for a ship."

Yatzil rested her fingertips to the bow of the crib.

"A ship shall place us further from the raton capital. I witnessed the concern Queen Sute failed to hide when I spoke of the palenore wearing armor like hers. And we must make certain of what Putma meant by two kingdoms."

Haseya gave Yatzil's hand a squeeze.

"Well, we won't go hungry thanks to your brother."

Yatzil rested her eyes on her child's face, and a name bloomed like flowers in Maua's hair.

"Yat-hig-seya."

"I like that one, my queen, but you need Maua as part of that name."

Yatzil stroked her nearly named child's brow, small wisps of hair kissing her hand.

"Mau-hig-seya-zil?"

"Remove the 'zil'" Haseya chuckled, "and we have a name."

THERE WERE sixty steps left by her count. Strain compressed the lips of guards who pressed their hands to the immense palm-n-oak doors sealing off the palace from the city beyond. They clasped heavy iron rings above them; the rust was visible even from a great distance. Clod remained hesitant, watchful, his breaths loud enough to be heard amongst the constant wind. The column of avalanche warriors to either side of them, she guessed, was what made him uneasy as he carried their supplies. The avalanche warriors were like a wall of flesh and shaped metal and kept their eyes fixed on her above the others. She bit her lip, releasing a breath from her nose, but the tension within her remained fine like the edge of each step beneath her sandals.

She found pride in her garb for it made her like the warrior queens of old but the gold eagle upon her nol crown enriched it further. Its weight seemed less and was cool against her brow. Yatzil dreaded if a nescaran dared yank if from her head for there was no iron to be found, but in the palace, and to have it stolen was too great to bear. Squares of gray whale bone were sown into the lumao about her waist. A breastplate of the same bronze was shaped to her abdomen. Her chest felt like it was in a coffin, but her skin was protected from the hard metal by layers of wrapped silks. Yatzil padded the thick belt completing her outfit. Its pouches held food and holstered Sparron's knife. A faint slosh on her left hip came from Ahigan's tortoise shell.

She remembered the final kiss she had given Mau-hig-seya and resisted retreating to see her once more. It was not a final goodbye because if she had to hunt for the tunnel Flor showed her, she would. Peering up the steps her child was well out of sight. Sachihiro had promised to keep her as safe as he would his own son. His queen took each step slower than the others, garbed like Yatzil, except her legs were wrapped in layers of dark fabric. Yatzil felt a throbbing in her throat and by Sute's expression, she too missed her child deeply. Yellow lightning glided down then vanished from the queen's eyes. Sute breathed easier than Yatzil did within armor, wearing the dragon scale breastplate of her father's kingdom. The wind danced with jade squares of Queen Sute's lumao as she caught up to Yatzil.

They neared the bottom when her wish to turn back swelled like a storm on the ocean. Yatzil took a hesitant breath before surveying the others. Maua's feet latched to every step like roots searching for room to grow. Haseya and Clod moved with a balance all Nol possessed. The light snow rested on her cheek like a tear, but it did little to calm her rising worry.

"I cannot praise you enough for not choosing a ship," said Sute, the talons of her crown wet from fallen snowflakes. "The Palenore may have taken Rinyu ... and I must be certain the opposite is true."

Yatzil swallowed her worry and gave her a nod.

"How can I refuse your wish for truth?"

The yellow lightning bolts ceased for a moment, giving splendor to Sute's long eyelashes but they vanished within lightning white like snow. Yatzil had little of her own tears left, spent by frustration for their task and leaving Mau-hig-seya behind. There was no changing her mind on Putma and Yatzil had made it a lasting judgement only an hour ago.

"Of what I have witnessed of our people's actions," Sute refocused on the steps, an unease on her lips. "Death is wanted for mercy. I wish to order all Niev to move beyond such a tradition but..."

"But it shall make your return dangerous."

Sute gave a slight shrug as their feet met the deepening snow. The dais between them and the doors had always made Yatzil nervous. It was as if her father, brother and even Putma possessed no escape if forced to climb the steps on public days. One word out of place meant riot yet she didn't understand how a family meant to be worshiped as gods was subject to such defiance. *Perhaps, I shall never know.*

"Nescarans honor brutality unlike a Raton does civility," Sute said. "We are cunning in violence, but we do not punish mercy with banishment and threats."

"I am pleased to be banished in a way." she said, wishing she hadn't. Sute gave her a charged look. "My family are meant to act as gods without flaw or breaking from tradition. I am glad to do the unexpected."

The guards ahead frosted and grabbed hold of the great

rings. Yatzil could hear Clod grumble behind her and braced as Maua took her hand.

"It will be fine, Maua." said Yatzil. She ran her thumb over the smoothness of Maua's hand, flakes loosened as she did. "No harm will come if we don't react."

"That will not happen for me."

Yatzil waved for the guards to stand at ease. The others stopped as the columns of avalanche warriors, lining the steps descended, filling the air with their footsteps. She embraced the northerner, demanding deep within herself to remain confident, but at this moment, wished they both had more time together.

"I am considered a traitor, but my brother's warriors shall protect us. You must remain calm." Yatzil raised Maua's chin. "For me?"

"They are under my order too, lady of the Lijani." said Sute. She rested a hand on Maua's shoulder, but Maua drew herself closer to Yatzil. "And you have me at your side if they fail."

"I thank you for that," Yatzil grinned. "But she must still remain calm."

Maua shook in her arms, flecks of bark slid down the armor measuring Yatzil's every breath. She would have to have Haseya loosen its cords if they survived what waited for them. They needed to leave and their path to Niev's gates was long. Yatzil had never paid notice until escorted to the palace by Putma's guards.

"I promised to keep you free. That shall not end, and neither will your life."

They stared at one another for moments but were interrupted by Haseya's panting and the crackle and boom of Sute's eyes. She brushed back some of Maua longer braids, finding her eyes had softened.

"You have kept that promise."

"So, you believe all will be well?" said Yatzil.

"Yes."

Yatzil smiled and waved for the doors to be opened. Their armored escort formed a channel as if to guide them as they proceeded. And as the doors slowly opened a thin glimpse of the streets gave way in time to carts pulled by old men in every direction.

When they passed through the palace gates, Yatzil fought the wish to flee back to Sachihiro and beg him to overrule the banishment. She peered back. The vast length and height of the doors left too long a run before they'd close. And to give in, to retreat would leave Maua abandoned like the others. She sighed as the doors boomed shut. The doors were too thick for even Clod's axe to pierce.

The Four's temples were distant but unmistakable beyond the mansions hindering her vision. Yatzil released a discreet breath as arch-less doorways to walled courtyards opened. Niev's nobles desired a look at who had spared their king's murderer. They bowed to Sute, unable to hide their curiosity at why their queen walked beside who they deemed a traitor. Their servants urged them to drop the stones in their hands as Clod gave one noble a menacing look. She hoped with Clod and the warriors lining her way that no previous threats saw action.

Light snow gave way to heavier flakes once beyond the arch marking the final row of mansions. People loomed unarmed from high farms shaded by in bloom bate-nich trees. Those giving the sternest expressions were older than she was. Children ran among the narrowed allies naked or in single fabric skirts flowing below their knees. They threw snow at one another, remaining oblivious to the world. Those who kept at their mothers' side stared only in anger from the whispers hissed by those elders among them.

Another hissing rose, setting her nerves bounding through

her chest as Niev's city center grew closer. Yatzil clenched her teeth to dam up a gasp as it formed a single word. *Weak.* It pounded on her senses like the drums of Non's temple before death had claimed her father. She gulped down her nerves but choked as children joined the old. Yatzil remained emotionless, eyeing anyone beyond the avalanche warriors for stones. Haseya was less reserved, muttering words that must have been Nol her lamodun thought improper for a princess. Sute remained poised though it was certain, as the wind drew back her flowing hair, that anger held her teeth in a vice. *Sachihiro is blessed to have someone so strong.* Yatzil thought.

No nescaran challenged her brother's avalanche warriors but as the chanting grew so did the street narrow. It was as if all Niev were slowly cutting off their escape, every avalanche warrior held firm, waiting for orders to kill if commanded but Yatzil doubted Sute wished it to come to that. Clod's face grew black from the wind as he cracked his knuckles. She released a breath in relief at his patience.

To be hated, she thought, for mercy was so foolish she wished she could have such belief banned. But such power belonged to her brother and even with their mother imprisoned, tradition still held him captive.

They were within the jade moon that connected the Four's temples. The chants of her weakness were loud enough to wake the dead nescaran deep below Niev's clean swept streets. A roughness brushed and sealed around her fingers. Maua's posture was firm like her grip with eyes bright as meal makers oven fire. A pride, almost passion for the northern rose within Yatzil's belly. Amongst the ocean of hate threatening to drown them, the desire to explore new wants swelled suddenly but there was no time. They kept pace with one another, eventually passing out of reach of the temples, closing in on Niev's gates.

"Why leave with a traitor, great queen?" called a man bal d across his scalp but with long hair around his ears. "Has our king banished you too?"

Before Yatzil could free herself from Maua's grip, Sute held up her hand, lightning ran over it gathering into an orb. Yatzil froze.

"I must make certain the traitor leaves our lands. And a new means of peace must be struck with the west." Sute remained poised with her hand fully a glow. Avalanche warriors closed in around them. "Our king trusts such an act to no other."

Yatzil's jaw dropped hearing Clod grumble, amongst the collective crackle of warriors frosting over. His fingers were bound tight to the shaft of his axe. Haseya pressed her back to Clod's, a pointed prison of ice spears surrounding them. Yatzil shielded Maua but the northern moved and did so instead, the tips of her fingers sharpened to points. A weight of disbelief heaved itself upon Yatzil's shoulders, dragging her down, but what perplexed her more was Sute. Amongst the lightning streaming down the queen's cheeks a smile flashed. Yatzil scanned to find if others had witnessed it but found none. And soon her brother's warriors had separated them from Sute.

The wind cut off the young queen's words as she spoke again and left only its howl to torment Yatzil's ears. A great roar out matched the wind as more snow fell. She returned her concern to Maua as the immense gates ahead opened. The northern was calm again, hunched a little to shield herself from the wind. Clod moved with unease as he slipped free his axe hand.

"We are near Niev's gates," Yatzil said and waved her hand. "Hold back your anger until we are beyond them."

"She's going to have us eaten," Haseya hissed, slowing her

pace as Sachihiro's statues loomed. "You said your brother keeps to tradition."

"My brother shall not have his city's guardians eat us."

"Oh, we'll be dead first," said Clod, grabbing and strangling the shaft of his axe with both hands. He grimaced at the avalanche warriors as they held firm their spears. "I'll make a mess of these—"

"You will do no such thing," Sute said, approaching with purpose in her steps. "I will not have bloodshed."

Yatzil rushed to demand what had come over her. Her brother's avalanche warriors thawed and retreated to the palace, leaving Sute unprotected. Maua leapt at the queen, but Yatzil grabbed her by the shoulders.

"She tricked us." Maua twisted with both hands forming long claws. The rage was unlike her as Sute cast a wall of lighting between them. "We trusted her to help us."

Yatzil flung her to the ground. Maua glared at her, confused, as Haseya helped the northerner to her feet.

"What's wrong with you royals?" said Haseya. "I thought we were supposed to work together, not kill each other."

"No one will see death, lady of the nol," said Sute, waving her hand over the shield of lightning, brightness blinking out of existence. "We must leave. The guardians will not keep our way open for long."

"It was a ruse." said Yatzil, finding herself at the center of a triangle of confusion. Clod hesitated then released his axe. Maua shrugged Haseya off. "It was clear to all that Queen Sute's presence with us was strange."

Yatzil gave Maua's shoulder a squeeze. To see so much rage in her brought a wish to relax Maua in some way. She ignored the rising feelings in her chest. Maua's fingers hissed back to the smooth slenderness they once had.

"I... I do not want to lose you," said Maua. "I mean Nema

cannot afford to lose who can aid in returning it to what it was."

"I know what you mean, yet... I am still unsure."

Her hand fell from Maua's shoulder. The need for what was put aside held her in its massive grip. To allow herself to love, and when so much remained left to do, felt like a distraction.

"I know you wish to learn more about me," Maua said before similar words touched Yatzil's own lips. "I am willing to wait a little longer."

CHAPTER NINETEEN

No more was said after that, and Yatzil found greater concern in what the others thought of Queen Sute than what both her and Maua felt. She sensed their resentment, but it was less in Clod for what reason she was uncertain. The queen kept close without a spark from her fingertips though Yatzil still held reservations. She wanted to trust the queen for Sute felt as she always did. A desire to return home and save her family from harm.

With a flash of the owl's eyes tattooed upon her hands, the guardians roared and slowly returned to their moat until the gates closed. If either massive serpent had passed any kind of judgement, they hid it by keeping to duty. Clod only let down his guard after the moat's waters had settled. With every step Yatzil led the way, snow crunched, flaking over the straps of her sandals.

It had taken them until midmorning when the sun had thinned out many of the shadows to cross the city. Beyond a short forest the Wrinkled River's rushing waters met her ears. She eyed Maua, watching the lijani girl sweep a hand over the under and overgrowth, it parted and withered away. Yatzil resisted meeting her eye, swallowed, and went about sorting her feelings for the northerner.

Maua was unpredictable and had been bolder than expected for someone who fell to pieces when challenged. Yatzil cringed but hid it, remembering last night Maua being unrelenting in her gaze upon Mau-hig-seya. But sleep had replaced her concern that night and she believed Maua watched her child out of concern. *She too had a hand in my child's emergence.* Yatzil thought, smiling as the river came into full focus, the rich soil of its muddy banks filling her nostrils.

She uncinched a heavy pouch from her waist, took a bate-nich from it and bit into it. There was a ripeness in this one, its juices traveled swiftly down her ice-blue chin.

Further up the river a congregation of frigagators lay on the riverbank. They were scaled in gold and made her wonder how they had not disappeared from over hunting. Haseya touched her arm, a hard line sealed her lips, eyeing the others and the frigagators.

"We need to talk about—" Haseya pointed at Sute with a thumb.

The queen formed a ball of cress crossing lightning and ignited a small mound of wood Clod had stacked. She backed off and folded her arms as the Nol giant gave her a nod. His mind seemed to have changed but Maua remained secluded to the river's edge for some reason.

"I'm still not convinced like Maua," said Haseya.

"I understand your mistrust in Queen Sute, but there is no time to search for another raton woman."

Haseya raised an eyebrow as they moved back into the forest. They kept their eyes to the ground for diamond fangs. After out of sight of the others they stopped, the wind swaying the treetops overhead.

"Do you know about the Gifnos?" said Haseya. "And how it killed many nol? It killed King Amteer's brothers and mother. His mother not only gave Sparron the knife but forged it too."

Yatzil shook her head, running her fingers over the knife's hilt, but then she remembered the rash gone from Amteer's face.

"I know little of that war's history." Yatzil recalled Ahigan mentioning it long ago. "What of it?"

Drawing a deep breath, Haseya gave her a look as if she had forgotten some important detail.

"Do you remember what Queen Sute said? Her people are smart in violence. nol attack at random but you know it when it happens."

Yatzil had dismissed such words earlier, the fear of judgement, of being mobbed had been a greater concern. She tossed her finished bate-nich in a bush. To what her lamodun taught of history, no mention of Nescarans invading the East had ever passed his glossed lips. The west fought amongst itself and the south at times. Usurpation and assassination clouded her dynasty and those previous were plagued by rebellions that had kept the Trunk divided until the first of her dynasty conquered all of it to assert his divinity.

"To what I know, no one has challenged the raton except... Did King Yanter do so?"

"Yes," said Haseya. Her brow merged as she crossed her arms. "We'd have won because Nol are too quick for raton lightning and their dragons had gone missing high upon the left Lid."

"But it was the Giftnos that ended it." Yatzil rested her hands on Haseya's shoulders. "You know the reason for Queen Sute's actions. And it saved us from my people's rage."

Haseya ran her fingers through the gray of her feathers

then rubbed her eyes. Yatzil listened for a moment at the distant river then breathed easy.

"You have grown, my queen." Haseya rested her hand on Yatzil's cheek. Her glove held hints of spices spent on meat they had shared. "More inside than out as everyone should."

Haseya brought her close and kissed her cheek. Yatzil returned her kindness with a kiss to the forehead. Her every breath was lighter, the brewing storm of concern deep within had settled. Her focus returned to the journey. A scream rang out, stopping her heart in mid beat as she realized it was Maua's.

As they rushed through the overgrowth, Clod swiped at three immense frigagators. Their six eyes widened, and jaws snapped at his feet. Sute lashed at them with her lightning like it was a whip, melting them into the ground. The snow boiled and filled the air with steam. Maua dashed toward Yatzil but stumbled over a peaking rock in the snow.

"Hide Haseya," Yatzil said.

Haseya didn't argue but eyed her with worry as Yatzil frosted. Yatzil smacked her fists together then pierced a frigagator through the jaws once the spear had surpassed her shoulders. Yanking it free the tip was cracked. Maua made it to her side, shaking in fear, making Yatzil search for the whereabouts of the brave lijani from earlier.

"Become as you were in Niev," said Yatzil. "Haseya needs your protection."

"Her knife will be enough. I must stay with you."

All six slender fingers Maua possessed thickened, growing points, the ember of her eyes reflected off them. Disgust slithered over Yatzil's tongue before both girls swung and jabbed their way to Clod. His axe cleaved off the long snout of a frigagator snapping at his ankle. The blade's resilience lessened her worry a little, but Haseya had no skill in battle.

"Do what I ask of you." said Yatzil, thrusting her spear. It snapped then broke off behind a frigagators jaw. Smacking her fists together again, Maua finished off the growling, snapping creature first. "We need Haseya for what must be done."

"No," Maua said. "She treats me like a lesser as Queen—"

A congregation of frigagators separated them. Yatzil swung with each step then scowled at Maua. Soon the Lijani was up shore, but Sute went after her. There were too many frigagators to count yet Clod had heard her pleas. He dashed for the trees as Yatzil found herself alone. The gold scaled creatures urged her toward the river. Her heart leapt back to her spine from their chopping jaws. She peered at the ice crusting the river, unable to believe Maua's words.

Yatzil fell and gasped, Sute calling out her name as the water swallowed all sound. A great blast of lighting forced her eyes shut. The current snatched her spear away like an angered parent. Yatzil thawed but the weight of her armor and crown made up for it. All of it gave a reminder to an enclosed courtyard not of her father's palace. Clawing, she failed to untie the armor and kicked to the surface. Her fingers found air, but she sank again. A wish for someone to pull her to shore came, but Flor wasn't there like before when bracelets, shoulder necklaces and gold arm bands weighed on her. The chiseled steps of a vacant mansion were replaced by a distant shore.

The shore grew blurry with no one in view. Yatzil had forgotten to take a breath as the water dragged her further from salvation. To give in consumed her but it was not what anyone, alive in her heart, or on snow covered shores wanted. Yatzil frosted, focused, shutting her eyes. They crystallized. The rush and swirl of current stopped. She climbed until both hands found air. Her confidence rose the more the water became shallow, breaking her concentration for a second as fatigue set in. She had eaten a bate-nich earlier but a desire to live, to finish what Sath spoke of, and find truth to Maua's words fueled her.

All became ice and she climbed then dropped upon a smooth slick surface. The frigagators had fled up shore, barely visible in what amazement she found next. Lapping water splashed over a short, jagged burg of ice before her. Yatzil quickly stood, fumbling with the breastplates cords but then realized what she had done. The berg was small but held back the river like a dam. Her father had formed larger ones to sink distant ships. But out of desperation, anger, and determination a berg of ice came from her not trained yet tested self.

HER GARB WAS HEAVIER from the gray whale bone inlaid lumao to the layers of silk under her armor. Yatzil moved at a fast pace across the ice to the shore. Her curiosity as to why so many frigagators had attacked was another mystery to solve. The fire had been snuffed out. Its freshly burned wood scattered, leaving black streaks reaching like the petals of a blooming flower. The others rushed to her side, Haseya further behind. Sute had her focus more on Clod, whose boot was pierced in places. His left glove was missing two fingers and bite marks lined the skin underneath.

Focus fell on Maua, and it wasn't just Yatzil's. The northern woman had become black mist wrapped in thorny vines. Her eyes flared amongst a coiled singular vine with a spiked tip. Yatzil gasped. The likeness of Maua to the Lijani on the walls of Wolfstrong was unmistakable but impossible for how aged the image had been. Yatzil felt Haseya's embrace. To have her close, and without a scratch gifted her with relief. She returned the embrace then approached Maua as the northern slowly returned to the form she had been familiar with. Vines formed into arms and legs, all clothed in leaves and berries not of the south.

"I know you wish not to hear it," said Yatzil, releasing the vice she had placed her teeth in, "yet I have no reason to care. You know what is at risk but defied my orders to protect Haseya."

Braids slithered from Maua's blackened scalp as she kept a rebellious glare.

"You are correct. I also was promised freedom and that comes with no—"

"Our lives were at risk," said Yatzil, ice filled in her skin, but her eyes remained their original color. "You left Haseya defenseless. I believed with what rage you showed before I—"

"Could use me like Queen Aagono her Palenore?"

Clod readied his axe. Popping, sizzling orbs encompassed Sute's fists. It was not her intention to make such feelings arise in Maua. She wanted them to become more than two pieces to something greater than themselves. The frustration keeping Maua's eyes burning bright halted more bark from filling in her face. A question surfaced, and though it was strange to ask, Yatzil knew Maua was too angry to give a false answer now.

"You were at the river's edge when I left. Do you know what brought the frigagators upon us?"

"I am curious about this too," said Sute, the heat of her power melting the snow. "They were far from us, and we gave them no reason for confrontation."

"She's right." said Clod, eyeing the scattered wood and absent embers of their fire. "And it's snowing too much for them to spot the fire."

"Why would they look for fire, Clod?" Haseya said with a

raised eyebrow. "You didn't see it my queen. Maua touched the water."

"And how can that...?"

And then it came to her why the diamond fang had attacked Maua. Yatzil knew Haseya enough that her actions were meant to teach. There was an edge to Haseya that had unsettled herself at first. It was the reason she had not relented despite Yatzil being her queen. A faint smile crossed her lips at all Haseya had done.

"You spoke of no woman holding the title of mother in the north." Yatzil stepped back, fully frosted, not willing to give in if Maua trampled her heart again. "You told me all this and wished to take Haseya over who bore me into this world."

"I... I was mistaken."

"We all have been," Haseya said, eyeballing Clod to put his axe away. He did so with a grumble, "kind to you. I'm not easy to be around, but I wanted you to be stronger for all..."

Tears swelled in Haseya's eyes as she laid a hand on Maua's shoulder, but the northerner backed off, black wisps running down her cheeks.

"Why not tell me what troubled you?" said Yatzil.

Maua's mouth dropped open and then slowly shut. Yatzil drifted back to when they were both alone in the forest. She bound her hands into fists, remnants of that kiss remained on her lips like a scar. Too much had Maua done without her consent from that moment. So much now, that she considered changing Mau-hig-seya's name. The wish to leave Maua behind and find another lijani grew with the silence.

"I wish to speak with Maua, alone."

"That's not a good idea, my queen." said Clod. His voice boomed so loud it made her flinch. "She almost killed us—"

"I know this." She craned her neck to Sute. The queen had lowered her guard but had balled her fists. "I do not wish to command you, but I must have Clod tended to. Can you take Haseya with you until I decide Maua's fate?"

"I believe leaving you is an unwise—"

Yatzil allowed herself to thaw, loosening the familiar tightness from her breastplate. Maua remained still, but even with the others around, Yatzil was uncertain the northerner didn't possess another trick.

"Please trust in me as you do my brother."

Sute gave a stern nod, a hint of worry unsettled her lips, and the lightning lessoned down her cheeks. Clod followed the young queen, cradling his half naked hand. Some marks on his fingers had begun to bleed. Haseya remained while the others crossed the jagged berg of ice.

"Give Queen Sute as much aid as you can to heal Clod," said Yatzil, resting a hand to Haseya's shoulder. "I shall find you but must do this alone."

Haseya sighed. "Whatever you do, please don't let it haunt you."

Haseya ran to join the others' unease and slowed her steps across the dammed river. Branches snapped and cracked; snow crunched until they were both alone.

"So., I know you more now," said Yatzil.

Silence fell for a moment with snow slowing its downward dance.

"Yes," said Maua. "You do. I did all of it to gain trust, to keep you safe, and end my loneliness."

Yatzil's brow creased, and lips pursed.

"You have done it in the wrong way."

A need to break into a rage rose as the prickle of ice scraped the back of her eyes like a knife sharpened on stone. She kept silent like Maua and found it fitting if the northerner would begin to wilt but Maua remained strong like an ancient tree.

"We cannot create another moon without you, but your care for me is too much of a risk for the others."

The words were like a flame blended with wood as bark fell from Maua's face. To search for another lijani would slow Sute's wish to see her family but there was no other choice.

"You," Maua dropped to her knees. "Are you leaving me?

Yatzil felt her throat close with emotion for the woman she wanted to love. But how could she love someone who cared more about her wants than the fate of Nema. Yatzil reflected on how she was once driven in the same way to avenge her father and rescue Sachihiro. It was in the past and as she parted her lips to speak, to pass sentence, pity downed her tongue like guards an unruly prisoner.

"I doubt any of my kind will help you."

"They were near victims of the Highnonstar when they traded you," said Yatzil. "Do not try to fool me. If they are as driven by their wants as you then I do not see reason to—"

"Please. Do not abandon me like they did."

Maua covered her face, sobbing, her braids withered as if succumbing to the cold. Yatzil edged a foot forward, compelled to comfort the woman her child partially bore the name of. She had kept her promise and desired to kiss Maua, to hold her. Maua glared up at her, both ember eyes burning red hot.

"I have no choice," said Yazil. "Too much is at stake, and I must … leave you."

A coarseness snatched her ankles, pressing the straps of her sandals into her skin. Snow crunched then enveloped her before a hint of grass grazed her neck. Yatzil frosted as Maua's eyes drew closer. She gasped as if in a nightmare as a growl rose from Maua's lips.

"You will not find another. I will not allow it.'

The Lijani was far enough away that neither could touch one

another but Maua's arms had somehow quadrupled in length. Yatzil dug her fingers into the snow, searching for purchase. She focused to freeze Maua from within, a cloud of breath released from the northern's lips but still Maua pulled. Smacking her fists together a spear formed, matching the hastened beat of Yatzil's heart. She aimed it at Maua and the Lijani released her. Yatzil scrambled to her feet, ignoring the chafing on her ankles.

"Surrender Maua," said Yatzil. "I no longer want what I have desired for so long."

Maua reared up like a serpent twisting into a mass of tangled vines and blackened mist.

"If you leave me, I will take what I made happen so swiftly. You would have died sooner if burdened with a chi—"

Snow suddenly rose and wrapped around Maua like a tree caught in an inferno. Yatzil tossed down her spear. The yellow of her eyes grew cold, crystallizing as a film of ice ran over her breastplate. Wind raced across her iced face in a torrent of snowflakes. Maua reached out but Yatzil swung up her hands with a fury and the vines stiffened and iced over. Her child was safe under her brother's protection but after what had happened, she believed Maua capable of anything.

"You are done," said Yatzil. "I wanted to give you another chance but now I do not care for you anymore."

With a sharp motion she ripped Maua's frozen arms off. A scream unlike any she had ever heard rang out. She refused to cover her ears, rage tensing every muscle. Maua charged, growing nubs then twin thorns from her elbows, but they shriveled from the cold. Yatzil remembered how Haseya had wrapped her child in furs. She reached out to the whirling snow then sealed Maua within it. The thought was demented but it held the woman she no longer cared for. She pulled until only the glow of Maua's eyes glared like a beacon through a storm. Yatzil snatched up her spear, lunged, and thrusted it through Maua's chest.

CHAPTER TWENTY

Branches dragged against Yatzil's bear arms, nicking the points of her crown. Her anger blurred all ahead with tears. No breath came from Maua, nor any struggle after the spear had pierced through. Yatzil dared not look back, running further and further north, searching for the sound of Clod's axe against tree limbs, or the pop and crackle of Sute's lightning. She felt ill somehow, as if killing Maua had been the worst thing she had ever done.

There was no sign of the others until eventually she found herself swiping at air. Branches rested in bushes and hung on low missed ones. Yatzil picked up her pace, hoping to find them soon and have Haseya soothe the ache of her heart. She stopped short of voices ahead, Clod's thinly feathered head visible through the trees. Yatzil drew in a deep breath, thawing, her frozen tears fell from her cheeks. Maua may not have been the one to finish their fight, but it felt as if the ice pear had pierced Yatzil's heart, tearing through it, ending hope and life in an instant.

"If Maua cared for me enough to hasten my child's forma-

tion, then why threaten Mau-hig-seya? Why not come to me
with her worries?"

There remained an emptiness in her despite the anger
surging within her belly, as if she had lost someone closer
than family. Tremors ran down her legs, both her knees
ready to buckle. A face appeared between downed branches.
It approached slowly and was hard at first to distinguish but
she knew it didn't belong to the person whose words
tormented her. *Don't let it haunt you.* Hands reached and drew
her close, the embrace filled her with a strength she desired
to banish away.

"I can guess you have brought our group down a
member." said Sute, the words colder than the snow at their
feet. "I'm sorry for your—"

Yatzil pulled away, staring down Sute. She clenched her
teeth and let out a scream that brought Haseya and Clod
racing toward them.

"I wanted ... so much to love her," Yatzil cried, "and have
what I never understood with Flor."

Yatzil collapsed to her knees, ignoring the looming faces
over her. She yanked off the iron feathered crown of her
position and threw it aside. Sute removed the hardened
expression from her face and embraced her again. Yatzil gave
in, resting her head against the young queen's chest. Haseya
glared down at her, then crossed her arms, and mushed her
lips together.

"I told you not to let it haunt you. I've never heard of any
woman loving another, but Maua must have meant more to
you than I thought."

The softness of Haseya's furs pressed against her cheek.
She wanted to return Haseya's embrace but hid her face in
her hands. She wondered if the same disappointment she felt
had been like Ahigan's after she had abandoned Amteer. It

must have been close, but the long white feathered nol had been stronger and with difficulty had learned to forgive.

"I had wanted to give it time yet her every choice... I did not know how to feel."

A slight ruffling brought down the shield formed from her hands as Clod picked up her crown.

"I never liked her."

Everyone turned to Clod, but none gave him a flustered look as in the past. Yatzil rested her eyes on his bandaged fingers.

"And you were right not to," Yatzil sighed. "I wished to aid her from the beginning. Now all I desire is to move forward." She eyed Haseya then Sute. The bolts running down the queen's cheeks changed to a shade of yellow. "And I know where next we must go. I am sorry, Queen Sute. I have delayed your wish to seek news of home."

Sute folded her arms as they stood, barely able to meet Yatzil's eyes.

"I will manage as I have in parting from my son. Let us proceed."

"Are you sure?" Haseya pulled from the sack on her hip Ahigan's smifta. "May we rest, Queen Sute? It—"

"I said let us proceed." Sute snapped. "The sooner we overcome the border the closer we will be to finding our fourth woman."

Yatzil nodded, not wishing to argue. And though she had discovered her will to live had made her more powerful, to challenge her brother's wife wasn't something she wanted.

"Put the smifta away, Haseya." Yatzil rested a hand on her shoulder. Haseya stared for a moment, perplexed, putting their shelter away. "Let us proceed until the next morning has come."

THEY HAD MADE it to beyond the border wall as the midday bought forest and their trailing footprints to full light. In the distance was a barren lakebed that had been full before Ahigan's death. Yatzil ran her fingers over his tortoise shell at her hip, deciding to conserve it a bit longer like he would. She eyed the white clay jugs on Clod's back and was unsure how long their water may last.

Sute frowned as she unwrapped his bandages. She had finally stopped her relentless march after they had bled through. His cuts were deeper than Yatzil thought. And as Sute held his fingers her own glowed. Clod let out a growl that disturbed the trees, sending birds fleeing south. Red smoking calluses replaced where the cuts had been. Sute took a handful of snow and ran it over his fingers.

There appeared to be an unspoken friendship between the queen and the now fully feathered head giant. Yatzil wasn't sure whether it was from when she had saved his life, or the tomb being constructed for his father by Sachihiro's stone masons. The more she thought of home the more an emptiness plagued her for being parted from Mau-hig-seya. She could have spent more time with her but worried the Highnonstar had desires to come south.

Snow scattered and clumps of dirt flung as Haseya backed from their growing smifta. Yatzil hesitated at the need to tell her what Maua had said. Of how the northerner threatened to claim her daughter's life, but the words tasted bitter and so she swallowed them to forget it ever happened.

"I forgot to return this," Haseya slipped Sparron's knife from her sack and held it to Yatzil. "I think I'll be safe with how angry your brother's wife is."

"I agree. Although..."

"Although what?" Haseya asked, the knife still in hand.

Yatzil sighed.

"I have stolen from her what I once desperately wanted. What I still want. To be home again."

Haseya kept the knife as the falling snow eased away to a chilling breeze. Beyond the distant dried lakebed, a glow marked where they meant to go next. A glow eagerly matching the sun pressing upon Yatzil's cheeks.

"I want to tell you a story," Haseya said, pulling the drawstring of her sack closed. "It's one many my age weren't allowed to forget. Before any of us were born, thousands of nescarans and raton fought on that lake." Haseya pointed as Clod left to find firewood and Sute removed her crown and entered the smifta. She gave Yatzil a stern glare before her long dark hair tumbled over her shoulders and concealed her stiffened lips. "Queen Aagono had killed all but the Nemamoon from your dream and the Palenore were spreading like the Giftnos. It took our ancestors a year to push them back. Many needed to leave family …, especially their babes to the safest places they knew."

Yatzil folded her arms. An invisible grip wrapped its fingers around her heart. Haseya raised her chin with the tips of her fingers and smiled. She sniffed back sadness, seeing where the old woman's story was heading.

"Many nescarans died in that lake and many more raton did when only they could help the Nemamoon imprison the First Son and Daughter with their Palenore." Haseya swallowed, as if her next words were poorly seasoned dried meat. "The … Nol were freed soon after. We are great warriors, able to forge the strongest weapons, but everyone else was given greater power."

Yatzil embraced Haseya, hoping to steady her shaking from the great surge of icy wind against their cheeks. She swallowed, afraid that those fleeing to the Gaping Mouth under her rule were in danger.

"I am sorry. I wish our people were blessed with more power."

"I." Haseya gave Yastil a squeeze before she wiped fresh tears from her eyes. "I let myself get caught up in history's choices, my child."

Yatzil removed Ahigan's tortoise shell from her belt. Now seemed best for its use as Haseya failed to clear her throat. After a quick swig and worried thanks, the old Nol spoke again.

"That lake feeds the west's rivers. Many dead nescarans filled it and after their family's said goodbye, the raton melted them to feed the west."

A shudder blended with a burst of heat down Yatzil's spine. She pictured what must have been millions of her people made formless, and the millions more forced to move on. She hoped Mau-hig-seya wouldn't have to do the same for her.

"Sute is right to go without rest."

"She is," said Haseya, filling her bottom lip with her tongue then letting it deflate. "If I was made out of a storm's anger like her, I'd be in the north by now."

Surprise washed over Yatzil's face to find the story her father had told was true. *"They are power within flesh,"* he had said. *"To anger what can shatter stone with a clap is unwise, and if you fight one, may your steps be swift."*

"We shall have to be wiser."

"Why so, my queen?"

"Because if another Lijani cannot be found, and we anger my brother's wife ... Nema is lost."

CHAPTER TWENTY-ONE

Heat pressed against her skin like a guard not permitting entry. Yatzil had taken Sute's advice with hope that a dragon could be found. Her hand ran over the ancient, dusty wall that outmatched Niev's own by sheer height. It acted as a guide to the Blastdooru gate from the coast where her last breath of ocean air had been taken. Sute was slower in her strides, and Yatzil believed it was the wall which by her tone in suggesting it in previous days, left the young queen feeling closer to home. When the young queen had suggested their route, Yatzil had mentioned the rumor Haseya spoke of, that dragons hid upon the Lid. To this her brother's wife said that she was taught the thunstruck language at a young age and would speak the ancient tongue if they found a dragon.

Yatzil's mind drifted to her dreams of late. They brought her to the noble's villa, to Maua on her knees pinning her pale green top since given a new purpose. She wanted a piece of Flor to protect Mau-hig-seya as if she were still in Niev. It was still home no matter her banishment, or its tradition against showing the mercy. The top's silks were rough from her journey south, but it had brought Yatzil luck. Yatzil kept the remainder of its frigagator teeth in a pouch on her belt.

She sifted through names for her daughter to replace the one shared with Maua. The road along the wall was smoother than the dry, rooted terrain from nearly two weeks ago. A name reached her lips as Yatzil raised Ahigan's tortoise shell to them, sensing its near emptiness. The name wouldn't be made the same as most nescaran names, but with her child far from her arms, she did not care. *Yat-hig-seya*. She smiled at how it sounded.

A shallow lake lay at the base of the Lid like the one Ringna had been captured above. A quick glance at the sky increased the pain she did not miss in her eyes. There was uncertainty within her that Ringna lived. None of her brethren patrolled the skies since they had left the south.

She went to ask Clod to aid in refilling his father's tortoise shell. A faint rattling whispered to her ear before she shook the jugs. Two of the three were less than a week full. She peered over her shoulder, spotting a red pyramid shape. There was a large dark mass before it and an even larger one Yatzil thought to be a man.

"To cover," she said. "Everyone."

They headed for the fallen and jagged woods to their left. Yatzil reached to remove her crown but realized both her and Sute's rested in Haseya's wagon. The weight of Yatzil's had grown unbearable and Sute worried both crowns may draw attention.

The rattling grew in pitch as patches of barren branches shaded them from the Highnonstar. Yatzil ducked behind some brush, worried that Sath had taken rest. Or with the First daughter unable to use Amteer to find her had Queen Aagono gone after the one keeping Nema alive. Sute focused on the shape ahead, her eyes widen, releasing long bolts down her cheeks.

"It's one of my people," she said, fear heightening her voice. "Though if my judgement deceives me, he has killed someone close to him."

"Wait." Haseya gaped. "How do you know?"

Yatzil found the shape was much closer when she focused on it again. It was pulled by a crimson hornbull large enough for Clod to ride. The bull had red close-cropped fur and a long sharp horn upon its brow. What it pulled looked more like a bate-nich farmers storehouse than a wagon. Sute's breaths increased, making Yatzil worry how dangerous was the man whipping the reins? He had puffy cheeks, tiny sparking eyes, and robes blacker than darkness. A red breast plate with a black dragon head emblazoned on it dangled from his chest, spewing gold lightning. There were ornately painted barrels tied to the wagon's sides, doused in dust from the road.

"When a raton marriage falls to ruin its stronger partner drains the weaker of all energies," said Sute. "The stronger partner grows in not just grief but girth too."

"No one should do that to their wife," Clod growled. "I'll make him pay for it."

Clod burst from his hiding spot. Yatzil frosted and climbed after him. The stranger leapt from his wagon and landed with a heavy thud. He was taller than expected as Yatzil called after Clod. Lightning skipped off the iron of his axe as the two giants locked fingers and wrestled each other for dominance. The stranger knocked Clod's axe from his hand with a jolt, sending it hurtling into the woods. There was a faint whimpering below the anxious bleats of the hornbull.

"Stop this foolishness, Clod," said Sute, firing a long booming lightning bolt.

"Do not let off another bolt or..." The stranger's voice trailed off, as if lost, his expression went from rage to confusion. He threw off Clod, only to be assaulted again. "The palenore will know of our location."

Yatzil made for the wagon's rear as Clod struggled to throw the stranger over his shoulder. There was a door with a small window where the whimpering grew louder. Yatzil climbed a narrow set of wooden steps below the wagon's door. A lightning bolt narrowly missed her chest.

"Keep away from there," called the stranger.

She ripped open the door and her heart stopped at a random scraping against the wagon's floor. Yatzil had heard such a sound before but against stone. A pair of glowing ember eyes shrank back from her. It was another, older, Lijani. Her braids were partially withered. In place of pointed fingertips, the Lijani held a dagger with a red gem pommel, black hilt, and sharp diamond blade.

The commotion outside had stopped as heavy footsteps sent her eyes toward the light. A great shadow filled where her silhouette lacked girth.

"The fight is over," The stranger's voice thrummed. "Tend to your nol, Storm Queen, and leave my wife in my care."

"Why keep her hidden?" said Yatzil. His face was clearer to her memory, though she was unable to believe it was the same man.

"I mean no disrespect of any kind. Allow me to calm her, and I will tell you why."

Flesh replaced ice as she released anger and sadness from her face. He made it to the ground to allow her to join the others and then climbed into the wagon. The stranger was deep within the wagon before she could say a word, whispering in a Lijani she didn't know. But when he had spoken to her, it was as if he was not the criminal or commoner Yatzil believed. Haseya rushed to her with Sute whose hands trembled, and chin was pressed to her chest.

"He keeps a Lijani captive yet says she is his wife."

"The northerner is as he says," said Sute, folding her hands as if afraid of something. "My father learned what the Lijani favor most among themselves. Companionship. So ... he wedded their leader, Busara, and opened our borders to the northern sisters. That man is ... my father."

Yatzil gulped. She had not seen King Inazu since he had come to make peace when the moon was in the south. The wagon creaked, letting off a whine as the king brought out his Lijani queen. All but Clod gasped for her face was like Maua's.

"I am not the first Lijani you have seen." said the queen, standing firm with thick bark on her face and hands. She wore weathered flowing red robes with a hand stitched black dragon wrapped about her narrow abdomen. The spikes along its back were sharp and angled, lined in solid gold. "Who was this girl and how did you come to know her?"

All remained silent until Clod's immense shadow passed Yatzil like a cloud summoned to form a storm. She reached for him, wanting to be the one to speak first, yet a great pain snared her tongue. *How do I tell her what Maua said?*

"You kind of look like her." Clod grimaced, then turned to King Inazu. "I hope she's not going to try and kill us."

"My apologies, Father," said Sute, stepping forward and giving a bow. "He does not understand our ways and attacked you for them. We... We had a girl we trusted ... even—"

"Loved." Yatzil interrupted. "I cared for her but every decision she made was strange. She ... threatened my child's life before her end."

A jolt of fear ran through everyone as they focused on her.

"Find your axe, Clod." Haseya hissed, storming past Yatzil. "We're going back and making firewood out of that bitch."

"There is no time," Yatzil grabbed Haseya by the wrist. "And I don't wish to look upon her face again."

"I must agree, Storm Queen, and I will pardon your nol," said the king. "It does not aid to move forward if you take a step back."

Yatzil raised the owl's eyes upon her, hands to him and, struggling to keep her composure. All she wished was to move on to the Blasdooru gate and end Highnonstar. Yatzil noticed the palenore dagger wasn't in the Lijani's possession.

"How did you come to have a palenore dagger?"

"And where," said Sute, keeping still like a tree. "Father is your personal guard?"

Queen Busara sighed but her husband answered.

"The palenore came soon after we received it," he said. "The dagger was sent as a threat before the Highnonstar left many blind. I have commanded all in my service to protect our people while I seek nescaran aid, Storm Queen."

Yatzil took in his words eyeing Sute. The young queen remained bound like a tightly knotted rope. A warm breeze brushed Yatzil's cheek, worsening the heat. She fixed her gaze on the Raton king and let out a breath.

"My brother will help you," said Yatzil, nervousness filling her throat. "If you wish refuge in Niev, I must teach you the entrance dance and you must wear the sacred glyphs of the Four upon your stomach."

Inazu nodded, gesturing to the wagon with two fingers thicker than her own. He gave her a suspicious arch with his eyebrow as they maneuvered behind the wagon.

"I have known your near silent pain." he said, removing his breastplate and hanging it on a hook near the wagon's door. "I have three loyal sons with mothers wishing them to take my throne. I gave each wife love and share of power, yet it was not enough."

"I gave her freedom and a purpose," Yatzil replied. "I ... do not wish to speak of it."

The king nodded and peeled back the battle licked layers of his robes. There was a foul smell about him that might have churned her stomach, but much weighed on her mind. A large patch of dark gray hair nestled above the king's immense belly.

"There is much space for the glyphs you spoke of," he chuckled. "Though if danger stands before me, less will be had with use of my bolts."

Yatzil smiled as the king's stomach rumbled with his laughter.

"You become like I remember through battle?"

"And with great speed." said the king, slapping his gut, sending ripples across it.

Yatzil's face went sour as she recalled the moves Flor had made her practice. The question she needed to ask clung to her tongue. She raised her tattooed hands to her head, but when her eyes met his again, the deep thunderous laugh he had been belting ceased.

"I need your queen. The last Nemamoon came to me in a dream and only by each kingdom's dance can we create another moon and defeat the Palenore."

"This is a great request of me." King Inazu refolded his robes across himself. "I have not known such devotion from anyone. Beyond of course, my own daughter."

Yatzil concentrated on the wagon for a moment, wishing she had never met Maua. *Does he know how fierce such devotion can be?* She returned her focus to Sute's father. He folded his arms and seemed to be thinking to himself as lightning cascaded down his swollen cheeks.

"I shall keep her safe the best I—" She panned her vision to the trees lining the road. Their leaves were faded, other trees stood barren and bent, "can, but it pains me to be around another Lijani, but I must put Nema over myself."

A smile peered from between the king's cheeks. It was slightly bitter but only just as he revealed his stomach once more.

"You are more like your father than your mother gave credit for." he chuckled. "Now. You have a dance you must teach me."

THERE WAS no one so large and light on his feet as King Inazu. His eighth attempt at the dance meant to please Niev's guardians was precise. Yatzil had no doubt Clod was outmatched from the earlier fight. The nol giant kept his distance after finding his axe, and he realized, as he returned with it, his misjudgment was his own fault.

Yatzil described every glyph to the king and traced them with a finger on his stomach. He ignited his finger and drew them out, wincing, but promised Raton royals were taught from a young age how to heal small wounds. It gave an explanation for Sute's healing skills. Yatzil sensed Queen Busara's gaze as the king slipped on his robes and breast-plate. She swallowed, dreading the queen's jealousy before refusing an encore from the king.

The king left her for his queen, allowing Yatzil to release a shackled breath. Yatzil went to make certain the food Sute's father had given them was secure to Clod's back. He nudged her behind him when the Lijani fixed them with another gaze. It was softer than the firm tug Yatzil gave the ropes of their replenished water jugs.

Sute approach her father with yellow lightning in her eyes. The young queen bowed, restraining her emotions like she was a nescaran noble girl. The king raised her to full height and brushed away the lightning from Sute's cheeks and embraced her. Emotion swallowed Yatzil's heart like a starving toad, a plump fly. She could not recall when last, she had embraced her father, but if she were able, it would have been out of sight of others.

Drawing in a deep breath those in her group followed her. She heard King Inazu's hornbull bleat as the wagon sped south. The rattle of the wagon's wheels faded, replaced by faint sobs from Sute, muting their lifeless repetition.

Yatzil hoped no resentment existed between Sute and her stepmother. The Lijani spoke to the young queen with a monotone voice, not relenting in her focus on Yatzil. She remained thawed, wanting to trust a woman she wasn't sure was any different than Maua. Yatzil pulled a chimry from a pouch on her belt and popped it in her mouth. It was from the king's wagon, and she had never seen one since they grew in the distant north. It was sweet with red and green swirls over its skin, possessing no seeds. Such fruit was a gift King Inuza could enjoy by sight since no raton partook in food.

They were soon at the Lids base, within a stone's throw of the lake, but to her surprise it was half full. She pictured Sath upon her feet as her hopes soared of the goddess dancing again. The trees were arranged upon the Lid like separated encampments of travelers. Clod pointed to an overhanging tree with multiple levels of branches and higher and lower canopies thick enough to house his father's smifta.

"We should camp under them, my queen." said Clod. He leaned close and whispered. "I don't want the stick queen in my father's smifta."

Yatzil peered over her shoulder to Sute. Sute no longer wept but listened to her stepmother speak of what sounded like her brothers. A small smile smoothed the crinkle of Sute's lips as her brothers resisted the Palenore. It made

Yatzil's heart leap to see someone in so... She turned away and looked upon Clod, burying a feeling that may further cause her pain.

"I will permit her the shelter it provides," she said, frustration intensifying her tone as Clod sneered. "Trusting her is not what I want but if I don't how shall another moon be possible?"

"You're thinking like a queen, and that's good," said Haseya. She had been preparing the smifta, planting it in the ground. "You have been since wanting to make up for before, but I have to agree with Clod."

"I can make my own shelter until I earn your trust."

All three spun, Haseya clamored to keep a hold of the smifta, and Clod grabbed the shaft of his holstered ax.

"Good," Clod said.

Sute narrowed her eyes, their lightning turned a faint shade of red.

"I promised your king I'd protect you, Queen Sute," said Clod. "I barely know queen thorn bush here."

The Lijani queen gave a deep throated laugh.

"I am beginning to wish I had not agreed to this." She turned to Yatzil and aimed a bark crusted finger. "You lead this group, Storm Queen. I agreed with my husband of its urgency and need for my dance."

Yatzil nibbled at the inside of her lip. She clung to the wish to part from her pain and live up to King Inazu's words. The budding leaves from the trees were plentiful upon the Lid. And then it came to her, something that may remove some weight from her shoulders.

"Do you help us, Queen Busara, for Nema, or to preserve who you care about most?"

As if having an epiphany, Sute stepped away from her stepmother. A half sneer contorted her lips as she stood beside Yatzil. Yatzil had to know if Maua's selfishness was in all Lijani. If they desired companionship and were willing to go to great lengths for who they loved, did this woman have the same drive. There was hesitation with each second the queen remained composed. Her lower lip edged out of place and then retreated under its partner. Slowly, Busara shut her eyes and opened them with a faint, unsteady flash. It was as if Queen Busara were about to weep, but Yatzil crossed her arms. Her patience had gone dry like her skin.

"I help to repair Nema."

CHAPTER TWENTY-TWO

The smifta was left up to Yatzil to bring down and its inconvenience for her to carry. But what kept Yatzil from appreciating the darkness of its inner walls an hour previous was Haseya not being at her side. The old Nol raked dirt and leaves from her gray feathers. It sprang out frazzled like the look Haseya traded with her. *She understands my trust in Queen Busara.* Yatzil grimaced. *Yet acts as if I had gone against my better judgement.* Some relief filled her to know Clod had stayed with Haseya while both slept under the tree Sute called a zei.

Scratches and tings against her breastplate doubled the struggle of stuffing the smifta in her belt. With a grunt, she managed it, then peered to find Clod and Haseya leaving without her and the other royals.

"The woman you call Haseya will have to trust me before the struggle we have ahead," said the Lijani queen. "I remember Nema's creation and when Lijani herself danced me into existence."

Yatzil and Sute stared in shock at Busara, Yatzil struggled

to keep her jaw from dropping. The queen smiled as all three picked up their pace. A deep throated laugh left Busara's lips.

"I appear young because Lijani wished for it," she said. "I was of her First Couple for she wished two women to aid in Mutafakara's existence."

"You must know then," said Sute. "If we have the strength to defeat this First Daughter the Storm Queen spoke of."

They were gaining on Clod and Haseya and the road along the wall had ended with overgrowth blocking further travel. Faint wagon tracks led from where Clod unhooked his axe and readied to swing.

"Your blade will be unnecessary, giant," said Busara, raising a hand in protest. "I will clear what I made to protect my husband." She slowly waved her hands then returned her brightening eyes to Sute. Faint scrapes against the dirt combined with whining branches, slowly revealing more road to travel. "I met her when she was your age, daughter. I do not know if we can defeat her, but our dances will create another moon."

Relief washed over Yatzil like the cool waters of a midday cleansing. The relief compounded as Haseya turned back to her with a smile.

"Why did you sleep away from me?" She watched Haseya approach. "I know you understand my decision. Are you angered by it?"

Haseya threw back her head and let out a raspy laugh.

"Oh. No. I didn't want to be jabbed by her feet," said Haseya. "Maua left scratches on my legs."

Haseya chuckled, raising her hide dress with its beads around the trim. Tiny cuts ran up and down her legs, but the rest disappeared into her boots. Busara and Sute smiled at this as another sensation of relief ran over Yatzil's chest.

"I'm too old to worry about someone being like another I don't like."

"I am glad you feel this way," Yatzil winced. The smifta's needles jabbed her leg. "I want to move beyond the past."

She struggled to slip the iron needles from her lumao. Haseya helped her ease the shrunken smifta from her belt and offered her Sparron's knife. Yatzil took it from Haseya's hand, peering down at her leg. No blood seeped into the fabrics of her lumao. She stuffed the knife in her belt.

"I believe that's a good idea." Haseya tilted her head to her then whispered. "I bet she doesn't kick in her sleep anyway."

BEYOND THE REACHING grass and over extended tree branches upon the road faint voices arose. Instead of Queen Busara clearing their way, the group climbed the Lid until within sight of the gate, hiding behind what wooded area was untouched by the remains of a battle. Palenore lay dead around them but there was no raton. Clod slumped down behind the base of a tower. Yatzil settled behind a thick mesh of dead bushes above him. She watched him get ready with his axe. The tower was like a smoking crown, its bricks scattered across the Lid.

The Blastdooru gate stood tall across from the domed surface of the Lid. Its every level was manned by palenore, making Yatzil wish she were wise in battle. Under the gates pointed archway a door lay many feet away, cracked and bent inward. Its underside was plated in rows of red dragon scales.

Yatzil peered over her shoulder to a moon shaped boulder further up the Lid. Haseya was safe there with Queen Busara, but for the first time, as ice replaced her flesh, Yatzil wished the old nol could join the fight. Their race long ago to save Amteer had proven Haseya was swift, yet to have her at risk offered too much uncertainty. And as she formed an ice spear its chill brought her focus back to the gate.

A heavy scraping joined the groans of what she counted to be a fifty palenore. They pushed with combined might the fallen door. Above them, the gate's Keep had red tiled roofing carved in diamond shapes and layered like a dense forest. The palenore were armored in fine dragon scale, patrolling the Keep's multiple levels that reached out to either side like giant claw marks. They were armed with bows and full quivers of black arrows. The shoulder plates of their armor had curved black spikes and upon their captains' quills no red could be seen through countless black rings.

A slight wisp brushed her ear, carried by a warm breeze. In the days leading to the present, Clod had taught her what he knew of winded words. It was an older nol, difficult at first to use, but the need for it was necessary. His words were, *"The men pushing the door don't have armor, my queen."*

Setting down her spear, she cupped her hands to her lips and said, *"But there are ones with armor to protect them. I shall be fine, but you can be harmed."*

Clod smirked at Sute, relaying what was said. She shook her head then whispered to him. He grumbled and cupped his hands again. *"We need the stick lady to join us."*

Yatzil frowned at the thought of leaving Haseya vulnerable. She eyed the palenore carrying long thick ropes to the door, to drag it. She noticed its hinges were melted. Hesitation gripped her as she observed how bent the door was, as if some great force had smashed against it. Yatzil gulped, then shook off her reservations and decided to take a chance, knowing Haseya knew how to stay hidden. She waited for another breeze then cupped her hands to where Haseya was. Yatzil gasped at a tap at her shoulder.

"Can you aid us against the palenore?"

"I will try," said Queen Busara. "I was brave for the first time in centuries when I was here."

Busara's braids curled up from her knees, thinning. Yatzil felt the need to comfort her but firmed up her chin.

"I need you to do so again." Yatzil said, giving the place Haseya hid another look. "We need you to aid Queen Sute against those archers."

Queen Busara glanced at the Palenore upon the Keep. Her eyes flickered like dying embers as her lips trembled.

"I will tr—"

"Please be better than those who broke my heart." Yatzil couldn't contain it anymore. It snatched her breath away as she failed to compose herself. "You are her elder and know what she has done. Be better. Help us."

The queen turned away for a moment, shuddered, falling silent as her hair released its leaves. She faced Yatzil again with her eyes filled with light. Bark broke away to black mist on her face, vines slithered from the queen's sleeves and low collar. Yatzil backed away and snatched up her spear.

"Let us go then." Busara hissed.

They dashed down the Lid joined by Clod's heavy foot falls. Palenore lined the Keep's higher levels along a black wood railing. Its posts were mounted by spiraling dragons spewing lightning. Sute scattered many on the Keep's lower levels with red clawing lightning bolts. Captains shouted to the unarmored palenore below to ready themselves. Yatzil's eyes widened as their mouths cocked open, flame churning behind their teeth. She threw her spear, piercing the shoulder of the closest man. He toppled over driving off his brethren with his flames.

A yelp rang out as pale flesh met Clod's axe. Yatzil smacked her fists together as the Lijani queen engulfed frightened palenore in vines. Arrows flew overhead, one nicking the end of her spear, another sliced across Sute's arm, but she waved for Yatzil to continue the fight. A Palenore charged as Sute's lightning cut through a row of archers. Yatzil threw her spear, striking the man down before her brother's wife could react. Those on the Keep scattered from the fight sending a jolt of relief through her, but shouts snatched it away from the gateway. She glanced at Queen Busara to find she was holding her own with eyes burning bright.

Amongst rising dust and screams she found Clod alone beside the fallen door. She leapt upon the door in a sprint. She shielded her eyes as a great flame soared. Yatzil dove on her stomach, her breastplate scraping wood as the flame passed over her. Its heat was too much but she refused to thaw. A heavy iron thud sent vibrations to her knees as the flames vanished.

"No!" she screamed.

Far from her, Clod collapsed to his knees, roaring and twisting, cloaked in flames. He gasped and reached and clawed toward her. The flames robbing his glaring eyes of clear direction until all his great strength was ... spent, and he surrendered to the heat.

CLOD'S HANDS lay outstretched but the life once within him was gone. A scream she barely heard amongst her grief rang out. Yatzil crawled toward him, ducking low of a torrent of flames. It was cut off by deafening red lightning and hissing, whipping vines. A shout came from ahead and high above only to be silenced once her fingers slowly turned to flesh to hold Clod's hand. Half his face rested on the ground with his eyes shut and the feathers of his head like burning grass.

Swift faint vibrations rushed across the door joined by gasping sobs. She felt fingers at her shoulders as if they were pulling her away. Yatzil resisted, shut her eyes, and screamed. Yanking at the laces binding her breastplate, her fingers fumbled but were calmed by Haseya's.

"Let me, my child."

Great heavy breaths leapt from her lips, watching Haseya swiftly unlace the breastplate of gray whale bone. After a moment, the warm metal against her chest was gone. She whispered the Four's names, demanding they make this all a dream, but they told her, soaring in a ring within her mind, resurrection was a magic no one possessed.

All care remained out of thought the longer she focused on Clod's darkened, smoldering body. From the corner of her sight palenore laid torn or burnt beyond recognition. She smiled quickly, struggling to cradle her friend's hand. Even in death it possessed great might. She had shaken hands with him once after she had taken the arrow for him. The rage she had been raised to show, but felt guilty to display, fueled her heart the longer she looked upon him.

Yatzil strained to lift even his thumb, to hold it close, to promise to turn them south and head forth to remove Queen Aagono from this world. She closed her eyes at the thought but then remembered what Ahigan had said. The palenore soldiers had killed Clod and not the First Daughter's own flames. She understood finally that only someone directly involved can be held to blame for the pain to follow. If the First Daughter were to answer for any crimes beyond placing Nema under her feet, it was for helping Highnonstar possesses Amteer.

Haseya held Yatzil close. Clod's thumb fell to pieces in her hands, revealing bone thick as iron.

"He was the best of us," said Haseya, dropping beside her. "Clod never apologized for who he was. I'll never give up…"

Haseya covered her lips and slammed her eyes shut, sobbing, unable to finish, but Yatzil knew what she meant.

Queen Busara rested her hand, returning it to its original form, on Sute's shoulder. Its bark screeching against the queen's armor, her glowing eyes a faint orange. Yatzil clenched her teeth, tempted to send them all from her sight and take on the First Daughter alone. It was unwise though, to put aside their mission, and she was not of great enough power to fight Queen Aagono alone. Her grief made her eyes and nose run swiftly like the Wrinkled River.

"You are right, Haseya." Yatzil rubbed her face, struggling to bring herself to her feet. The heat zapped less at her strength knowing they had to move on. "We must never submit, yet how shall we bury him."

"Though he did not trust me," Queen Busara said. "I will use the roots of trees to part the dirt and allow him to be *buried* as you call it."

Yatzil rested her eyes on the Lid's climbing dome mass, and then to Busara. The queen backed away, leaves falling from her braids. Yatzil considered how someone Clod never liked would dare make such an offer.

"Allow her to do it, my child," said Haseya. "Kindness can come from more than just friends."

"But…" Yatzil remembered what King Inazu had said, then of how forgiving Ahigan had been long ago. "Do you know what traditions the nol perform for the dead, Haseya? I know only the royal way if Amteer were to die."

"There's no ceremony," Haseya ran a finger below her eye to catch a tear, "for nol outside the royal line, but a feast is what honors our dead best."

Yatzil embraced her as tears ran over the canals that were Haseya's wrinkles. She turned her thoughts to what remained of the Keep. Scorch marks blackened where palenore lay, flames danced on the ends of splintered railing. Its vastness must have held food if the palenore had taken it.

"Do what you can, Queen Busara," said Yatzil. "I trust you."

Queen Busara smiled, leaves blooming in her hair.

"I will not leave you disappointed."

She swallowed with a nod, moving to the end of the door, leapt from it, landing in upturned dirt, but decided then, instead of collecting food for the feast alone, to ask for Sute's help. With sorrow slowing her movements, Sute rose to join her. Her thin cut ran across her right arm, sleeveless, like the other, with no cold to fend against. Sute covered the cut as it sizzled and seeped light.

They took slow steps to the Keep. Yatzil peered back after a few moments, finding thick roots breaking from dirt and gathering Clod like a great hand as other roots parted dirt for a pit. Haseya's calls for the queen to be gentle reached her ears, and unlike Maua, Busara was a better listener. This she grew a little suspicious of with a royal being ordered around by a non-royal. *It is different with Haseya and me. She is a mother to me.*

Entering the Keep, stairs to the left and right lead up into its inner barracks. There was a long tunnel ahead that cupped the light at its end like a rabbit trapped in a giant's grasp. Sute chose the staircase to their left. Yatzil made sure again that Haseya was well.

Up turned roots acted like a wall around a long open pit. Yatzil smiled, and followed Sute up the steps, finding Haseya shouting orders parallel to Busara over the pit.

"I have chosen well in trusting Queen Busara," said Yatzil, noticing the sizzling again before they met the first landing. "How can we heal you?"

"We are both unfortunate in requiring someone with unique healing gifts." said Sute, referring to Niev's glace healers. "A hizunu is needed if this were worse, and all of you would have to leave but this is small enough to manage."

They stopped on a second landing, taking in the well-placed brickwork of the tunnel floor. Its dustiness enhanced their footprints with its thickness.

"Why must we leave?"

Sute grimaced, rubbing her eyes. Their light removed the darkness Yatzil found her feelings trapped within. She yearned to embrace her brother's wife like Flor had when hope had nearly vanished. But unless under specific circumstances a queen of Niev was to be touched only by her... Sute pressed her lips against Yatzil's, their warmth almost unbearable yet exceptionally soft. They left as quick as they had come as Sute drew her in close. Yatzil had to resist, to remind herself the queen belonged to Sachihiro.

"Because if not, I will be energy with great and terrible reach."

"You are Sachihiro's bonded one." said Yatzil, resisting the urge to press Sute against the railing and thrust her tongue into her mouth. "You have given him an heir. I do not understand."

"I love him, and my son is most precious to me, but I desire you too."

Yatzil searched for reason, picturing Sachihiro high upon his throne. She imagined Sute in his arms instead of her own. Yatzil leaned in close, asking, begging herself to resist. Sute kissed her cheek and guided her up the steps until they met a hall with rooms on either side. A set of steps climbed up its middle to the rooms above. Yatzil felt her heart pounding against her chest.

Sute pulled aside a curtain, leading her in, and slowly undressed herself. Yatzil thought of what they had come to do, but for some reason, as Sute untied the knot of silk at her side, she found herself aiding what she knew was desire. A glimpse of light came from a window high above a bed. It reminded her of what needed to be done, yet soon, Sute's fingers were gliding down her unclothed chest.

A slow pull undid the knot binding Yatzil's lumao. Its bronze squares covering soft silks clunked on the floor beside Sute's discarded dragon scale breastplate. Yatzil ran her thumbs down Sute's smooth stomach. She hesitated when her fingers found the knot meant for Sachihiro. *This is.* Her fingers undid the knot, and before she knew it, dark hair surrounded by pearl flesh pressed above what wetness surfaced between her legs. They collapsed upon the bed, Yatzil on her back, gazing upon Sute's eyes, finding herself self-conscious of how she smelled.

"You have come this far," said Sute. "Much concern clouds my mind, but I trust all will be well if we allow ourselves peace."

"I... I am unsure but..."

Yatzil kissed her, pulling the young queen's flesh against her own. A hand ran over the scar on her temple and into her hair as both traded positions. She weaved her fingers through Sute's and tried to lock them but winced. A jolt of pain went up her arm giving a reminder of the diamond fang's mark.

A faint voice drifted from the window, growing in strength, clearing her mind of wanted pleasures. *Haseya.* Yatzil rolled off Sute, leaving the queen breathless.

"We have delayed our search." Yatzil stood, out of breath, staring down at Sute, half wishing to ignore Haseya's calls. "Dress yourself before she finds us."

Sute sat up and narrowed her eyes, their lightning fading to a faint yellow.

"I agree," she said, slight disappointment in her tone. "We must find what we can for Clod's feast."

The queen crawled off the bed then snatched up Yatzil's

lumao and handed it to her. Yatzil reached to take it, but Sute cocked her hand back.

"But remember the nol woman does not disapprove of your choice of love making. And though she is like a mother to you, I do not care what she thinks."

Yatzil gasped, grabbing her lumao from the queen. A need to frost crept through her ice blue skin.

"I tell her everything." Yatzil dressed, looking Sute up and down then tossed her clothes at her. "I should never have given in. Maua's betrayal haunts me and now I have betrayed my brother."

Sute dressed slowly for some reason, giving Yatzil longer looks of the queen's curves. Yatzil edged a foot forward, every breath catching, but then it ended as applied her breastplate.

"You have done no such thing." Sute pursed her lips. "Only I will be to blame if we survive what is to come. He knows I always make the first move. He knows how you care for him."

They left the room following the long hall past the staircase. A rankness slithered into her nostrils like a host of chamber pots had been left filled. Once they made it to another set of stairs, she hesitated to gain Haseya's attention. Haseya was nearly to the tunnel as words reached Yatzil's lips, but Sute called out instead.

"You worry more than any rutoe should." said Sute, eyeing Haseya kindly as the old nol climbed the steps. "Trust in what I have said and let us honor our fallen friend."

CHAPTER TWENTY-THREE

They searched the Keep, feeling doubt in their hearts of finding food for Clod's feast. And along the way, Sute had gone from the bold girl whose lips felt as if they had never left Yatzil's, to one near in tears. The armory had been tossed about and looted. Statues of her father in elegant robes and in more slender form were melted to his feet or smashed in a training area fit for one hundred men. Every door except the one they found at the Keep's highest level was smashed inward. Yatzil took a deep breath, peered back at Haseya and Sute then lifted the door handle.

Scaping footsteps came as bile fowled her tongue and the others gasped. She swallowed it, gaging as the bark of Busara's face went pale. Yatzil turned back to the room's long wide table of thick dark wood. Limbs, bones, and organs covered it with small clouds of flies overhead. The room must have been for holding council in time of war. Ornately carved chairs lined its sides, their cushions ripped or missing. A chair possessing a tall back to it at the end aligned with a skull. Haseya screamed. The skull had long black feathers and a small, sheathed knife lay next to it, crafted in the nol style. Haseya clasped her hands over her lips and raced to it. Yatzil noticed the knife's brow tie was a shorter one than on Sparron's. There was writing down its hilt she couldn't make out.

"They are worse than I remember!" Queen Busara cried, black mist tears running down her cheeks. "The palenore once fed only on the will of Highnonstar himself."

"They are monsters." Haseya held the knife to her cheek. "They... They killed my daughter. This is her knife."

Yatzil felt her knees buckle, their strength fleeing her as Haseya placed the knife in her sack.

"How can you be certain?" Yatzil turned to Queen Busara. "If this was because of my wound in Niev. I am sorry."

Queen Busara readied to speak but Haseya cut her off.

"I know it's hers. Her name is on the hilt. She was always losing what I gave her. Nol return what doesn't belong to them." Haseya sighed, then met Yatzil's eyes. "Our king is no longer a Nol, Yatzil. I don't blame you for being wounded."

Yatzil went to Haseya's side, avoiding puddles of blood and scattered feathers toppled by Haseya's agony. She felt as if she were the mother now, bringing Haseya close. It made her miss Yat-hig-seya more just to think of it. Tears ran down her cheeks as she noticed both queens had left the room. Perhaps they wished to give them time alone, or maybe to search for what may aid in the journey ahead.

It was quiet with just the two of them amongst what she believed had been Haseya's village. Her heart dropped to her stomach, hoping against every thought splashing upon the shores of her mind that Sparron had escaped somehow. The little girl was brave, possessing the talent of a meal maker, and had been fortunate to miss losing her sight to the High-nonstar.

They were down the hall, ready to descend the worn

wooden steps. Yatzil slipped Sparron's knife from her belt and held it to Haseya. Emotion sealed her throat, the knife seemed to triple in weight the longer she possessed it.

"I cannot carry this knowing I can no longer keep my promise."

Haseya kept her eyes from Yatzil for a moment. It was as if what they had found had drained her of all strength. Yatzil readied to speak but instead replaced the knife in her belt.

"I can only hope what you said isn't true." Haseya met her eyes, rolling her lips inward until they quivered. "I'm tired of loss. I'm … just tired."

Yatzil was tired of loss too, desiring more than ever to end the lingering chaos around them. Blame no longer clung to the brickwork of her mind like an unwanted weed for her past selfishness. No matter her past choices, Amteer was no longer the man she knew. His new queen had seen to it.

"I understand." She took Haseya by the hand, finding some resistance. The old Nol huffed but gave in. "Let us rest in what rooms remain untouched."

"I can't imagine there is any."

The stairs were narrow and made several sharp turns. Yatzil kept her grip firm around Haseya's hand and listened. Haseya spoke of Busara being gentle with Clod's body. Of how the dirt buried him like it had a mind of its own. And though it was out of place in such circumstances, Haseya mentioned their supplies beyond the Keep.

"I'll retrieve them," said Yatzil. "You need not worry."

They were at the hall leading to the barracks. Yatzil rubbed her brow of sweat as both descended the steps. It was warmer within the stone walls of the Keep than outside. The room she and Sute had intertwined within gave no breeze from its window. She kept that moment to herself, not ready to burden Haseya with more troubles.

"You do that, my queen." Haseya said, a small smile

crossed her lips. "I have missed what a bed feels like. You nescarans truly know comfort."

Yatzil held her close, stifling a chuckle. Some tiny measure of happiness was always under the surface with Haseya. They parted. Haseya pinched her nose to search for a room. Yatzil went further down the hall and found both queens had settled in. Sute gave her a nod before lying down. Even on the narrow frame of the bed to the left, Queen Busara was already asleep. Yatzil rubbed her nose then whispered, "thank you," in nescaran. She pulled the curtain shut, finding Haseya's words had rung true. Kindness can come from more than just friends.

IT HAD BEEN a long time since last Yatzil could remember being alone. She hiked up the Lid, strain grasping at her calves. Sharp edged rocks and steep incline jarred her into full awareness. Her sandals found the crunch of dirt more than the fine green of grass. It weighed her heart with disappointment, speaking of Highnonstar's doings. She had wept after returning home. The temptation to do so now played with her eyes, but like loss, tears were something she no longer wished to experience.

Far down the Lid, Clod's graved rested untroubled by the heat. She intended to visit it once she had retrieved her group's supplies. Dirt gave way as she maneuvered around the moon shaped boulder. She forced herself against its surface, spotting the water jugs. She weaved her fingers through each rope that bound them. Yatzil lifted them, dirt crumbled and hissed, a weakness gripped her knees. She fell against the boulder, shutting her eyes, strain escaping their sealed lids. The mass of the boulder was uneven, and in places pitted. Its weight though not upon her shoulders felt like the responsibility entrusted to her.

"It is too much," she said to herself. "I do not know how our combined dances shall do what Sath says."

She looked to the trees and bushes. Their green was all but gone. The task of finding a dragon to travel further east weighed on her and she wanted to believe their journey would lead them to one. She gulped at how large the one in her dream had been. Sute had made mention before the battle if you met a dragon's eye, lighting was certain to strike you dead. They both possessed potential to be struck down, but not by a dragon's lightning.

Sachihiro's face surfaced in her mind as sleep crept through her body. It was twisted in disappointment at the truth she felt compelled to tell him. She remembered once loving him like she had Maua and to great measure Flor. Yatzil pushed that feeling to the past. It could not be used to play on his sympathies if she told him of her and his queen. If he were to raise a hand and give the order for her execution, nothing could compel her to plea for mercy. *I do not deserve it.*

She spat at the thought of allowing Sute to touch her ever again. Resting her head against one of the sacks at her side, it was not love with Sute, nor the possibility for it with Maua. Sleep laid its fingers on her eyes as they shut. A need to be alone a little longer was no great demand of the women she hoped were asleep.

"You have come so far, Yatzil."

Yatzil gasped, bolting upward. Thick clumps of wet sand clung to her skin as she found herself on the shores of another dream. Ahead, the shoreline went on for miles, visited and abandoned by surf. She made it to her feet, sinking with the tide, the waters nipping at her balance. Another wave licked the hem of her lumao. Yatzil pulled herself free and spun to find Sath lying on her back. She forced herself to her knees beside the goddess, blood coated

Sath's lush lips. Her long black skirt was tattered from flames. Sath pressed the folds of her shawl to her chest. Another wave reached her scalp, darkening her hair to that of a night sky.

"You must stay strong," said the Nemamoon. "What you see is my future if you allow doubt and grief to slow you."

"Is... Is this by Aagono or Highnonstar's hand?"

Sath groaned and clasped her chest, taking Yatzil by the hand. Her grip was weak and clammy as if this was not a dream. But with there being no sign of Highnonstar, and the trees with the island's center untouched by heat, there was no doubt this was a dream.

"It was my daughter's." The goddess clenched her teeth. "The former Storm King will take no part. Highnonstar made one great sacrifice for her, and it costed him."

"And... And now she has him back against Amteer's choice."

The Nemamoon shuddered into a coughing fit. Yatzil noticed the burns against Sath's skin had left her brittle and slow, chipping away at her memory of how graceful Sath had once been. She frosted her hands to numb the pain of each burn but drew back, realizing it was useless.

"I admire your wish to sooth me, Yatzil." Sath smiled. "Yes. Highnonstar has returned. But not as the First Son, Aagono knew. Possessing someone has never been tried. It has turned him mad." Yatzil brushed Sath's hair from her eyes. Another coughing fit took hold of Sath then released her. "You must not doubt yourself. If you do, the others will follow and Highnonstar will lay barren Nema."

"Is there no other way?"

"Yes. Although I am unable to absorb the no longer existing parts of myself which defined Nema's vast kingdoms."

Yatzil was growing impatient as she tried to banish doubt from her thoughts. Grief kept its grip upon her heart, but she took a deep breath and released it.

"I shall never see my daughter again if I cower. Will I?"

"Nor" said the Nemamoon, lifting her head from the sand, "will you keep your promise."

EVERY BLADE of grass was green, and the trees hid the light with leaves. Yatzil scrambled to her feet, frosted, and heaved all three jugs and three sacks over her shoulder. It was as if the Nemamoon's final words had given her new hope. The jugs were heavy, and each sack was light. The sacks' lightness lessened the hope driving her steps, knowing it would not make a worthy feast for Clod.

She stopped within inches of his grave. Its sides were lined with thick roots like a coral reef she had once seen as a child. Until his death, Yatzil believed that Clod had been invincible.

"Trust was your greatest challenge. I was uncertain you would overcome it with me, but I am honored you did."

She rested the supplies at her feet, thawed, and then presented the owl eyes upon her hands above her own. Slowly, Yatzil whispered Urra, the Four's goddess of war. She prayed the fiercest of Urra's panthers would protect Clod as he ascended to what the nol called Peaceful Thunders. The panthers were the goddess's servants and were assigned this position after the Four were remade into owls. Where Clod's soul went, all nols did, and she prayed that what remained of Amteer had gone there too.

Ice replaced flesh. She shouldered her group's supplies again. She bit her lip and wondered if they would consider what they had worthy of their friend. *He deserves a feast to surpass any I have attended.* Yatzil drew in a deep breath then headed for the Keep.

She had made it into the barracks. The foul smell of waste was gone. Searching each room for Haseya, Yatzil guessed she had tired herself by removing the chamber pots. Faint laughter touched her ears when at the final room. She rested the supplies between two doorways and pulled back the curtain.

Tears formed in her eyes, flooding them to see Haseya holding her granddaughter upon the bed. Ice receded until she was flesh and blood. Smiles formed on the faces of grandmother and grandchild, but Yatzil couldn't accept their joy. *Does she know of her mother?* She did not know why this thought had rushed to her mind. Every thought should have been in relief rather than worry. The little girl's feathers were longer and messy compared to when Yatzil had last seen her. Her legs hung well over the bedside and were slightly bruised. Sparron smelled of a foulness, like an animal and there were healed blisters littering her feet.

Yatzil stepped into the room, a small smile formed across her lips. Sparron leapt from her grandmother's lap. She kneeled to embrace her and noticed Haseya had given Sparron the beaded dress she had been sowing for days. It was soft, possessing a natural sheen, made from fur of a green boar. The fur was the rarest to be found in the south for hunting such a creature required keener sight than most possessed.

"Grandmother says you are going to find a dragon," said Sparron, pulling away and giving a blank smile. "I only know about them from stories."

Drawing the knife from her belt, Yatzil held it gently by the hilt.

"We are. And believe I have a promise to keep." She searched the young nol girl for the scabbard containing the likeness of Amteer's mother and found disappointment on Sparron's face. "What happened to the beautiful woman meant to protect your knife?"

The little girl sighed, giving Haseya an unsure look,

receiving a gentle nod before trying to contain her tears. Yatzil set the knife aside, and Sparron spoke of what she feared had come true. Ahigan's nomadic people, and Haseya's village were captured within sight of the Gaping Mouth and robbed of all possessions. But before it had happened, they had received winded word of a large mass of nol holding strong in the mine. It was a whisper of hope Yatzil held close to her chest.

When both village and nomadic people marched south to the capital, Sparron said, the white toothed cities were black and smoking. Sparron stopped to rub her nose and wiped her eyes of tears.

"The First Daughter lives in Wolfstrong with the mean king." Sparron sniffed. "I think I know him, my queen. I saw somebody on an eagle like him, but he was nol. Is he the same one, grandmother?"

Haseya hesitated but kept her lips sealed, shaking her head. Yatzil dared not say otherwise. Sparron shrugged, speaking of how the cities were raided down to what explained the hand cast chamber pots within the Keep, and that she had been spared to empty them. She finished with the long march east and the dead left behind. Sparron fell silent, keeping her eyes on her knife lying beside Yatzil.

"My ... mother wanted to go with you like I did." Sparron's lips trembled, each breath quick and short. Tears ran down the little girl's cheeks before facing Haseya. "That stupid mean king is the one I saw isn't it, grandmother?"

Haseya readied to speak but couldn't.

"Isn't he?" Sparron screamed. "He's who commanded us to go west, right?"

Yatzil remained silent knowing it wasn't her place to speak. What anger filled so young a girl was stronger than even her own. Haseya finally answered but it was like the words were from someone begging at death's feet.

"Yes, my child. He is the … king I told you about."

"He is who I left to save," said Yatzil. "I failed. And for that I am to blame for your mother's death."

Yatzil sank to her knees, feeling ashamed within Sparron's gaze. She wished to frost and hide her emotions but knew cowering was the worst she could do. All the blame she had banished from her heart returned in full force. Yatzil eyed the knife at her side, contemplating handing it to Sparron. The girl's fists were bawled, shaking, and teeth were in such a vice it was too painful to imagine. Putma had pushed her to similar extremes. But it was Yatzil, Storm Queen of the nol and princess of Niev that had begun her people's suffering. And without understanding until now, hand in hand with Queen Aagono.

"I want to leave, grandmother."

Haseya gasped.

"My child. Our queen isn't the reason the Highnonstar killed our people."

Yatzil breathed easily upon hearing this. Sparron leapt forward, slapping her, and screaming through a storm of tears.

"I was there when you tricked us. I know what you did. You left to get what you wanted. YOU LIED TO ME."

Slap after slap hurt more than any pain she ever experienced. Haseya climbed from the bed, grabbed her granddaughter, and fell back, holding the last of her family against her chest. The scratches across Yatzil's face felt deep and countless. She touched them and winced, wanting it to continue, believing she deserved such pain. Yatzil glared at Sparron's darkening face, its youth warped by vengeance.

"I never lied." Her throat filled with emotion like water in a drowning man's lungs. "I wanted to save him, to tell our … king, how sorry I was. But if I had stayed with him there would be no doubt the same horrors would have happened."

Yatzil picked up the knife and offered it upon her palms like a guard to a king about to deliver an execution. She deserved death from such rage breaking through Haseya's grip. It was a choice she would have been given if a traitor were placed at her feet. Sparron broke free, seized the knife, and raised it. Haseya screamed as if she had been stabbed. The sound of it frightening Sparron. The knife fell and clunked on the floor.

"Goodbye, grandmother."

Sparron fled through the door. A hissing followed the little girl's footsteps until there was only silence. Yatzil gazed up at Haseya, her tears mudding the old Nol's stern expression.

"I'm sorry. I gave her the choice I thought—"

"You should not have given it," Haseya said. "Nema is still in trouble, and if she had killed you, I'd have lost you both."

Trying to rise, Yatzil eyed the knife as it lay between them, tempting her, begging her to answer for her selfishness. It rose from the weathered floorboards. Haseya held it at her side and then threw it out the window.

"You were stupid. No child should ever be given a choice like that."

Yatzil's head shot up, glaring at Haseya, as if by instinct. Confusion struck her mind, sending the room spinning for a moment. *I would have. And if I refused banishment was certain no matter my birthright.* Yatzil stood but her knees shook. It was not the same for children of the west.

"I agree," she said, turning away. "I shall go find her then."

Haseya snatched Yatzil's wrist forcing them face to face, the old Nol's was clenched like a spent cloth. She stared into Haseya's eyes, confused by such an action that kept her from finding the one rutoe that hated her most.

"I told her our plans." Haseya released her wrist. "If

Sparron doesn't want to be alone she will find us. nol can sense family from great distances."

Yatzil rubbed her tears away and searched her mind for how best to apologize. She hoped Haseya would still share a room with her, but when she wiped her tears away, and her lips had parted, Haseya silenced her, for the first time, with a raised hand.

"I'm not angry. I am disappointed you allowed a child to decide your fate when she has lost almost everyone she has ever known. You have forgotten what Ahigan taught you."

"I—"

"Rest here, my child. Wake me when you want to find that dragon."

CHAPTER TWENTY-FOUR

A feast for Clod's passing was harder to imagine. What sound had followed Sparron's footsteps was a water jug and sack of food, robbing them of bread. There remained only a sack of chimries leaving all in her group disappointed. Yatzil felt even more disappointed as she handed Haseya a chimry. Sute sat across from her, yellow merged and parted with red in the lightning of her eyes. Haseya folded her arms, mumbling to herself. Busara raised a chimry to eye level, admiring at it.

They were within a room that gave a view of the tunnel. In its corners dust laden dragon scale armor stood assembled like guards. Yatzil guessed the room must have been left alone for the Highnonstar and his queen. Its floor was of finely finished wood, and they sat around an ornately carved table on low cushion armless chairs. At the table's center rested what remained of their chimries.

Haseya had given no instruction before they had begun. No special words, blessings, or rituals to be performed. But when Yatzil had woken earlier Haseya was lying in the bed across from her. She allowed herself to breathe easier for it, knowing she had not been forced to sleep alone.

As they ate, and spoke of Clod's final act of bravery, Yatzil told them when their task was done Clod deserved a grown name. It left the room in a shroud of silence, tears surfaced in Haseya's eyes and yellow lightning met Sute's fingers as she clasped her hand over her lips. Busara wiped away black mist from her cheeks, holding a chimry between her fingers.

"Queen Busara," said Yatzil, in a dignified fashion, though her idea tore at her. "Maua could form fruit by the tip of her finger when I needed it most. Can ... you perform such a task?"

The queen placed her last chimry in her mouth and swallowed it like a serpent a mouse.

"The girl must have been well fed for one attempt. I will need all the food we possess." She eyed the remaining water jugs like they were well preserved palm wine. "And one of our two water jugs to replace all of what we have eaten on this journey."

Yatzil finished her chimry, eyeing Haseya. Haseya wiped her lips and crossed her arms. A racing feeling went up Yatzil's spine, waiting until everyone's eyes were on her.

"Can you fill the sack upon the table?" Yatzil said, finally. "I do not know if a stream exists on the Lid's other half, but if so, I shall take the risk."

Haseya shot her a glance, wide eyed and nostrils flared.

"You can't take that risk."

"I have no need of nourishment, Storm Queen," said Sute, eyes electrifying with boldness. "But the trees are green once more. I'm not certain if a stream upon the Lid exists and have not been beyond my husband's palace until recently. Take the risk. We have little choice."

Yatzil tensed her fingers over her knees, every inch of her filled with uncertainty. She delayed them with further silence. It was true a risk had to be taken. She ran her fingers through her hair and found it dry and tangled.

"We shall take the risk." She met Haseya's eyes. "And I shall keep to Ahigan's words and hope you are right about Sparron."

Haseya glared at her for a moment and then eyed the near empty sack. Ten chimries remained and only one of the jugs was completely full. A smile formed on the old nol's lips.

"Do you not know this already, my child?"

Yatzil turned her head, unsure of what Haseya meant.

"A mother is always right," Haseya said, smiling. "Grandmothers most of all. Take the risk and if my granddaughter returns, we will teach her what you have learned."

A spell of laughter leapt from Haseya's lip, and soon, Yatzil felt the need to laugh too. Her eyes watered from it, chest aching. The two queens failed to seal their joy away with a hand over their lips. She pushed the sack to Busara. The lijani sprouted red flowers with orange pistils in her hair. Yatzil went to retrieve the lesser filled jug for the queen but then the light through the window slowly began to fade. Darkness claimed the room as the others noticed, suspicion rising in her like a growing flame.

"The Highnonstar is leaving the west." Yatzil gasped, bolting out of the room. "Please let it not head south."

Her heart thundered within her chest as she raced down the hall and to the balcony above the barracks. She took two steps in place of one down into them, footsteps pounding above her. Haseya popped her head over the railing and called her name. There was no time to stop and before she could recognize how far she had gone her fear had placed her in the tunnel.

"Storm Queen!" Sute screamed. "Wait."

Yatzil traced Sute's voice to the wide window high above.

"I must know where it is going."

She refused to stop, wishing the air wasn't so dry, yearning to move swiftly on an iced path to the buildings coming into focus. The light was all but gone and all she could summon in her mind was her daughter's glowing eyes and tiny face warmed in layers of furs. Her brother frosted and in full gray whale armor upon his throne. A thought surfaced above those she loved. Queen Aagono had found out somehow that Putma had lost hold of Sachihiro. It would explain what Putma meant about only North and South.

Every breath grabbed at her belly as echoes of the women she had left behind chased her. Finally, the tunnel had ended, the Highnonstar was distant and moved at a speed the moon had never achieved, moving further and further east. Homes possessing red tiled pyramid roofs blocked most of it from view, filling her line of vision with a climb to their height that proved the east, Crizalbolt, was one vast city. Yatzil dropped to her knees, the brickwork beneath them aged and cracked. She struggled to regain spent breath, knowing her child was safe. Her brother and his child too had been spared the Highnonstar's wrath. But her dream of Sath near death was coming closer to being fulfilled.

Footstep filled her ears, falling silent as she listened and rub her eyes and brow of flooding sweat. A familiar touch rested over her shoulder, and another engulfed the other, but the second was slender. Yatzil was too upset to shake off Sute's kind gesture.

"We must find the dragon quickly or," She looked at them then returned her attention to what remained of the High-nonstar's light. "My last dream shall come true."

There was silence amongst them before it was broken by Busara's heavy breaths. Bark fell from the queen's face shattering on the brickwork, giving way large sections of black swirling mist upon aged cheeks.

"It will happen as before, Storm Queen." Queen Busara said. "It will come to mother against daughter."

Yatzil rose, as Busara explained it took Sath's need to absorb what remained of the nemamoons to dance the first son and daughter behind the moon, imprisoning them and their armies. Yatzil opened her lips to speak but fell silent. From what she had learned from Busara and Sath, it explained what Aagono had said of killing Nescara.

"We can no longer delay." Yatzil turned to Sute, storing away every bit of regret for the moment. "We know my brother and our children are safe. Let's continue north."

Sute turned south as the shadow from the wall blended with the sky. The sky turned black, broken by the glittering of stars. Everything was clearer and the remnants of the Highnonstar was all but gone.

"If we stay close to my ancestors wall it will guide us to the Lid like it did before."

All agreed, though as much as Yatzil wished to be there in an instant there were alleys, streets, and homes to slow their way. She turned back to the tunnel. Two dragons, like the one of her dreams, climbed the arch formed from the tunnel entrance. They locked claws and roared angrily. Busara gave her a curt nod then proceeded down the tunnel. Yatzil called out to her but like the others she realized their food would not grow itself.

<hr />

THERE WAS no return of Sparron, no patter of youthful feet within the narrow streets of what her lamodun called Crizal-bolt. Regret plagued Yatzil the more the young girl remained absent. Abandoned carts half filled with straw, shuttered homes with black painted doors and every sixth structure or so there stood a Singlebolt temple with lightning shaped pillars surrounding opened entrances. Yatzil found herself jealous for all nescarans. They were permitted to worship at the very base of the Four's temples, being unworthy of entrance since none were royal or of devout servitude to the owl goddesses.

Haseya kept close to her, admitting how she hated the closeness of their surroundings. Yatzil let out a breath to calm herself. A screech came as they stopped between a temple and a tall structure littered with outreaching balconies. There was a scent from it that made her feel like being caressed by someone beautiful, another screech sent her racing for cover. A swift, immense shape blotted out the stars, then vanished.

She rubbed her brow finding sweat didn't dot her hand. The air was cooler and though it would ease travel, suspicion churned in her belly that time was running out. Her group went further, bearing sacks on their shoulders of what Busara had grown. Yatzil carried one filled with bate-nichs. Haseya had hers filled with apples. And for the queen herself chimries.

Everyone flinched at the second screech. The stars vanished for seconds, the mass of another eagle came and moved on. Yatzil peered over her shoulder, resisting shielding her stomach. Sute moved at a slow pace, the weath-ered ropes keeping the water jug to her back dug into her palms. The queen's boundless energies kept her upright, untroubled by the weight she carried, but the task clearly annoyed her.

"There is no need to come to aid me, Storm Queen." Sute pulled away as Yatzil frosted and reached to help her. "You had best keep to such a form if hiding is your intent."

"I am hiding nothing," Yatzil whispered, biting her lip as she met Sute's narrowed jolting gaze. "It bothers me nescarans are forbidden to lay with someone not theirs, and you are—"

Smash.

"Cease your worry for Singlebolt's sake."

Haseya and Busara rushed up to them. Yatzil stepped back, palms raised, wishing she had left Sute alone.

"I love my husband," said Sute. "He is more than I can ask of any man. I wish to love you too."

Yatzil had nothing to say, no anger to release, finding that like herself, Sute had been driven by lust. Her flesh replaced ice, watching what remained of their water run down the street. The risk she had chosen to take doubled and Sute wanting her only made it worse.

"Your brother will make sure you stay banished," said Haseya, leaving Busara behind in her shock. She narrowed her eyes, the redness given by the Highnonstar had all but gone from them. "I know she's beautiful." Sute smirked but only Yatzil noticed. Haseya threw up her hands to regain her attention. "But why? We won't be able to see Yat-hig-seya again."

Busara cleared her throat before Yatzil could answer. Thorns formed in her braids, her eyes flared an orange and yellow like miniature suns.

"You have to mend what you have done, Sute, but we must stop Queen Aagono first."

"I have told the Storm Queen I will," said Sute. "I will make my husband and king understand…"

The ground shook followed by distant screeches, drawing everyone's gaze to the immense green mountain that formed the Lid. A storm churned and faded over it, its thundering and lightning like one of her dreams.

"We shall settle this later." Yatzil took off, covering four to five bricks with each stride as ice replaced the flesh of her tensed body. "Busara is right, we must defeat Queen Aagono first and the dragon we need is in danger."

The others raced behind, each home and shop grew lower and more at an angle. The city expanded up onto the Lid. As they passed under a pointed archway a lightning bolt cracked so loud it rattled the trees ahead. Overgrowth slowed Yatzil's pace as thunder roared. She quickened it again, spying Sute beside her. The queen glared at her, silent, a snarl raced then vanished across her lips. Yatzil shook her head at their misjudgment.

The storm boomed and expanded the higher Yatzil went, but then, as she ducked low branches and leapt over roots Sute stopped in her tracks. Yatzil stopped too, her legs aching, every breath a chore to regain.

"It cannot be," Sute said. They both scanned the skies, neither felt the ground shake. "It cannot be dead. So, few remain, and they hide so well."

Yatzil searched the Lid to find Haseya had outpaced Busara. Her lamodun had taught her dragons merged with clouds and required tribute of criminals to be appeased like the Urra for an audience.

"We'll never make it if it's at the top," said Haseya. "It's too far."

"No listen." Busara made it to Yatzil's side, her flower petal ears twitched. "The rumbling is close."

There was a faintness to it, dirt shifted under her feet, and a warm breeze came and swept over her ankles.

"It's this way," said Yatzil.

She chose a slower pace and returned to flesh form. The Lid was in darkness with the clouds hiding the stars, and the Highnonstar too far to reach it. Busara had spoken yesterday of the palenore being unable to see even with stars out during night. Palenore required their leader's brightness unlike the rutoe of Nema. Bushes clung and tugged Yatzil's lumao, skimming the skin of her calves. The air grew cooler with time and the further she went the damper the air became. She felt the strength to form an iced path return.

Vibration raced under her feet before she crouched behind a thicket. Far ahead torches were spread in a great, long shape barely hindering a black and gold scaled dragon, possessing narrowed eyes the size of a ship. Haseya crouched beside her. Her jaw had dropped to as low as Yatzil had ever seen it. Sute and Busara joined them before she returned her amazement to the dragon. *There was no way,* she thought, *a creature of such size could hide within the clouds.*

The dragon loomed at a distance, large enough to rival one of Niev's guardians. Its hot breath blew her hair back. Circling its mass torch light reflected upon its gold scales. Its head was covered in an array of jetting black lightning bolts and its eyes were a solid green, absent of pupils, eyeing its captors. A forest of tall zig zagging spikes lined its back. But what unsettled Yatzil most was the countless thick chains pinning it to the ground.

Haseya nudged her as a screech sent a rush of heat down her spine. Eagles of great size circled overhead, their beaks large enough to gobble her whole.

"There are too many, my child," said Haseya, shuddering in her words. "How will we free the dragon now?"

Yatzil clenched her stomach and shielded it, wanting to crawl behind a tree and hide. Ten eagles soared above by her count, doing so in a widening formation, sporting metal tipped talons. The palenore upon them were surrounded by feathers and wielded long shafted spears tipped with diamond points. Flashes of her near forgotten nightmares placed Yatzil upon her back, arms pinned by an eagle's talons. The bird's beak tore at her belly. A grim feeling slithered across her skin. A feel she guessed her father may have experienced before death. She swallowed her fear, refusing to let it surface again.

"We must free the dragon."

Haseya gasped and gulped loudly covering her mouth and peering up to see if she had been heard.

"What?" she said, uncovering her lips. "It'll kill us."

The dragon let out another ground shaking breath as Yatzil eyed Sute. The queen had a foul look upon her face. Yatzil cursed under her breath.

"I must ask you, Queen Sute, to maneuver close to the dragon to calm—"

A rush of wind scattered them amongst the overgrowth. Yatzil frosted as Haseya ran for cover. Lightning leapt from Sute's fingertips. Busara warped her hands, making them thick tree roots, striking like a whip at the palenore's eagle. She stayed with Yatzil, but Sute was soon far off. An eagle swooped down and then flew off to reveal a tall palenore layered in muscles and thick armor. He swung at Sute with his long spear. Her lightning skipped off his breastplate.

Yatzil cringed as another eagle circled close. Her nerves tensed as Busura seized the tall palenore with thick thorny vines. He ripped them off and plowed forward, laughing at Busara's gritted teeth.

"Look out, Yatzil," Haseya cried.

She caught a glimpse of Haseya from behind a tree, a crushing grip tore her from the ground. It flew high, snatching her breath away as she witnessed the others struggling from her hesitation. Haseya called out to her again but then a palenore grabbed her and mounted an encroaching eagle. Fear forced Yatzil to thaw, to give in. A crack of lightning startled her from panic with the eagle swaying left to avoid its red fury. She looked down and saw the tall palenore's head roll off his shoulders.

The eagle's talons closed tighter and tighter, her stomach

pressed and retreated from their grasp. She wished she had kept her breastplate, yearning for its impenetrable fine craftsmanship. The pain was worse than her nightmares. The eagle dove toward the dragon, Haseya's screams tormented her like a stinging insect. *I must not give in.*

Yatzil frosted then smacked her fists together and with great speed the spear shot from the ends of her fists. With a thrust she pierced the eagle's hind legs, loosening its grip. Another thrust was answered with a diamond tipped spear before the eagle lost its grip and she fell. The blade scraped the edge of her shoulder, losing flecks of ice. The glowing burn within her eyes lashed against her cheeks. The dragon grew from her descent, replacing the moment of pain in her shoulder.

She sent her concern to Haseya. The old nol struggled hundreds of feet ahead within the palenore's grasp. Yatzil stretched out her hand, shutting her eyes, focusing on how to form a path, feeling the damp and cool of the air. Ice released from her fingertips, pulling at her bones.

She touched the path's surface with her feet. It was so cold she felt as if she were in the south again. Yatzil kept her fingers pointed and closed like a spearhead. She pointed her hand down but kept her arm straight, her other hand wielding her spear. Haseya was feet below, calling to her, wrestling to be free. The palenore's fingers went to his throat. Haseya pulled back her fist, a strangely shaped object clutched in it. Haseya shoved the palenore off balance. He rolled off and fell, striking, and splitting in two upon one of the dragon's spikes.

"Head for the others," said Haseya. She narrowed her eyes into slits and grabbed the eagle's feathers. "Go. I can fly this bird better than they can."

A turn of her wrist sent the ice path toward the remaining eagles. Yatzil peered back to find Haseya had lost her fear of the dragon, flying down toward it. Her own fear was absent as she harnessed the air's coolness. Sliding onward, she thrusted her spear into an eagle before it could smash her path. Its rider took leave of his senses and jumped but let out an inferno from his mouth. His eagle flailed its wings and smoldered his safe passage to the ground.

Ice touched grass darkening its blades and muddying the exposed dirt about it. Yatzil smacked her fists together and drew them apart to form another spear. Confidence rushed through her like an arctic wind in a cavernous tunnel. A rustling came from her right, but she ignored it to begin another iced path. Climbing once more into the sky another eagle brandished its talons, but she pierced one of them, wedging the spear between two of its toes. Yanking it free the eagle's breast was exposed so she thrusted again, but the bird's size forced her to back off. The eagle collided with another, cut in half from a lightning bolt. Several of the palenore retreated, leaping to the trees as Busara's vines throttled their winged mounts.

Yatzil slid to find the queens. Busara returned to her woman like form, bark and leaves fell from her face. She dropped to her knees before Yatzil's feet touched dirt.

"It is over, Queen Busara," said Yatzil. "You can rest now."

Sute turned to her, parting her lips, but the ground shook. A rush of heat scattered the panicked eagles overhead. Chains thudded against the ground in a storm of clangs. Yatzil's ears rang before they caught a faint shuffling. Haseya waded through the bushes at a great speed, clutching what Yatzil realized had been a key from earlier.

"Tell it I just wanted to help," she said, out of breath and wild eyed. "Queen Sute. Say something."

Yatzil pushed Haseya behind her and leered at Sute. Sute's hair shrouded her face like a thick curtain, dirt and grass clung to the jade squares of her lumao. There was a deep scratch across the gut of her breastplate, and for the first time she was panting. Everything grew dim as Yatzil felt the dragon continue to rise, its size consumed the clouds and stars behind it. Sute swallowed, reciting words in thunstruck faster than any language Yatzil had ever heard. She focused on it, but it was too old and swift. And through the sharp, evenly placed words spoken the young queen kept her eyes to the ground.

"Keep your eyes to the ground before it—" Sute fell silent.

The dragon cocked its head up, opened its jaws, releasing an infinite amount of lightning that made it as if the High-nonstar had returned. The light dissipated; smoke shrouded the dragon's face in a cloud smelling of burnt flesh.

"Do as she commands," said Yatzil, placing her focus on the ground. "Now."

Haseya reflected on Busara who had heeded Sute first. Yatzil edged to Sute's side, realizing for the first time that in none of her dreams had Sath told which island she had been on.

"Tell it we wish to find the nemamoon." Yatzil focused on a patch of grass matted down by the fight. "We do not know where she is."

"I know I-I will. He_ Puh-please. I beg your forgiveness," Sute stammered.

Yatzil couldn't meet her eyes, they remained hidden behind her hair. The dragon eyed them with judgement like they intended to chain him again.

"We must not speak of this—"

"He has sensed what you dreamed but will not carry us."

An unsureness crawled across her skin to learn the dragon somehow knew what the young queen had done. She had allowed it to happen, and to swallow or breath felt as if it may anger the dragon further.

"He knows I cheated on my husband with you," said Sute,

meeting her eye. "I was wrong to want more, to add to your pain."

She thought on Sute's words, closing her eyes to think. Yat-hig-seya surfaced in her mind's eye, forcing her to wonder if she dreamed of her mother or … had the wet nurse she had selected taken her place?

"I forgive you. I am at fault too." Yatzil took Sute's hand and held it tight. "I still feel guilt, but for now, I care more about returning to my child."

They faced one another, embraced, then Sute spoke again to the dragon. Yatzil went to Busara's side as the dragon nodded, the motion unsetting the trees. The short rest had restored the northern queen, but thicker bark had grown over her face and hands. Every braid was as thick as two of Yatzil's fingers. Yet as Yatzil and Haseya aided her to stand, red petal flowers bloomed behind her ears.

"You have made your father proud daughter," said Busara.

The ground shook before Sute could respond. The dragon reached out and laid his hand in front of them. Yatzil helped Haseya up first, then with Sute, aided Busara. A cool breeze kissed her cheek as she followed Sute, telling her to wait, but Haseya was too close to need winded word. And then a small voice caught her attention once she found balance upon the dragon's hand.

"Grandmother."

CHAPTER TWENTY-FIVE

Yatzil ran for the edge of the dragon's hand, calling for Sute to stop it, but an immense storm formed enveloping its spikes until they vanished. She shook off her surprise but lost her footing short of Sparron's reach. She crawled toward the girl reaching her hand out. Haseya dropped beside her with a thud, knocking Yatzil to the side but Sute dropped beside her, halting her struggle. Haseya called Sparron, and the little girl jumped but fell short. Long serpentine shadows reached amongst the flashes of distant lightning.

"I have her, Storm Queen." Busara said.

Sparron shrieked. Yatzil took her hands, and Haseya soothed her, running her fingers over the girl's feathered head. Once Sparron was safe, they moved to within the dragon's grasp, much of its body had vanished within its storm clouds but its head, belly and muscled arms remained visible.

"You've forgiven me?" Yatzil asked, thawing as she regained her breath. "I am—"

Sparron silenced her with an embrace, wind sending her long, dirty feathers into a frenzy. Yatzil said no more, frustration and sorrow drained from her, hushing the raging storm above.

"Can we look at the city, Storm Queen?" Sparron gave her grandmother a hug then faced Yatzil again. "I want to see it."

Yatzil stretched out her hand.

"Yes."

They moved hand in hand close to the dragon's thumb, finding the tops of shops and temples. With the dragon's speed increasing, scorch marks peppered the city. Towers of smoke climbed into the air like circling staircases, eclipsing miles of red shingled homes. Flames fought against streaks of lightning in alleyways. Rebellion had caused the city's outer limits to be abandoned. Far south the city remained untouched, but for how long Yatzil dared not guess. She felt a press against her chest, finding Sparron shielding her eyes.

Entire stretches of homes were consumed by blackness and flame, the breadth of the devastation wide enough to engulf Niev. Sute braced herself against the dragon's thumb, weak in her stance. Yatzil reached out to help but Busara eased Sute down. Rinyu, the raton capital, was in ruins.

"My ... home." Sute pressed her fists to her chest. "How can this be?"

Four towering statues shaped as elderly men in elegant robes were face down within a walled city separated from the rest by legions of scorched zei trees. Yatzil shuddered for a royal to be found face down at death was a disgrace. There was defeat and embarrassment to receive from it. She reached for Sute's shoulder, but the queen cried out in the tongue of her people. Busara held Sute close and stared without aim.

A grand palace lay at the capitals center with towers collapsed and burning. At its center, the palace rose from the immense mouth of a golden dragon, its teeth glimmered, made of silver. The collapsed palace released a tower smoke as if the dragon were alive, clouding the sky ahead in a darkness she feared to be within. Yatzil looked to Sute, and her heart stopped, realizing the statues had been Sute's ancestors.

"We shall punish the first daughter," Yatzil said, the words something she had kept inside for some time. "Can you call to the dragon to fly faster?"

Sute rose, breaking the embrace of her stepmother like a fist the surface of a pound. Lightning formed over her hands, blurring them. Yatzil stepped back as her heart leapt to her throat.

"Yes," Her words buzzed, both eyes merging with light. "But there will be no 'we' after I have given the command." She turned and called to the dragon. It gave a great nod then flew higher into the sky. "The First Daughter has doomed my ancestors and forced my brothers to scatter. I will split her in two."

Yatzil swallowed.

"But if she can make the moon unlike what it once was," Yatzil asked, "then how shall you do it alone?"

"I will find a way."

"Only Sath can do it alone," Busara stood between Yatzil and Sute. "Queen Aagono is older than I am and knows much of Nema's secrets. She and Highnonstar were imprisoned for wanting to bring an end to Nema. And they would have if not for Sath." Busara turned to Yatzil, the flowers weaved amongst her braids wilted. "We are what remains here and now to represent the nemamoons lost to Aagono's anger. I joined you not for my husband or Nema's sake. I did for only I can heal Sath if her daughter gains the upper hand."

"Then," Yatzil gasped. "Five women are needed to save Nema?"

"Yes. Your dream is true in every way. The other nemamoons wished to fight alone and only joined Sath when Nescara died."

Yatzil looked at Sute. Her eyes eased to a soft glow and her hands were visible once more.

"Do you see, daughter, why fighting alone is foolish?"

"I ..."

Yatzil embraced Sute as if the queen were the lost and angered reflection of her past self.

"I believed once I could do what was needed alone, but I was wrong." she sighed. "I wish not to lose you."

Yatzil raised Sute's chin. And without hesitation, nor painful regret of a future that may never come. Yatzil kissed her.

"Together?"

"Yes," Sute said. "Together."

NEMA GREW distant behind them while on the horizon a radiant glow slowly rose. Sparron passed Ahigan's tortoise shell back to Yatzil after taking a tiny sip. She gathered herself into Haseya's arms that were draped in boar furs. Yatzil held it to her lips but did not drink because little water remained in it. Her lips were dry, and constant wind kept her hair behind her shoulders. A day had passed with her sleep coming briefly when long moments of thunderous darkness replaced constant distant lightning. She pushed the cork stopper into it and rested it beside her. Her group sat in a circle at the center of the dragon's palm. Its towering fingers were like faceless guards protecting them from the ocean beyond.

Yatzil asked Sute to plead with the dragon to make rain fall to replenish the canteen. Sute told her the storm clouds were not meant for rain but was what manifested for the dragon to fly.

Her thoughts returned to the island ahead. It was too

distant to fully see, but image after image formed in her mind of a small piece of land. Lush trees filled its center and Sath fought on its shores in remnants of her long skirt and yellow shawl. Yatzil had seen all this in her mind, as if Sath were calling for aid. A bolt of lightning went off nearby, briefly painting her face in light. The ocean swelled beneath them, compelled by the dragon's storm, yet beyond its shifting clouds was a calm and placid sea.

"The dragon must go faster, daughter," said Busara. "I have seen in days beginning, larger dragons cross Nema in less than a day."

Sute huffed.

"I have offered it palenore to feast on if it must fight but—"

"It's afraid," Haseya interrupted. "What else can kill a dragon but a goddess?"

Yatzil frowned as the dragon's head vanished and appeared from the clouds like a leaping fish. Clouds covered its face again, making Yatzil wish Haseya were wrong.

"Are you saying," Yatzil said slowly. "That she killed the others? That the First Daughter is why so few remain?"

Haseya nodded, forcing down a dry swallow. Sparron reached for Ahigan's tortoise shell but was pulled deep into the gray boar fur protecting them from the wind.

"No, my child. We must save it."

"But you are—"

"I'm fine." Haseya croaked. "Though I wish I had a weapon to fight the First Daughter."

Yatzil buried her chin into her chest for a moment, contemplating giving Haseya an ice spear, but remembered when Clod had carried her from the villa. His body had shook, and his fingers had nearly fused to her frosted legs. Haseya's wagon was behind her, stacked with furs sorted by color. Something poked from beneath them. It had a dark color and appeared as thick as her arm. There was a slight bend to where it disappeared into an assortment of green boar fur.

"What protrudes from your wagon, Haseya?"

Haseya turned back. Yatzil moved toward it. It took some effort, but she managed to slide out to her surprise Clod's bow. She handed it to Haseya. It was twice the old Nol's height. Yatzil searched for arrows, yanking her hand back at the bite of a sharp edge. The bow's string was loosely bound around what to her disappointment was two arrows. She slid them out and found they were not damaged. They were long and round by their shafts. Their points spread down into four sharp blades.

"These shall allow you to aid us, Haseya." Yatzil sighed, mourning Clod. "We must hope Clod's arrows shall strike true."

"I… I'd forgotten he had given me these." Haseya eyed how the bow loomed over her. "I used a bow once but not for hunting. Clod was unlike other nol, so I—"

"His weapons are so elegant." Sute said, admiring the bow's smooth surface and its arrows' dark fletching. "We have no use for weapons in the East, but I have wanted to see a nol bow be—"

"I can't use this at all." Haseya scowled. "No one can."

Everyone froze as Haseya twisted her lips from a scowl to a pout. Yatzil had never used a bow nor had any nescaran. She pictured how Clod had pulled the bow's string with ease, remembering the loud twang when he released an arrow. She worried Haseya may be harmed if she pulled the bow back.

"What if you use an arrow like a spear, grandmother?" Sparron took it. Its fletching brushed against her toes. She held it tight, overwhelmed by its length. "I … can use the other … one."

"No, Sparron. I can use an arrow like a spear, but you won't be fighting."

"What?" Sparron's lips quivered. She dropped the arrow, but Sute caught it. "How will I help you? I must, or else, I won't earn my grown name."

Yatzil was taken aback by Sparron's courage. She focused on the light ahead, still distant, but growing in brightness. The dragon stayed on course, raising her hope that it had decided to be brave like the little girl before her. She had denied Sparron the chance to earn her grown name long ago. It was less desperate then, and to earn a grown name a Nol had to be grown in body. The chance to grow older may not come though, and thus, to prove brave with a blade.

"Give her your knife, Haseya."

Haseya spun to her in shock. Sparron abandoned her pout to a smile larger than her face. Yatzil raised her hand as the little girl ran up to embrace her.

"I want you to have protection if we fail." She drew in a deep breath to summon the confidence needed to believe her next words. "But we shall not fail."

THE ISLAND WAS CLOSE, but Haseya had distanced herself after Yatzil's last words. She was forced to squint again with the Highnonstar hanging like a great eye in the distance not far from the sun itself. Their food was spent with another mouth to feed, and Haseya had taken her wagon by pooling its string. It had snapped and whined, shifted, and shrunk, then flew up into Haseya's hand. The old Nol then marched off in her frustration.

Yatzil held Sparron's hand in hers. Haseya's knife hung, wrapped in a torn piece of red boar fur from Sparron's neck. There were flashes in the distance, growing brighter the faster the dragon flew. Yatzil gave Sparron a hug then sent her to be with Queen Busara. She had no real plan but believed her drive to live may aid against Queen Aagono somehow. She summoned the wish to hold Yat-hig-seya again as her motivation, and after some time she found Haseya.

The old Nol leaned against the dragon's middle finger, silent, except for the message Yatzil understood by choosing such a finger. She had secreted such a gesture at Putma when scolded for improper posture at court. *I was different then.*

Beside Haseya laid one of Clod's arrows. She reached for Haseya's shoulder but then withdrew her hand.

"You drag your feet more, my queen." Haseya glared up at her. "Since when I first met you."

"I intended not to surprise you," said Yatzil. "I wished to tell you we are close, and that I hope we are not too late."

Haseya returned to the choppy ocean beyond the dragon's storm. There were more islands aligned with where they were going, like a boundary meant to keep someone from exploring the unknown.

"I'm glad." Haseya faced her, planting the arrow to steady her footing. "I'm not mad at you, my child, only disappointed that you have put a blade in my granddaughters' hand again. She isn't ready for a fight."

"I want her safe. I do not believe we shall fail if we work as one like Queen Busara said."

Haseya sighed and grimaced.

"No harm shall come to her. I promise."

"I believe—"

A force flung them to the ground, sending Haseya's weapon sliding out of reach. The dragon roared and a wall of dark clouds surrounded them, shielding against bright flames. Yatzil covered her ears at a thunderclap and shut her eyes. She opened them to find three faint figures drawing close. Ice ran over her flesh as she stood with Haseya. The others were close, but she took off to where the light had been brightest. Her vision was blurred, and she risked falling, but had to know if Sath lived. Footsteps trailed behind her; shouts grew in pitch with each second her hearing returned.

Yatzil rubbed her eyes as the scent of the ocean filled her nostrils. She stopped short of dark waters; red flashes reflected off them. A crackling, hissing spoke of Busara changing form. Loud, frightening cracks and snaps revealed Sute armed with orbs of lightning. Sute called out to the dragon. It descended, dragging its storms like a long cloak. Yatzil peered down to find Aagono frozen in mid motion, wearing a flowing black skirt and a red dragon scale breast-plate. Her flames roared from her hands toward Yatzil but were stilled, swirling just below the dragon's hand. Something small and star shaped slipped off the First Daughter's head as she twisted to be free.

"We are nearing the island, Yatzil," said Sute. Her voice battled against the roaring inferno. They both steadied themselves as the dragon circled the island. "Sath has stalled the First Daughter somehow."

The dragon neared the sand, but from what Yatzil could see, the Nemamoon was weakening. Sath bent her fingers and planted her feet. Her shawl bound tight to her breasts, and her skirt, black as her hair, clung to her legs, tattered like a damaged sail across two bowing masts.

"Follow me when you land." Yatzil stretched out her hand, releasing a stream of ice. "I must go before my dream comes true."

She leapt from the dragon's hand, finding the lower it went the more its storms faded from sight. Ice jetted from her fingertips in a narrow wave as her feet slid onward. Shouts came but Yatzil couldn't make them out. Blackened trees formed a maze ahead, but no patience was left in her to weave through it. Cocking her fingers upward she sailed over them. Far ahead, Queen Aagono remained trapped, but as Yatzil cleared the island's center a bright flash blinded her. Her vision slowly cleared but she gasped before a wave of flame, its heat licked the very bottom of her ice path.

Yatzil peered back, her breath catching in her throat. The flames vanished before the dragon landed. It took off and circled, conjuring another storm, through the smoke and flame orbs of light shown. She smiled and faced forward, waving away smoke, and then there was a crackling. Yatzil stiffened her fingers to keep the path solid, to not allow the heat to win, but the path gave way.

CHAPTER TWENTY-SIX

She was not dead like she expected, nor had any Palenore come to take her prisoner. Yatzil sat up breathless and found she had thawed. There was no sound of a fight as she ran. The blackened burning trees crackled behind her, joined by crashing waves beyond. She swiped at smoke; the dark sand weighed her sandals. A figure with long red quills glared at her, panting, looming over Sath.

"You should wait for aid before challenging me," the First Daughter said. "Mother will be lost to us soon. If not for her wish to reason, your band of royals and insects might've had her aid."

Ice replaced her flesh for what Yatzil hoped was not the final time. She listened for footsteps and searched for Amteer, but he was nowhere to be seen. Sath reached for her and bled from a burn at her side. Her eyes slammed shut, struggling to speak, but the sea's roar drowned her words.

"Where is Amteer?"

Aagono smirked for a second. Her eyes hinted at disappointment but quickly refocused as if nothing was the matter.

"You still care for him despite severing the connection you both shared? Why bother?"

Yatzil raised her hands to form fists, but the fall burdened her limbs with pain. There was no care left for the man she knew. Finding so many nol made into a meal had ended that.

"Answer my question," Yatzil said.

She kept her eyes fixed, feeling more strength return to her hands as she reached out to the surf retreating from Queen Aagono's feet. But her heart was more with Sath, whose words she could finally make out.

"You must stop this daughter," said Sath. Her voice was hoarse. "You have doomed the world I made for you to live—"

The First Daughter slammed her foot against her mother's wound. Sath screamed so loud Yatzil had to cover her ears. Aagono rammed her heel into her mother's cheek. Sath coughed and whimpered, begging with her eyes.

"Finally, I have silenced you." Queen Aagono's eyes widened slightly. Yatzil spun to find Haseya and the others. "He is ... where I wish him to be." Fear nipped at the queen's words. "Now, I will remove you all from—"

Great fearsome jaws engulfed Aagono, trailed by an immense wall of gold and thunderous clouds. Thunder filled the air with deafening noise. Lightning flashed and dark clouds filled the sky until the Highnonstar vanished from sight.

"You made it," said Yatzil, thawing and embracing Haseya, Sute, Busara and Sparron. "I feared you were trapped on the other side."

"Save relief for later, Storm Queen," Busara said. "We have been given time and Sath is in need."

Yatzil shook her head then ran to the Nemamoon,

clasping her hand over her lips. Sath's breaths were faint with her face swollen, only one eye remained open. The blood had ceased from her burn, but pale veins reached from it in the hundreds.

"Can you heal her as you said, Queen Busara?" Yatzil said.

A roar sent her worries to the distant islands north of where she stood. The dragon was in a knot of its own body. Its storm narrowed, and its throat bulged. Momentarily, light smothered darkness. Every one of its scales grew red hot as the dragon twisted and turned. Queen Aagono appeared to be strangling it from within.

"Hurry!" Yatzil cried.

Busara threw herself over Sath, forming into a blanket of vines, black mist, and raton robes. The change hardened to the Nemamoon's slender shape, drawing in her long black hair toward her face. Black mist rose like steam as ember eyes swirled within it.

"Prepare yourselves," said Busara, in a hollow voice. "I will be unable to help you for some time."

"But we..."

Boom

Yatzil ran to the shore, the ocean's waters running over her feet as she stopped and stared. The dragon fell. A gaping hole in its throat releasing clouds and lightning through a wreath of flame. Tremors ran down her spine as she frosted and firmed up her face, bracing herself. The dragon's body struck the ocean with such force a wave formed, chasing a glowing orange orb.

"Hide, Sparron," said Yatzil. "Wherever you can."

There was no protest, only the rushed steps of a girl, Yatzil hoped may earn her grown name in the next life. She turned back to find Busara's vines had doubled in layers of bright green moss.

"I don't think I can stop it."

"You must," said Sute, taking her hand, wincing at its chill. "You are the strongest of us. I have witnessed it."

The wave gained on the orb, climbing higher and higher. Yatzil strained her vision, finding within the swirling orb the First Daughter aiming her fist directly at her. She turned back to Haseya, the old Nol's face begging her to be strong.

"If I fail—"

"You have no choice but to succeed." Sute rested a hand to Yatzil's cheek. "All you care for depends on it."

She gave Sute a rushed nod, feeling Sute's tense fingers leave her cheek. They had been warm, almost too warm, as if Sute had been prodding her to put aside fear. Yatzil reached out to the towering wall of water, its rage and might could wipe the island clean from existence and swallow them whole. She bent her fingers, strained, and with great effort pulled. The wave remained at its pace, and then she pulled again. It crashed and consumed Aagono, silencing the first daughter's terror. The glowing orb protecting her shattered as a chill bristled Yatzil's eyes. She let out a painful scream, bawling her fingers to fists. A burg of ice formed, gathering the sea at its base. Within the bergs center Aagono reached to the sky, her pale skin and glowing eyes faded like a dying ember and then went dark.

Yatzil dropped to her knees, striking, cracking the ice, trapping the tide. The island's shore was wreathed by jagged icicles. Every breath was a struggle, but cheers kept her from collapsing. Queen Aagono remained without motion, dead she hoped, for the berg of ice was her biggest yet.

A hand rested on her shoulder as she thawed. It was neither warm nor wrinkled but familiar and unreal at the same time. She raised her gaze from the faceless ice to Sath, whose beauty had returned, and her skirt and yellow shawl was untorn, dancing in the wind.

"Come dance with us, Yatzil." Sath offered her hand. "A

moon must be born so the old, corrupted one may fade into legend."

"Is ... she gone?"

The Nemamoon kept her hand offered. An unsureness swirled deep within Yatzil, but she took the goddess's hand.

"Yes," said Sath, holding her hand with a firmness that reassured her. "Now shall we dance."

"Yes."

They joined the others before the island's ravaged jungle. Its smoke rose, twisted, and gathered over the surface of the Highnonstar, but the orb's brightness far exceeded the blackness blanketing it. Sath asked them to form a diamond around her, saying her dance would give the strength not possessed within themselves. Haseya rested her spear beside her, taking a position parallel to Sute. The young queen shut her eyes and folded her hands across her stomach. Yatzil dropped to a squatting position and shaped her hands like panther paws. And like she was the beast during a hunt, suspicion crawled up her back. She made certain the First Daughter was dead, finding no movement. The light of the Highnonstar filled the berg of ice until it was like a yellow flame.

Sath began first, striking her feet to the sand with precision, both hands running down her stomach, and then they leaped to Busara. The queen rooted her feet into the sand, flinging her arms up and allowing them to sway forward and back like branches in a storm. Sute threw up her fingers, taking a step forward, and then back, lightning releasing from her fingers then retreating from Sath's own.

Yatzil molded her face, imitating a snarling panther, but a faint cracking caught her attention. Haseya held her arms up like an eagle's wings. Yatzil crept toward Sath, as if enticed to mate.

Boom

Large chunks of ice flew up and fell, smashing the ice surrounding the island. Queen Aagono emerged engulfed in the flames, her rage sped toward Sath. The flames about her person skimming, melting, and reducing the icy water to steam. Yatzil frosted, smacking her fist together, then gasped. Haseya stood rigged, caught between the Nemamoon and a daughter trapped in a fit of rage.

"Get down!" Yatzil cried, sand slowing her steps. "Please."

Haseya dropped as the others were almost to her. Sath ran to shield her, but Aagono was too close. Anger contorted the First Daughter's lineless face, flames roared from her hands...

"Ack."

Yatzil dropped her spear. Sute's lightning faded from sight. Busara's vines retreated, forming bark laden fingers. Clod's arrow had pierced through Aagono's chest and out her back, steadied deep in the sand. The flames were gone, and with their disappearance, Sath was on her knees, holding...

"No!" Yatzil cried. "It cannot..."

Haseya laid in Sath's arms. Her hands readied as if they still held the arrow pinning a crying, groaning Aagono. The First Daughter clasped at the arrow, yanking, and pulling. Yatzil fought back tears, every part of her was pained beyond reason. She bent to one knee, reaching to hold Haseya in her arms, but the noise was too much. She tore her eyes from Haseya and narrowed them upon the queen.

"You have failed," Aagono said. Her stomach heaved and her toes gripped at sand. "I will remove the arrow and all you from—"

"Careful daughter." Sath peered from Haseya's blackened, motionless face with contempt. "You're trapped without servants or a husband, and I am at full strength. I suggest you beg—"

"Ack," Aagono cried.

Yatzil plunged her spear into Aagono's pale stomach, its flesh pushed somehow against the spears' chill. She caught a hint of boars' meat on the queen's breath. The First Daughter's eyes begged, as if she feared her mother's warning.

"You made this all happen," Yatzil said, as a chill ran over her eyes. Her iced fingers found Aagono's throat. The queen's throat throbbed in her grasp. "My father. My marriage. Using Putma to control my brother. Give me one reason I shouldn't allow Sath to finish you."

Aagono forced a swallow, but Yatzil increased her grip. The First Daughter bunched her face and aimed to spit, but Sath had risen and placed Haseya in Sute's care.

"I can help... Please." Aagono cried. "I can act as if I were Nol."

Yatzil loosened her grip, holding her spear steady. Aagono's flesh seized it and pushed. Regret swelled in the black iris of the queen. Light footsteps came with a scream Yatzil would never forget.

"How?" Yatzil turned and found Sparron on her knees, sobbing, Busara holding her close. "You possess no compassion like them. Nor do you look like one."

"Release me. And I will show you—"

"Kill her." Sparron ripped herself from the Lijani queen's embrace, grabbing Yatzil's spear, pushing, fighting its chill like it were a storm. "I'll dance instead."

Sparron's rage brought Yatzil to her old self. She thawed and pulled out the spear. She took Sparron in her arms and refused to let go.

"Great Nemamoon," Sparron said. "I can do it. I've seen it done."

Yatzil bound her arms tighter, finding it harder and harder to not retract her decision and avenge the nol. How many like Sparron remained in the Gaping Mouth? Haseya was gone from her, just like Clod and Ahigan. Just like her father entombed so far and deep beneath the ground that it seemed like years since the faint *plop* had changed everything. Sparron pushed at her chest. The Nemamoon's contempt was gone from her face. Yatzil bit her lip, unable to decide if revenge was so wrong this time.

"These dances are for birth, Yatzil," Sath said within Yatzil's mind. *"A child cannot do such a thing and the one you hold knows it. Allow my daughter to be what she once was before her hatred for Nema's rutoe consumed her."*

She hesitated. Haseya was gone because of Aagono but with no moon how long would Nema last? She thought of what King Inuza said, of overcoming her worries about Queen Busara.

"Free her."

"No." Sparron turned in Yatzil's arms then punched her in the face. "Let me go, you monster." Yatzil shut her eyes against Sparron's blunt nails. "She took my mother. My grandmother."

Yatzil released her, the pain in her eyes forcing her to narrow her vision. Uncertainty halted the others from following her decision. They watched Sparron bend and seeth, tears blazing trails down the young girl's cheeks.

"How can you do this?" Sparron said.

They looked at her for a moment and then went to work. Part of the arrow's shaft had punctured Aagono's back. Sath grasped near the point, bending it until it cracked from tension. Sparron ran up with Haseya's knife and thrusted it. Yatzil gasped but Sath caught the little girl's wrist.

"You will never earn your grown name by revenge," Sath said, kneeling in the shadow of her daughter, squeezing Sparron's wrist. Sparron cried out and dropped the knife. "I am disappointed that one of nol's creations has not taken heed to her teachings. Yatzil. I request you decide on the punishment that fits this girl."

"She's not my Storm Queen."

Yatzil couldn't take it. Sparron had lost much but losing her kindness outmatched it all. Something she guessed Queen Aagono had lost as Sath placed Sparron's wrist in her hand and then aided the others. The little girl pulled and scratched. The sting from her earlier frustration pained her less than her disappointment. There was only one punishment her lamodun spoke of for such anger and betrayal.

"I am your Storm Queen." Frustration deepened in her voice as she said it. "Every nol must remain trustworthy and strong. You have lost much but it doesn't excuse the dishonor you've brought your mother and … grandmother." She looked at Haseya and couldn't help but wish to grant Sparron's request, but there was nothing to learn from it. "You are stripped of your right to a grown name."

"No, please don't—"

"No act of bravery with a blade can erase what you have done. And so, by the laws of nol herself I, Yatzil, Storm Queen of the nol and Princess of Niev banish you to as far west as can be traveled."

Her chest felt as if it had been crushed. Sparron dropped to her knees. Aagono cried out as the spear head was broken and the others struggled, slipping her off its splintered end. No blood coated it as the queen's flesh knitted itself together. Yatzil drew in a breath, wanting to allow Sparron to say goodbye to Haseya, but her decree required execution immediately.

"You cannot send her west," Aagono said, panting. A jagged ring of metal revealed the pale flesh of her breast where the wound had healed. "My husband controls all but the south. He believes your mother still controls your brother."

The relief from hearing this was comparable to the taste of a bate-nich. But there was still a punishment to execute and a moon to form. Sparron went and kneeled beside Haseya. Yatzil drew her gaze to the healed First Daughter, seeking to control things, to have time to mourn Haseya, The Highnonstar's heat sent sweat beads down her brow.

"Are you unable to control him like you did before? I must keep to what I have said for a Storm Queen's word is a promise."

There was a long pause, smoke stung her nostrils from the island's ruined remains, the sea's current beyond the ice relaxed her only so. Sparron buried her face in her hands.

"I no longer can," said Aagono. "He needed controlled when your bond existed with him. But with it severed, he grew distant and wanted me less." she sighed. "I will stand with you to stop him and help carry out your decree."

"I am proud of you, daughter," said Sath, tears filling her eyes. "I know you cannot return to the girl I knew, but you still can be her in your heart."

Yatzil smiled when Aagono did. Her heart filled with hope to witness centuries of anger ending. It kindled hope at ending the differences between her and Putma. Taking one last look at Haseya, her heart fell from its high perch. *You will be buried with high honor.* She placed her hands above her brow, their owl eyes unmoving unlike her own. *May the Four, no, may I give myself strength.*

SATH CALLED all of them to a part of the beach distant from the tide and jungle. They positioned themselves as before and began to dance. The Nemamoon extended herself to Queen Busara. The queen rooted herself and swayed back and forth. Next came Sute, both goddess and queen inter-twining lightning bolts, stepping forward and then back until their fingers were a breath away. The First Daughter raised her arms like wings, raising one foot to calf height with perfect balance.

When Sath faced her, an energy filled Yatzil like it had before. An aura enhanced the ice blue of her skin as she crept like a panther to Sath. Sparron dropped her hands, and like her grandmother, her jaw followed. A loud crack sounded from the Highnonstar, echoing, the sky went dark, and from it blooming and spreading a blue sky of scattered clouds. The unbearable heat vanished, and in the distance over Nema the sun appeared. An ear-piercing crack raced down Highnonstar, splitting it in half, fading until gone from sight. A silver orb solidified in the Highnonstar's place and spun away at great speed. Its destination went west for a time, and then darted south, stirring the ocean in its wake.

"Why does it travel for the Trunk, Sath?" Yatzil said. "We've traveled for so long. It should have gone to the East."

Sath parted her lips, but Queen Aagono cut her off.

"My control over it has ceased. You counted your days like those who opposed me long ago I suspect. Your brother will be blessed with the first light of a new moon."

The moon rotated slower than the Highnonstar. Its direction spoke to her of a want needing fulfilled. She felt her stomach, its smoothness returned from so long a journey. A familiar scent returned to her nose, replacing the dampness of the silks bound about her abdomen.

"What troubles you?" said Sute, weaving her fingers through Yatzil's. "Do we travel south for Niev? Or is our next purpose to find Highnonstar?"

Yatzil faced her, eyes dry and salty from sweat. There was too much ahead to worry about, but all of it could wait.

"I wish for us to honor Haseya first. And when that is done to hold my child again."

"I wish to see my son too. I ... now understand Haseya's importance to you."

"I don't know how you shall enter the palace," said Sute. "And the way to the royal shipyard is guarded."

"I know how you can," said Aagono, peering over to her mother. The Nemamoon graced her with a look of pride. "It was blocked when first I came south as my Palenore laid siege to the Lijani."

Leaving Sute, Yatzil stood face to face with the First Daughter. The wind sent her hair across her lips, hints of smoke and sweat polluted it. She parted it to find sadness consuming Aagono's face. Yatzil sensed her guilt and realized it had been Queen Aagono who had held her back in Non's temple.

"I remember a great quake when I was fifteen," said Yatzil. "I went that way no longer after it."

Aagono panned her solid black eyes to a distant coastline where the east's immense city stopped, her chin sank. Yatzil stepped before the First Daughter, raising her chin, drawing in a breath.

"I must see my child before repairing what you have done. I remember the tunnel began in the palace throne room."

"Yes," said Aagono, her voice heightened. "And ended at a stretch of stone where snow never remains for—"

"Long."

Yatzil remembered how warm those stones were, and that there were two large tunnels below the city walls. She knew where to go, but first her promise needed to be kept.

CHAPTER TWENTY-SEVEN

D eep inside grief held her heart in a tight embrace. New trees rose among fallen timbers as Sath danced at the island's center. Yatzil found some hope in giving a dance. She watched the new trees with wide splayed leaves pierce crumbled wood. The island's center looked to be the place Haseya may have liked. *She treated me as a mother should.* She rested her hand on Sath's shoulder.

"Yes, Storm Queen," said Sath, lowering her hand just as trees were sprouting from the dirt. "I have land to cover still and fruit to grow. I intend to stay here with my daughter and mend what I can."

"I wish to bury Haseya upon this island. To do so in the land she grew old in would be—"

"A risk I dare not have a Storm Queen make." Sath motioned for Busara. The lijani queen kept an eye on Sparron like Yatzil did. The little girl knelt huddled over her grandmother with arms folded as if she were cold. "You spoke of your journey while I was in your care, Busara. Can you honor Haseya with a grand burial?"

Queen Busara turned from Sparron. Her braids faded to a pale green but remained long and thick.

"Yes," she said. "Though I am still weak from healing you."

"I can create a few chimeries if needed," said Sath.

Yatzil smiled a small smile then embraced them both, peering over them. Sparron's eyes were reddened from tears, the silver over skin a flushed gray. She passed between Sute, who remained where her stepmother had left her, and Aagono, who leaned against a tree not far from Sath. Sute remained silent and focused on the First Daughter. Yatzil sensed the decision to free the palenore queen had been an unfavored one. But as she drew closer to Sparron, Sute's eye emitted white lightning in place of red.

A whining and turning of roots through dirt far off began. Tremors ran under her feet halted short of Sparron. The little girl remained undisturbed, rubbing her eyes and nose before returning to her huddled position. Yatzil shook Ahigan's tortoise shell at her hip, finding what remained within was what Haseya encouraged them to preserve. Every step made clear what Aagono's flames had done, and again, she wished she had allowed revenge for so many nol. *Sparron nor any of us would learn from it.* She turned back to Sute, unable to understand her restraint, yet maybe, it was possible that the young queen trusted her decision. *And so, must I.*

Yatzil knelt beside Haseya and searched for words to ease Sparron's grief, but with the night encroaching upon the island, the little girl appeared angrier than last they were alone. The right words grew distant from her tongue. Sparron licked her lips, eyeing Ahigan's tortoise shell. Yatzil rested her hand on it, but the young Nol girl returned focused to her grandmother. Haseya had mushed her lips together in her final act of bravery, but her eyes had closed. She was glad they were for if Haseya could see, she would have been ashamed of her granddaughter. Sparron's face was blank as a block of granite.

The banishment was final and non-removable by nol law like that of nescaran. And though it pained her deeply to punish Sparron like this, she dared not justify sparing a life as better than wanting revenge.

"Am I going to be sent west, Princess?" said Sparron. Her tone was like Haseya's when Yatzil had been caught in the hut belonging to Sparron's mother. "Will you send me to die?"

"I … I have no." *I cannot. I will not place her in danger.* "I shall not send you where death is certain."

Yatzil met Sparron's eyes. They remained hardened as if the little girl before her knew what Yatzil was deciding next.

"You shall remain with Sath."

Sparron bunched her nose and got to her feet, backing away.

"I'd rather be sent to the west," Sparron said. "I don't belong so far from home."

Yatzil pursed her lips, reframing from telling the little girl what they both already knew. Sparron grabbed at her chest for Haseya's knife, her little fingers clutched only red boar fur.

"You have no way of shaming yourself anymore, Sparron." Yatzil rested a hand to Haseya's forehead then returned her eyes to Sparron. The little girl took a step forward but quickly froze. "And if you did, would it be before we bury your grandmother, my … mother."

The ground ceased its tremors, and the whine of roots fell silent. The little girl knitted her brow with her lips twisted in a snarl. Yatzil wanted to take such anger away somehow, but death remained eternal in Nema. Although, from the tall trees surrounding them she saw reason to believe otherwise.

"I have not spoken to Sath of my choice" said Yatzil, sighing. "She wishes to mend ways with her daughter. They may wish to join me against the Highnonstar."

"I'll be alone then." said Sparron, clenching her teeth, ignoring the wind ruffling her feathers. "I hate you."

"I do only what I must." Yatzil huffed, standing, remaining composed in Haseya's presence. She stared her down, tears prickled in the corners of her eyes. "I did not wish to do this but how shall you be safe? Sath can make certain you go without hunger."

"If she can do that," Sparron reflected on her grandmother, tears ran into her lips. "Then why can't she send me home?"

"You have been told why—"

Sparron grabbed handfuls of her feathers then dropped to her knees.

"I don't want to be here." she cried. "Please don't banish me. Take me with you."

Yatzil hated herself the more Sparron wept. Every muscle ached to hold the little girl in her arms. She was a queen but what point did her divine position serve if she was unable to rescind a decree? A decree that teared at her heart. The others approached limiting what time they had left.

"If you had kept to…" *No.* The word was poison on her tongue and had dominated most of her life. Sparron seemed ashamed by her very words. Anger and sadness shaped the little girl's face, aging her beyond what her dark feathers proved. "You will stay here until you have remembered what being a nol means and then—"

"You're going to allow me to earn my grown name?"

Sparron's face brightened like Yatzil's did when her lamodun had shown kindness instead of a blank face when she performed a wrong. But the man in long white silk robes, whose head was without a single strand of hair, would have done the opposite of what Yatzil readied to.

"Yes. But keep my decision to yourself and remember what I told you."

The others were within ears range. Sparron snuck a nod, returning her face to the blankness it was before.

"Come, child," said Sath, yanking Sparron up. The little girl winced, feet digging into the sand. "You will bear witness to what has been made for your noble grandmother."

They headed for the island's center, but before Yatzil and Busara could lift Haseya, Sath looked over her shoulder.

"I recommend the child stay with me, Yatzil. A dance for a stream to drink or fruit to eat is an easy task."

Yatzil nearly shook her head but restrained herself. *She was listening.*

"I wanted to ask that of you," said Yatzil. "I do not wish to put her at risk when much of Nema is under Highnonstar's control."

"A wise choice, Storm Queen. And once we have honored Haseya, a way to bring you to Niev will be needed."

Yatzil bent down with Busara, finding the need to slap herself for being distracted by emotions. She had no way home. No way to hold Yat-hig-seya once more before life grew complicated again.

DESPERATION RAN THROUGH HER HEART. She struggled to hold Haseya, unable to imagine how getting home was possible. She did not know if there was another dragon, and Aagono had ridden no eagle in her drive for revenge. The First Daughter kept her head down, remaining a few paces behind her mother. She felt conflicted about the First Daughter. Busara turned to look where Yatzil did.

"Do you pity Queen Aagono?"

"What?" said Yatzil, shaking her head. "I am mourning

Haseya. What care should I have for Aagono if I can find a way home?"

Busara glared at her, her ember eyes flaring.

"She is a goddess without worshippers now. While you reasoned with Sparron, the First Daughter spoke of a feud with Highnonstar. He is worse than his past self. We have witnessed it. It is not your fault that battle severed your bond with the Storm King, but it is the cause of your present loss."

Yatzil reaffirmed her hold under Haseya's shoulders, putting the battle out of her mind.

"Must I make another blood trade with him?" Yatzil found herself growing tired by the second. To frost would make carrying Haseya easier but she didn't want to hide her sadness. "He would have killed every priest to prevent such a thing."

"I will not add weight to your grief. And I do believe it is possible to reach Niev ."

"What? How…?"

Towering ahead, a statue of twisted vines stood in Haseya's image. Leaves of a pale green jetted back and down from her head like feathers. A light gray wood made up her face, with detail down to her toothless mouth.

They rested her upon the ground, sand hissing and leaves crunching. The likeness of Haseya held what remained of Clod's arrow, its point replaced by her knife, well out of Sparron's reach. *She has no use for it now.* Yatzil thought. At the statue's base thick brown roots ran down into a pit like a muddied waterfall.

"I … cannot thank you enough, Queen Busara," Yatzil said.

"Storm Queen, to give Nema its moon back is thanks enough."

Yatzil embraced her before receiving one from Sute. The

young queen shut her eyes, resting her head on Yatzil's shoulder.

"I will make right my deed when we are south once more."

"I'm not worried about it now," said Yatzil. "I wish to bury my mother first."

Sute nodded as they watched Busara raise her hands above the pit. The roots streaming from Haseya's statue shook to life, hissing across the ground. Yatzil and Sute to back away from them. A hand of three fingers formed and slipped under Haseya, closing, and weaving, forming a coffin. Yatzil had seen nobles of Niev placed in ones of stone. Her father had one of gold, its lid formed to his body, leaving an open place for his face and the jade mask to rest upon it. The coffin lowered into the pit, roots pierced from its ends and sides, filling the pit at a hunting serpent's pace. Yatzil strolled slowly to the foot of the pit. She shuffled and gathered the right words, hoping they would be perfect.

"I came north to seek an army for revenge, knowing its success meant much for who I had left behind. I lost a friend for it; someone I had loved without knowing. And yet my greed grew despite this loss." She gazed upon the statue, swallowing sadness. "And then I met Haseya. I gave her every reason to doubt me, but she found strength to forgive me before I could myself." Yatzil faced Aagono, the First Daughter was deep under the tree's shade. She folded her arms and pressed her chin to her dragon scale breastplate. "I will do the same and release my reservations. I forgive you, First Daughter."

The first daughter stepped forward within feet of Haseya's grave. There was a lightness in Yatzil's heart as the goddess met her eye. Letting go was never what she intended but deep within she knew Haseya would. Haseya was strong when needed, ruthless when someone she cared for was in danger, but no grudge held a firm grip over her heart. Aagono's face remained dry of tears, but a slight quivering plagued her full lips.

"I will not disappoint you, Storm Queen." Aagono nodded, rubbing her eyes, and once she was done, it was as if the fierce scarlet quilled goddess had gone for good. "I cannot carry any of you to Niev without burning you, but there is another dragon to perform the task."

"Where? Why has no one—"

"It resides not far from where you saved the other from my Highnonstar's palenore. Can you summon Crimson Spike, Mother?"

"He will sense you are here, Daughter," said Sath, a wind rushed through the trees, catching the end of her skirt. "And that you have killed one of his own, one I wear the colors of."

Aagono rolled her eyes.

The dirt settled over the crest of Haseya's grave. Knowing Yatzil would never see the old Nol again pressed on her heart. She took Sute's hand, squeezing it to remain strong.

"I'm willing to trust in what you have planned." She peered over to Sath. The Nemamoon merged her thin eyebrows. There was a tightness in her jaw which made Yatzil reconsider leaving Sparron in her care. "Is what your mother said about Crimson Spike true?" "Yes," said Aagono, "but I will leave this island for another to aid you."

Sath loosened the frustration she had placed her teeth in.

"That will require you to either place yourself within Highnonstar's borders or—"

"Or" Yatzil squeezed Sute's hand, its heat made her wince. "go meet us outside Niev itself."

"I will go to the southernmost part of your island, Mother, to prepare."

"I would rather you stay, Daughter." Sath spun her left hand, then in an instant was nose to nose with Aagono.

"There are other ways. I want to make up for what I have done to you."

"Then trust me like you have the storm queen."

Yatzil watched Aagono brush past Sath without another word. It would work yet in that moment she became uncertain of the Nemamoon. She hoped as the First Daughter marched past Haseya's statue into the thickness of the island's jungle that the Palenore Queen had a plan for Niev's guardians.

oncern blended with worry on Sath's face as
Yatzil left to have one final word with Aagono.
From Yatzil's last thought, suspicion raced
through her mind for Sath. She wondered if this Crimson
Spike had been the one she had ridden in her dreams, and if
it was, why had Sath not sent it to aid the dragon bearing the
colors she wore? The black and gold dragon had even battled
the First Daughter alone, and still, Sath had not sent for
Crimson Spike's aid. Yatzil allowed these thoughts to churn
when she caught up to Aagono. The tide consumed and then
released Aagono's black sandaled feet, their slender shape
half buried in wet sand.

The Nemamoon had guided Yatzil, helped her see life in a
better way. But the closer she came to the First Daughter, the
more she became an ally rather than a forgiven enemy. The
goddess stood unmoved by the tide, its waters rising with
each encore of wave, licking the hem of her skirt. There was
a thought, no, more a question which had risen in her mind
after forgiving the people less queen. But when Sath had not

stopped her earlier, she guessed the Nemamoon knew what it was.

A breeze hissed across her face, gaining strength as if Sath had second thoughts. It had to be, for a brief second earlier the wind had come from her left. She pressed on, ignoring how the sea breeze reminded her of home.

"I must ask you something before your mother calls forth Crimson Spike."

Aagono faced her. Her ringed quills clicked like tiny claps of thunder. She sent a firm glare to the trees. It lessened the wind, and the tide lowered gradually, both making it seem Sath didn't wish to be ignored.

"What is it you wish to ask me?" Aagono said, through clenched teeth. "Pardon my frustration. Mother wishes to mend ways yet doesn't trust my judgement."

"Was it fear of death that made you help us, or was there another reason? Queen Busara spoke of difficulties between you and Highnonstar."

Aagono rested her eyes on the hole where Clod's arrow had pierced her chest. It was jagged and twisted but no blood lined its dragon scale, a glimpse of her pale left breast shown through.

"It was not to preserve my life." Aagono met Yatzil's eye and then both caught sight of Sath, shielded by bushes, and shaded by branches. "If you were so intent on understanding me when we fought, Mother!" she shouted, tension hardening her jaw, "Then why not trust my wish to aid those I have wronged?"

The Nemamoon remained still for moments, increasing the wind's strength. She nodded and turned, vanishing into the jungle. Yatzil sighed when Aagono did, finding much more needed repaired between both goddesses than she thought.

"I think she will trust you long before Putma will me."

"Your mother makes my own appear tamed."

Yatzil chuckled. The goddess looked at her with softness in her eyes.

"I must unfortunately disagree," said Yatzil. "Putma was far worse and put many through torment."

"Be grateful for her rage, Storm Queen." Aagono took Yatzil's hand in her own. "My mother paid more mind to Nema than me, and for it I caused greater pain than can be matched."

"I am sorry she placed duty over you."

Yatzil slowly freed her hand from the heat of Aagono's.

"No need." She smiled. "As to what you have asked, my reason for aiding you is long, but I know no other." Aagono sighed, an unsteadiness ran through her slender fingers, forming a fist. "My husband sacrificed his life for me and our palenore. We were meant to rule as First Son and Daughter had we succeeded but our prison behind the moon kept such a dream from us. And with his sacrifice a part of him remained with me until I found him a host. One fit in both body and blood."

"And this is why you chose Amteer?"

"Yes." Aagono focused on the islands leading south. Their alignment like a necklace of jade beads. "But you know why I had difficulty and why it became easy to do so later. The scar upon his palm remains even with Highnonstar in control. He was changed after seizing control. Where I wished torment and enslavement for my mother's creations for depriving me of her, he wanted their complete extinction. They resist even now."

Yatzil stepped in front of Aagono, remembering Sute's father, brothers, and the Nol of the Gaping Mouth. Hope filled her heart for a moment, finding mist running down Aagono's cheeks like tears.

"You did not wish to be alone," said Yatzil. She raised

Aagono's chin with a curled finger. "You knew one way to make certain of it. I promise you shall not be alone from this day on."

She raised her hands and presented the owl eyes upon them. And as she lowered them, she saw Sath amongst the bushes.

"She has returned," said Aagono, with a wry smile, "hasn't she?"

"Yes. And I believe there won't be any need for you to leave her. I am going to see my daughter."

Ice ran over her flesh, crackling as it met her fingertips. Aagono's eyes grew wide.

"How?"

"I shall need food and water to keep my strength, but I can freeze a path from island to island until I reach southern snow."

"I…"

"You have a chance to repair what is more important than Nema." Yatzil hesitated for a moment, finding a favor needed from the goddess. "Protect Sparron for me. Help her remember what being Nol truly means."

"I … will do what I can."

Aagono raised both hands like she was presenting an offering and then left. Yatzil wondered if the sacred nol gesture meant more than an offering. When last she used it, it was to pay respect to Ahigan. It must have meant more, for this time it felt as if the First Daughter were sealing a promise.

The current ran through her sandals then retreated, uneven like Aagono and Sath's relationship. The Nemamoon spoke to Aagono to which Yatzil could not hear but a curt nod from the goddess brought a smile to Sath's face. Yatzil tensed her fingers for a second as Sath approached. *She has heard everything.*

"I have heard your last thought and that is all," said Sath. "I decided this time to pry like that of a mortal. Now, will I be summoning Crimson Spike, or do you have another way to see your daughter?"

Yatzil faced the chain of islands leading south then swallowed. The first island was close enough to see but worry sank in of every possible problem her father and brother had faced in their voyages up Nema's coast. Her heart retreated to her spine like it was being chased to think of fish thieves and storms. But she had offered Aagono and Sath a chance to mend their relationship, and Sparron needed another nol to guide her from revenge, even if it was from who killed her grandmother.

"There is no need to bring him out of hiding," she said, sniffing back her nervousness, facing Sath again. "We require food though, and I have only Ahigan's tortoise shell to hold water."

"What do you have planned?"

A faint ruffling followed a snap, sending Sath's focus from her to Busara, and then with a loud crack Sute.

"You were reading my thoughts, weren't you?"

"No," said Sath, in a hushed voice. "But my guess is that my daughter spoke of your plan to them."

"Then you do not know what I plan to do?"

"Yatzil. I kept Crimson Spike away because neither dragon you have seen is from this world. He is the last of his kind, and I hoped you would save Narningold."

The others were with them now. Yatzil's face bristled. Its ice crackling from the sharp movement. She was tempted to bring Sparron with them, but too much danger lay ahead. Sath had told the truth and was listening.

"Keep out of my head," said Yatzil. "I am trusting you to protect what little remains of the nol."

Sath bowed her head.

"If you need me, I will answer. The girl is safe with us. I will find a way to supply you however you wish to travel."

"Good," she said, firmly. "We shall need whatever can be provided until the south's cold is on our skin."

"I will need protection against such a cold," said Sute. "I left what warm clothes I possessed in…"

Yatzil looked down to where Sute's lumao halted at her knees. She knew why the young queen's words had trailed off. It was apparent Haseya's wagon had perished with their crowns too. All of it burned to ash in the old Nol's final act of bravery.

"I shall find some way to keep you warm."

"You must go now," Sath said. "I will help where I can but even now Nema is closer to being how Highnonstar had envisioned it. You have but two advantages."

"And what are they?" said Yatzil. "What can aid us against a god?"

"Me. And he is no longer in control of the moon."

CHAPTER TWENTY-NINE

The three queens took their time along the shore, the surf running over their feet and retreating swiftly to the sea. The water was warm running under the straps of Yatzil's sandals, coating the ice of her feet in thin foam. The clouds slowly shifted, gracing them with darkness and the distant light of stars. She focused on the water, reaching out like she had the wave of hours previous. The water stretching out ahead quieted, but only until her thoughts raced to what may happen if she failed.

She shook her head and shut her eyes, remembering her daughter's face, the strength in her hand when she squeezed Yatzil's finger. *I miss her so much.* And with that, Yatzil focused, the breathing of both queens the most prominent sound. Faint were the waves in the distance as she opened her eyes. A solid stretch of ice wide enough to allow two carts side by side withstood the ocean current. Great thick jagged bergs of ice held the bridge like support towers and were dark like stone from the night. A narrow path she had envisioned weaved through it all, yet it left room for only one of them at a time.

"You have done it," said Sute. "We are closer to our children now."

"Yes." Yatzil whispered, thawing. "Let's move with care."

The ice was slick in places, and some of it gave off a faint shifting sound, setting her nerves on edge. Yatzil dared not think of how much water was halted by her efforts, or how long the ice may hold. The queens followed her lead as they had long before a moon was born from their efforts. She sifted through her mind as to why her confidence was fleeing. Their journey was to the one place her heart ached for, but she doubted its completion. Sute rested a hand on her shoulder, slowing her steps.

An unsureness was in her feet, shortening the lightning of her eyes, revealing her eyelashes. Queen Busara held Sute by the hand, but like Yatzil didn't struggle on the ice. Yatzil guided them with her teeth clenched. Wherever her own doubt was coming from, it had no place in what she wanted. And then, her thoughts went to Sath as the island ahead drew closer.

"We need to go back." The words surprised her after she had said them. "I think we had better do as Aagono recommended."

The queens blocked her way before she could leave. Confusion twisted and pulsated the lightning around Sute's eyes. Yatzil peered over her shoulder to Sath's island.

"Why?" said Sute. "You have gifted our former enemy with what she truly needed."

"Your daughter must see you before Highnonstar can be beaten." Queen Busara tilted her head, her eyes relaxing to a faint glow. "Sath is innocent of whatever your mind may tell you, Storm Queen. You have allowed Aagono's long held frustration to taint your trust in who has only ever wished to help you."

"I ..."

She turned from them, running her fingers through her hair. It was well over her shoulders, and she had paid no mind to it since leaving Niev. *They are right.* Yatzil removed her fingers from her hair and then focused on what needed to be done. On the journey lying ahead and Yat-hig-seya. *I won't allow her to grow apart from me like the goddesses did one another.* She took a final look at where they had come from.

"Let's go on then."

THEY HAD MADE it to a second island with her strength spent. The clouds had parted to reveal faint morning sun amongst a cloudy sky. She had pushed them to walk all night, yet despite their haste, the ice slowed them. She slid down the surface of a boulder, moss running over it like continents on a map. The sand cushioned her stop, whispering with her movements. The ocean's endless whispering din overpowered it. Her head thrummed from so much use of her magic. If she could have Non command of the ocean be parted, she could save her strength. Yatzil sighed, her brother had the Four under his will and she had only the ability to seek their counsel. The last few times she had asked for it, none of it was pleasant.

Yatzil's eyes fluttered shut, then opened, catching the distant crunch of footsteps. The queens carried what Sath promised. Busara had taken Ahigan's tortoise shell to fill as well, leaving her spit to be savored. A hint of doubt lingered about something the queen had mentioned a day past. It was of not wanting to add weight to her grief. Her eyes edged on closing, and then what the Lijani queen spoke of sent her sitting straight up.

"I don't wish to see her again," Yatzil gasped, remembering. "No. Maua is dead. There is no way she can mend my blood trade with Amteer."

Snap.

Yatzil cocked her head to the approaching queens. They were passing through trees pointing to the ocean like a finger. Busara led while her stepdaughter trailed behind. Thoughts of how permanent death was running to her tongue, making her wish to question what the lijani queen meant.

Sute sat beside her with a handful of bate niches in one hand and chimries in the other. The tortoise shell's sloshed in the lijani queen's grasp. Queen Busara caught the look in Yatzil's eyes. She rested with slight uneasiness beside them.

"Are you troubled by something, Storm Queen?"

"Yes." She didn't want to sound forceful but the mere thought of having to confront Maua was too much. *She is dead.* "I believe I know what you meant by not wishing to add to my grief. How can someone dead mend a severed blood trade?"

Queen Busara didn't answer but instead focused on the chimries in her hands. They were smaller, unlike the one Yatzil first tasted. It would have been large enough to swallow whole if she had been brave enough.

"Stepmother?" Sute nudged Busara's elbow with hers. "It is not possible to return someone to life. Is it? And if so, can one not a nol restore what Yatzil speaks of?"

The queen rested the chimries in her lap, rubbing her hands together before meeting Yatzil's eye.

"Resurrection is possible in only one place. It is hidden in the ruins of Mutafakara. The girl though cannot mend a blood trade."

Mutafakara was as far north as one could travel but none of this explained what the queen meant a day ago.

"What shall burden me with grief as you have said?"

Busara took Yatzil's hand. "I wanted to speak of this after you both spent time with your children."

The long thick braids making up her hair withered a little, losing leaves. Yatzil struggled to make sense of whether Maua may need to return to her life again.

"Please tell us now." Yatzil begged. Every beat of her heart ached not to know the truth. "Why should we seek the resurrection of who threatened my child?"

Queen Busara released her hand and buried her face in her own. The bark over her knuckles crumbled, a deep sobbing breath escaped her lips.

"Because she is my daughter."

THE STONES WERE WARM, small, and countless under her feet. How the south's arctic chill permitted such a disturbance perplexed her. Snow fell in great sheets every day they spent along the Trunk's coast. With great regret, and further insult to her people, she had robbed a fisherman's clothing string of a seal fur rug. It gave warmth to Sute, who ignored its itchiness against her skin. None of them appeared royal in their travel worn garb leaving little choice.

The snow finally slowed but only a little, wind keeping it from settling upon the ground. Yatzil turned back to where they had come from. She traced a line through her mind to the map of the Trunk from her lessons. Her lamodun spoke of Niev's harbors, of the royal one containing her father's fleet. It was far from where they wished to go. Each smaller harbor possessed traditions for when the morning catch was brought ashore. The stars were at their brightest in the sky, some hidden by clouds. She listened for the possibility of a fang blast to summon the fishermen. Fangs were said to be from the guardians' yearly shedding of old teeth. Just one was large enough to be blown by a man with powerful lungs.

Fffffmmmm

It was distant but she realized the tunnel they headed for was close to a fish market.

"If we take the way we do now," she said to Sute. "It shall place suspicion on you if you are recognized."

"I am willing to risk it for my son and husband." she said, holding the seal fur tight around her shoulders.

The fang blast ended with Sute's words, and another would come to send men out for the selling of their catch. Yatzil sighed, admiring Sute's determination.

"Then we must be quick. I remember where to go, but once within the tunnel, I am unsure of how far the entrance is to the throne room."

They continued until finding an immense boulder pressed partially into a cliff side making up the moat around Niev. Its top was jagged and broken, but when she steadied herself to its lower half, its surface was smooth, like something had rubbed against it for an extended time. The heat was worse here as stones were fewer and separated over damp dark sand. Snow melted before reaching the ground within seconds. There was a mugginess to the sea's scent as it splashed upon the shore, it surf dark from both night and the cliff face residing before it. Yatzil's jaw dropped. to

Two twin caves, both large enough to swallow an entire fleet loomed.

"I have never traveled this far south, Storm Queen." Queen Busara stopped ahead of her, wiping her brow. "But this must have been how Nescara brought the Four's guardians to the moat."

Sute let drop her fur rug. The cave sent a slow rush of heat toward them. Her pearl skin reddened slightly from it.

"Why do the caves act like a man's nostrils, Stepmother?"

"Sath never told me much about her creation of Nema, but she did speak of a beast with a long nose. She rode it for an age before wishing to settle amongst the stars."

Yatzil moved closer to the caves, for some reason her heart quickened, and her mind raced at why Busara had not taken revenge for her daughter. Did the queen see no fault in her defending Yat-hig-seya from Maua's threat? And did Busara desire to bring Maua back? Yatzil frosted but it was like the villa when Aagono had scorched the grass. She focused harder knowing they only had to pass both caves. To go until the scent of cod brought in after the fang's blast welcomed them. It was too much but she resisted with each step slower than the previous.

"What are you doing, Yatzil?" Sute grabbed her by the shoulders and pulled her back. Her touch added to the heat. Yatzil shook herself free and backed toward the sea. "You will cause harm to yourself."

"I wanted to ready myself."

"What madness do you speak of? We are so close to our children."

Sute glared at her with red in her bolting eyes. Yatzil was unable to find what words to say. She removed Ahigan's tortoise shell from her belt to quench her thirst, but Sute blocked its mouthpiece.

"What are you readying for? We have been through much. What heat comes from those caves keeps me warm, but you, I wish not to think of it."

"I want to be ready, Sute." Yatzil removed the tortoise shell's stopper then drank until she choked. "I want to be ready to face, Highnonstar, but..." She looked to where they needed to go. "I just do not know."

"You venture too far ahead," said Queen Busara, giving Yatzil's arm a soft squeeze. "And you worry about bringing my daughter back and that task is up to me."

She turned away for a moment, taking another draft from the tortoise shell. The great burden that lay ahead was truly something she could not rush to face. She was so close to holding Yat-hig-seya again. *It may be for a final time.* She shook the thought from her mind and found herself in need of council from someone no longer able to give it.

"I am sorry." Yatzil replaced the tortoise shell's stopper. "I am lost without Haseya. I feel I have tried to make the right decisions. If you wish to revive Maua, Queen Busara, I ask one favor."

"And what is it you ask of me, Storm Queen?"

Yatzil met the queen's eager glowing ember eyes.

"Stay with us until we are home again."

"I would be honored. I—"

With a spin in the sand every breath grew heavy as images of when last Yatzil saw Haseya filled her mind. She refused to weep but so sudden an action would arouse concern. She could hear the snapping and popping of Sute's eyes, the scrap of Queen Busara's feet through the sand. There was no hand to yank her back or words to ask what troubled her. But Yatzil guessed both royals understood why she had left so abruptly.

CHAPTER THIRTY

A long stretch of sand and stone separated them from the palm-and-oak wood shacks. Docks stretched out across the water like a creature with tentacles tied to ships of great length and many levels. Men pulled carts weighed by cod, muscles, and crab. Yatzil peered from behind an aground ship to a cave shaded by a thick cylinder of white granite. It held stable a section of Niev's thick outer wall. Such weight of stone to her was nothing in comparison to how she felt.

"The secret entrance is this way." She pointed, taking in the harbor's saltiness to calm her nerves. "We have only to head for the—"

"Guards."

The call was faint by the clatter of wheels and distance, but a balding man let the handles of his cart drop. He pointed then called again. Yatzil pushed off from the ship and ran for the cave.

"This entrance is not so secret if anyone can wander to it," said Sute.

Yatzil cocked her head to the harbor, catching the frosted

faces of their pursuers until she and the royals with her were out of sight.

"This is not it," said Yatzil.

She frosted and pressed her hands to a smooth stretch of rock tucked beside the cylinder of white granite left of the cave. It gave her right revealing a narrow tunnel sloping steadily upward.

"This is—?" Sute cried.

"Just go daughter!" Busara yelled. "The guards will catch us."

Yatzil grabbed the door's edge and pushed once they were all in. The shouts and footsteps fell silent, the door booming shut. Yatzil pressed her back against the door. It was made of thick palm-and-oak, worn, and crumbled in places.

"How could you open this as a child?" Sute stared at it with her red bolting eyes fading to white. "It is larger than any child can manage."

Yatzil dropped her chin to her chest, thawing.

"I had Flor."

"You... You loved her then?"

"Yes." She gazed at the tunnel ahead, unable to conjure up how far they had left, dwelling instead on the past. "I will always keep her close to my heart."

Sute parted her lips but slid them back into place. Yatzil embraced her, resting her cheek to Sute's own. It was warm and smelled of salt.

"We must move on and find our children." She took Sute's hand. "Come."

The tunnel incline increased for a time, warmer than upon the beach and cavernous. Parts of the ceiling and floor were melted once they reached a small landing. There was a narrow gap ahead, forcing them to go one at a time. Heat from when last Aagono had been here remained trapped somehow, sending sweat down Yatzil's brow. A faint cool breeze relieved her, flowing down from a set of finely chiseled steps.

She stopped short to the top at a familiar voice accompanied by another breeze. Sute let her hand go and sped past her.

"Wait, Sute," Busara said.

They chased her, finding another door of palm-and-oak stood in their way. Yatzil grabbed Sute's wrist and yanked her back. The voice was clearer, Sachihiro's, but he wasn't alone, and it had come to Yatzil what, or rather, who was directly behind the door.

"I am not certain I can go further."

Sute wrenched her from Yatzil's grip.

"What keeps troubling you the closer we come to our wants? You know what must be done to save Nema. And our children will be separated from us when we leave again."

Yatzil pictured Putma contorted and frozen upon her throne. Unable to speak or witness her actions by what she knew of imprisonment. And then her thoughts churned over what Sute had said, finding what brought her such nervous feelings. There was a faint numbing tingling in her palm. As if something sharp was slid across it, weakening it. A gripping of dread came over her then went away, returning the strength in her hand.

"I know we have much ahead, Yatzil." said Sute "And I have told you once you worry far more than any in Nema should, but I understand why. Tell us. Tell me. What scares you now?"

"My ... Putma is imprisoned within the gray whale beyond the door." That was not it, yet she could not understand why her hand had been pained. It was familiar but hadn't ravaged her hand to the point of rendering it useless. "She reminds me of my banishment. But... Oh."

She shot past Sute balling her fists to fight back surfacing pain. Her eyes widened as the veins under her ice-blue skin ignited yellow, burning. She frosted and ripped open the door. Sachihiro spun to face her. He was slimmer, ornately dressed and his crown wasn't snug on his head.

"Yatzil!"

There was a pause in her steps, seeing Putma in the pain she had left her in. Her own pain overtook her hesitation. She edged around the throne and out of the gray whale's jaws, embracing her brother. A sharp slice robbed her hand strength, the same hand containing her damaged blood trade scar. *It cannot be.* She cradled her hand with the other, shaking still from the diamond fang's blood.

"What ails you?" Sachihiro struggled to hold her steady. Her balance led them to the gray whale's jaws. "Your hand is cracking. I will call for a—"

"No," she said, thawing. "Bring me to, Yat-hig-seya."

She looked to find Sute and Queen Busara at her side. Queen Busara's eyes grew to half the size of her face. Whispers and harsh looks came from nobles and generals crowding the throne room's columned vastness. The Lijani queen took her hand and released a deep shuddering breath.

"Highnonstar has found a nol priest." She cupped both her hands over Yatzil's. Yatzil winced and seethed. It felt as if a bone needle continuously punctured then withdrew from her open hand. Her numbness faded but every stitch sent a shrill scream from her lips. "And a powerful one but I sense you are bonded with a raton."

"A raton?" Yatzil shut her eyes. "He must not wish to lose control again."

The pain subsided yet her confusion plagued her. *Why a raton?* Her strength steadily returned as she rested her head upon Sachihiro's chest. He was clothed in soft pale green silks and around his neck was a jeweled owl. Its wings were spread like swooping for a kill. Nowhere was Sute's father amongst those eyeing her with suspicion.

"Out. All of you. I command it," said Sachihiro. The nobles and generals remained. "Go or be executed by my hand."

They took to his brutality with dull expressions. And even in her worry for King Inuza, she cursed her people's way of being. The room emptied at a slow pace as Busara released her hand.

"Please, brother," she cried. "Bring my daughter to me."

"I will find her, Yatzil," said Sute, then realizing what Yatzil had. "Where is my father, Husband?"

Sachihiro raised an eyebrow.

"No one has entered Niev since all of you left for Crizalbolt."

Sute gasped, giving Yatzil a look of worry, yellowing the lightning of her eyes. As the young queen left Yatzil stared at Busara's stitch work. Three scars crossed paths with one another, and blood coated her fingers. Sachihiro held her close, sadness fought to escape his painted eyes.

"I grant you many blessings, lijani woman," he said, resting his gaze upon Busara. "You are not the one my sister came south with before. What reason has the king of the raton to enter my kingdom?"

"She is queen to King Inuza." said Yatzil. "His kingdom has been overrun by Highnonstar, Brother. He was coming to seek your aid." She peered back to Putma in her twisted state, sighed, and decided only for him. "Our mother. She formed an alliance with the First Daughter and kept you under her control as part of their agreement. Highnonstar knows where I am by this scar."

A creak came from the distant doors beyond the room's forest of columns. There was a shuffling, and then from behind the closest one, carved in the shape of a sitting panther, came Sute with a wet nurse. Sachihiro parted from her but as he did her heart swam with joy. Eyes a complete glowing yellow framed by jet black hair over little ears. Yat-hig-seya had grown from the little babe she remembered. A tear ran down her cheek to see her child so without care and searching the room with curiosity.

"She is more beautiful than I remember." Yatzil took a step, desiring to hold her child close, but Yat-hig-seya clung to her wet nurse. "Give her to me."

The wet nurse tried but Yat-hig-seya groaned and fussed, twisting the closer Yatzil came to her. *Does she not know me?* She raised the hand branded by the new scar upon her palm, wondering if the blood was to blame. Yatzil met her child's fearful gaze, there was something in it confirming her previous worry. Yat-hig-seya calmed when she backed away. Her child rested her head on the wet nurse's shoulder.

"I have been gone too long," Yatzil said. "And longer still now that he is coming."

"No." Sachihiro took her in his arms. He held her close, drawing in a breath. "I will make a sacrifice to summon all Niev's forces to keep you safe."

She kissed his cheek, smiling a small smile to reassure herself to keep from falling into despair. Yet even with her pain gone her confidence wavered. Yatzil parted from him to look once again at her daughter. Yat-hig-seya rested her head on the nurse's chest with suspicion in her eyes.

"Do so brother," she said, a lump of emotion forming in her throat. "I do not know when Highnonstar will come but we must be ready."

THERE WAS no place for her to go but her bedchamber, even with Sachihiro placing all who had witnessed her trespassing on house confinement. The doors of her bed chamber were frozen over, and men of Sachihiro's personal guard manned them. Her daughter had been returned to her room amongst dozens of others made open for her brother's future heirs. The children of their father, who remained silent and loyal to Putma, had long been banished with their mothers to an island far south of the palace. She pulled the sheets of her bed over her shoulders, hoping Yat-hig-seya had at least not learned to walk yet. Such a precious moment for a nescaran meant readiness to worship at the Four's temples. But from what she knew of the goddesses her child learning to walk was something to be remembered.

Yatzil ran her thumb over her new scar. The stitch work was tight, and the scar was smaller than the others, but those didn't foreshadow war. She rolled over, finding sleep refused to greet her. A chilling breeze brushed her hair from her eyes, revealing the swift encroachment of night over the city. Her brother had made a sacrifice to Urra, thus rallying every avalanche warrior to fight. By doing this he promised battle would come south before the moon cycled north. Nearly a month had passed and Highnonstar had not trespassed beyond the ruined border wall. At this thought she hoped Niev could stand strong even in defiance of tradition. She thought of what Sath said, of no moon in the First Son's being an advantage and of her being there to help. Yatzil put her every thought of late on the goddess, wanting to dream of her, seek her help, but nothing came of it.

A faint crackling arose from the doors. She wasn't expecting anyone and Sute had been in her son's company since they arrived. He didn't act as if the queen were a stranger, and Yatzil suspected it was her haste to head north that deprived Yat-hig-seya of such a solid bond. Queen Busara was gone too, traveling north, intent on returning to life someone Yatzil dared not think about.

"Open these doors, Yatzil," said Sachihiro, pounding on their thick palm-and-oak.

Yatzil climbed from her bed and realized she had not selected a dress. None lay about her bedchamber and leaving it her bed felt pointless unless the city was attacked.

"My guards have removed the ice barrier. I will open them without your say if you do not. I know what you have done."

Yatzil gasped. Why would Sute tell him about the Keep? She yanked the sheets from her bed, hoping their pale green silks may conceal her nakedness. She moved with haste to the doors, gathering words to say. *How could Sute take my forgiveness and toss it aside?* The young queen's guilt seemed to have disappeared before passing the immense tunnels. Gripping the iron owl shaped knob, she lifted it and pulled. The door took on a life of its own as Sachihiro burst through it. She fell upon the room's boar furs, ones still lingering of palm wine from the day Yat-hig-seya was born.

"You laid with my queen!" Sachihiro fumed. "She is my bonded one."

"I ... did not force myself upon her."

"But you did not resist." He scowled and strolled toward the bath. His face took on a darker shade of ice blue. "Gather yourself up. You ... distract me from my purpose here."

Making it to her feet she pulled the sheets tight over her shoulders. It felt as if their softness were a net cast by him. Like she was a seal upon his ship waiting to be put out of her agony. It pained her to see him angered as he bawled his fists and faced her with a flare of yellow in his youthful eyes.

"I apologize for allowing this to happen," she said. "I ... I believed her and I were no longer in conflict about it."

Sachihiro folded his arms, pressing them tight until his face went blank.

"You know what tradition demands of a nescaran laying with another nescaran's bonded one."

"Then," Yatzil said, guilt forcing her voice to a whisper. "Take my life. I am without a way to defeat Highnonstar. Your armies are our only hope."

Yatzil eased to her knees and pressed her forehead to the floor. Much depended on her regarding what was to come but long ago she promised not to fight him if it came to this. Sachihiro let out a deep shuddering breath. Ice crackled over his skin and the scrape of his crystalized fists was like the sound the wolf's paw made against her temple.

"She told me how you resolved things. I... Why must I keep to tradition?"

There was sadness in his voice, she knew without looking that he was failing to mask it. Her mind went to all they had gone through, of those who depended on her victory over the First Son. He loomed over her, his feet, sandaled in the finest boar leather, inlaid with jade squares. Yatzil licked the jade squares upon her teeth and braced herself, wishing in this moment to change the past.

"Because you are a good king," she said, "and for all your life a good brother."

A swift hiss and crackle nipped at her ears, leaving her confused. A chill clasped her wrapped shoulders, forcing her to stand. The ice dissipated into her brother's skin as she looked up into his eyes. Her heart swelled at his change of mind, the sadness in his delicately painted eyes calming. She fell into his embrace and found him firm in his stance.

"I had no intention of executing you," he said, flashing a faint smile. "But you were quick to make it so."

Yatzil parted from, halting at her bed to pull a pillow from it to eclipse more of her nakedness. There was a need to thump herself on the head for such a rush to be punished.

It would have cost all she knew, everything if his intentions had been different.

"I am grateful for it." She made a fist then released. A faint numbing surfaced, fading to just a whisper of sensation. "I can feel whose hand I suspect is in mine, but he is far away."

Sachihiro's face went blank for a moment, and then he stiffened his jaw. He was free of Putma's influence and had grown thick in confidence and lean in body. He slipped a scroll from his jade inlaid belt she had not noticed during their argument.

"This came with an eagle who refuses food or water, and remains in fury with a white ring of fea—"

"Ringna!" Yatzil pressed the pillow firmly to her chest. "She lives."

"Yes," said Sachihiro. "The eagle delivered this in its beak. No one has been able to get close to it since."

Yatzil took the scroll and then sat upon the cushioned bricks of her bed. It was sealed with gold stars on both ends. Unclipping them, she read until her mind fell upon Sute.

"He has King Inuza," she said, gulping back fear. "Ringna is to take me to where I left Amteer, and I am to come with no aid."

"How can you fight someone who is a true god?"

She rested the scroll at her side, rose, and took a deep breath. Fear refused to come this time, and all had been laid out before her from forming another moon to seeing her child once again. There was no giving in, no time to waste if she were to form the bond she lacked with Yat-hig-seya. She felt her brother's arms encompass her, acting as armor she couldn't wear upon a battlefield but inside her heart.

"I will find a way," She swallowed, remembering Haseya, whose bravery wounded the First Daughter. "And I can only hope it works."

SHE HELD HER CHILD CLOSE, taking in the precious moment as the wind remained silent. Behind her Ringna stood in the company of the Four's gold likenesses, eyeing her as it had when they first met. Yat-hig-seya slept in her arms, bundled in many layers of boar fur. A wet nurse stood at a distance from them, both Sachihiro and Sute had said their good-byes. It hurt her like a hand clasped around her throat to be parted from them. But the pain of being parted from her daughter was worse, like being sealed in a stone coffin and bound in the coils of a diamond fang.

Yatzil kissed her child's cheek, calling the wetnurse forward. The thought of being only able to hold Yat-hig-seya in this way was a dagger to the belly. She checked the cords of her breastplate. It was made loose to fit her for Sute had offered her a dragon scale one. It was stronger than the bronze of a gray whale and lighter. She bound her hair back with the top from her marriage. Its silks were thin from wear and no frigagator teeth remained to it. And about her waist a lumao inlaid with iron squares.

Ringna amongst all other eagles she had seen possessed all its feathers, as if some part of Amteer remained. A holding back Highnonstar's wish to make ugly the young bird. Ringna turned her head away and lowered for her to mount. Yatzil knew they only needed to fly north for the distance and location of Lid remained in her memory. If Ringna had flown south alone, she supposed it needed no guidance.

Soon they were in flight but this time it was not to flee from danger. Yatzil refused to look down upon Niev as the chilling wind lashed against her face, flooding her nostrils. She didn't wish to think of the city or even the palace, deciding the company of Yat-hig-seya and Sachihiro was her home.

The eagle passed the city entrance where she found the guardians remained submerged in their moat. They were the few who didn't look upon her with disgust from the start of her banishment. Perhaps they were wiser, less brutal in thought than those they protected.

The forest was soon all Yatzil could see below. Far in the distance a thin gray line marked the border wall, snow slowly fell in sheets, blurring it. Ringna was faster than last, she rode it, as if the moon's return gave her strength long missed. The eagle screeched. The call not frightening Yatzil like before, piercing the snowflakes ever so, clearing the sky ahead for many yards. Such a trick would have fascinated her long ago if fear had not forced her eyes shut.

She thought of Flor and Sute. Another screech cleared a mile of downward snowflakes as she wrestled with how she felt. Flor had been more than a friend for so long, and even now she cursed herself for hiding her feelings, unlike with Sute. She swallowed, relieved at least, such confusion between them was resolved. Deep within though, as another stretch of snow was frightened away by Ringna's cry, her heart felt as though it may rest with no one. She massaged the hand stained, pain from the diamond fang's blood. *I must return my focus to what I can control.*

The border wall was drawing closer, its winged statues of the Four clear from the woken sun of midmorning. Long behind her was the Wrinkled River, growing thin and distant, urging her to search the forest for Queen Busara, and ask if she had done what she intended. The trees were too clustered to see the Lijani queen, and for this, she was grateful.

Yatzil swallowed. The scroll said to come alone, and at the speed Ringna flew at there wasn't time to dream of Sath. She shut her eyes, focusing on the goddess, remembering Sparron was on the island with the Nemamoon. Yatzil clenched her teeth, understanding if the little girl were to remain safe, she had to battle Highnonstar alone. She gripped Ringna's neck feathers then kicked her heels into the eagle's sides. It screeched, flying faster. She pushed aside all confusion of heart, all fear of failure. The rush of the eagle's speed scattered snow from the Four's wings, showering the fallen statue of Limpe, whose stern eyes for once gave Yatzil strength.

CHAPTER THIRTY-ONE

S now had given way to rain, slowing Ringna. In the distance beyond the blackened Wolfstrong a ring of flames glared at her like an eye. The rain pounded her shoulders hard enough that she frosted to her waist. She feared the chill may cause Ringna harm. Yatzil released the eagle's feathers, raindrops tapping so loud off her frosted limbs it was deafening.

They were nearing Lake Wet Iron at the Lid's base, its once shallowness overflowing. Every tree she had seen until now was rich with green, but those surrounding the ring of flame upon the Lid remained barren, as if Sath's dance couldn't touch them with new life. The dome shaped mountain shifted faintly somehow. Yatzil rubbed her eyes to find scarlet covered with a faintness of white, and then, a roar of indiscernible voices erupted. She gulped, realizing what it was, or to her mind who. Palenore covered the Lid at its top. A figure stood within the fire ring; his star crown reflected the flame's light. Beside him at his knees a lean figure who could have towered over Highnonstar was bound at the wrists and ankles with chains. She gasped, recognizing King Inuza as he once was.

As Ringna drew closer the scent of burning wood flooded her nostrils, but she refused to weep from how it stung them. The ground was close with the palenore around her falling silent at her landing. Her mind searched for why the First Son had chosen this spot but decided nothing mattered at this moment except his defeat. Yatzil dismounted to find Highnonstar armored like her but with shoulder plates mounted by hooked black spikes. His breastplate was formed to his muscles and his lumao was made of black leather.

"You've come as I have asked," he said. "Do you wonder why I chose where you betrayed my host for your death?"

A united marching of feet sent her eyes to the Palenore. They opened their mouths wide, spun and released flames, consuming the mountain in heat. Yatzil frosted her whole self as Ringna took off. King Inuza eyed the flames, lips trembling. Trees vanished in the fire as the palenore crept down to the mountain's base. His bolting eyes a weak sparking yellow.

"Free King Inuza," said Yatzil. "I do not care about your reasons for anything."

Highnonstar grimaced then narrowed his black eyes, gold flashed around their irises.

"You have a sharp tongue like Nescara," he said, releasing a frustrated breath from his nostrils. "She was demanding too."

She watched him unfasten a key from the thick belt around his waist. The key was small, possessing short nubby teeth. Both wrist and ankle chains fell away as the Raton king rose then moved to her side. Inuza had been stripped of his robes and given only a soiled loincloth to wear. The glyphs to enter Niev had shrunk on his belly.

"I resisted with all I possessed, Storm Queen."

"Are you well?" Yatzil eyed the dirt and mud being washed away by the rain, revealing long lash marks he must have healed himself. "If I lose, you will be the first to feel the pain from it."

King Inuza raised his hand, clenched it into a fist and then gave her a stern look.

"Not so much as others will, Storm Queen." He rested a hand on her shoulder, ignoring its chill. "You have strength beyond measure in you. Do not let Nema's suffering carry on."

She focused on his hand as it shook from the chill of her shoulder.

"Let's begin, Storm Queen," said Highnonstar. "I have the south to conquer with no recent news from the nescaran Mother of the King to stay my might."

Yatzil gave King Inuza a sharp nod, stepped forward and slammed her fists together. The points of her ice spear raced past her shoulders, cutting short the journeys of falling rain-drops. Her heart pounded and mind envisioned Yat-hig-seya, Sachihiro and Sute. Faces of the Nol she had failed flashed before her mind's eye, followed by the emotionless glare even of the nescarans who called her *weak*.

"I won't let you make it off this mountain," said Yatzil.

"We will see, young one."

Thump. A diamond bladed sword landed upright in the dirt at Highnonstar's feet. Yatzil peered up to find four eagles circling like irritated buzzards over a carcass. Every bird eyed her with rage as the First Son pointed the sword at her. She swung, and he countered, ice flaking off her spear. The sword was like a spear, transparent and sharp, but diamond was stronger than ice. Yatzil dodged a swipe at her gut.

She thrust for his face, but Highnonstar struck her cheek with the red gem pommel of his sword. Yatzil backed off, pressing her hand to her face, finding a thin crack linked with the scar on her temple. She was no avalanche warrior and knew only how to throw her spear, not wield it like they could. Yatzil went at him again, rain muddying the glow of her burning yellow eyes. Every move was pitiful in her mind until Highnonstar knocked her spear into the flames and kicked her to the ground. She crawled backward, pushing with her hands like the nescaran prince she once learned of who had proved mighty in words, but once struck down had crawled just the same. She did not weep as he did or have a dagger like he did under her garb as a final effort.

"You are beaten, Storm Queen." said Highnonstar, aligning his sword with her widening eyes. "You possess none of Nescara's skill, and soon, you will be without life like her."

With a gulp, she refocused her fear into rage clenching her teeth. The air was thick with heat, but Yatzil forced with all her might to freeze him from within. His fingers loosened their grip on his sword for a moment, both his well-shaped lips trembled as he tried to shake off her attempt. Yatzil crawled to her feet, reached out her hand and climbed the air upon an ice path. King Inuza called after her but when the First Son found focus again, he released great white lightning bolts from his fingertips. Highnonstar toppled into the flames as Yatzil dodged in coming eagles.

"Leave her." called Highnonstar, rising from the flames. His lumao smoked and burned. "I will have your head, Raton king, after I have melted the southern royal."

Swordless, Highnonstar raised his hands and drained the flames from the Lid, launching like a shark from a roaring sea into the sky. Yatzil dodged another eagle as the Lid lay dormant, only the jolting of the king's eye pieced the smoke. She readied to form an ice spear, but the First Son gave chase. The air was exactly right for her to keep up her pace but to run forever was useless.

She turned and gagged. His fingers squeezed her throat, steam ebbing from their tips. A long tale of flame kept him within flight, strangling her ice path and shattering it.

"You should have gone against my instruction!" Highnonstar laughed. "Sath is of better use off that island where my wife lost my namesake."

Yatzil pounded at his arm, refusing to thaw, daring not to ask how he knew of Sath being alive.

"She protects the one who I failed."

"Then," said Highnonstar. "Once I have taken your frozen home, I will rid myself of further rivals and the one you—"

Her eyes ignited brighter than ever before. She focused on the rain, remembering what she had done to the ocean. Countless droplets froze over Highnonstar's pale skin, loosening his grip. She struggled free and started another ice path. Steam rose from the First Son, melting the forming ice. Soon layer upon layer of ice snared him and snuffed out his trail of flames to form a berg of ice. She kept her ice path going, using the rain to reinforce its travel, circling the collective, glowing spearhead shaped berg. Making a fist she yanked it from the air and watched the First Son fall to the lake.

Yatzil aimed her hand toward where she left King Inuza. He met her as her feet touched the blackened grass.

"We must hurry to the lake, Storm Queen," he said.

"Why? He is trapped. We have time to find a way to—"

"No. We do not."

They raced down the Lid meeting no resistance before a faint glow snatched her breath away. She ran faster, finding neither could go a step further. Palenore encircled the massive ice chunk bobbing at the lakes center. They aimed their flaming breath to free their First Son. Inuza lashed lightning from his fists, scattering and cutting palenore in half. Yatzil winced. The lightning was louder than Sute's, but then she thought of a way to aid him as the flames melted Highnonstar's ice prison. She reached up, picturing hundreds of ice spears then a combined crackle met screams as the palenore fell. Many of them fled out of her range, bleeding, while others reached to her out of mercy.

A crack raced down the berg of ice, splitting and glowing. Highnonstar stood garbed from waist to shoulders, his every breath a struggle for some reason, as if the part of him that was Amteer limited him somehow. And then he flew backwards into the regrown forest. A red lightning bolt vanishing from where it sent him.

"He was weakened, King Inuza," said Yatzil, letting the rain be itself again. "I wished words with him before I finished things by myself."

Inuza turned to her with a jolt of red in his eyes.

"You truly are like your father. Wishing to deliver a lesson to an enemy before ending them."

"You are not what you were when we last met."

"Look at me, Storm Queen." he said, raising his arms, displaying the marks on his skin. There was a scar over his left eye she had missed somehow. "I have been disgraced. Nema has been disgraced."

She looked on ahead, past the lake to find Highnonstar crawling to his feet. He didn't stand tall and proud as he once did, and the more she thought, the more the memories of those nol eaten in the Keep surfaced. Memory of the foul smell Sparron was subjected to as the palenores servant. *I must end him.* She thought, churning up the words of Haseya, that Amteer was no longer a Nol. Yatzil slammed her fists together, ending more journeys of raindrops with its speed.

"Let's end him."

King Inuza smiled as they charged forward. Yatzil began another path, soaring over the lake as Highnonstar conjured flames over his fists. Red lightning raced across the lake, striking the First Son's armor as he released a torrent of flame. Highnonstar fell on his back as rain pattered his face. Yatzil seized the rain again, pinning his quills to the ground.

"This cannot happen!" Highnonstar cried, tugging to be free. "I will not die exposed and to a mortal."

Yatzil ended her ice path short of his head and then raised her ice spear. Highnonstar reached for the heavens. Eagles screeched. Their immense bodies dove at her but were cut from the sky by lightning.

"You have killed so many of my people," said Yatzil, a lump formed in her throat, seeing his gaping petrified face. "I shall end you for—"

"Do not delay!" Inuza called, breaking her focus.

Flames erupted from Highnonstar's mouth, landing her on her back at the lake's edge. He ripped himself free and dove at her, eyes blazing. Yatzil thrusted her spear into his shoulder. He toppled over her into the lake. She made it to her hands and knees, panting, finding him on his knees in the shallows, grabbing for the spear. Yatzil put her hands in the water, freezing it until the spear end submerged and was wedged in ice and mud.

Yatzil hugged her stomach, pulling her arms away to find Sute's armor had saved her, but the force had knocked the wind from her body.

"You…" Highnonstar shivered. "I was supposed to rule Nema. It belongs to me! How…? How could a traitor like you do all this?"

Yatzil made it to her feet in time for King Inuza to join her. She thawed as he took her weakness in need of support. The towering Raton king kept her steady as she realized Highnonstar was still only slowed. But the way First Son shivered was like nothing she would have expected. Palenore surrounded them with fewer than twenty in number.

"Because it was what a true Storm Queen would have done."

"You will not have your chance." he shivered again, struggling to remove the spear. "Finish me. Palenore attack!"

All at once they rushed but King Inuza released her, spun, and struck the ground with his fists. Every palenore screamed in horror as lightning struck like blades and split them in half.

"No," Highnonstar cried. "You will pay for—"

Yatzil leapt upon the lake, frosting, pulling out and then thrusted her spear into the First Son's throat. He coughed, stumbling backward. She backed away to the shore, deprived still of full breath. The king went to her support again as she thawed. Highnonstar's skin darkened until it was silver with the red marks of the Giftnos. Each gold ring clinked on the surrounding ice as his quills shrunk to erect black feathers. The rain slowed with time to a drizzle as First Son's Raton armor hung loose on his body. Amteer was like a lean, yet muscled skeleton compared to who had held his body captive. And then the one-time king, the one-time god, collapsed, exhaling one, final breath.

"You have done what I failed to, Storm Queen," said King Inuza. A smile carved its way across his chiseled face. "I will head south with you, if company is what you wish."

"No," said Yatzil, breath regained. "You have the east to…"

Before them lay the bloodied and burned bodies of nol. They wore the dark loincloths and leggings of Palenore with some in stolen raton armor. It had never struck Yatzil from when first seeing the palenore how much alike they were to nol. Faces remained in horror as they were before the king's lightning. Feathers smoked from those lying face down in the mud.

"By Singlebolt's wisdom and mercy," said Inuza. "Had I known who the palenore truly were I'd…"

"There is no way either of us could have known this." Yatzil swallowed. Her body felt as if the wind had been struck from it again. "All this time we were fighting my own people."

King Inuza rested hand on her shoulder, the scar made by the priest smooth against her ice-blue skin.

"I will not go east at present," said King Inuza. "My heart weighs me, and if those who were once palenore still live, my sons will spare them."

"How can you be certain?"

He gazed down at her with the smile she knew him for.

"Above all King Yanter's madness he made a wise enough decision to sue for peace in the end."

Yatzil pursed her lips. It was only after suffering the Giftnos this had happened, but she refused to reopen the flesh of an old wound.

"I am glad the west is at peace with your people," she said. "I feel I must hold a feast for those nol recently lost to honor them. But I must first…"

"You must first, what, Storm Queen?"

They faced one another, every breath still a struggle in her chest. He raised her chin with a curled finger like her father used to, and it made it worse, knowing the struggle remained south.

"I must choose a grown name for a friend lost to me and find a way for my child to love me as I her."

The king brought her close, yellow lighting cascading down his cheeks.

"You will choose well. And there is one way to earn love, Yatzil."

"What is it?"

"Patience with time."

PLEASE LEAVE A REVIEW

Customer reviews allow independent authors to continue sharing their stories. If you enjoyed this book, please leave a review wherever you normally would.

Thank you for reading!